Water Magic

Three Moon Falls
Book Two

Katie O'Connor

Water Magic

Three Moon Falls Book Two

Katie O'Connor

-Water Magic-

-Three Moon Falls Book 2-

This book is a work of fiction. Names, characters, places, and incidents either are products of the author's imagination or are used fictitiously. Any resemblance to actual events, locales, or persons, living or dead, is entirely coincidental.

Published March 2021 by Snarky Heart Press and Katie O'Connor

(katieohwrites.com)

ISBN: 978-1-989816-15-8 (Digital Edition)

ISBN: 978-1-989816-17-2 (Other Digital Editions)

ISBN: 978-1-989816-16-5 (Print Edition)

ISBN: 978-1-997548-10-2 (Alternate Print Edition)

Design and cover art by Raquel Lyon, Crooked Sixpence Book Covers

Copyediting by Terri St. Clair

Contents

Dedication

This one is for the great teachers in my life. Thanks for all you taught me. I wouldn't be here without your help. Your patience and understanding helped shape who I am today.

It's also for every shitty teacher I ever had. For those of you who treated me poorly because I didn't meet your standards of perfection. Kudos to me...I grew up and I flourished, despite you. I'm a successfully published author with over forty titles to my name. To quote Toby Keith: "How do you like me now?"

About Water Magic

Will the fear of water be her undoing, or can a water witch overcome her past to save her soulmate?

Hazel Hawk is desperate to obtain employment in a town reluctant to hire anyone from a family of reputed witches. A descendant of sixteen generations of magic wielders, Hazel controls water and channels it to her own purposes. There's only one problem, she's deathly terrified of water and terrified someone might use this to their advantage.

After Dennis Belanger discovers his ex-fiancée was trying to control his mind and manipulate his will, he vowed never to get involved with another magical being, and moved to Three Moon Falls to start over, and soon his garden center is thriving. Unfortunately, he's exhausted and half a year behind on his accounting. Out of options, he hires Hazel as his bookkeeper, despite her reputation as a witch.

They've barely scratched the surface of their irresistible mutual attraction when an enemy with supernatural powers intrudes on their relationship. With lives in danger, paranormal skills must be used to defeat the foe bent on destroying Hazel, her family, and Three Moon Falls.

When Dennis's life is threatened, Hazel must face the one thing she's more afraid of than losing her soulmate – water. Can she overcome her fear or will they both die in battle?

Chapter One

Hazel Hawk smoothed her favorite ocean patterned skirt, straightened her bejeweled T-shirt, and lightweight cotton sweater, huffed out a breath and took two steps forward. Dang, she'd forgotten her resume. She'd emailed one, when she'd applied online for the position, but it didn't hurt to have one with her anyway. She glanced around the parking lot to ensure she was alone, and with a quick flick of her fingers, cast a spell that had the resume flying off the passenger seat and into her hand through the open window of her ancient, lime green, Ford Fiesta.

She gave her car's rusty hood a fond pat. She loved this car. It didn't look like much, but the gas mileage was incredible, better than a lot of newer cars. While the car wasn't sound of body, it was certainly fuel efficient, and in excellent working order. The engine and drive train were perfect. Last week, the old car had passed her emissions test with flying colors.

"Okay, Hazel, enough procrastinating." For all the bravery of her words, she couldn't quite make herself move toward the customer entrance to Get Growing Greenhouses. She'd been here a million times, and loved wandering the aisles of flourishing plants was peaceful and relaxing. But she'd never anticipated being here for a job interview. Everything was riding on this.

As the youngest of four sisters, she was the only one who wasn't gainfully employed, and it was starting to rub her the wrong way. Her family had never mentioned it, it was her own stubborn pride fueling her desire to make her way as a bookkeeper, now that she'd aced her final exams. She wanted to contribute to the household expenses, not just cause them to increase. She wanted, no needed to earn her way.

Unfortunately, her hometown didn't present many job opportunities, especially for someone with her reputation. It wasn't that Hazel, or her family had done anything bad, it was just their reputation for being odd. Being from a family of witches, even private ones made you an odd duck. Occasionally, when weird things happened around town, her family was given sly, accusatory glances. Their newly opened metaphysical supply shop hadn't helped their reputation.

Now, after sending out a hundred or more resumes, this was her only interview. Not having options sucked. She could probably get a job at the gas station or convenience store working nights, but she'd finished her education and wanted a real job. She didn't want to have to travel fifty miles to the next town for work as a bookkeeper, and she sure didn't want to move away from the home she'd grown up in.

When this job had come up, she'd asked around town about the garden center's new owner, but nobody knew anything about him, beyond his name. Dennis Belanger was an enigma in Three Moon Falls and that was unusual; in this town, everybody knew everyone else, except this guy. She'd hoped to learn something about him, but had come up dry, even on the local gossip grapevine. The gossip breakdown could be a point in her favor, maybe he hadn't heard of her either and she'd be able to leave her family's reputation for weirdness behind, at least long enough to secure the job and prove herself.

Shaking off the self-defeating thoughts, she headed toward the doors.

"He could have called me for the interview, rather than just emailing me. At least I could have tried to get a feel for him that way." Her ability to get a "feel" for people was limited, she wasn't gifted in reading people the way her sister Lazuli was, but she might have picked up something by speaking to him. She wasn't totally without magical empathy.

She forced her feet into motion and fueled her steps with all the confidence she could muster. Fake it until you make it was her motto for the day. "I'm going to ace this," she bolstered herself.

"Pardon me?"

The unexpected male voice sent her heart lurching into overdrive. Why hadn't she noticed him when she checked the lot? Hopefully he hadn't seen her *spell* the paper into her hand. The magic council wouldn't be happy if she were caught performing magic in front of a mundane. Last year they'd bound a witch's magic when she zapped a mundane with a spell. Hazel couldn't imagine life without the magic she'd known all her life.

She whirled round, hand against her chest, crumpling her resume. "What?" she squeaked. The underground sprinkler to her left spit out a rush of water. Crap. She needed to control her emotions, or she'd call enough water to soak them both. Not cool. At least her water control hadn't caused the thick clouds overhead to open up and dump on him. Unrestrained emotions were the bane of a witch's existence. It took years to learn to experience emotion without letting their side effects run rampant. Luckily, a witch's powers rarely came in before she turned twelve or thirteen, although there were exceptions in her family.

"You said something, were you talking to me?" A grin tipped up the right corner of his mouth, giving him an adorable, lopsided grin.

By the Goddess, he was gorgeous. Over six feet tall. Damn, she loved a tall man. Her heart skipped happily. Ocean blue eyes, golden brown hair and bulging biceps. She swallowed a wave of attraction and couldn't stop her gaze from examining him from head to toe. Snug blue jeans emphasized his long legs, and his chest was accentuated by a form fitting Get Growing T-shirt...

Whoa!

Get Growing? No way. She was not ogling her potential employer and he had not just caught her talking to herself. No way. No how. Heat flooded her face. Maybe he was just an employee.

"Um. Hi. I was just thinking out loud." She almost stumbled over the words, and the edge of a sidewalk block simultaneously. *Shit. Get a grip Hawk.*

"Do that a lot, do you?" His smile grew exponentially. Laughter made his eyes shine. He didn't seem judgy, just amused.

Would the earth just open up and swallow her already? Did she talk to herself a lot? Absolutely, but he didn't need to know that. "No, not much. Sometimes. A little. Yeah." Great, way to make a good impression. She sounded like an idiot. How was she supposed to impress him if she couldn't form a coherent sentence?

"Nervous?" His deep laugh was more of a growl and sent a wave of warmth flooding down her spine.

Grasping for an intelligent response, she blurted, "Nope. Not me."

He laughed again. The sound was so infectious she joined in.

"Okay, maybe a bit." She thrust out her hand, her resume poked his chest. "I'm Hazel Hawk. I'm here to see Dennis Belanger for an interview."

He tugged on the wrinkled paper she'd forgotten was in her hand. She yanked it back and shoved it into her other hand. "Sorry." She offered her hand again as heat stole into her face. She was blowing this, big time.

"Nice to meet you, Hazel Hawk. I'm Dennis Belanger."

"Dang. I was hoping you were just someone who worked here, and I hadn't made a total ass—jerk—of myself." She barely resisted the urge to roll her eyes at her ineptitude. "I swear, I'm a competent bookkeeper. I'm just nervous."

"Come inside then. We'll go into the office and discuss the position." He placed his hand lightly on her shoulder and urged her toward the building.

Beneath her sweater, her skin prickled where he touched her. Whoa! That was a first. What man's touch had ever affected her so strongly? None. Sure, she'd been attracted to men, but wow. Good looks and electricity, Dennis Belanger was lethal. And his laugh was enough to make her crazy, in a good way.

The automatic doors opened and she stepped inside, Dennis right behind her. Tempted to pause and absorb the healing atmosphere, she kept moving and inhaled deeply, taking in the moist air, and the aroma of fresh greenery and damp earth. Her nerves stilled as she grounded herself as she walked forward.

"My office is this way," he gestured to the left.

She followed him through the retail area, noting, not for the first time, the wide array of products. Plant pots of all types, ceramic, glass, wicker, plastic as well as a few cement ones. Flower and vegetable seeds. Fertilizers and tools of all shapes and sizes. There was even a small section with trinkets, mugs and other gardening related gifts. She adored the fairy and dragon statuettes.

"Oh, those are new." She paused and picked up a tiny dragon with teal and purple wings. "She's adorable."

"Those came in yesterday. There's another box full in the back. I hope they sell, I wasn't sure, but the sales rep talked me into them."

"They'll be a big hit. It's almost my sister's birthday. I'll have to get her one." She set the statuette down and looked up at Dennis. "Sorry. I'm not here to shop, I'm here for the interview. I just got distracted. Lead the way." She followed him through a winding chain of six interconnected greenhouses and back outside. They crossed a small expanse of yard toward a large white bungalow with dark green shutters.

"We're going into your house?" she blurted.

"My office is just inside." He held the door open for her.

Weird. Why wasn't the office in the greenhouse somewhere? Or why hadn't he conducted the interview there, rather than in his personal space? This had the potential to be uncomfortable and unprofessional. She paused on the back step. Reaching out, she tried to get a feel for his intentions. Dammit, why wasn't she more adept at reading people. She should have gotten her sister Lazuli to check him out in advance.

Well, nothing ventured, nothing gained. If the office was in the house, that's where she'd be working, so no sense dithering about it. Besides, her entire family knew where she was. She wiped her feet on the wicker mat and stepped into the back entry. The small space was pristine. The walls were pale sage green, the trim gleaming white. A row of coat hooks hung on one wall, a neat shelf of footwear below it. To the left she noticed a small washroom, the office was to the right. Straight ahead, a set of French doors with frosted windows separated the entry-office area from the rest of the house.

"In here?" She asked, waving toward the office. She bent to unbuckle her sandals.

"You can leave those on, if you wish." He wiped his feet on the mat.

She did the same and went into the office. She stood across from the untidy desk until he sat behind it and invited her to sit. Her stomach churned like a fountain had erupted inside her belly as she slid into the chair. Discretely, she wiped her damp palms on her skirt, the resume in her hand crackled. Dang. She'd forgotten all about it. It was a wrinkled mess, the corners curled and damp from perspiration. No way she could give it to him now. The interview hadn't even started, and she was already blowing it. Searching for calm, she glanced around the room. Books lay crookedly on the shelf alongside messy stacks of paper and open boxes of office supplies. His desk was strewn with documents and catalogues held in place by dirty coffee mugs. She'd have to get rid of those right off and clean things up. She hated working in a mess.

"You're the fourth person I've interviewed for this position."

Her heart sank at the words. The fourth? Seriously? This wasn't going to be an easy job to get.

"Honestly, I debated even giving you an interview. You have no experience and I need someone who knows what they're doing. Is that you?"

Tempted to beg for the job, she held her tongue for a moment before answering. "I have just graduated. Top of my class to be honest. My GPA is on my resume. I'm familiar with the major computerized accounting programs and can use a manual spreadsheet. I'm not an accountant, but I know the tax categories they use and what should go where. Additionally, I have more than a working knowledge of plants and their care. I can be an asset to you. I'm also willing to work the floor if you need the help."

His eyes narrowed, leaving her wondering what she'd said wrong. The resume crinkled in her hands as she bunched them together.

"Is that your resume?" He asked.

"It is." She handed it to him. "Sorry it's wrinkled."

He took it and slipped it into the shredder. The grinding of gears and paper destroyed any hope she had of getting the job. Her heart sank to her toes and she stood.

"Where are you going?" His voice was curious, but not unkind. "I have more questions."

"But, but--you shredded my resume." She gestured vaguely. "I assumed we were done."

"You emailed me a copy. I've read it. I shredded it for privacy purposes. I assumed you didn't want to keep it, it's a little crumpled."

"Oh." She sank back into her seat, willing herself not to blush, say anything stupid or jump to any more conclusions. Something about him made her jumpy. Not in a bad way, but in a way she couldn't quite understand.

"I've heard rumors about your family. I'd like to discuss them."

And there it was, the death knell to any chance of employment. She was going to have to leave Three Moon Falls to get work. She suppressed a wince. "Okay." What choice did she have but to answer the questions? It was either that, or risk not getting the job.

"Your family runs the new store, the new age place?"

"Yes, we've just opened." His tone was neutral, but she suspected he had a reason for asking.

"Unusual store. Why aren't you working there?" His hands rested easily on the desk.

She studied his expression. The man was unreadable. Did he think they were crazy? She didn't have enough information to know what was going on in his head. He might not care about the shop at all. Those lovely blue eyes didn't give her a single hint as to what he was thinking.

"I do work there. My entire family does. All three of my sisters as well as my grandmother. It's a family business. I'm looking for more. I'll still work there when I'm needed, and I'm not at this job." She floundered for a moment, struggling to express herself. "I want to be independent from my family and the shop. I need to make my own way." Oh, she sounded totally lame.

"That I understand." He took a deep breath. "Tell me about the unusual nature of the shop?" he prodded.

"There isn't much to tell." She fought back a rising sense of frustration and despair. She flattened her hands against her thighs to keep from twisting her hands together. "New age, metaphysical beliefs are making a comeback. They're increasing in popularity. We're capitalizing on that market. Our market research shows tourists are interested in a lot of what we sell. Books, statuettes, stones and gems. Divination items."

"And you do you believe in all of that metaphysical business?" His tone was slightly accusatory.

"Frankly, I don't see how it is any of your business and it certainly isn't relevant to the job you advertised. Plus, questioning my belief system could be construed as questioning my religion. Unacceptable." She stood quickly and looked down at him. "Thanks for your time, I'll show myself out." She was in the entryway before he spoke.

"Hazel, wait. Please."

She pivoted on her heel and looked back at him, trying her best not to glare.

"Can you assure me your beliefs won't impact your work?"

By the Goddess, the man was rude and insufferable. How could she even consider working for him? "Would you ask a Catholic, or a Christian that question?" He had the grace to flush and glance away. She'd scored a direct hit, so why didn't it feel good?

"I apologize. The question was unworthy of you and of me. Can we pretend I didn't ask it?"

He had to be kidding. That made as much sense as a judge telling the jury to disregard the testimony, as if you could unhear something. Reluctantly, she nodded, but didn't return to her chair. If she didn't need this position so badly, she'd be gone faster than water through a burst dam; but she did need the work. Financially, and for her own self-worth.

Chapter Two

D ennis waited for her to come back into the office. After a long, tense pause, it became apparent she had no intention of sitting back down. She stood in the doorway; arms folded over her chest, staring at him. He'd crossed a line. When he left his past, his ex-fiancée, and Drayton Valley behind, he swore he'd stop letting his ex's actions color his perception of the world. Big fat failure there. He was here to make a fresh start and only half a year in, he'd blown it already. He needed to get his business in order and hiring a competent bookkeeper was the first step.

His better judgment told him to apologize, again, and let her leave. Instead, he found himself asking her to sit down. She eyed him warily and perched on the edge of her seat. She reminded him of a nervous bird who might fly away at any second. He could hardly blame her.

It wasn't just her beliefs making him nervous; after his ex, Natalia, he was cautious around women. He had no desire to start a relationship and Hazel Hawk was entirely too attractive for his peace of mind. The sun streaming through the window to her left lit her light brown hair with gold and red highlights. He wondered if they were natural or costly upgrades like his ex indulged in. He had to stop judging everyone based on Natalia's behaviors. Hazel didn't appear high maintenance. She looked...wholesome.

Unless he missed his guess, those beautiful brown eyes and high cheek bones were unadorned by makeup. Her clothing was simple and earthy. She was a tiny little thing, barely over five feet, maybe five two or three. She was thin, with a curvy, feminine look to her. Judging by the name Hazel, he'd been expecting someone—older. Maybe a mother returning to the work force when her children went back to school. Or even a grandmother. The rumor mill had neglected to include her age.

When he saw her in the parking lot, his attraction had been deep, and instantaneous. It had floored him. She'd been talking to herself, and it was cute. Her blush when she realized his identity was adorable. Her quiet anger at his later rudeness was justifiable and only raised his opinion of her.

Yeah, he had to stop his libido from controlling his brain. He should let her go and continue his search for a bookkeeper elsewhere; yet he found himself wanting to get to know her better. Plus, he was six months behind on his books and busy enough he'd never catch up alone. Get Growing was booming and had the potential to be a thriving success, if he didn't screw it up by losing track of his finances. He had two choices, hire Hazel and fight his attraction; or start working twenty-four-hour days to catch up. He was already exhausted. He never would have thought running a garden center was this much work. His yard-care business hadn't been nearly this mentally taxing. Physically, yes. Mentally, not so much.

She cleared her throat, bringing his attention back to the moment at hand. His grandfather would say, "Time to shit or get off the pot." His best friend would tell him to "man up." They'd both be right.

"Tell me about your knowledge of plants." He had a thousand other questions he'd like to ask her, none of them job related.

"My family has our own greenhouses and extensive gardens. We grow herbs and flowers for teas and salves. I grew up around plants. I can identify almost every native Alberta plant species and sub-species; although there are a few I only know by their common names, rather than the scientific ones. I'm trained in the medicinal uses of plants and herbs as well as which plants to grow together for optimum benefit. I'm not trained in botany, but I've taken a number of correspondence classes. However, I thought I was here for the bookkeeping job."

"You are. But you mentioned working the floor."

"Do you need help on the sales floor? Did all your staff start with a wide floral knowledge base? Or are they just regular retail staff you've trained?" She squinted at him, as if daring him to annoy her again.

Damned if he didn't like the way she put him on the spot. She was straightforward and no-nonsense; he admired that. He ignored her question about his employee's knowledge. "I am looking for staff, but my primary purpose in interviewing you was, and is, for the bookkeeping position. But it's nice to know you have other skills which would benefit my customers."

Her eyes narrowed further, as if she didn't believe him. She had such an expressive face; he wondered what she'd look like in the throes of passion.

Not happening.

He had zero interest in women or relationships. Certainly not in the type that involved close physical contact. And yet he couldn't stop himself from imagining her glorious hair spread across his pillow. He cleared his throat to remove the ball of desire lodged there.

"When can you start?" He'd meant to ask something else, but the question exploded out of him before he'd consciously made a decision.

She leaned back in her chair; arms crossed over her chest. He'd expected eager acceptance, judging by how she'd explained her need for the job.

"What hours are you offering? What is the wage? If I work the floor will I be paid the same wage as for bookkeeping? A bookkeeper does earn more than regular retail staff. Are there benefits?"

He stifled a grin; he admired her spunk. Her professionalism was miles above his. She'd be an asset to his fledgling business. He named a monthly wage. "Full time, forty hours a week. Benefits after a three-month probation period. There will be no sales work until the books have been brought up to date. After that, we'll discuss it."

"Wait. Just how far out of date are your books? You've haven't been open long." She sounded wary. Justifiably so.

He flushed. Time to fess up and hope she didn't refuse the job. Two of his earlier prospective hires had refused when they saw his shoe-box accounting method. "Let me put it this way," he smiled his most disarming grin, "I've been open for seven months, and I'm six months behind on paperwork."

"You're telling me you haven't paid bills for six months? How are the lights even still on?" Her eyes bulged and her mouth dropped open. She blinked rapidly and snapped her mouth shut.

This was where she walked out on him. He held up a hand. "Wait. I didn't say I haven't paid bills. I have. I'm up to date on payments. I pay them when they come in. I just haven't entered anything in the computer yet." He winced at the admission. Frankly, it was a miracle he was even still open.

"That's a relief. Do you have a business plan? Projections for the future?" She paused and eyed him skeptically. "Do you even have the money to pay me?"

He laughed. He totally deserved her scorn and doubt. He'd made the right decision offering her the position. She'd keep him on his toes. "Yes, I have a plan." In his head, but he wasn't going there. "I have adequate funds to pay your wages, and that of my other employees." Why was he defending himself? He had run a successful yard-work business and sold it for a tidy profit. He had more than enough money to keep the greenhouse afloat for a couple years, or longer. Though his plan was to grow quickly into a profit.

"Where are your receipts? Your cheque book? How are you recording your purchases, wages, income?"

"In my head. The receipts are here." He pulled an overflowing box off the shelf behind him and dropped it on the table with a thud. Loose papers flew everywhere, and he scrambled to stuff them back in the box.

"Are you out of your mind? You can't run a business like that!" She jumped to her feet and grabbed the box from his hands. "I'm going to need a place to spread out. This paperwork is a disaster. I'll need room to sort receipts. Somewhere it won't be disturbed for a few days, until I get it organized and entered. There isn't enough room in this office to do it right."

He jerked back in his chair. What the devil? This could be a mistake. She was going to be the type of woman to step in and take over his business which wasn't what he wanted. All he needed was a competent record keeper and someone to handle bill payments. He wasn't a business newbie. Although admittedly, he'd had a partner who'd handled most of the paperwork before they sold out. Maybe he shouldn't have been so quick to offer her the job. Hell, he hadn't meant to offer it. He'd intended to send her on her way and keep searching. In his exhaustion, he was losing control over his ability to make rational decisions and stick to them.

His goose was cooked. Rather than admit he'd screwed up and was still leery of her new age ways and lack of experience, he again brought up the probationary period. "There's a three-month trial period. If, at the end of, or during that time, I'm not satisfied with your performance, I have the option to terminate your employment." Suddenly, it was of utmost importance that she agreed to his terms. He didn't want to run into issues when he had to fire her later on. "I have paperwork for you to fill in before you start."

"Can you even find it?" Her tone was light and teasing.

"Yes. I can find it," he shot back defensively. He'd printed it this morning. She wasn't even hired, and she was giving him the gears. This could be a colossal mistake, or it could be fun.

She chuckled, obviously not believing him. Her laughter brightened the room, like the sun coming out from behind the clouds. Dammit all to hell. He wasn't attracted to her. He refused to be. He didn't have time for women, especially witchy women.

She was an inexperienced bookkeeper and new age to boot. He'd had enough magic shit from his ex. He was not going to get caught up in it again. One thing for certain, you couldn't trust a witch. They had unnerving skills and didn't hesitate to use them.

"One last thing," he said, pulling the forms she needed to fill out of the printer's tray. "No magic on the premises."

"What?" She gaped at him like he'd grown three heads.

"No magic. None."

"I'm sorry, what do you mean by magic?"

"You heard me. Your family has a reputation for being magical. I'm asking you not to perform spells on my property." God, he sounded as paranoid as he felt.

"I have no idea what you're talking about. Besides, why in the world would I need magic when I'm entering numbers into a computer and balancing your books?"

Shit, now she was defensive again. He liked her better when she was smiling and teasing. His head started to ache. He massaged his temples. "I'm familiar with witches and magic. Yes or no?" *Damn. He had to get a grip on himself, and his biases.*

"I promise, on my honor, I will not use magic on your property. Not that I believe in magic." Her eyes shifted away as she talked. "I assume someone who had the ability to cast spells wouldn't just go throwing them around in public." Her brows scrunched together, and her hands curled into balls.

Yeah, she was pissed off and somehow her agreement wasn't reassuring; but he'd try and take her at her word. He reminded himself she wasn't Natalia; she was her own person and hadn't given him a reason not to trust her. Yet.

It crossed his mind that if she was an actual, living breathing witch, she might be influencing his decision, the way Natalia had. He opened his mouth to ask her if she was, and snapped it shut. No sense going there, if she was, she wouldn't admit it anyway. Another of his grandfather's expressions crossed his mind. "Trust first, doubt later." He wished the old guy hadn't passed away three years ago, he could use his advice about now and he definitely could have used it when he realized what Natalia had been up to.

He slid the papers across the desk. "Fill these in and I'll find you a place to work."

"Unmagically." The single word was a shot, but he refused to take the bait.

Chapter Three

Hazel danced into Four Seasons Metaphysical, her family's new age shop. Peace and calm washed over her as she breathed in the fragrant air. Lavender, rose, sage, lemon. The aroma came from bundles of dried herbs and the scented candles they sold. She loved it here. She adored every metaphysical book and new age trinket on the shelves, especially the rocks and gems. She grabbed her sister's hand and spun her in a circle, laughing like she was nuts.

"Wow, you're excited," Amber said, grinning widely. "I gather you got the job?"

Hazel released Amber and hugged herself. "I did. I start first thing in the morning," She couldn't stop a tiny frown from pulling her brows together. She was still miffed at her new employer's attitude.

"I hear a but in there. What's wrong?"

Amber was just coming into her clairvoyant skills, but she was Hazel's closest sibling, and knew her moods well.

"Aside from nearly accidentally soaking his feet with the automatic sprinklers? He's a total witchaphobe. He actually warned me not to use magic on his property. As if I would! Can you believe that?" His gall still irritated her. She sensed he had his reasons, but he didn't reveal why, and she refused to ask. "It pissed me off. I barely managed to stop myself from admitting I was magic."

"So, he believes then?"

"Yup." Was a grumpy believer any better than a non-believer like Amber's fiancé, Kody, had been? Probably not. If he'd had bad experiences, it was probably worse, much worse.

"At least he knows about our world and you don't have to worry about accidentally exposing yourself to him. You're already out of the broom closet," her sister commiserated. "That has to be reassuring."

"I guess. I mean I didn't actually confess, so he's still guessing." His bias against magic was upsetting. You'd think she'd be used to it by now. Most of the world were non-believers or people who considered magic evil and the tool of the devil which just wasn't true. Speaking for her family, they were nature lovers tapped into the power around them and trying to be good people.

"It's not like you'd use magic at work anyway, right?" Amber paused. She shifted some amethyst crystals on a glass shelf and gave her sister a sly look. "What aren't you telling me? I'm sensing more. Fess up."

Damn. She must be giving off strong emotions if Amber was picking up on them this strongly. Lazuli was the family empath, not Amber. Hazel tried to rein in her unchecked attraction to Dennis. The trouble with being part of a family of witches and empaths was sharing a strong connection. Emotions, especially fear, desperation, and excitement flowed easily through their connection, particularly when she forgot to block them. If the emotion was strong enough, it could be felt over a long distance. Miles.

As kids, all four of the Hawk sisters had learned to shield their emotions from each other, and their grandmother, most of the time. Eventually, the block had become habit, done without thinking. In her excitement, she'd let the block slip. Hastily, she threw her mental wall back up.

"I'm just excited to have a job, nothing more," Hazel fibbed. She spun away and hurried into the store's back room. Unfortunately, because she had no customers at the moment, Amber followed.

"You are such a liar. What are you hiding? You might as well tell me. One of us will get it out of you." She sat on the small red sofa in the staff area.

"Smells good in here," Hazel deflected.

"She was making lavender candles," a disembodied voice complained. "I can't abide lavender. Calming, my left butt cheek. It gets my hackles up."

"What's wrong with lavender, Ev?" Hazel looked around the room trying to locate the speaker. Evelyn Woods, the former owner of the building, was one of the store's two resident ghosts.

"My grandmother, the old hag, always used lavender soap. Every time I smell it, I see her grumpy, judgmental face and get annoyed." Ev appeared at the tiny kitchen table with a small popping sound. A second pop heralded the arrival of Kansas McGuire, the shop's second ethereal resident.

"I adore it," Kansas piped in. "I might not have gotten hooked on drugs and OD'd if I'd learned about calming herbs. Even now, it helps me chill."

"You would have had to stay in school and not drop out for that," Ev countered.

The duo had a love-hate relationship. They'd only revealed themselves to the family a few weeks ago and they'd been bickering good naturedly since. Despite their constant arguing, the pair had steadfastly refused to admit why they remained on the physical plain rather than passing through the veil to the spirit world. Being tied to the building had to get old after a while.

"Get used to smelling lavender," Amber warned. "It's my best-selling candle."

Ev and Kansas groaned in unison. "I love the smell, but not everyday. When you make candles, the smell is so overwhelming."

"Back to the matter at hand." Amber flicked her long, dark brown hair over her shoulder. "Fess up, Hazel. What actually happened at your interview...besides getting the job?"

"Oh, I smell gossip," Ev chimed in.

"Ugh. I think I liked it better when you two kept yourselves hidden." Hazel glared at the duo. Ev shrugged and Kansas stuck out her tongue. They were an entertaining, if impudent, pair.

"Hazel," Amber taunted, "don't make me call Laz."

"Fine." She dropped onto the couch beside her sister with a groan. "He's cute."

"How cute?" Amber teased.

Sisters were such a pain in the ass. "Like trip over my tongue and the sidewalk cute," she confessed, burying her head in her hands.

"So, totally hot then?" Amber pressed.

"Way too hot. Good thing he works the floor, and the office is in his house." Shoot! She hadn't meant to reveal that little detail.

Amber and both ghosts gasped.

"Is it a good idea to work in his house?" Her sister asked, all evidence of teasing gone from her voice. A frown dimmed her teasing smile.

"It isn't exactly in the house. Well, it is, but it isn't." She snapped her mouth shut hoping Amber would let it drop. She should have known her overprotective sister would interfere. She always did.

"Explain." The single word was a demand. "I won't have my sister working in unsafe conditions. You don't need a job that badly."

Being the youngest of four girls felt like a burden. Everyone else thought they could run her life and were ridiculously over-protective. "I do need the job, no matter what you think. Technically, the office is in the house." She held up a hand to stop the protest she saw coming. "But it's in a porch-entry and separate from the real house. I doubt I'll see much of Dennis anyway, he's short staffed and works in the garden center itself. Okay?" She held back a wince at the belligerence in her voice. She was looking forward to seeing him every day.

"Can you trust him? Did you get any bad vibes from him? Do we need to send Gramma or Laz over to read him?"

"Don't even think about sending them. I can handle this. I swear. Honestly? I didn't get much from him, but there wasn't anything overtly negative or dark and certainly no signs of magic or evil anywhere I looked. And I did look."

White, or good magic left a residue behind, sort of a sparkle, which other magical practitioners could see. It faded over time until it disappeared. Dark magic, what some people called black magic, left darkness, as if all light had been sucked away. She hadn't seen evidence of either.

After their recent run-in with a dark sorcerer named Keres, the entire family was super careful. With a lot of luck, and skill, they had managed to defeat Keres, barely. Hazel nearly died that day when Keres conjured a swarm of wasps. She was deathly allergic to them. It had taken every ounce of her sister Hyacinth's healing skill to save Hazel. She might not have made it if not for Amber's fiancé and his grandmother's help.

Death had walked too close to them, to all of them, during the battle. Only their ability to blend and combine their magical skills had saved them. They'd injured Keres badly, and in the aftermath, he'd been arrested by the Witch's Council and taken to a secure center for incarceration and healing. Part of her found it hard to believe he was gone, and not coming back.

Keres had been searching for something, an item he claimed her ancestors had stolen, though he'd never revealed what it was. In the weeks since his defeat, they'd spent dozens of hours searching family records without finding a clue.

Both Amber and Lazuli had experienced visions since the clash. Amber's involved a cloth wrapped item and running water. Hers seemed to come to her from the past. Lazuli's were vague visions of a potential future and more threats to their family. None of them would fully relax until they discovered what Keres had sought.

Consequently, Dennis's bias against magic was both a comfort and an annoyance. At least Dennis wasn't magical. Now, all she had to worry about was her strange attraction to him and how his casual touches made her feel alive.

"I guess your new boss seems safe then? Not a threat or potential threat?" Amber persisted, arms crossed over her chest, her face set in a serious, slightly threatening mask.

Hazel considered the question. "Yes." The only danger she could perceive was her attraction to Dennis. "There's no magic there, despite the greenhouse having the healthiest plants I've ever seen, anywhere, except in our own greenhouses. I've been there dozens of times since Dennis took over from the previous owners. There's a peace there, a serenity, that wasn't there before he arrived."

"You think it's natural?" Ev asked. A former witch herself, she was well versed in magic.

"You took the words right out of my mouth," Amber laughed.

"I think it's due to proper care and watering. Those plants feel loved, but it's not magic. I think he might be genuinely gifted with growing things."

"Be careful anyway," Amber advised, obviously taking her big sister role seriously. "We need to keep our guard up."

"Are you keeping yours up now that you're practically living with Kody and not safely at home with the rest of us?" She was joking. Sort of. Kody's apartment was the suite above their shop. Both spaces were magically warded for protection and to prevent unwanted entry. The comment would get her sister's goat, and as the youngest, she loved teasing her siblings as much as they loved bossing her around.

"At least we have privacy here," Amber retorted, half angry. "At the house there's always someone interrupting our privacy. We're never alone which isn't healthy for a new relationship."

Sasha, the shop cat, hopped up onto Hazel's lap. "And they need their privacy." The cat chirped. "They're always all kissy faced or making out."

Sasha, a black and white cat with a grey sash across her chest, had wandered into the shop one day and declared it her home. Somehow, she had magic enough to get from the shop into the apartment through closed doors. Amber's fiancé had been the first to hear Sasha talk. Recently, she'd begun talking to them all and never missed a chance to blurt out something sarcastic or inappropriate.

"You could always move out," Amber suggested. "Move into the house with everyone else."

"And leave my fans? My people need me." Sasha let out an indignant meow. She and her brood of kittens were favorites with customers. All six babies were already spoken for and would leave for their forever homes in a couple weeks.

Hazel elected to ignore the cat's vanity. "Time for a celebratory tea. I've got a job!" She set Sasha on the floor and rose to fill the kettle. She had the ability to move things telekinetically, but usually did things the normal, non-magical way. Especially in the shop where a customer might come in at any time. Additionally, it would be way too easy to become dependent on magic. Besides, she was a highly active person and staying still for too long made her antsy. She loved being on the move. Dancing, jogging, yoga, walking...it didn't matter, she loved it all. Except swimming. She could do without water sports.

She was a water witch with the ability to locate and control water. That didn't mean she liked it. Once upon a time, she had loved it. But after nearly drowning when she was ten, she avoided anything deeper than a bathtub. The only exception to avoiding water was the nearby creek. She loved wading in the creek, but only when it was running slowly, and she could clearly see the bottom. Nothing deeper than mid-calf.

When Keres blew up part of Raven Falls during his reign of terror, she'd joined the rescue team on the lake. Barely functional due to her fear, she'd survived the day only by channeling her strongest will. Her fears had taken a back seat to the lives of others.

"Seriously," she put the kettle on the burner and turned to face Amber. "When are you guys coming home? The house seems empty without you. It misses you. I miss you."

"Probably never, except to visit. We're going to build our own place, as soon as the plans are finished. Frank Perrum, who owns the lumber yard is also a draftsman. He's working with us to create our dream house."

"Oh." Sadness overwhelmed Hazel, squashing her elation over finally landing a job. She'd slept in the room beside Amber's every day of her life. It didn't feel right that her sister was breaking up the family for a man.

Amber walked over and hugged Hazel. "Cheer up, Sis. I won't be far. We're building on the family land. Down by the orchard. Close enough to come mooch dinner as often as we can. Nobody can cook like Gramma Pearl."

"That's good. I guess." As much as her three older sisters were enormous pains, she loved them. Hell, she loved Amber's Kody too. Her favorite sister was moving out. It felt worse that she begrudged her sister's happiness.

"There was a time when I didn't think I'd ever want to move away from my family." Amber explained. "Times change. Kody's my family too. If we're going to make our relationship, and our marriage work, I need to spend time alone with him."

Logically, the words made sense, but deep down, in her heart, she felt...abandoned. Family was everything.

"Besides, don't you want a niece or nephew to spoil?"

Hazel jerked out of Amber's embrace. "Are you pregnant?" She asked excitedly. Wouldn't that be amazing?

"No. Not yet." Amber grinned.

"Are you trying? A new baby to cuddle would be fabulous."

"We aren't actively preventing it," Amber replied with an unusually shy smile.

"Did you tell Kody all Hawk babies are female?" In all the Hawk family records, there hadn't been a single male child born since the Salem Witch Trials.

Their family was, by accident, or design, based on a matriarchy. With no sons, the women had kept the Hawk family name, passing the name, along with their magical knowledge and skills onto their daughters.

"He figured it out for himself, but he's hoping to beat the trend. I warned him not to get his hopes up."

"Oh, I can't wait," Hazel said with a chuckle.

"I can." After her sarcastic response, Ev popped out.

"What was that all about?" Kansas asked. "I better check on her." Slowly, she faded away to wherever ghosts went when they weren't visible.

The bell out front jangled and Amber hurried to serve their customer. Hazel poured the water over loose-leaf pineapple-orange tea and breathed deeply, drawing the familiar, comforting scent in. What a day!

A new boss. A handsome, sexy one to boot. Her sister moving out. Her sister trying to have a baby. A hot boss, who was a witchaphobe. Up. Down. Up. Down. A crazy emotional rollercoaster and it was grating on her nerves.

Mug of hot tea in her hands, she sat back on the sofa, crossed her legs and closed her eyes. Breathing calmly, slowly, she centered herself and took a moment to count her blessings.

Her eyes popped open. Tomorrow morning, eight o'clock sharp, she went to work for the hottest man she'd ever met. Oddly, excitement flooded through her.

So much for calm.

Chapter Four

"Is Dennis in?" Hazel asked Rosa Hunley, the lady manning the garden center's cash register. Rosa had worked at the garden center for as long as Hazel could remember. In her mid-fifties, she was an institution and knew almost as much about plants as Hazel.

"Hi, Hazel. He's up at the house. He said he'd meet you in the office."

"Thanks, Rosa. How's your Mom?" After a few moments of small talk, Hazel hurried toward the office, it wouldn't do to be late on her first day. She'd have loved to stop and smell the flowers and enjoy the calm and quiet, but work waited. If she wanted to linger in the greenhouses, she'd have to remember to make arrangements to start later or leave home earlier.

She rapped on the back door with her knuckles and let herself in. Dennis wasn't in the office. She looked around for a moment, wondering where he was. Dust and stale air assaulted her nose. The outside door, like the office window, was shut tight. The place needed some fresh air. She opened them both, letting the breeze blow through.

Better, but not enough. A short, wide, three-wick candle sat on the shelf behind the desk. Dennis's or a remnant of the previous owners? She walked around and leaned in to smell it. Lovely. Lemony and outdoorsy. Two of her favorites. She cleared some room and moved it to the desk and rummaged around in her purse for a lighter.

She'd barely lit the first wick when Dennis arrived.

"What are you doing?" He demanded.

"Lighting a candle?" Why was he so upset? "Is that okay?" Guilt flooded through her. She shouldn't have touched his stuff without asking.

"I told you, no magic. Put it out." He crossed his arms over his chest and scrunched his brows together.

Anger replaced guilt. "What?" She blew out the candle. "It's your candle. It's not magic, it's just a candle. It's stale in here, in case you didn't notice. I'm sorry if I offended you by using your candle to freshen the room," she snapped.

She didn't give him time to respond. "Is this how it's going to be? You questioning my every move? If so, you can stuff your job up your..." She bit back the last word, realizing she, like him, might be overreacting. "I agreed to no magic. I meant it, Dennis. I'll keep my word. I don't know why you're so dead set against it and it's none of my business, but I promise you I will not do anything even remotely magical on your property. Ever." She breathed deeply and forced her clenched hands to unfurl. She needed to get a grip.

She looked down at the desk at the water bottle she'd brought with her. Bubbles perked their way up from the bottom. Shit. She struggled for calm. She'd let her emotions run away. She looked up at him and crossed her arms over her chest, mimicking his posture. "Are we good? Or shall I go?"

His mouth opened and snapped shut. He closed his eyes and rubbed the bridge of his nose. "We're good. I apologize. Go ahead, light the candle; it is stale in here," he admitted.

She bit back a snarky comment. If this were her family, she'd have let it fly, but she was trying to be professional, and she'd already failed. His paranoia about magic was off the charts. He must have known an unethical magic practitioner. Someone who dabbled in dark magic or had hurt him with their magic.

Dark magic wasn't her style, nor was it her family's style. They practiced white magic and never used it to control others, but she'd met people who did. One of her family's cardinal rules was, "Do as you will, with harm to none." Except for teenage angst and hissy fits directed toward her sisters when she was younger, she abided by that rule and she resented his implication that she might behave otherwise.

"I'm sorry." He shuffled his feet and looked down at the floor. "I'll try to contain my bias."

She didn't know how to respond, so she nodded her acceptance. "I'd like to get started if that's okay?"

He blinked rapidly. "Okay. I set you up on the dining room table, inside. You said you needed room to sort paperwork. It's the best, largest, space I've got."

In his house? So much for the idea she'd be safely away from his personal space. "You're the boss," she replied after an uncomfortably long pause. "I won't light the candle then." She returned the candle to the shelf after reassuring herself it was extinguished.

"The receipts are inside. And the laptop. Do you mind telling me your plan for sorting this mess out?"

"I'll sort everything by date first. That'll allow me to enter each month's bills and reconcile with the bank statements before moving to the next month. Less chance of carrying forward errors if I go one month at a time."

She followed Dennis into the house. When he removed his shoes, she removed hers. They walked through a small entryway, past the kitchen with a green and white wood table. Adjacent to it was a tiny breakfast nook with seats built into the bay window that faced the long row of greenhouses. He came to a halt just inside the dining room, beside a massive oak table that could easily accommodate a dozen people. Three eating areas in one house. Incredible. She'd known the house was large, but wow. Just wow.

"Your table is huge," she blurted.

"It came with the house. I guess the old owner must have liked to entertain. He lived here with his wife. No kids." He shrugged. "Everything is here. There's fresh coffee in the kitchen, help yourself."

"Thank you." She stared at the massive box of receipts. "Are those all business expenses?" She couldn't fathom accumulating so many receipts in six months.

"Um. No." His face turned pink. "Set aside the personal ones and call me if you can't tell. My number is on that sticky note." He pointed to a neon green note stuck to the laptop. "I'll leave you to get started. I'll be in the greenhouse. Thanks for this."

"You're welcome?" The statement turned into a question as she stared at his rapidly retreating back. By the goddess, he had a nice ass. "Okay then. Coffee first, then work."

She poured coffee into a black and white checkered mug she found hanging below the cupboard and debated with herself for a full two minutes before she went searching in the fridge for milk. As much as she adored coffee, she preferred it milky white. Tea was black, coffee well doctored. Besides, he wouldn't want her to drink it black, would he? In her mind, offering coffee implied permission to add the fixings.

Coffee at her side, she dug into the receipts. There was absolutely no organization. Right side up, upside down. Folded. Flat, wrinkled. Scrunched into little balls. Yesterday's receipt lay atop one nearly six months old. Unopened bank statements. It was absolute chaos. He must have spilled the box, at least once. Probably repeatedly. She was in heaven sorting it all out. Bringing order from chaos was fulfilling and soothing. She wished she was one of those extremely rare witches who could zap things in order. She wouldn't have, but it might be nice to have that option.

She was barely into the deep box when he returned for lunch, accompanied by the enticing aroma of pepperoni and cheese.

"Sorry to interrupt. I need lunch. I skipped breakfast. Want some pizza?"

She recognized the gesture as an olive branch. "I'd love some, thanks. It smells delicious." She rinsed her coffee cup and set it in the sink. She grabbed a cola from her insulated lunch bag before joining him in the breakfast nook. She hadn't been sure of her lunch plans, so she'd packed food, just in case she didn't get home.

They ate right out of the box, not bothering with plates or forks. She was finished her second piece before she spoke.

"What brought you to Three Moon Falls?" She grabbed another slice and took a huge bite to keep from spewing out more questions. She was curious about him and wanted to pester him with questions.

He chewed for a moment and swallowed before answering. "I wanted to try something new."

"What did you do before?" Dang her wayward mouth. She couldn't keep it shut. Luckily, he didn't seem to mind.

"I was a partner in a landscaping business in Drayton Valley. I liked the work, but both my partner and I were tired of the relentless physical labor. Manning a shovel is for the young. We decided to sell the business."

She sipped her cola. "Why Three Moon Falls?" She grinned. "Yes, I'm nosy."

He chuckled. "The greenhouse was for sale. I had no real ties to Drayton, except friends. I have friends near here, and my brother lives on a farm west of town. He's got three kids. I wanted to be closer to them." He gestured vaguely. "And here I am."

"What brought *you* to Three Moon Falls?" He shot her question back at her.

"Born here. The Hawk family has lived here for generations, about a hundred years." She nibbled on her pizza. Her family connection went deeper. Their use of magic had seeped into their land and property, infusing it with a magic of its own.

"Town founders then? I read the town's website, it's not much older than a hundred years."

"Not quite founders, from what I understand, but close. Mom's married to Trevor Moon. His family were founders. They used to own practically all the surrounding area. Some kind of government grant. They named the town after the series of falls flowing into the lake and sold off a lot of the property when times were tough."

"I guess your mom being married to a founder makes you important around here."

There was a tone in his voice she couldn't quite identify. Not a simple question, not derision, but something. She chalked it up to curiosity and chose to ignore it.

"Important? That's funny. The only time the Moon name is valuable is on Founder's Day. Besides, Trevor is my stepdad. I'm not a blood relative." She wrinkled her nose. "I'm a nobody around here."

"That's not the rumor I heard." He slid the last bite of a slice into his mouth and wiped his fingers on a napkin.

And there it was. She was certain he was referring to her family's magical abilities. She'd wondered how long it would take him to bring it up. Her family was important in the magical community. They weren't part of a coven, but they had provided magic supplies long before their store opened to the general public.

"You're referring to our standing in the magical community. How did you find out about that? Typically, magicals keep their mouths shut." Learning someone was gossiping about her family was aggravating and disappointing. Problems happened when witches were outed. Big problems. Just look at Salem.

"I just overheard some stuff at the café when I first moved in, that's all."

Which no doubt led to his bias against witches. "You make a habit of listening to gossip? Do you believe everything you hear? Most of what they say is total bullshit, if you'll excuse the language." She'd expected better of him than listening to the rumor mill. The delicious pizza was starting to weigh heavily in her guts.

"Typically? No. But I've known some less than ethical witches, so I paid attention even though, at the time, I didn't think it would affect me. At least not until your resume landed in my inbox. Then I arranged an interview and chose to judge for myself."

"I sent my resume in almost a month before you replied." She'd long since given up on hearing back before he returned her email. She couldn't quite keep her voice from sounding accusatory. Apparently, his bias against magic was a bigger deal to him than she'd realized. Familiar with the discomfort of being judged, she tried not to judge others and now, she was being a cow. "Sorry. I'm extra defensive today for some reason."

Dennis sighed and stood to make a fresh pot of coffee. The dark liquid flowed, and the glass carafe was full before either of them spoke.

"In the interest of honesty," he said, "If I could have found someone qualified without a reputation for magic, you never would have gotten an interview."

How did she even respond to that? "Ouch. We're not all unethical." She was beyond hurt that he'd labelled her without knowing who she was.

"Which is part of the reason why I decided to give you the benefit of the doubt."

"That and your total desperation to get your ginormous stack of receipts under control." She closed the lid on the empty pizza box. To her shock, Dennis laughed.

"True enough," he replied when his mirth faded. "Guilty as charged. My need for organization outweighed your reputation and judging by the many piles on the other table, I made a good decision."

"Thank you. I promise you won't regret hiring me. Do you mind if I make myself some tea? I'm not much for coffee in the afternoon."

"I don't have any tea bags. Sorry."

"No problem. I brought my own. I rarely drink commercial tea. I prefer our family blends." She dug in her purse. "Wow. Didn't that sound pompous?" She stood and filled the kettle she saw on the counter. "I'll just make this and take it back to work with me. I can't be caught slacking off. My boss is a no-nonsense hard-ass." The joke was out before she realized it was coming. Damn.

"I think he might cut you some slack on your first day." Dennis chuckled. "But no slacking on your second day," he shot back.

She turned and saluted him impudently. "Yes, sir. I'll keep that in mind, sir."

He threw up his hands in mock despair. "I get no respect around here." He winked. "Talk to you later. I'll be in the greenhouse; I've got a string of interviews scheduled. I'm hiring for the summer rush."

His wink went straight to her heart. He hadn't meant anything more than teasing, but it felt—personal and entirely too good. She hadn't expected this magnetic attraction between them, despite the crazy pull she'd felt the first time she saw him.

"Good luck. I'll let you know if I have any questions." He dawdled in the doorway.

She poured hot water into her mug. Not boiling water, full boil could draw out the bitter in the delicate herbs in her mug. Instantly, the fresh aromas of apple, mint and chamomile flooded her senses.

"That smells good," Dennis commented. "Almost good enough to make me try it."

"Four Season Metaphysical Teas will surprise you and convert you to a tea drinker. Want a cup? I've got lots."

"Maybe later, thanks. I need coffee to brace me for interviewing. It's my least favorite part of this job, well, except for accounting. I better go, I've lingered too long already. I'll be back later." He filled his coffee cup, grabbed the empty pizza box and left.

The man needed a single cup brewer, or an insulated carafe for his coffee. He'd wasted most of two pots already.

Dennis threw the pizza box into his compost bin. He had a shredder for processing the larger pieces, so the organics became usable more quickly. His personal and garden center's compost went into making his own soil enhancers. He wasted as little as he could. Recycling and composting were a natural part of his day. He wondered if Hazel cared about the environment. Probably, if his ex was any indication, magicals seemed to care a lot about mother earth.

He'd have to ask her. It would give them something to talk about tomorrow at lunch. He paused mid-step. Was he planning on making lunch with Hazel part of his daily routine? He resumed his journey toward the greenhouse. Why not? She was attractive and a decent conversationalist. She was in his house.

While he made a point of talking to every one of his staff members each day, a lot of them were young parents or college students and he didn't have much in common with them. Despite knowing Hazel was a witch, he was comfortable around her and wanted to get to know her better.

He stopped to pull some small weeds from an enormous, potted, chestnut vine. Could Hazel be affecting his mind the way his ex, Natalia had influenced his? He didn't think so. He wasn't getting that weird ache in the back of his skull. The one he'd learned to associate with Natalia trying to twist his mind.

He reminded himself he was giving Hazel the benefit of the doubt. She had promised not to do magic on his property, and he was going to try his best to trust her. He probably needed to try harder.

Ten people were waiting for him in the staff room. Eight college kids, a woman who looked to be in her late-thirties and a man about the same age.

Dennis introduced himself and started a full tour of the greenhouse property. Ten minutes in, one girl raised her hand.

"Yes? You have a question?"

"Um. Am I gonna have to, like, lift those bags of dirt? Or can I just, you know, run the register? I like to stay clean." She brushed some imaginary dirt from her skirt.

He noticed her stiletto heels for the first time. She mightn't be the best fit for a job which involved dirt, and if the weather was bad, mud.

"Yes, you'll be lifting bags of soil. The heaviest is only thirty pounds." None of his other staff had trouble with the bags. "Everyone works the floor, the yard, and the register. Except Evan who is in a wheelchair. He's excused from lifting. You will get dirty, but you'll also have an apron to protect your clothing."

"Oh."

He saw the disappointment and disgust on her face. "If this isn't what you expected, you don't have to stay for the interview. No hard feelings." He smiled brightly, trying to reassure her. No sense hiring someone clearly unfit for the job. He thought he'd made the job duties clear in his advertisement, apparently not.

She looked at the ground and shuffled her feet. "Okay. Bye then." She hurried away.

"Anyone else?" When no one responded, he finished the tour and walked them back to the staff room and set them up with cold drinks, and cookies from the local bakery.

One by one, he took them to his secondary office at the end of the retail space for an interview and narrowed the group down to six. Two girls, two somewhat rowdy guys and the two adults. The young men might need a bit of extra supervision at first, but he could tap into their energy and turn them into good, strong employees. He'd done it before.

The university aged girls seemed steady and responsible, he hired them, and the boys, on the spot as he finished each interview. The adults were another story. Hiring and firing kids was one thing. Adults who might have dependents were another thing entirely. He wanted to be certain he had the right people. For his sake, and theirs.

For his landscaping business, he'd done all hiring in conjunction with his partner. He trusted his ability but liked the comfort of having a back-up opinion. Too bad he didn't have that option now. Unless...

"Are you okay to hang around for a bit longer?" Dennis asked the remaining two candidates. "I'd like to have you talk to my office manager before I make a final decision. It's part of the hiring process. With their agreement, he hurried to the house to talk to Hazel.

She was concentrating hard, a small frown on her face. She looked adorable.

"Hey, I need a favor," he stated as soon as she noticed him in the room.

"Sure, what can I do for you?" She returned a handful of receipts to the box and focused her attention on him.

Her total concentration was unnerving and attractive.

"My interviews are going well. I've hired a couple kids and declined a couple more." Now with Hazel standing in front of him, asking for her help didn't seem like such a great plan. It was like admitting he didn't know what he was doing or didn't trust his own decision-making ability.

"How does that factor into a favor?" She asked.

He'd already asked for help, he couldn't really back down now. Might as well forge on ahead and ignore the potential blow to his ego. "I have two people left. I'd like to get your take on them."

"Me?" Her eyes widened in surprise. "Why me?" Her mouth snapped shut. "You're not asking me to read them...magically, are you? Right after you told me no magic? I don't have that skill and I wouldn't use it if I did." She propped her hands on her hips, clearly waiting for his response.

Oh. She sounded pissed. He'd mishandled an already bad idea. Why was he always sticking his foot in his mouth around her? He grasped for a good, non-offensive response.

"No. Not at all. Just a normal second opinion." She relaxed slightly, so he went on. "I'm considering two adults. I want to be as certain as I can before I hire someone who might have dependents. That's where you come in." He'd left them until last, and for the positions requiring more hours than a typical teen would like.

"You don't trust yourself?"

He winced when she hit the nail on the head. "I do, but I used to hire in conjunction with my partner. We each interviewed a few candidates. If they passed their interview with me, they had one with my partner and vice versa. All hires were joint decision. We rarely disagreed." He looked Hazel square in the eye. "One of today's interviews is a single mother who let her status slip during the tour. I think she'll be a good fit, but before I hire her, I want to be sure."

"You're asking me, a virtual stranger, who has worked for you for," she looked at her watch, "for six hours, to back you up? You know that's nuts, right?"

"Probably, but will you do it? I don't feel comfortable messing with her life if she isn't going to last." Hazel hesitated so long he thought she was going to refuse.

"And no blame on me if they don't work out?" Her steady gaze caught his and challenged him to agree.

For a moment, he was so tangled up in those lovely brown eyes, he forgot the question.

"Well?"

"Yeah," he blurted. "No blame."

"And I get to ask questions?"

"You get to ask questions," he affirmed without a moment of doubt.

"Fine then. I'll help. What positions are you hiring for?"

He explained as they walked to the staff room. She asked a few questions to clarify what he was looking for, impressing him with how serious she was taking the task. Except for the two prospective hires, the staff room was empty. He introduced them to Hazel who hid her surprise at being called his office manager.

"Mathew, why don't you go out and familiarize yourself with the sales floor while we talk to Sarah? We'd finish in my office, but it isn't big enough for three people." Dennis suggested. "This won't take long."

After asking Sarah to be seated, Hazel sat across from her, leaving Dennis to take a seat at the end of the staff table. "Sarah, tell me what makes you a good fit for Get Growing?" Hazel asked kindly.

The tall, thin, blonde woman folded her hands together and set them on the table. Her knuckles whitened as if she were trying to still her nerves. "I love plants. I had a large garden before I was forced to move. I've taken several online horticultural classes, and before I had kids, I worked in retail for years. I was a manager for a ladies wear store."

Hazel jotted some notes on a notepad she'd brought along. He thought she'd meant to use it as a prop. Apparently, he was wrong.

Hazel fired questions at Sarah, one after the other and made more notes. "I have a couple of final questions and we're finished." She took a deep breath. "Legally, I can't ask you this, so feel free to decline, it won't hurt your chances of getting this job if you choose not to answer."

What the hell? Dennis gave Hazel a wide-eyed look. She shook her head slightly.

"Go ahead," Sarah said. "Ask away."

"How many kids do you have, and who watches them while you're at work?"

"Jesus, Hazel, you can't ask that." Dennis groaned.

"It's okay," Sarah said with a smile.

"I only ask because you mentioned children earlier, and I, we, want to be sure we're keeping their best interests in mind. I know you're new in town and childcare can be an issue."

Her words and tone were kind and compassionate. Dennis relaxed slightly. But what was she thinking? These questions could put him in deep trouble. It was illegal to ask them.

"My husband passed away seven months ago. I have three-year-old twins. One of each. We're living with my aunt. We moved here so she could help us get back on our feet. It was her idea. My own mother has passed and my aunt has no children of her own. We're making ourselves a new family. She'll be watching the kids for me."

"That's wonderful for you and your children. Thank you for your honesty," Hazel praised. "I'm glad you're finding a way to get along. You'll love Three Moon Falls. We're a very supportive community."

Hazel looked at Dennis and nodded slightly. He rose to his feet and offered Sarah his hand. "Welcome to the team. If you're still interested, we'd love to hire you."

"Oh! Thank you so much. I'd love to work here. When do I start?"

They quickly worked out the details and she was on her way.

"I think we did well." Hazel smiled at Dennis. How could he have missed Sarah's potential? She thought he'd have a heart attack when she asked the final question. "I think she'll make a fabulous employee."

"That's what I thought. Though I can't believe you asked her those personal questions. We could have gotten in legal hot water."

"Maybe. But she had a sense of calm eagerness about her. I took a risk. She didn't have to answer me. I didn't think it would be a problem if I focused on our concern for her children."

"You probably shouldn't have taken the risk, but at least it worked out okay. I'll go get Mathew. Try not to ask him personal questions. Okay?"

"No guarantees, but I'll try." She grinned.

He shook his head and left. While he was gone, she got herself a glass of water. Dennis was back in less than five minutes. He re-introduced her to Mathew, a short, stocky man in his thirties with black hair, icy blue eyes and pale skin. He smelled vaguely of incense and cigarette smoke.

His smile was completely fake and his handshake excessively strong. She disliked him on sight. Something about him made her skin crawl. It took everything she had not to leave the room. Still, first impressions could be deceiving. His negative vibe could easily be because he was tired of waiting for the interview process to be complete. It had been hours since Dennis said he was going to start them.

"Where were you last employed?" she asked, getting right down to business.

"I was a gardener and landscaper in Edmonton." He named a wealthy businessman who had recently passed on. No easy way to check the details.

"And before that?" she asked ignoring Dennis's raised eyebrow at the blunt question.

"I worked there for eight years. Previously, I worked at Home Depot. The information is all on my resume, including my supervisor's name and number."

"Are you seeking long-term employment? We're hiring for part-time seasonal at the moment." Dennis said.

"I'll take seasonal to start. Preferably full time. I'm confident I'll prove myself to you, and potentially turn seasonal into long-term."

Confident? He sounded arrogant to Hazel.

"Would you accept seasonal, part-time?" Hazel asked.

"Absolutely. I came to Three Moon Falls because of the mysteries of the lake. I'm learning diving. My previous position included room and board. I have a substantial nest egg. I like to be busy, and I love working with herbs." His smile was probably meant to be reassuring but it left Hazel cold. Working with herbs was often a euphemism for performing magic, and for smoking drugs.

Everything about this man set off warning bells in her mind. From his smell and cold eyes, through his uncheckable employment, and right on to the way he said mysteries of the lake and working with herbs. She'd bet her last candle that he was magic, dark magic, though she couldn't get a read on it. He had a wall up and it made her nervous. After Keres, she was cautious, maybe excessively so. Hiring him didn't feel right. She gave Dennis a slight shake of her head.

His brows pinched together. Obviously, he disagreed. He continued to ask questions. On the surface, the answers ticked all the right boxes, but her witchy senses were screaming like she was caught in a tsunami, like she was drowning all over again. Mathew Brown wasn't what or who he seemed to be.

"Please give us a minute to discuss this," Dennis asked.

"Absolutely. I'll be outside. Take your time." Again, the perfect answer, but it reeked of insincerity.

When he was gone, Hazel shut the door, and took a moment to shake off the willies he'd given her and turned to Dennis.

"I like him," Dennis declared. "What about you?"

"He makes me uncomfortable," she replied honestly. "Something about him sets my nerves on edge. I can't put my finger on what."

"I already talked to his Home Depot supervisor. He is highly recommended."

She winced. "Maybe so, but that was years ago, nearly a decade. If I were you, I'd pass on him."

"Is this your normal opinion or your witch opinion?" He scrubbed a hand over his face. "Sorry. I worded that poorly."

"Frankly, I'm not good at magically reading people, but he makes my witch radar scream. He might not be who he claims he is. Or he might be hiding something. That's my magical and my *human* assessment."

"Thanks for your honesty, but I still like him. He's got experience, he's strong and fit. I'm going to take a chance on him."

"Doesn't his story set off any alarms for you?" He made her skin crawl; she didn't even want to be in the same room with him. It was probably irrational, but it was what it was.

"None. I'm going to hire him."

She wondered why Dennis had even asked her opinion if he was going to disregard it. Oh well, she'd be working in the office, and wouldn't have to deal with Mathew often. She'd be damn sure her guard was up when he was around.

"I guess that's your choice. I'll just head back to my accounting."

Wandering back to the house, she wished the garden center was haunted by a friendly ghost, like the duo at the shop. Occasionally, ghosts could pick up different vibes from humans or witches which would be handy right now. Of course, there was no way she'd be able to explain her skill at talking with the dead to Dennis.

She put the matter from her mind. His business, his employees. His problems.

Chapter Five

Dennis stood, hands on his hips, staring out over a sea of potted shrubs. Most he grew himself, though there were several varieties he'd brought in from local tree farms. He'd like to grow them all, but time, space, and staff were limited commodities. He was proud of what he was building here.

Firm steps on the gravel path came from behind him, breaking his enjoyment of the rare moment of peace.

"Hey, dude." The familiar voice had Dennis whirling around to greet his old friend.

"Bert. Good to see you." They clasped arms and slapped each other's backs in a cozy man-hug. "What brings you here? Looking for some shrubs? I've got whatever you need." He gestured at the products he'd been admiring.

"Got time for a brew?"

"Always." Dennis checked the time. Eight-forty-five. Darn near closing time. "Let me check with the girls out front. If everything's good, we can head to the house and crack a couple of cold ones. I'll toss some steaks on too." It had been entirely too long since they'd shared a beer. He could use a good bullshit session.

"That'd be great."

Dennis glanced at his tall, blond friend as they strolled toward the greenhouse. His usual farmer's smile was missing. He looked haggard and exhausted. This was about more than beers between friends. Something was up.

Nothing required Dennis's immediate attention in the retail shop, so before long, they were settled on his deck, enjoying a cold beer, and the last of the sun's rays.

"What's up man? You look stressed." He'd broken the guy code by asking but didn't care. Having prompted him and knowing his friend would talk when he was ready, Dennis leaned back in his chair and sipped heaven's nectar. The bottle was a product of a small local brewery. Not top of the line imported beer, but quite delicious.

"You called it," Bert said, frowning. "You were one hundred percent right. Do you have any idea how much that pisses me off?" He groaned and dropped his head back against the chair.

"I'm always right. What, specifically, pisses you off?" Dennis laughed, and crossed his ankles where they rested on the railing.

"Laura's gone." The toneless words spoke to the depth of his friend's pain.

"Shit." Dennis dropped his feet to the deck and leaned forward, elbows on his knees. "I'm sorry man. That sucks." As much as he loved being right, he didn't want it to be at the expense of his friend's happiness or relationship.

"Decided she didn't like rural life. Up and left. Left all those stupid llamas behind. I shouldn't have let her talk me into them. I'm a cattle rancher not a damned llama herder, farmer or whatever."

"Sell them. No reason to keep them if she's gone. Is there?" Laura leaving was a bugger but selling off three dozen llamas shouldn't be an issue.

"Already taken care of. Auction came to take the lot."

"What aren't you saying?" Dennis stood and opened the barbecue's propane valve and lid before hitting the igniter. It lit with a whoosh and the scent of burning meat. Damn. He'd meant to clean it after he ate last night. He grabbed the brush and scraped down the grates. Good thing the residue would burn clean while their foil wrapped potatoes cooked.

"I've got one llama left."

Dennis pivoted to stare at Bert. "Why didn't you sell them all?"

"The auction house wouldn't take them all. This one's a genetic anomaly, or something. They took one look at her and refused."

"What exactly is a genetic anomaly?"

"She's in the truck. You have to see it to understand. Throw some spuds on. I'm starved. Then we'll go look."

Puzzled, Dennis prepped some potato and onion packages and threw them on the grill before following Bert to his truck. The white Dodge had been fitted with a large wood-slat enclosure. Inside stood a pure white llama.

"She looks fine to me," Dennis said, walking around to look at her from all sides. "What's wrong with her?"

"This." Bert opened the end gate and slammed it shut with an enormous bang.

The llama's eyes closed, and it dropped onto its side, narrowly missing the edge of the box.

"What the hell? Did it just faint?" Dennis stared at the fallen animal and then at his friend.

Bert grinned like a damned fool. "Yup. Stupid thing is scared to death of loud noises and sudden movements. Faints every time. What the hell am I going to do with a fainting llama?"

Dennis laughed until he was out of breath. "Only you could end up with a drama llama." The words sent them both into fresh peals of laughter.

"What am I going to do with her? She'll be lonely at my place. I thought you could take her. For the petting zoo you talked about when you arrived in town." He flashed a hopeful smile.

"Hell no. She'd be lonely here too." He shook his head wildly back and forth. The petting zoo was a concept to go along with the small play park out front. Something to draw families in. He'd planned it for the future, not for now. There was space for it, but not enough staff.

"Come on," Bert urged. "She's great with kids and pot-bellied pigs. Chickens, whatever. I'll even teach you how to look after any other animals you buy to keep her company. I just want her gone. Her drama reminds me of Laura. Hell, I'll even give you the companion animals."

The naked pleading in Bert's voice was Dennis's undoing. They'd been friends since university. Bert had never asked for anything. Ever. *Shit.*

"Fine. You supply and build proper petting zoo pens for all of them. Llama, pigs, chickens, goats, whatever. Then, I'll take the stupid thing off your hands. My barn will work for winter, but not for daily interactions. But I better not regret this, or you'll pay." He'd planned on a petting zoo, next year. Not now.

"Thanks, man."

"Drive her down to the barn. It's empty but it's sound. She can live there until you fix her up a spot." They climbed into the truck. "I can't believe you're foisting a drama llama off on me."

"I can't believe you agreed." Bert roared with laughter. "I appreciate it. I'll find a way to repay you. I promise."

"I'm going to hold you to that. Fricken drama llama." He turned toward Bert. "why didn't you tell me about Laura? How long's she been gone?"

"Eight weeks." Bert put the truck into gear.

"Damn. I've seen you half a dozen times since then and you never said a word." He didn't really blame Bert; it wasn't easy to admit your choice in women sucked. Lord knows his ex was no prize. Funny thing was, he hadn't liked Laura, and Bert hadn't liked Natalia.

"We're going to have to start pre-approving each other's dates." Dennis sighed.

"Don't bet on me dating any time soon," Bert grumbled as they pulled up to the barn.

"Me either." Especially since he now had a petting zoo to look after. No time to get all his work done, and dating was even farther down the list. For a second, Hazel's face flashed into his mind. Nope. Not happening. One, she was his employee. Two, she was magical. That made her doubly off his list. Even if he had enjoyed having lunch with her

.

He must have muttered aloud because Bert said, "Enjoyed lunch with who?"

"Nobody."

"Who'd you have lunch with?" Bert pressed.

"My new bookkeeper."

"Is she hot?" Bert climbed out of the truck and walked around back to release the llama who had managed to regain her footing when they stopped.

"Ya. She's hot. But totally not my type. She'll never be more than an employee." He wasn't sure if he was reassuring himself or explaining to Bert.

"Right. Grab the hay." Bert helped the llama down a ramp he'd placed against the truck.

Dennis carried the bale to the barn and opened the door and flipped on the light. He breathed deep, enjoying the smell of hay and dust. Luckily, the place was clean and didn't smell like manure. Unlike his friend, he didn't much care for that particular smell.

Bert sliced open the bale and tossed half of it into a stall and carefully disposed of the twine which held it together. "She's set for the night. She'll just need water. I'll be back tomorrow with lumber and more feed."

They closed up the barn and got back into the truck. "I could use another beer," Bert said as he backed up. "And details on your hot new employee."

After they finished their steaks, Bert brought up the subject of women. "That steak was incredible. You're a barbecue master. Tell me about your new employee."

Dennis had hoped, in vain, that his friend would let it go but he knew better than to think Bert would let up now; the guy had the determination of a pit bull on a pork chop. Dennis launched into details. "I hired six people today."

"Whoa there. I only care about the hot one. You're not going to fall for her, are you?" His tone landed smack-dab between joking and dead serious.

"No chance of that. Hazel's a witch. I'm not riding that broom again." Even if she was pretty, sexy and smart.

"Hazel?" Bert's voice rose in alarm. "Hazel Hawk? You hired a witch after what Natalia did to you?"

"I'm giving her the benefit of the doubt. She seems competent." Aside from her reputation as a witch, she hadn't done anything upsetting. "I heard rumors, but nothing concrete."

"Just watch yourself. They've never done anything to me personally, but I've heard stories. Plus, after the falls blew up, some guy was found partially burned on their land. Rumor has it he blew up the falls and they retaliated. He's in some kind of special hospital now."

"Are you freaking kidding me?" This was news. He had heard about the explosion. The entire town had shuddered with the blast. People had died. He hadn't heard much after that. Could Hazel have been involved in the explosion, or with the guy getting burned? She didn't seem the type. She'd struck him as kind and caring. She'd been great with Sarah earlier.

"I'm not saying she was involved," Bert hedged. "I'm saying it is a bloody big coincidence." He sipped his beer.

Dennis rubbed his chest where stomach acid was giving him heart-burn before deciding he wasn't overly worried about Hazel's beliefs. She had a sense of calm kindness about her that he liked.

"I'll watch myself, and her," Dennis said at last. "I'm not dating her, she's an employee and as long as she doesn't do any magic here, I don't care what she does." Plus, they had a probationary period. "Have you ever met her, or her family?"

"Personally? No. I've only been in the area a few years, you know that. I'm not in town often. I know they have a new witch supply shop and it's doing well with locals and tourists. But they found some guy on her family's land. Police say he was camping there, illegally, and the guy with him died. It's suspicious if you ask me. Since you already hired her, I don't know, maybe watch your ass and try to give her the benefit of the doubt?" He shrugged. "And keep your dick in your pants."

"First, you're warning me against her, then telling me to try and trust her? You're insane."

"I know. But even after my divorce, I try and see the best in everyone. But there are rumors. You need to be aware of that."

"I'll be cautious. Plus, I'm swamped with customers and now I have a damned petting zoo to look after. It better bring me customers or I'm going to kick your ass."

"It will, guaranteed." He raised his beer bottle in a toast. "I can keep you in babies along with adults. Switch them out as they grow. Nothing cuter than a baby goat or pig."

Dennis raised his too. "To success for me and being free of a drama llama for you." They clinked bottles together and drank.

Dennis pondered Bert's advice as he sipped his beer. Keeping his distance from Hazel would be easy...if only she wasn't so easy to talk to and so damned attractive.

Chapter Six

Four days later, Dennis pulled his red Jeep Wrangler through the enormous, elaborate wrought iron gates onto Hawk land.

What the hell was he doing here? Hazel had invited him to her family's Summer Solstice celebration, and he'd said he wasn't sure he'd make it.

Way ahead, past the sea of vehicles parked on the neatly mown grass, an enormous Victorian style house rose into the air. It looked welcoming and strangely intimidating all at once. Kind of like Hazel. He parked at the end of a row of cars and sat staring at the large crowd gathered beside a cluster of tents and a roaring bonfire. It was barely one and they had a fire going already. Hazel had mentioned the event lasted until the evening. It seemed odd to have the fire going already.

Through his closed windows, he heard a classic rock song morph into a popular country tune. He searched the crowd and found a local DJ's van at the edge of the event. The enticing aroma of grilled meat tickled his nose. He might not know much about Hazel's family, but it looked like they put on a good party.

He hadn't really wanted to come, yet here he was, sitting on the sidelines, debating going home, without learning more about the Hawks, which was his true purpose for being here. He'd balked when Hazel invited him. What would he do at a witch's celebration? He'd caved when she explained the party was for everyone, magical and mundane. The family would have a private summer solstice celebration later, after everyone was gone.

This was crazy. He had no desire to be here. He wouldn't know anyone. He should just go home.

Motion outside his window caught his eye. His newest employee, Mathew Brown, stood beside the jeep, smiling. Dennis rolled down the window.

"Hey boss. You here for the party?" Matt asked with a crooked grin,

"Yeah, I guess." It surprised him to see Matt. Over the past few days, Hazel had stuck close to the office and turned away every time she saw Matt. She'd disliked him on sight and avoided him. When Dennis had Matt up to the house a couple of times, Hazel left immediately. That made him wonder how Matt had gotten invited to a special celebration. "I didn't expect to see you here."

"Me either." Matt's eyes narrowed. "But I was at the café and I heard about this solstice party. I guess it's kind of an open event. Come and go. So, I came by. Did you get a formal invitation?"

There was something hard in his voice which spoke of jealousy. Dennis flashed him a look and Matt's frown morphed into a grin.

Weird.

"I got an invite, but on second thought, I've decided to give it a miss. Think I'll just go."

"Come on. Let's go socialize. Meet some townies. Have a drink or two, eat some free food. It'll be a blast." His smile didn't meet his eyes. Maybe he was nervous about crashing the party.

"Why not?" He rolled up the window, shut off the jeep and climbed out. He'd snoop around a bit and see if he could gather any intel on Hazel. He suppressed a tinge of guilt at the thought of spying on her. He was invited, dammit, and everyone snooped a bit the first time they came over for a visit. Right?

The music was louder outside the jeep and the scent of barbecue tripled, making him salivate. He'd skipped breakfast and was long overdue for lunch. Whatever was grilling would fill the hole quite nicely.

They were silent on the short walk past the vehicles to the party. Matt's head pivoted back and forth like a dog at a tennis match.

"Looking for someone?" Dennis asked, his curiosity getting the better of him.

"Naw. Just checking this place out. I googled the county land maps. These guys own a ton of real estate."

Who googled land maps before attending a party?

"They've lived here for decades," Dennis offered without meaning to.

"Probably snatched the land up while it was cheap," Matt grumbled.

"I don't know. I got a great deal when I bought the greenhouse. I don't think land values here are as crazy as they are in the city. You looking to buy?" This was the weirdest conversation he'd had in a long time.

"Maybe. I like to get a feel for a place before I commit to living there."

That statement didn't seem to mesh with his last employment of nearly a decade, but maybe living in one place so long made him cautious. Personally, Dennis hadn't hesitated to relocate after he'd sold his business. He was already settled in and starting to make friends. He'd probably make a few more today.

He scanned the crowd for familiar faces. He saw a few customers and a couple people he'd call more than acquaintances, but not quite friends. He'd remedy that right now. "I see some people I know. I'm going to talk to them. You coming?"

"No. I'm going to hit the food first. I'm starving. Catch you later."

Matt hurried off leaving Dennis staring at his back. He disappeared into the crowd. Matt was nice enough, but a bit odd. It didn't matter, he was a hard worker.

Strolling forward Dennis studied the decorations. Pots of bright flowers in every possible color were scattered about the yard. Red, orange, and yellow ribbons decorated the trees. Lanterns hung from portable wooden posts topped with metal hooks. A few guests wore butterfly costumes.

Dennis spotted a familiar, long grey braid. Mayor Quinton was easily recognizable by her braid and wild clothing. Today she wore a poppy print shirt and blinding white pants which ended eight inches above her orange hipster sandals. He wandered over to the tent where she stood talking to a small group of people. She stopped mid-sentence when he approached.

"Hey, everyone. This is Dennis Belanger. He owns the garden center." She didn't pause for anyone to respond. "Those rose bushes you sold me are incredible. I barely planted them when they started blooming. I'll be by next week to get some herbs. My lavender and basil could be doing better."

"Glad the roses are doing well. Ask for me when you come by. I'll help you out personally." The positive feedback pleased him.

The mayor introduced him to everyone in her small group and they talked about plants and gardening.

A soft breeze brushed against the back of his neck. Hazel. He had no idea how he'd known she was approaching, but he knew he'd see her when he turned around. He pivoted, and there she was, looking bright and summery in a short, flowing, blue and green floral dress. Despite the flowers, it made him think of a softly flowing creek meandering its way through the grass. He shook the image off as too fanciful. But, man, did she look fine.

"Dennis," she greeted him with a smile that felt like he was coming home. "I'm glad you made it. Did you get a drink? No. Your hands are empty." She laughed. "Excuse us, everyone. This man needs a drink." She grasped him by the elbow and tugged him forward.

"Nice meeting you," he called over his shoulder and allowed her to lead him away.

"I'm so glad you came," she repeated. Her hands wrapped around his bicep and she pulled him to her side. Warmth flooded through him. She had a powerful touch. Her hands were soft and warm on his bare skin below the sleeve of his T-shirt. Nice, but not magical.

Great, now he believed he could tell a magic touch. Something about Hazel made him off kilter, tilted his world off its axis. Was she using magic or was it just Hazel the woman who affected him? Time would tell. He liked her bubbly enthusiasm and how she stuck to her guns when their opinions differed at work, but he'd keep his guard up all the same.

Before he realized it, he stood in front of a large table covered in enormous tubs of ice, each filled with bottles or cans. Soda, beer, coolers, juice, bottled water. If you wanted it, it was on the table.

Behind the table a pretty woman dressed in a lacy gold and green dress grinned at him. She pushed her glasses up with her index finger and thrust out her hand. "Hi. I'm Hazel's big sister, Lazuli. Call me Laz. You must be Dennis. Nice to meet you. Welcome to our Summer

Solstice party. Can I offer you a drink?" Her endless chatter flowed over him, pulling him in, easing the discomfort lingering in his shoulders.

"Hi." He accepted her handshake, wondering how her hands were warm while handling all those cold drinks. "I'd love a water, please." The day was warm already and promised to be a scorcher. He took the bottle she held out to him. "I might be back later for a beer, but I better eat first. Thanks."

"You haven't eaten?" The sisters chorused in musical unison.

Lazuli whistled. "Hey, Cynth, Get over here. This man needs food."

A tall, thin, blonde pivoted around and jogged over to them.

"Hazel, why haven't you fed our guest?" she chided. She turned to Dennis. "I'm Hazel's biggest sister, Hyacinth. I'm on food today." She threw her arm around his shoulder. "Come on, let's get you fed."

"Ugh. Sisters." Hazel groaned. "Geez Cynth. I'm pretty sure I can find my way to the food with him."

"Maybe. But Dennis grows plants, and you know I'm the best with all things growing. Well, plants and babies." She laughed lightly.

This family had the happiest attitude he'd seen in years. It was uplifting.

Hazel hurried to keep up. "Don't you have a baby to birth? Or something? Cynth is a midwife and healer," she explained. "She thinks it's her job to look after the entire world. She's wrong."

He bit back a laugh at their family dynamics and sibling rivalry. It was so much like the teasing he shared with his sister and brother. He'd have to call them and check in when he got home. Too often, he let life get in the way of his relationship with them.

"Hey, Gramma Pearl," Cynth greeted the woman manning the barbeque. She looked to be in her early fifty's, not nearly old enough to be their grandmother. "Give this man a steak." Cynth turned toward him. "You look like a medium-rare guy."

"Um. Yeah. Sure. Okay." He turned to the girl's grandmother. "Hi. Pearl is it? Nice to meet you. I'm Dennis Belanger. I own the greenhouse. Hazel tells me you have your own greenhouse. I'd love a tour sometime."

"Not today, but another day for sure." She handed him an enormous platter-sized T-bone and grinned. Her smile was wide and assessing. He felt like she could see right inside of him and read his thoughts. Hopefully not the ones about kissing Hazel.

Pearl's grin morphed to a frown as an ache started in his head. Oh, hell no! He looked around. Nobody was within earshot, except the sisters. "Did you just read me?" Dennis demanded.

"Not magically. No. But I could if I wanted to." There was a hint of warning to the older woman's voice.

"Really, Gramma? We don't do that," Hazel chided. "Don't listen to her, Dennis. We're Wiccan, white witches. Our cardinal rule is "Do as you will, with harm to none. She won't actually read your mind." She fixed her grandmother with an angry glare.

"Good to know. Thanks for the steak." At least they claimed to believe in not harming anyone else; although he suspected Pearl might occasionally bend the rules and he'd be cautious around her. He was one hundred percent certain she'd stuck her nose into his head, despite claiming otherwise.

"The rest of the food's down here," Hazel tipped her head left. The music morphed again to something jazzy as a cool breeze blew through the yard, fluttering Hazel's hair so it ticked across his arm.

Cynth's phone chimed. She pulled it out and typed something and slid it back into her pocket. "That's my cue. Baby's coming. Dennis, I'll catch you later. Be nice to my little sister." She winked and jogged toward the house, leaving him with Hazel, alone at last. At least as alone as they could be in a crowd of party goers.

Dennis piled his plate with a loaded baked potato, salad and asparagus. Hazel led him to a semi-isolated table and sat down. He savored a juicy bite of lightly charred steak before he spoke to Hazel who had, disappointingly, sat across from him.

"Does your family pounce on everyone?" he asked. They were intimidating for a gaggle of women. Simultaneously caring and daunting.

"Yes." She hid her face in her hands for a second. "They're always like that. I'm the baby and they're crazy overprotective. They completely scared off the first half-dozen guys I tried to date, and there aren't many eligible bachelors in Three Moon Falls." She glanced around to see if anyone was in earshot. "They even used magic to frighten away one particularly persistent guy. I didn't date for real until I went away for school." She shook her head sadly, but grinned. "Trying to date around here is a double-edged sword."

"Do they think we're trying to date? Are you asking me out?" The words flooded out of him. He shoveled a scoop of potato into his mouth to keep it busy and shut himself up.

Funny, until he mentioned dating, he hadn't given it much thought, beyond ruling it out. He'd never date an employee. The idea had a certain undeniable appeal, except for their working relationship. He was comfortable talking to Hazel, like they fit together.

"No," she said at last. "We aren't trying to date. You're my boss and I'd never date my boss." She blushed, bright pink, from neck of her blouse to the roots of her light auburn hair.

Her blush was adorable. Her answer, disappointing.

No. It was a good thing, he reminded himself. They had nothing in common. Except a love of plants, and shared family values as her relationship with her siblings demonstrated.

Wow. That was more than he realized. They also shared a belief in magic, though she eagerly embraced magic and he rejected using it.

"But I would like to be friends." She tilted her head in inquiry.

Lord love a duck! The friend zone. Death to any hope he may have harbored about a relationship between them taking root and blossoming. He swallowed the enormous mouthful of steak he's just taken and chugged half his water to wash it down.

"Friendship is good," he said at last.

Her smile was radiant. His lips turned up in response and he forced his attention back to his food to keep from staring.

"What the actual hell?" she blurted.

His head snapped back up. "What?" Had he done something wrong?

Her attention was fixed to a point to his right. He turned his head. Matt was ambling toward them.

"Who the hell invited him? Did you bring him?" she demanded.

"I ran into him when I arrived."

"Why didn't you tell me? I don't want him on my property. We never should have fully deactivated the wards to let everyone in." She leaped up, knocking her chair over. She stormed toward Matt.

Dennis's water bottle rocked on the table and tipped over, dousing his plate. Crap. She was beyond mad. He dropped his silverware on the table and hurried after her.

She stopped, hands on her hips, three feet in front of the uninvited guest. "What are you doing here?" Anger infused her low-pitched voice.

"I came for the solstice celebration. I thought it would be nice to celebrate with likeminded individuals. The café was abuzz about your event. Someone said it was open to everyone, so I came." He threw his arms wide open in a look at me gesture.

Hazel crossed her arms. "You are not welcome here. Please leave."

Wow. She was incredible when she was pissed off. Dennis's foot got wet. He looked down. Water spurted from an underground sprinkler,

soaking his feet and ankles. He'd heard about water witches. She needed to calm down. He reached out and placed a hand gently on her
shoulder.

She whirled toward him and glared. "What?"

"Calm down." He tipped his head slightly toward the ground. She
looked down and her face went red.

"He needs to leave. Now!"

More water surged up to soaked Dennis's foot.

"I'm sure Matt didn't mean any harm." He gave Matt an expectant
look.

"No harm intended. I just wanted to share the solstice. I'll go."

"I'll walk you out," Dennis suggested. "We'll leave Hazel to get back
to her guests."

T he two men walked toward the parking area. She wasn't going
to turn away while they were in sight. Matt Brown, whoever he
really was, was up to no good. She knew it as surely as she knew her
own name. His appearance here was no coincidence. He was checking
out her family and property. What in the world was he up to?

"What's the matter, Hazel?" Amber asked, striding up to her. "I felt
your anger all the way up at the house. Even the cats felt it and started
meowing and screeching."

"I told you we should keep the wards up. That guy," she gestured
to the distant figures of Matt and Dennis, "Matt Brown, Dennis hired
him, heard about the celebration and showed up. He gives me the hee-
bie-jeebies. If the wards were up, he never could have gotten in. He's up
to something. After Keres, we should have known better than to fully
drop the wards." The wards were their defense mechanism. Powered

by magic which seeped into their home and land over generations of magical practice, they were a defense to kept ill wishes off their land.

Renewed yearly, they could be adjusted to admit neutral people, like most of the party-goers today, or they could be fired up in full to keep everyone away. Yet, for this event, they'd dropped them entirely because it required less magic than filtering for limited entrance. That might have been a mistake.

"If we kept them up, half the people here wouldn't have gotten in, only our closest friends. We do it every year. It's a risk we choose to take." She stepped in front of Hazel and massaged her shoulders.

Hazel brushed her off and stepped to the side, her sandals squishing in the sodden grass. Shit. She turned her attention back to Matt, making sure he left.

"Hazel Pearl Hawk," Amber barked out. "Chill. Can it right now! Before you soak all of our guests."

"As soon as he's gone, I'm going out to the main gate and warding it to keep him out. A specific ward directed at him. By the Goddess, he worries me, and you should be scared too." Relief flooded her when Amber didn't argue. She was closer to Amber than to any of her other sisters. They shared a special, non-magical, closeness.

When Matt and Dennis disappeared from sight, she relaxed her shoulders and plastered a smile on her face. The pestilence was on his way out. She was trusting Dennis to ensure he left their property. Now maybe she could get back to enjoying the celebration. Right after she pushed some of the excess water back into the earth. She focused on the ground at her feet and slowly, the water seeped away until nothing remained but a bit of dampness.

Exhausted from the exertion and her vacillating emotions, she grabbed a burger to refuel her flagging energy.

Summer Solstice, June twentieth, every year, marked the end of spring and the start of summer. Next to Samhain, Halloween, it was her favorite holiday. She didn't want to let one man steal her joy.

"I'm going to ward the gate, find Dennis, if he didn't leave, and get back to the party," she said when the burger was gone.

"He's special then?" Amber asked softly.

"He's a nice guy, except for his aversion to magic, and for hiring Matt against my advice. I like him." The admission wasn't hard. She shared everything with Amber and knew she'd understand both the attraction and her unspoken doubts.

"One thing I learned with Kody, is that you can cure witchaphobia. It's not always terminal." They chuckled together.

Kody Wilkins, Amber's fiancé, was a died-in-the-wool witchaphobe until he had to channel the magic he didn't know he had to help the family defeat Keres. They couldn't have done it without him. Believing there was hope for Dennis's change of heart lifted Hazel's innate, but flagging, optimism.

"You want me to walk you to the gate?" Amber asked.

Hazel appreciated the show of support. "I'm good. You go back to the party." Some of their magical guests might get suspicious if they both wandered off. Many of them were sensitive and empathetic and would have felt her magic surge out of control. She could re-ward alone and it would give her a chance to apologize to Dennis for soaking his feet.

That, in turn, would require some explanations though he'd probably already concluded she was a water witch. She pushed out a breath and trudged toward the gate. Being a witch wasn't always making sparkles and sunshine. Frankly, it could be a pain in the ass, but she wouldn't give it up for anything. Ever.

Chapter Seven

Hazel had barely seen Dennis since the Summer Solstice. She'd found him in the impromptu parking lot after he'd walked Matt to his car. She and Dennis had returned to the party together after she warded the gate.

Surprisingly, he hadn't asked her what she was doing. She was cautious about being seen by mundanes, and the ward she created was temporary, just enough to keep Matt off the property until the family could do a proper job on July's full moon. Even then, a powerful enough witch might possess the skills to counteract the wards. Dennis had stood respectfully quiet until she was finished. They'd been side by side for the rest of the party, mingling and socializing. That was Saturday. It was late Wednesday and he'd been like a ghost. She missed him, not seeing him for coffee and lunch left a hole in her chest, an ache her family couldn't fill.

With one staff member out sick and Dennis busy training new staff, her boss was swamped. She felt sorry for him, he must be run ragged. Even from a distance, she could see he was looking tired. She'd gotten tired of waiting for him to show up at the house and decided to chase him down, wherever he was. She had work to do, and he was holding her up. Besides, she wanted to see his smile and spend a few minutes absorbing the energy his presence gave her.

"Dennis," she called out as she hurried toward the newly created petting zoo. He was deep in conversation with Sarah and a young man Hazel hadn't met. Hazel heard Dennis's groan from twenty feet away. She mentioned her reason for seeking him out anyway. "I'm going to need your help to go over some receipts with me today. I've gone as far as I can without your input. When is good for you?"

"Can it wait?" His shoulders slumped in exhaustion.

"It's up to you, but I'd rather get started on the actual data entry. If you pick a time, I'll be here."

"My days are over-filled already. Would you be willing to trade a few evening hours for time off during the day? Could we work in the evening?"

She did a mental scan of her appointments. "Tonight works for me." She was scheduled to work the family shop Thursday and Friday evening, and he'd be even busier on the weekend.

"Yeah," Dennis said defeatedly. "I can make that work. How about six? If you bring take-out, I'll pay for it." He dug out his wallet and handed her a bunch of cash. "Get whatever you want. I'm not fussy."

"Sure thing, boss." She slid the money into the pocket of her denim skirt. "See you later." She turned to walk away, when a weird humming sound made her turn back. "What was that?"

Sarah laughed. "You won't believe it," she exclaimed pointing to a paddock to their left where a llama's white head poked over the top of its enclosure.

"Oh, a llama. I've never seen a live llama." Hazel hurried the enclosure. "Can I pet it?" She asked.

"Yes, you can pet her." Dennis said. "Like this." He moved slowly, holding out his hand, fingers tucked under. After the animal sniffed him, he scratched the side of her head and between her ears.

Hazel copied him. "Oh. She's so soft. I didn't know what to expect."

"I researched llamas," Sarah said, moving to stand beside them. "Some have soft fur, others have stiff, wiry fur."

"That's so cool. Does she have a name?"

"Not yet," Dennis said.

"What? She needs a name. What's your name, girl?" She fondled the llama's ears.

The animal made a loud humming noise and fell over.

"Oh! What's wrong with her? Is she sick? Should we go in the pen with her? Should we call the vet?" Panic raced over her. She had no idea what to do, or what she'd done.

"She's fine," Dennis said with an eye roll. "She does this, although this is the first time I've seen her do it without being startled."

"She just falls over. That's crazy? There must be something wrong with her."

"It's hilarious," the youth who'd been standing with Dennis earlier said. "It cracks me up every time. Yesterday, someone dropped a tin bucket, and she went down like a rock. Two minutes later, she was fine. Kids are going to love her."

The petting zoo was set to open on the weekend. Outside of each enclosure there was a coin operated machine which dispensed the proper food pellets for the animals. The area would be supervised by trained staff who would talk about the animals' habits and uses for each type of animal.

"Are you sure she's okay?" Seeing an animal drop over for no reason was startling and worrisome. "I can call my sister, she's great with animals. She could come check her out. I know she wouldn't mind."

Dennis explained the story of how he'd acquired the llama and ended with, "and now I have an entire petting zoo, including this drama llama."

Rustling sounds alerted them to the llama's recovery. She popped to her feet as if nothing had happened.

"That's incredible," Hazel exclaimed. "You need a name don't you girl."

"Go ahead. Name her. Let me know what you decide. I've got to get back to work. Come on then." He gestured for the other two people to proceed him. "I've got instructions and animal information for you in the office. See you at six, Hazel."

"Later," she responded and turned her attention back to the llama. "You really need a name. Don't you?" The animal nodded as if she understood. Well, stranger things were known to happen. Her family's shop had a talking cat after all.

"Who gets a pet and doesn't name it? Although you weren't a pet until you got here. Maybe we should call you Ursula" The llama shook her head. "That's a no then. I think you actually understand me." Another nod. "Well then, I'll just run through some names. Let me know when I get to one you like." Hazel listed name after name. each met with a negative response. Perhaps the animal didn't understand after all. "Fine then," she said in exasperation. "I'm going to call you Jellybean."

The llama dropped to the ground. A soft laugh bubbled out of Hazel. "You really are a drama queen."

The animal jumped to her feet. "Why you little faker. I'm calling you Jellybean then. Jellybean the Drama Llama Queen. I think you like it." When Jellybean nodded, she added, "My sister, Lazuli, is a carpenter.

I'm going to get her to make a name plate for your pen. In fact, since I have to work tonight, I'm taking the afternoon off. I'll ask her right now."

H azel juggled a bag of Chinese takeout, her purse, and a six-pack of beer and opened the door between the office and Dennis's living space. She'd pulled her car around to his private driveway rather than toting everything through the entire greenhouse. No sense alerting the world she was eating with her boss.

"Dennis? Are you here?" There was no response, so she continued to the kitchen. The low tones of the countertop radio almost drowned out the sound of a shower running down the hall. "Guess he's not ready yet," she muttered.

She slid the beer into the fridge and turned the oven on low to keep the food warm. If they were going to work before they ate, she'd rather it stayed hot. Nuked food was never as good as fresh. She set the kitchen table and poured them both glasses of ice water. Even with the windows wide open, it was stifling hot in the kitchen. As June rolled on, the days were getting warmer. She loved the heat and the sun. At home, they'd be eating outside in the fresh air. Somehow, an idea which felt too personal for a working dinner.

The shower shut off and ten minutes later, Dennis strolled into the kitchen smelling of soap and leather. A snug T-shirt emphasized the breadth of his shoulders. Tanned legs and feet were displayed beneath his casual shorts. She was fairly sure he was oblivious to his sex appeal. Heat pooled in her abdomen. Suddenly, she was ravenous and not for food.

He smiled broadly. "Sorry to make you wait. There was an accident with a pallet of bagged manure, and I got coated."

She chuckled. "I'm glad you chose to de-stink. The smell might make me lose my appetite. Let me know how much was destroyed. You can write it off." An idea hit her. "Since you can't sell it, you could donate it to the community garden plot west of town. Fresh, natural fertilizer would really benefit the families who garden there."

"Great idea. I'll have someone shovel it into a trailer and haul it over. My gardens have plenty already. Now, let's eat. The food smells amazing."

"Beer?" she offered. "I brought a few. On my tab, not yours."

"I'd love one, but later. I missed lunch. Food first. Beer later."

"Again? How many meals have you skipped this week? It's not healthy. How are you going to keep this place going if you're too weak to stand?" The man needed an assistant. Or a keeper. Someone to make sure he ate and got enough rest. The bags under his eyes were enormous. "Sit down. I'll grab the food."

She bustled around, filling the kettle and turning it on before pulling the food from the oven. When the kettle was hot, she made him a cup of restorative tea. She'd picked it up earlier, when she stopped to talk to Lazuli about name plates for the petting zoo.

"Drink this with your dinner," she commanded and sat across from him.

"Tea? Coffee would be better." He wrinkled his nose and leaned forward to smell it. "Yuck that's awful. It smells like dirty grass. What is it?"

"My own special blend. All natural, restorative. It'll boost your energy naturally. I'll leave you a different one to help you sleep. Drink up." She grabbed a spoon and ladled generous portions of fried rice for both of them. "I drink it all the time, especially when I'm run down."

He sipped the tea and looked at her. "It might smell like lawn clippings, but it tastes okay."

She gestured with the spoon for him to drink. "Suck it back and eat. We've got work to do." He seemed barely functional, he needed to pep up before they got to work.

She wasn't that eager to dive into the paperwork. As much as she loved her work, she'd much rather sit here and talk to Dennis. Taking care of him, feeding him and making tea for him was a bonus. It filled her natural nurturing side. Like her sisters and grandmother, taking care of others was a normal part of her life, and a way to pay back the universe and the Goddess for their wonderful lives.

Dennis literally shoveled food into his mouth. He barely took time to chew. He had to be starving to eat like that. It was rather off-putting and amazing all at once.

"You're going to choke to death if you don't slow down. Or your stomach will be so bloated you can't move. Take it easy. You can eat leftovers later when you're hungry again."

He paused, fork halfway to his mouth, rice dribbling back onto his plate. "Yes, Mom."

She laughed. "I do sound like Gramma Pearl. But, seriously, eating too fast isn't good for you. Nor is skipping multiple meals. Although the odd missed meal doesn't hurt."

"I can't help it. I'm swamped. In fact, I'm shocked they haven't called me to solve some crisis yet. I get a couple calls every evening, if I'm not already down there. I can't recall the last time I took an evening off. I'm going to have to hire more people."

"You need to delegate more. Split up your senior staff. Put someone in charge of each shift. Have them try and solve the issues themselves. It might cut down on your workload. You'd be surprised at how increased responsibility can motivate people."

He blinked and set his fork down. "Why didn't I think of that? We did it in Drayton. We had an office manager, and each team of workers had a designated leader. I've been running this place like a helicopter parent."

"Maybe you're too close, and too tired. You can't see the forest for the trees. Eat up." She served them both more veggies and a second spring roll.

"**W**hy is my dining room table covered in rocks?" He stared at the table. Dozens of piles of receipts of all sizes were held down with fist sized rocks.

Hazel laughed. "I learned the hard way that if you open both of those windows," she pointed to the left and right at two windows directly across from each other, "you get a fabulous cross draft. It's so gusty I had to pick up and re-sort a couple dozen receipts the first time I opened them."

"Where did the rocks come from? I don't sell anything like this." He lifted a water rounded stone from a pile.

"From the creek behind your barn. I found it on my noon walk. I took a couple buckets down and gathered myself some paperweights. I'll put them back when I'm done here."

He didn't have a response. She had a way of looking at things and finding solutions he'd never think of. He would have suffered through the heat with the windows closed to avoid the breeze messing up his piles.

"Want a beer while we do this?" He could use one. All the piles of paper made his stomach hurt. He had a solid idea of his finances and kept track of his bank balance, but he detested paperwork and accounting. He understood it fine, he just abhorred doing it. He'd much rather be digging in the dirt, or crossbreeding flowers. If he was lucky, he might get back at creating a striped, pink daisy before the snow flew. It had been way too long since he'd done anything beyond water the plants in his personal greenhouse.

"I'd love a beer."

"What?" Her words pulled his mind back to the conversations. "Right. Beer. Need a glass?"

"Naw. Bottle's fine for me. But grab a couple napkins to set them on, to keep the condensation off the table and paperwork."

He liked how she cared for his possessions as they were her own. He grabbed the beer and napkins and sat beside Hazel at the table. "Let's do this."

"You don't have to sound like we're going to a funeral. This is the easy part. I show you a bill or a receipt, you tell me if it's business or personal. Easy peasy." She picked up a receipt. "Like this one. Jeans and work gloves. Both could be personal, or work related. Which is it?"

She handed it to him, their fingers touched. Barely a brush but he felt it to his toes. Her skin was soft and warm. He inhaled deeply to push down the urge to touch her. Her soft, feminine, lemon scent washed over him.

Damn. He was going to have to stop breathing. How could something so simple as lemon go straight to his groin? *Focus, Belanger.* He looked at the paper in his hands, dated for the day he took possession of the property. He fumbled to recall the day. Right. He'd torn the backside out of his jeans leaving Drayton and needed gloves to move into his new house. It was frigid cold and blowing snow, he hadn't wanted to freeze his fingers or nuts off. "This is personal," he said, handing it back to her.

She waved it away. "Put it over there, top row, under the third stone. That's for November personal bills."

"Can't I just pitch it?" Why would he want to hold on to old receipts? He had his personal funds and spending well in hand. No worries there.

"I'm going to log your personal expenses separately. That way, if you're ever audited, we -or rather you- have backup paperwork. You'll be able to prove you keep business and personal separate. You'll probably never need it. In the future, you'll want to get separate credit cards and bank accounts for your personal expenses, to keep the lines clear."

Holy shit. He'd given a virtual stranger access to his entire life. Every penny he spent, what he spent it on. His credit card numbers, bank accounts. She basically had free run of his house. She could clean him out.

He almost laughed aloud at his paranoia. Somehow, deep inside, he trusted her honesty, even if she might have magical ways to reshape reality, ways he probably would never even imagine.

"Dennis? If you'd prefer, I can just discard the personal ones. It's up to you." She scratched her chin nervously and focused her attention on the stack of receipts between her fingers.

"Go ahead. Track them. I'll apply for a business credit card right away and use this one for personal. You're right."

One by one, they went through the receipts needing clarification. With each one, their hands touched. Often enough he wondered if it were deliberate on her part. Unlikely, as she appeared unaffected by the casual touches which were driving him crazy.

Two hours into the sorting, she leaned back and took a long pull of her beer. She set the bottle down and licked a tiny drop of beer from her bottom lip. Blood rushed to his groin, leaving him lightheaded.

Damn. He was losing it.

"Want to keep at it?" She asked. "Or take a break and go for a walk? It's cooling off out there and I could use a breath of fresh air. We can walk to the creek and back. I'll show you where the rocks came from."

Getting outside, away from her heady scent and touches, seemed like an excellent idea, until she bent over at the waist to buckle her sandals, pulling her denim skirt tight over her ass. He groaned.

She pivoted, without standing, to look at him. "Are you okay?"

"Um. Yeah." He punched his fist into his chest. "Indigestion. Guess I did eat too fast."

She straightened and touched his shoulder. "I can make you some mint tea to ease the discomfort."

"I'm good. Thanks." Tea was not going to solve his problem. "Maybe, if it doesn't improve, I'll try tea when we get back." Tea, right. Kissing her might help. Either that or make it worse. Yeah, kissing an employee was sure to help. He was losing his mind and it was all her fault.

They walked, side by side, across the lawn toward the barn. Occasionally their fingers brushed. He fought the urge to capture her hand in his. His mind knew better than to get involved but his body had a different plan.

"I probably should have asked before I started walking around on your property without permission. I am sorry if I overstepped."

Her apology fell into the silence between them. He considered her words before replying. "It's okay. I have no secrets." At least not any she'd find behind his barn. "I would prefer you didn't mention it to my other staff. I'd rather not have people wandering all over my personal space. That's why there's a fence around the business portion of the property. He referred to the split log, rail fence marking the end of the greenhouse land and start of his personal space. He owned it all but liked the distinction the previous owners had established.

"I didn't think of that, but I can see where random people wandering around could be problematic and could blur the lines between your personal space and the business."

"It could. I've started interviewing in the breakroom, rather than the office, to maintain the distinction. I'm trying to establish a line. The tiny space I call an ordering office, the one in the greenhouse, isn't big enough for more than just me." The space was nothing more than a closet he'd converted to hold a tiny desk.

The path narrowed behind the barn as grass turned to brush and then to trees. He paused and gestured for Hazel to go ahead. It took solid determination to keep his eyes off her curves and the length of her legs. She was short, but her legs were well toned, tanned and attractive.

The wind blew past him, carrying her scent. He'd hoped being outside would help avoid it. He groaned in frustration.

Hazel paused to look at him. "Are you okay? Is your heartburn worse?"

"What? Oh, no. I'm good," he lied. He was far from okay. His mind and body were in an argument over what to do with Hazel. Fighting his attraction was nearly impossible and demons from past relationships hounded him.

"You sure? We can go back. I don't mind." The concern on her face was touching.

"Let's keep going. It's been ages since I was down this way."

She nodded and kept walking. At the creek, she slipped out of her sandals and carefully stepped from rock to rock until she reached a large flat rock in the center of the stream. He ditched his shoes and followed, seating himself beside her, both with their toes in the water.

"It's funny," he said, "how easily you forget the blessings in your own backyard. When winter broke and it started warming up, I was down here every few days, but I haven't been here for weeks."

"Oh, I know. One of Three Moon Falls' waterfalls is on our property. Chickadee Falls, and I haven't been out there since before winter."

Her soft, ironic smile brought out his own. "Let's make a pact to enjoy the gifts close to us more often," he suggested.

"I agree. One hundred percent." She slid to the edge of the rock until she was into the water, almost to her knees. Her hands were flat on the stone, her arms stiff, her backside firmly against the rock. She reminded him of a bird ready to launch into flight at the first sign of a predator. Timid and overly cautious came to mind.

Wasn't she a water witch? Her anger at the festival had tumbled his water bottle and made the sprinklers leak. But here, she seemed almost afraid of the creek. Maybe the water was colder than she liked, though to him, it was quite warm. He'd ask about it, but he didn't want to upset her if it was a sensitive subject. Maybe when he knew her better.

He stood up and stepped into the pool at the base of the rock. Cautious not to lose his footing on the slippery bottom, he ambled around the pool.

"It feels good. Come, join me." He held out his hand.

She leaned away from him. "I'm good. Thanks. Enjoy yourself." She scooted back until she was fully on the rock, hugging her knees.

"You sure? I won't let you fall in. I'll hold your hand. It really takes away the heat of the air."

Her brows knit together, and she squeezed her arms around her legs. He was about to walk away when she said, "Promise me you won't let me fall?"

"Scout's honor." He flashed a boy scout salute. Yup, she was definitely afraid of the water. A thousand questions followed.

"Were you even a scout?" she asked doubtfully.

"Actually, yes. From Cub to junior leader to winning the Chief Scout's Award. Someday, when I have a son, I'll be a leader." The words must have reassured her, she inched forward on the rock.

"If I fall, I'll never trust you again. You know that, right?"

"Relax, Hazel. You'll be fine."

"I just don't want my clothes getting wet, that's all." She reached for his hand and rose slowly to her feet and took three tiny steps forward.

The water rose to her knees. Another step and it brushed the hem of her short skirt.

"Shoot, it's cold. Damn. My skirt's wet." She backed up half a step.

He'd forgotten how short she was. Of course, knee deep on him was thigh-high on her. "You really are short, aren't you? I hadn't realized."

"I'm the perfect height," she said, hands on her hips. She probably didn't realize she'd released his hand. "My legs are exactly long enough to reach the ground."

It took half a second to realize she was joking. "Funny."

"It's the truth," she said indignantly, a smirk spoiling her façade of anger. She reached down and rolled her hem up twice, revealing more of her legs.

If she rolled it any higher...

He tipped his face up, studying the sky to keep from ogling her. Unbidden, his gaze returned to her. He forced himself to look away. She was too damned attractive for his peace of mind. Add funny and kind to the mix, and she was irresistible.

He looked again. She was so pretty, sexy and nervous, he could almost feel his attraction for her growing like a flower bud opening under the morning sun.

"What's wrong?" she asked. "You look like someone ran over your dog. Are you okay? Is it the heartburn? We should go back for tea."

He opted for partial honesty. "Just wondering what it is about you that is attracting me." Her frown had him blurt out an explanation. "I mean, I'm not looking for a relationship, particularly not with an employee, but there's something about you..."

He stepped closer to her and released her hand. "Something makes me want to do this." He reached up and slid his one finger down the curve of her cheek. He rested one hand on her cheek, the other on her shoulder and took another step. He leaned toward her, eyes open, watching for a sign, any sign, that she didn't want this.

She smiled up at him, tilting her head to the right. Her tongue darted out to lick her lips, her pupils dilated. Unable to resist a second longer, he brushed his mouth softly against hers.

Her sigh whispered across his lips, stealing his breath, battering his control. He kissed her again, softly, and straightened to smile at her.

She brushed her finger across his lips, the corners of her mouth turned up. "I think we should go back to the house."

His heart soared.

"And get back to work," she finished, crushing his desire. "I don't want to delay catching up any longer than I have to. I'm sure you don't either."

She walked back to the rock and inched her way back to shore. Shoes in hand, she rushed, barefoot, toward the house.

Frozen in place, he stared after her until she was out of sight. Jesus. He could have sworn she was interested. He'd given her ample time to turn away, to object. And she'd pressed against him for that second, heart stopping, kiss. And she'd caressed him before racing away. Talk about mixed messages.

Was she okay?

Slipping dangerously on the rocky bottom, he raced after her.

By the Goddess, she was an idiot. She'd let him kiss her. He'd given her a chance to object, to turn away and she'd let him do it anyway. What was she thinking? They had a professional relationship. He was her boss. She shouldn't want this.

But she did.

Every fiber of her being was aligned to Dennis and having the chance to kiss him, she wasn't going to pass it up. Except now that she had, she wanted more, much, much more, and there was no way she could continue to work for him.

She doubled her pace, hurrying toward the house. If she ran, she could be gone before he got back to the house.

"Hazel, wait," he called from behind her.

She pretended she didn't hear him and sped forward. She might not escape, but she'd have half a moment to collect herself before facing him.

He stormed past her and stopped, facing her, blocking her way. Regret clear on his face.

Great, he regretted kissing her. That might be worse than kissing him. Her heart plummeted. She stumbled to a halt and stared at the ground. She couldn't bring herself to meet his eye.

"Are you okay, Hazel? I'm sorry if I overstepped." He swallowed, the sound loud in the silence between them. "I apologize and it won't happen again."

Disappointing. She liked kissing him. She forced herself to stay calm. No sense letting her turbulent emotions activate the sprinklers or draw in a rainstorm. She hadn't accidentally made it rain for years.

"Hazel?" His voice was soft with worry and regret.

"I should have said no." She twisted her hands together. "You're my boss."

"The fault is mine. As your employer, you're off limits. But honestly, you're so damn irresistible. I wanted to kiss you from the first time I saw you in the parking lot. It's a miracle I resisted this long."

She fought a smile at his confused confession. Inappropriate or not, it was nice to feel attractive and desired. Indecision warred in her head, battling her heart. She'd love to start something with him. Something not just physical. A friendship? A relationship? She had no idea. But the moral dilemma of doing so with her boss was immobilizing her.

"If you don't quit, I promise to leave you alone. No more kissing." His voice was husky with emotion. He mumbled something under his breath which sounded a lot like, even if it kills me.

Seventeen competing thoughts raced through her head, colliding and confusing her. The one that made it to her lips startled her.

"I wanted it too." She looked up and him. He stared back, his mouth gaping.

"Where does this leave us?" he asked, mirroring her thoughts.

"As boss and employee," she stated making a that's it motion with her hands. "I keep my job; you keep your distance and it never repeats. We forget it ever happened."

She could have sworn he felt the disappointment dragging her down. But it had to be. Their beliefs were miles apart, even if they didn't have the boss employee dynamic to worry about. Some couples were not meant to be.

"Agreed," he said at last, his voice filled with defeat.

"Thank you. Now, let's finish those receipts before it gets any later."

"After you." He waved toward the house and stepped aside.

As she passed him, she saw regret in his face and felt it in her heart.

Damn. One of them must have pissed off karma to end up in their awkward position. Probably both had unwittingly done something and the universe was torturing them in return.

Why was she disappointed? She was keeping her job; he wasn't going to kiss her again. She'd gotten exactly what she wanted.

Right?

Chapter Eight

H azel clutched a strand of beads in her hand. She'd strung herself a gemstone mandala using stones chosen for their magical properties. Smoothed bumpy freshwater pearls alternated with amethyst ovals. The water association of pearls grounded her, the amethyst soothed her irritability and anxiety.

At least that was the theory. Today, it wasn't working, and the stones had never failed her before. This morning she'd broken her habit of parking right outside Dennis's home office in favor of taking a calming walk through the interconnected greenhouses. Her stretched nerves needed the serenity of plants. She had yet to get out of the vehicle.

She fisted the beads in her dominant hand and pressed them to her roiling stomach, hoping they would ease the heavy ache lodged there. She didn't usually avoid uncomfortable situations. Typically, she made a joke and lightened the tension. Today, she had procrastinated getting out of the car and going to the office.

What if she ran into Dennis?

What if she didn't?

Both options were equally unappealing and crazily tempting. Either way, she had work to do. After their kiss last night, they'd worked side by side and sorted the last of the questionable receipts. Every accidental touch had been agony and delight.

Unless she missed her guess, he was as uneasy as she was. Conversation was stilted and uncomfortable until it faded to virtually nothing. For the last thirty minutes, they'd worked in virtual silence. She'd hand him a receipt; he'd give a one-word response. Personal or business.

The dead air was tight and aching with sexual tension and unspoken questions. He'd walked her to her car, and she drove away. Before she turned from sight, she'd risked a glance in the rearview mirror. Backlit by his yard light, he lifted his hand in a wave and was still standing there, arm raised, when she rounded the corner.

Now, here she was, back in her car, half scared to see him again. How could she be so confused, so conflicted, over a man she barely knew? Sure, he was attractive, friendly, polite and fun to be with. He had a gift for dealing with employees and a phenomenal green thumb. So what? Tons of other men had similar traits. Her attraction was bizarre, especially since he was a mundane with no respect for magic and witches. Although his attitude had quieted on the issue he seemed more disinterested, and ambivalent, than hostile. It was nice to see him coming around, sort of.

She should walk away. Now, before she fell for his charm.

Right. That was going to happen. Not. She couldn't walk away, and she couldn't let him get closer, no matter how much her heart and soul cried out for him.

With a couple twists, she triple wrapped the elasticated beads and slid them onto her wrist. Purse and lunch bag in hand, she climbed out of the car and waved at Sarah who was in the petting zoo, outside

Jellybean's pen. She'd like to check in on Sarah and see how she was enjoying her new job, but she had delayed long enough. No sense being late. Instead, she strode through the automatic doors and into the greenhouse, feigning a confidence she didn't feel.

Both cashiers were busy with early shoppers as she raced by. She hurried through the retail area and the first two glass enclosures. In the third, she stopped to admire a display of artfully dyed orchids. Even knowing the bright blues and lavenders would turn to white when they bloomed again, they were stunning.

The entire row beside the orchids was pansies. The next was a cascade of lobelia and sunny marigolds. She paused to breathe in the moist air and enjoy its peaty, damp scent. Floral undertones made it pleasant. House plants nestled alongside bedding out plants. Ivies beside flowering African Violets.

Slowly, her tension ebbed. Hyacinth might be the family's earth witch but connecting with nature and grounding was important to all of them. Small town life and their isolated land made it easy.

Today with her tension off the chart, the blossoms and leaves were her sanctuary. There had been a time when she turned to water for soothing. Not anymore. Water was her enemy. Disappointment washed over her at the sound of footsteps. She didn't want to be interrupted.

"Good morning," Dennis greeted her carefully.

She turned toward him. "Morning." She fumbled for something else to say. "Did you sleep well?" There. That was an innocuous question.

"Terrible. Thanks for asking, though."

So much for a decent conversation starter. "That's too bad. Did the heat keep you up?" She hadn't slept well herself. She'd been too busy reliving their kiss, like a teenager having her first crush.

"Not the heat, no." He straightened a few plant pots and smiled at her.

"Bad dreams?" By the Goddess, she was an idiot. She shouldn't be trying to have a normal conversation with him. He was her boss, and they'd crossed a boundary into personal territory last night. She had to return to the professional and not think about how his kiss affected her. They were miles apart and one hundred percent incompatible.

"Weird dreams. Good, weird though." He smiled at her. "About you."

Heat flooded her face. Not good. She gestured vaguely down the aisle and he walked beside her for the length of the row. "Oh," she said unable to format an even remotely intelligent response.

His hand on her elbow stopped her forward motion. She glanced at him.

"Look," he said. "I know we're different and I realize you're my employee which makes what I'm about to say totally inappropriate, but I'm going to say it anyway and hope you don't take offense."

Good grief. Where was he going with this? She didn't like where she suspected he was headed. "And, if I don't care for what you have to say?" She needed this job; she didn't want and couldn't afford to lose it. Rock, meet hard place.

Dennis tipped his head up toward the glass roof and sighed. "If it's a problem, I'm hoping you'll forgive me and forget I said anything."

She laughed wryly. "That's like asking me to unhear it." She shrugged. "Go ahead. I expect you're going to say it anyway." Her stomach roiled. She shifted her purse and lunch bag into her left hand and used her right to rotate the strands of beads on her left wrist.

"Okay, here goes." He looked around the greenhouse before continuing. "I find myself attracted to you." He huffed out a breath. "As you might have guessed. I didn't think I could be attracted to a magical person, but I am, and I'd like to get to know you better. On a personal level. Like a date. Or something."

Wow. He had a unique approach. Insulting who she was while asking her out. He was off his rocker. Nutso. Would he fire her if she refused?

"You're right. It is inappropriate, and rather insulting," she responded to give her mind time to assimilate all the implications of her answer. Hell, she needed to find an answer.

"I warned you." He grinned unsurely.

"Can I think about it?" Delaying her answer was cowardly, but if she were honest with herself, she was torn and didn't know what to say.

"Sure. I guess." He sounded disappointed. "I'll walk you to the house. I missed breakfast. That darned llama was kicking up a fuss."

"Jellybean. Her name is Jellybean." Great, so much for finding peace and grounding herself among the plants. "Was she okay?"

"A couple magpies were stealing her food. Honestly, I'm not sure I'm cut out to be a farmer, rancher, zoo operator. Whatever I am now. My hands are full enough with the greenhouse. Even my hobby has fallen to nothing."

"It's tough when everyday life gets hectic and steals away the small pleasures," she agreed. "What's your hobby?" They walked slowly toward the house. The tension between them should have been off the charts. Instead, there was a weird sense of companionship and attraction. She was genuinely interested in his off-work life.

"I crossbreed flowers. It's time consuming and finicky, but it relaxes me."

"Then you should find time to do it," she advised. "How did a former landscaper get into breeding flowers?" They strolled down another row and into the next building, before heading outside into the yard. A cool breeze brushed her skin, stealing away the excess heat from inside. She glanced at him; his face was lit with a soft smile. Obviously, this was more than just a hobby.

"Random really. I saw some dyed flowers in the grocery store the same day I stumbled upon an old genetics textbook in a used bookstore. It got me thinking. I loved genetics in high school, so I bought the book and started to study..." he trailed off.

"Where do you work on them? Surely you didn't abandon your work when you moved here. What are you growing now? And where?" She blurted the questions; crossbreeding flowers would be fascinating.

"I use the small greenhouse down by the barn. I rebuilt it when I arrived. It wasn't in the best shape. I can't work in the main buildings. There's no way to stop cross-contamination or to keep people away." He quick stepped ahead of her and unlocked the door to the house. He held it open for her.

"Thanks." She walked inside and slid her sunglasses off. "I'd like to see your flowers sometime. Coffee?"

"I'd like to show them to you." He launched into a passionate explanation of his work while she started coffee and put her lunch in the fridge. His passion and excitement were infectious. She enjoyed listening to him. He bandied around words like genes, alleles, locus and a handful of others she vaguely recalled from high school biology. She was only catching a third of what he said, but it was fascinating. Eventually, he paused.

"Sorry. I get carried away. You're a good listener."

"It was interesting. You're very passionate." And...then all she could think about was how passionate he might be in bed. His enthusiasm and obvious caring would probably transfer to his lovemaking. Her body heated.

She grabbed two mugs and poured coffee: her hands trembling. Damn.

"Well, I best get to work. My boss is a tyrant." She grinned to let him know she was teasing. She hadn't expected to feel this comfortable around him, but they were both avoiding yesterday's incident which left them in a less awkward space.

"I expect he'd cut you some slack. Stay for breakfast?"

His question felt low key and no pressure. She was tempted. Too tempted.

"I already ate but thank you. Maybe another time." She grabbed her purse, and coffee and headed for the office.

How in the world was she supposed to fight her attraction when he was so damned nice? He was her boss. A mundane. Magicals didn't get involved with mundanes. It was an unwritten rule. Practically a law. At one time, you had to ask the witch's council to marry outside of the magical community. It wasn't about purity; it was about maintaining the secrecy they needed to survive.

On the other hand, he was kind, compassionate. He took in stray animals. He was attractive. Last night's kisses had rocked her body and muddled her brain. That kind of attraction had to mean something. Surely the Goddess wouldn't put an attractive man in her path unless she was supposed to spend time with him. Right?

For every reason not to get involved, she found at least one reason why she should. She pinched her forehead and sighed.

Yes, it was inappropriate to start a boss-employee relationship. But, by the Goddess, she was tempted. Too tempted. Loath though she was to admit it, she was going to have to hash this out with someone. Maybe Amber. She'd fallen for Kody who they'd believed was a mundane until his latent powers kicked in, just in time to save her sister's life. Yes, Amber might have some sound advice.

With a sigh, Hazel turned on the computer and began entering data.

He'd made a colossal mistake asking her out and he'd doubled down by inviting her to breakfast. He'd unnerved her, put her on edge, he could tell by the way she raced from the kitchen.

He set a frying pan on the stove and pulled out some bacon and laid half a dozen strips in to cook.

He could easily lose a talented employee now. She'd demonstrated her skill as she organized his receipt disaster and in the questions she'd asked. Last night her suggestions had been right on point. She knew what she was doing.

Losing a valuable employee was one thing. Chasing away a new friend was another. Especially with his desire to get to know her better. Much better. Even with the awkward unease between them, he felt peaceful when he was with Hazel.

He wrapped the leftover bacon and returned it to the fridge as the strips in the pan sizzled and popped.

He couldn't believe he'd told Hazel about his passion for breeding flowers. He chuckled realizing he'd rattled on for ten minutes or more. She'd listened and asked questions, as if she were interested. Natalia had considered his hobby too girlie and frivolous.

What did it matter if it wasn't masculine like cage fighting or hockey? It was a hobby. A challenging and fulfilling one. Hazel hadn't dissed it. She'd been enthusiastic and supportive. Just as he'd be of her hobbies, assuming she had any.

The popping of bacon fat in the pan caught his attention. He should focus on the task at hand rather than the woman in his office. In his chair. He could picture her there, hands flying across the keyboard as she entered receipts and made notes. Her brows scrunched together slightly, as she concentrated.

It wouldn't take her long to catch up for the year. Then what? He'd need to find a way to keep her around, especially if she turned down his offer to date. Of course, once she had his books up to date, there would be less for her to do and he could put her in the greenhouse where she'd be closer to him.

He groaned and leaned against the counter, half his attention on the meat in the pan. He'd asked her out. He was a colossal idiot. All he could do was wait for the fallout. He'd follow her lead on how to go forward. Ignore the attraction. Try dating. Or if she quit, beg her to stay and promise to behave professionally.

He flipped the bacon, his appetite vanishing like smoke in a windstorm.

Chapter Nine

H azel parked at the back of her family's shop, Four Seasons Metaphysical. The recently added screen door let fresh air flow inside but was latched tight from the inside. The soft scents of sage, roses and cinnamon drifted out. Amber must have been making candles again. The popular scents were hard to keep in stock.

Sandals flicking against her heels with each step, she headed down the alley toward the customer entrance out front.

By the Goddess, she needed tea. Badly. Something to ease the ache in her head. Worse, she needed to talk to her sister about Dennis. She had no idea what to do and wasn't trusting her instincts right now.

"Hazel, how are you?" A familiar voice greeted her as she exited the alley.

"Mayor Quinton, what brings you around?" Hazel asked, suppressing a wince at Three Moon Falls' unconventional mayor's outfit. A lavender and teal floral blouse topped a pair of fluorescent pink leggings. Her ever present hipster sandals were black and red, and her long grey hair hung over her shoulder in a neat braid with an orange scrunchie at the end.

"I needed tea. Mango mint this week." She waved a bulging bag in front of her. "And a couple other things. I do adore scented candles," she added as the manager of the grocery store went by. Then the mayor winked at Hazel.

Like the Hawk family and many others, Mayor Quinton was a witch. Few of their kind flaunted their beliefs and the mayor kept hers a secret, claiming there was no sense alienating potential voters. She was probably right. Nothing frightened people more than something they didn't understand.

"Have you tried the cranberry-passionfruit tea? It's got a hint of mint and is almost a dessert by itself."

"Your lovely sister gave me a sample. I can't wait to try it. What's up with you?" She looked around the street before adding, "Your aura is off. It's all red, shot through with grey. Want to talk about it?"

Hazel sighed. Damn. Dennis had really thrown her off-kilter if her aura was messed up enough to cause comment. "It's nothing some family advice and meditation won't cure, but thanks for asking."

"Anytime, my dear. Anytime. You know I consider you girls and your grandmother my family. Speaking of family, any word from your folks? How are their travels?"

"They called a few days ago. They're on the move again. Leaving India and headed for South Africa. They still haven't found what they're looking for." There was no need to explain further. The mayor and most of the magical community knew Lily Beth Moon, Hazel's mom, and her stepdad, Trevor Moon, weren't vacationing. They were following clues in hopes of finding and stopping a witch killer who was murdering witches and stealing their powers.

A few weeks ago, the girls and their grandmother had battled Keres, an unethical magician who claimed they had something he needed to resurrect his dead wife. Banding together, the family had defeated him. Barely. He was now locked up in a metaphysical prison for magical offenders.

They never did figure out what it was he wanted. An item? A spell? Herbs? They had no clue. Though they continued to search the family records, an enormous collection of personal and family grimoires dating back to the 1600s, they'd found no real clues.

"I wish them luck in their search," the mayor said. "I'll ask the Goddess to help them."

"Thank you, your support means a lot."

The hair on the back of Hazel's neck stood up. She glanced behind her. Matt Brown strolled toward them; his icy blue eyes seeming to slice into her skin like knives. He hadn't done anything wrong, but he still gave her the creeps.

"Crap," she whispered.

"Who's that? The short stocky guy? I don't like the looks of him." Mayor Quinton said.

"Matt Brown. He works at the garden center. New hire. He makes me uncomfortable," Hazel confessed, feeling bad for judging without concrete reason.

"I can see why. I don't see any indication of magic on him, but he reeks of something dark. Maybe even evil. I'll be keeping my eye on him. I'm going to let Leticia know about him too."

Leticia Stone, local RCMP detachment head, was magical, though few other local police officers were. Some of Stone's magic fell into the grey area. Not quite white or good, but not dark either. She was a Voodoo Priestess who knew techniques and magics few other understood.

"I'm not one to judge on first impressions," Hazel said, rubbing her hands up and down her arms, her purse dangling from her shoulder. Even the sun wasn't chasing away the chill Brown gave her. "But, honestly, I can barely stand to be within sight of him."

"Trust your gut, dear. The Goddess gave us instincts for a reason."

The mayor's words made Hazel think about her attraction to Dennis.

Brown stalked up to them. "Hi, Hazel."

"Matt," she greeted him coolly, wishing he'd just go away. Far away. "Meet Mayor Quinton."

"Nice to have you in our little town. Where are you from?" The pair shook hands, Brown winced at the strength of the mayor's grip.

"Oh, here and there."

"I see," the mayor's voice turned to ice. "Enjoy your stay in Three Moon Falls. We look after each other here, we're a friendly, close knit town." The words were a clear warning.

"Good to know," Matt said. "Talk to you both later. I have things to do." His tone was rude and dismissive.

They watched him walk away.

"Am I wrong? Did that feel like a warning to you Hazel?"

"It did. I'll be watching my back. You better watch yours too." Every instinct she had was clanging away. Matt Brown was trouble. Keres style trouble.

"Indeed. Duty calls. A mayor's work is never done. Talk to your sisters, dear. Perhaps one of them can help you muddle through whatever's on your mind and mucking up your aura. Oh, and tell your parents I said hello. I'll let some other magicals know about Mr. Brown. We'll keep our eyes on him."

Hazel said goodbye and hurried the last few feet down the sidewalk and into their store.

"Your tea is ready," Gramma Pearl greeted her when she entered. "Some willow bark for the headache, chamomile and mint to calm you, a few rose petals and a bit of this and that. It'll cure what ails you."

Goddess bless her grandmother who had just enough clairsentience to know when her family needed her and the discretion not to peek in on too much private business. Although sometimes, her snoopy nature got the best of her.

Hazel threw her arms around her maternal grandmother, hugged her tight and breathed in her familiar scent. How she smelled like the ocean in the middle of the Canadian prairies was anyone's guess and she wasn't telling. "What would I do without you?"

Having family who knew she needed them without having to ask was both a blessing and a curse. Occasionally, they interfered before she was ready to talk. Luckily, that wasn't the case today. "Is there cake?" Hazel asked.

"Lemon meringue pie," Amber responded coming from behind the wooden cash desk, her high heels clicking on the tile floor.

"Wow. Look at you, all dressed up. And heels? I didn't even know you owned heels and I live with you. Or I did."

"The shoes are new," her older sister explained. "What do you think of the outfit?"

Hazel studied Amber's leafy green patterned sundress. It fell to mid-thigh, much higher than her usual ankle length skirts. Snug, but not tight, in all the right places. The dress accentuated all her curves and brought out the green in her eyes. Her blondie-brown hair was piled on her head in a complicated careless up-do which had probably taken an hour to achieve.

"Stunning. Kody's going to lose his shit when he sees you. I mean, wow. That outfit is totally not you, and at the same time, all you." She laughed at her cryptic response. "Hot date?"

"Yup. Kody scored reservations at Heaven."

Heaven was Three Moon Falls newest eatery and difficult to get a reservation for. Open only from five to midnight, the high-end restaurant was always packed. Kody must have booked ahead or gotten lucky in securing a reservation.

"I can't wait to hear how it was," Hazel enthused, forgetting her own dilemma for the moment.

"Enough about me." Amber's hand was cool on Hazel's elbow as she led her into the back room. Pearl followed them. "Time for tea and pie. And to tell us what's on your mind. Even I can hear your worry. Laz is on her way. Hyacinth is off delivering a baby, or she'd be here too. I can't believe the number of babies lately; we're having a mini population boom."

"And I hoped to talk to you alone," Hazel grumbled, only half meaning it.

"Fat chance." Amber laughed. "When does this family ever leave anyone alone with their problems?"

Out front, the shop's bell jangled merrily as someone entered. "Just me," Lazuli announced herself. Seconds later she burst into the back room on a wave of fresh sawdust scented air. "Sorry I'm late. I got caught up in a commission." Her jeans and T-shirt were spotless, but, as always, bits of sawdust clung to her hair. "Supper first?" she asked.

"Pie and tea," Hazel corrected. "I need pie and tea for this headache."

"That bad? Oh, baby sister, that sucks." Laz's embrace nearly crushed Hazel's ribs.

"Ah. Go easy. I'm fragile." Accustomed to hauling around lumber and custom created furniture all day, Laz was well muscled and strong, but still entirely feminine. Even if she failed to realize her own strength.

"Sit. Sit." Pearl encouraged them and gestured toward the shop sofa and chairs. Before opening the shop, Amber had created a comfortable kitchen and seating area in the store's workspace. Often working twelve- and sixteen-hour days as the store got onto its feet, she needed a place to relax and unwind and sneak in the occasional nap.

A steaming pot of tea and four china mugs sat on the table. Pearl bustled around at the fridge and counter and served them all generous slices of bright yellow lemon pie topped with thick piles of golden meringue.

"This pie looks amazing. Thanks, Gramma," Hazel said.

"You're welcome." Her grandmother sat with the grace and flexibility of someone twenty years younger than her age of sixty-five. "Now, tell us what's up."

"Yes. Tell us. We never hear any news," two voices chimed from behind Hazel.

Kansas and Ev sat on a workbench grinning eagerly. Hazel rolled her eyes.

"Yes. I'm here for your entertainment," she said, sarcasm dripping from her voice.

"You should be. We waited seven years for someone to move in and keep us company. Do you know how much it sucks to be here with only an old lady for company?" Kansas asked.

"Hush," Ev argued. "It's worse to be stuck with a petulant teenager."

"I'm nineteen. I've been stuck at nineteen for years."

"Exactly, a teenager."

"Shut it!" Lazuli yelled. "Don't make me look up a banishing spell. We could kick your asses across the barrier to the other side in a heartbeat."

"Fine," the ghosts pouted in unison.

"Thanks, guys," Hazel said. The last thing she needed was two bored ghosts sticking their noses in her business. Not that she could keep them away especially since they couldn't always be seen, leaving her with no idea if they were around or not. If Amber hadn't needed to keep the store open, they'd have done this at home.

Hazel needed to get the discussion going, but she was reluctant to admit she had feelings for a mundane. Magicals were supposed to fall for magicals. Or, in a worst-case scenario for the non-magical children of magical parents. Magic wasn't always passed down.

"My boss asked me out," she blurted.

"Sweet."

"No."

"Unprofessional."

"Yes."

The one-word answers battered her from all sides, too quickly to determine who said what.

"That helps," Hazel groaned. "Not."

"How do you feel about it?" Amber asked, patting Hazel on the knee. Like Hazel had expected, Amber understood her dilemma better than most.

"I can't date my boss," she wailed. "What if it sucks? Then I'd have to face him every day. Or risk getting fired when I dump him after a bad date."

"Does he seem the vindictive type?" Laz asked. "Would he really fire you?"

Good question. Dennis was always kind and patient with his staff. The only unkindness she'd seen was his absolute hatred of magic which had eased since their first meeting. She'd found it awkward between them after their brief kiss, which was to be expected. She looked deep into her emotions. Honestly, she didn't think he'd be vindictive, but that was her gut, not a rationally thought-out answer.

"Honestly? I don't know. I don't think so." She rubbed the ache in her forehead. Setting her tea on the table beside her pie, she leaned back and scrubbed her face with her hands. Why did things have to be so difficult?

"Do you like him?" Laz got right to the point.

"Yes."

"So, date him then. What's the trouble? I say go for it. If crap goes south, you can quit and get a new job," Laz advised.

"Jobs aren't easy to come by," Gramma Pearl stole the words from Hazel's mouth. Of course, if Pearl had her way, her granddaughters would die single, virgin spinsters.

"Are there sparks, physical attraction? Because the first time I saw Kody, I was in lust." Amber nudged Hazel.

"Gross. I do not need to hear that. You're my sister. Ew."

"You should kiss him and check for sparks," Kansas threw in her opinion.

Heat flooded Hazel's face. If only they knew. Thank heaven they didn't.

"Tell me you did not kiss a mundane," Pearl demanded. "You know better. I raised you better."

"It was a tiny kiss. Barely a kiss at all," Hazel protested. *Would the earth just open up and swallow her whole?* "Just a touch of lips, more a brush, really." A grin crept over her face.

"And you liked it!" Amber crowed. "Date him. Do it. If there are sparks and he seems like a decent person, you should try and see where it goes. Risk it."

"But he's a mundane and he doesn't like witches. Magic is a no-go for Dennis. I need to find someone magical."

"I thought so too. But Kody was mundane."

"Not a fair comparison, Amber. He was only mundane because his powers were blocked. I'm one hundred percent sure Dennis is mundane."

"I still say go for it. The ban of magic-mundane relationships is antiquated," Amber said and took a bite of her pie.

"It was put in for our protections," Pearl snapped. "If a mundane knows and the relationship ends badly, he could expose us."

"Pfft," Amber said. "And who would believe him? It's not like we aren't halfway out of the broom closet anyway."

"There is that." Hazel considered her sister's words. "What's your opinion, Laz?"

"Tough call," she said wisely. "I think if he seems decent and there is attraction and chemistry, you'd be doing yourself a big disservice to dismiss it out of hand. We aren't living in the dark ages, or the Burning Times. Besides, he already knows about us, right?"

"He does." All their opinions weren't helping her make a decision, even if they were making her look at the question from different angles. At least her sisters, two of three anyway, didn't think she was nuts to consider dating Dennis. Gramma Pearl, on the other hand, was dead set against it. Of course, she was against Kody at first and now he was like her long-lost son.

With every thought, the throbbing in Hazel's head intensified. She picked up her tea and chugged it down, barely tasting it. If Hyacinth were here, Hazel would get her to work some healing magic to ease the pain. But she wasn't and the tea wasn't doing enough. Conventional meds it was.

"This isn't helping me decide." Hazel walked to the kitchen, set her empty plate in the sink, and rummaged around in the cupboard above the fridge for Advil. "I keep reminding myself that none of our fathers were magical, and none have outed us, even if they don't all talk to us anymore."

"Aunt Opal married a mundane, and they're happy," Hazel said aloud. They'd been married for longer than Hazel had been alive and were proof that mixed marriages could work.

"I say go for it," Ev piped in. Hazel had forgotten the ghosts were even there.

She swallowed a couple tablets and leaned back against the counter; eyes closed. Being a witch was such a mixed blessing. She could control the flow of water and pull it from the air. She could levitate dishes, read Tarot cards and so much more. But she had to hide half of what she was from everyone and had to choose friends with extra care. Her Wiccan background told her to do what she wanted without harming anyone, even if they deserved it. She'd love to use magic to chase Matt Brown from town but forcing him to act against his will was considered harm. Plus, she had this whole dating dilemma to figure out.

She'd love to read Dennis's mind and find out what he was thinking. Again, a no-no, even if she had the skill, which she didn't. The universe had a damned twisted sense of humor, putting her in this situation.

Her cell phone vibrated in her pocket. She pulled it out and glanced at it.

Dennis.

She sighed and opened the text. ***Three staff have gone home sick. They have food poisoning, probably from the sushi tray someone brought in. It's just me and Sarah. She has to get home to her kids. Can you please come in and work the floor so I'm not alone? It's crazy busy.***

Yup. Fate was pushing them together.

"I have to go to work," she told her family as she texted him back.

On my way. I'm going to get a burger. Want one?

Yes, please!

"Thanks for the pie. I'll grab some real food on the way to work. Thanks for your opinions. You've given me a lot to think about." More than they'd ever realize. She poured her tea into a travel mug. "I'm not going to decide right away. I'm going to think about it first."

As she hugged everyone goodbye, she wondered if they knew she'd lied. She'd already decided, just that moment, to give Dennis a chance. How could she resist a guy who used proper grammar and punctation in a text? Her inner book nerd was tickled.

Chapter Ten

"That was insane." Dennis leaned against the garden center conveyor belt and glanced at his watch. "Nine thirty." He thrust his hands into his pockets. "I didn't think we'd ever see the last of them."

"Are you sure there isn't anyone lingering in the greenhouses?" she teased.

"Don't even think that." He groaned. She was right, they still needed to close up all the buildings, check the animals and cash out the registers. "You should go. I really appreciate you coming in."

"No problem. I was glad to help. I didn't expect it to be this crazy. Was there a sale I didn't know about?"

Her shoulder brushed his when she leaned beside him. He resisted the urge to lean against her.

"No sale. I think we're just slower than the usual clerks." He smiled at her. She was adorable in her Get Growing apron, with a smudge of dirt on her nose. "Go on home, Hazel. I've got this."

"How about I close up the greenhouses and you cash out?" She paused. "Then you can buy me more dinner for being a good sport." She stared at her shoes, revealing her uncertainty.

"Is this a boss-employee dinner, or something else?" He couldn't keep the question in, not if he wanted to maintain his sanity. They'd worked side by side for hours without obvious discomfort and he wasn't sure if they were okay, or just too busy to think about the electric tension between them.

She looked up at him and grinned. "Do we have to put a label on it?"

Her smile stole his breath. She was mesmerizing. "I guess it can go unlabeled. I'd love to take you to dinner." The leap in his heartbeat told him how thrilled he actually was. Too much so for his peace of mind.

"I'll lock up, you count the money." She hopped onto the counter, slid off the other side and jogged through the retail area, the bracelets on her arm clacking together musically with each step. She'd hadn't ever formally locked up, but he'd shown her where all the exits' dead-bolts were.

"Want to get takeout and come back here and eat by the creek?" She asked a few minutes later as they drove into town. "It's a beautiful night, the moon is almost full." Before he could answer, she added, "It's an outdoor girl thing, not a witch thing. I love being outdoors."

"We could," he said uncertainly. "But the bugs would eat us alive. The mosquitoes are insane this time of year."

"True. But I *could* protect us. If you didn't mind a tiny smidge of magic?"

He winced. Was this her way of forcing him to accept her magic?

"Never mind. I can see it's not a good idea. Dinner inside will be lovely."

She sounded sincere, if a bit disappointed. She was nothing like Natalie who never asked, just told, or went ahead and did what she wanted. Maybe he was being unreasonable.

"What the hell. It is a nice night, and the moon is gorgeous. Let's do it. A late dinner under the stars sounds nice." What it sounded was romantic, but he wasn't going to mention that.

She stared at him, her mouth open a fraction of an inch, as if he'd shocked her.

"Are you sure? We don't have to. I mean, I know magic makes you uncomfortable."

"I'm sure. Call ahead and order something. We'll gas up and pick up the food." They discussed options and she placed their order. Before he knew it, he was toting a small crate containing their food, wine, and glasses while racing to keep up as she rushed ahead, picnic blanket slung over her arm.

"You know this is crazy, right?" He asked as she spread the blanket on a smooth area beside the creek.

"Why? The rocks are small. I sit on the ground all the time. We've even got a blanket." She sat and patted the blanket beside her. "Join me."

He set the bin on the edge of the blanket and lowered himself beside her. Close, but not quite touching. "I meant it's almost eleven and we're having a picnic. Strange." He swatted a mosquito as it crawled across his leg. "Normal people don't picnic in the middle of the night."

"Lighten up, Dennis. This is fun. Just look at the moon, and those stars. Glorious. Besides, it's bright enough it's almost daylight. After the craziness of tonight, can't you just feel the moonlight washing away your stress?"

He'd never heard of moonlight reducing stress. Sunlight, yes, that was something to do with vitamin D.

"Come on," she urged. "Lean back and turn your face up. Try it. What have you got to lose?"

Since she'd suggested dinner, their relationship was on a firmer footing and he didn't want to shake the foundation. She leaned back on her elbows, her legs stretched out straight, and crossed at the ankles. Her face was lifted to the sky, a soft, relaxed smile on her lips. She looked...peaceful. She reminded him of the Sphinx but flipped over.

What the hell, he'd try it. Mimicking her pose, he leaned back.

"Breathe slow and deep. Picture the stress seeping from your body into the earth." Her voice was low and mesmerizing.

He tried. He gave it an honest shot. A sharp stone poked into his thigh. He shifted. Now one dug into his backside. He moved left a fraction of an inch, and sighed. This wasn't working. His stomach growled.

She laughed. "Fine. Let's eat. Maybe after I feed you, you'll be able to settle."

"Sorry. I'm starved. It's been five hours since I ate the burger you brought me. Remind me to pay you for it. Plus, I'm not really an enjoy the moon kind of guy."

"Meditating isn't easy at first." She sat up and twisted the screw cap off the wine and poured it into two stemless glasses. She handed him one and then passed him a cardboard takeout container. She lifted her glass. "A toast. To new friendships."

"To new friendships," he agreed and touched his glass to hers. "May they grow strong and true."

"Absolutely. Dig in."

They ate in silence, enjoying the creamy pasta and breadsticks, sipping on chilled white wine. Slowly, the tension slipped from his shoulders. She was good company. He didn't feel the need to put up his guard, which surprised him. He glanced at her, her long brown hair shining in the moonlight. She sat, cross legged, her torso perfectly upright, yet she appeared totally relaxed.

"How do you do that?"

"Do what?" She smiled at him.

"Perfect posture but completely relaxed at the same time?"

"Yoga. Lots of yoga. I used to slouch but years of yoga straightened me right out. It's easier to breathe when your body is aligned. You should try it."

"Yoga is a chick thing." He popped the end of a breadstick into his mouth.

"No, it's not. A lot of the best yoga instructors are men. Even here in town. The yoga studio is owned by a man. He teaches all male classes too. You should sign up; you could use it. You're all tight and wound up." Her smile told him she was teasing.

"I'm totally relaxed," he lied. He was more relaxed than he had been in ages, but still tense. But that was her fault. This crazy midnight picnic was relaxing, but his attraction kept him on edge.

Hazel set her dish aside and rose to her knees. She knee-walked behind him and put her hands on his shoulders. He fumbled his fork and stiffened his back. Her hands were warm through his shirt.

"What are you doing?" he blurted.

"Chill out. Breathe. I'm going to help you relax." She dug her fingers into his muscles. "Wow. You're more uptight than I thought. Super tense."

Tense? Of course, he was tense. A beautiful woman had her hands on him. He was lucky he didn't jump out of his skin or turn around and kiss her. But damn, her hands felt good. Too good. He shifted to loosen the sudden tightness in his jeans.

"Dude, you have to relax. Close your eyes. Enjoy the moon and the massage."

Easy for her to say. "Fine." He breathed deep, trying to do as she said. A whiff of wind carried her scent to tickle his nose. She smelled of sunshine, lemon and earth. He wanted to bury his face in her neck and memorize the aroma.

"If you're a water witch, why do you smell like earth?" He couldn't resist asking.

"What should I smell like?"

"I don't know. Rain? The ocean?"

"Are you saying my sister who controls fire should smell like ashes? Maybe brimstone? I smell like dirt because I work in a garden center."

He liked the way she teased; he heard the smile in her voice. "Okay, stupid question."

"There are no stupid questions," she said piously, making him grin.

"I suppose. Hey, I just noticed. The mosquitoes are gone. Did you do that?"

"I said I would. I just didn't make a big deal of it."

"But I didn't notice you do a spell. Don't you need a wand...or something? My ex always used a jeweled wand. She spent five hundred bucks on it."

"Your ex was magical?" It was a half question; she didn't wait for a response. "Some witches do use wands. Even me. A wand is a tool to focus your intent. As is a verbal spell. I am using a spell to keep the bugs away. I created it and said it in my head."

"How do you hold it?" He twisted to look at her. Her response fascinated him. She was being very open about something normally kept secret.

"I am pulling power from the earth. Honestly, half my mind is focused on the shield, the other half is on you and our picnic." She moved away from him and picked up her food. After a few bites, she continued. "It's tough to do, but Gramma Pearl forced us to practice dual focus, though not to keep bugs away. Eat." She gestured with her garlic toast toward his food.

She'd ordered bowtie pasta with Alfredo sauce and chicken. He'd chosen Spaghetti Bolognese. Not your usual picnic food, but delicious.

"You learned from your grandmother, not your parents?" The idea brought up a dozen questions about her family life.

"Our Dads weren't around. We lived with Mom and Gramma Pearl until Mom married Trevor Moon and moved out."

"That's right, you married into the founding family."

Her eye roll at the comment amused him.

"Mom was...a free spirit. Four kids, four dads. She wasn't promiscuous. We were all conceived deliberately with men she cared for."

He heard the embarrassment in her voice. "Hey, we can't control what happened before we were born."

"I guess." She scooped some pasta into her mouth as if blocking her words. A minute later she spoke again. "Mom and Trever knew each other all their lives but didn't fall in love right away. Or maybe they did. Mom doesn't talk much about her early life." She shifted so she wasn't quite facing him and sipped her wine. "What about you?"

"Born and raised in Calgary. University in Edmonton. Moved to Drayton Valley. Now here. My brother farms west of town. My sister and our folks are in Edmonton. I came here, to the garden center, hoping to have more time to breed flowers."

"How's that working out for you?" She looked up at him and winked.

"Like shit. I'm always swamped. We're open twelve hours a day, six days a week and eight on Sunday. I'm working twelve, sixteen, sometimes eighteen-hour days."

"Wow. It's impressive but must suck to live it. I'm happy with my six-hour days and the few hours I put in at the shop. But I guess with a new business, you don't have that luxury."

"Not at all. I'm taking your advice. I'm going to break the business, figuratively speaking, into two parts. Retail and growing. I'll hire or promote managers to each division and put someone else in charge of the petting zoo. Then, eventually, I'll be able to step back. I think there's money to be made from my crossbreeding, though I do it for fun, not profit."

God, he was baring his soul. He barely knew her, and he was spewing his guts, his dreams, out to her. She was ridiculously easy to talk to. A mosquito buzzed his ear. He swatted at it.

"Sorry. I guess I let that guy in. I'm having a bit of trouble holding the shield."

"Is it hard to maintain?" There was no way he could split his focus the way she was.

"Harder than I expected. Casting for two is way more difficult than for one. At home, I wear a pendant with marigold oil in it – keeps most of them off. This is a little physically and mentally taxing. Magic has a price."

"Let it go then. I had no idea it would strain you." Guilt wracked him. She'd done this, built an invisible barrier, for him. He was clueless about magic. He shouldn't be, Natalia had flaunted her skills, though in hindsight, she'd never revealed how magic worked, or indicated it could be difficult.

"I'm okay. I'll fuel up later. Let's enjoy the moon a while longer. I'm enjoying myself, enjoying the company."

Fuel up? What did that mean? "I'm enjoying being here with you too. I have a huge bay window; we could enjoy the moon from inside." Her face paled as he waited for her answer. Had he offended her somehow? She paled even further and dropped her fork.

"Sure. Let's go inside." She sounded relieved. "Pack up first. They'll be back with a vengeance when I drop the barrier. Another cost of holding them at bay. Nature is all about balance." Her voice trembled.

He threw everything into the basket and folded the blanket. "Let's make a break for it."

"Now," she blurted and took off, leaving him behind to catch up. She jogged ahead, wobbling unsteadily. She weaved left and right, staggering like a drunk.

He fumbled, one handed, for his keys as they raced toward the house. Inside he turned to look at her.

"Couldn't you have held the shield while we walked back?" He was curious, not upset.

"On a good day? Probably." Her face was colorless, and she leaned against the wall. She looked totally wiped. "It's late. I'm tired and I managed to hold it for nearly an hour." She bent over, panting, her palms resting on her knees. "Got any chocolate?"

"Sorry, no."

"Ice cream? Cake? Cookies? Steak?" Her eyes drifted shut and she listed sideways.

He dropped the bin with a crash and grasped her shoulder. Her eyes fluttered. "Come inside. I'll find something." He wrapped his arm around her and led her to the kitchen. He had no idea keeping bugs away would tire her so much. Was this temporary or permanent? He'd made her exhaust herself like this. He'd fix it. Somehow. "Sit. I'll find food." She said she needed to fuel up, he didn't realize she meant right now. "You literally refuel with food?"

"Ya." She rested her head on her crossed arms on the table while he sliced some cheddar and found some whole wheat crackers.

"Here." He pushed the plate in front of her, silently vowing to stock up on high calorie snacks for her. Rummaging around in the cupboard he found a boxed mug-cake mix his sister had left behind. A minute later, he popped the mug into the microwave. She perked up at the smell of chocolate. Or maybe from the food she was downing like a starving man. Was she literally starving?

The cheese plate was empty, so he poured her a glass of orange juice and handed it to her. She chugged the juice, ate the cake and the additional cheese he sliced before color began to return to her cheeks.

"Thank you. Sorry to eat you out of house and home." Her blush was accentuated by her pallor.

"You should have told me," he said, trying to hide his guilt. He wouldn't have let her shield them if he'd know the price. She'd done it without complaint, knowing it would drag her down. He slid into the chair across from her.

"I would have, but it hit me like a wall. I was fine, then I was done. Like my strength was sucked away or—" She fell silent. After a moment she scraped her mug free of crumbs.

"Or what? What aren't you telling me?" he asked, keeping the fear clawing at his back out of his voice. She was hiding something.

"Nothing. I'm fine. The food helped. Thank you. I better head home." She stood and trembled on her feet before dropping back into her seat. "I'll call my sister for a ride."

She didn't move to get her phone. She must be too drained to do even that. No way was he letting her leave until she felt better. This was his fault and he'd fix it, even if she was hiding something.

"Why don't you stay here, in the spare room? Let your family know you're out all night. I'll defrost a steak and feed you before you sleep." Would steak help? She'd asked for one earlier, he thought she'd been joking. Something was seriously wrong here.

"It's too late to cook. Do you have ice cream?"

"Why ice cream?" Junk food didn't seem the best idea for refueling. He'd prefer to give her something with more nutritional value. "How about salad while we wait for a steak?" Greens were high in nutrients.

"I need calories and the staying power of fat. Ice cream is perfect. Sugar for the instant boost and fat to reduce the crash afterward." She leaned back and closed her eyes. She was still pale, though a bit better.

"Ice cream it is. Then steak and you're going to bed. No arguments. I'll be right back."

Chapter Eleven

B y the Goddess, she'd made a colossal mistake putting up the bug screen. It wasn't something she did often, but she'd never had a crash like this after. It was more than expanding her personal block to cover two people. She'd felt the normal slow drain of her energy, and the food she'd been eating had kept her strength up. But after a while, the food hadn't sustained her. Weird. She hadn't had enough wine to affect her skills.

It was something else. She shivered, dread coursing through her.

Something, or someone, had fed on her power. The question was, who?

Not Dennis. She'd have felt the connection. Besides, he didn't have the slightest glimmer of power. He was one hundred percent mundane.

Shit!

She bolted out of her chair.

Keres!

Her heart pounded. Could he have escaped custody somehow? Would his injuries and burns even be healed yet? It had only been a couple months since he'd attacked her family. How long did it take major burns to heal?

She glanced at her watch. One-thirty. Way too late to contact Constable Stone and ensure Keres was still under wraps.

Maybe it was someone else. Surely word that her family possessed something, whatever Keres had been after, hadn't spread. Was someone else coming after it? Or them? Damn, she wished they'd been able to unearth what he was after.

She dropped back into her chair and scraped her fingers into her hair to massage her aching head. She was too exhausted to deal with this right now. She needed more food and sleep. Gramma Pearl's special energy balls would be perfect. She was going to have to start carrying them in her purse.

"Rocky road, or black cherry?" Dennis strode back into the kitchen with two tubs of ice cream and a brown paper package.

"Cherry, please." Her favorite. She'd expected him to be a vanilla guy, he'd surprised her. Half a minute later, he slid a heaping bowl in front of her.

"Chocolate sauce?" He wiggled the tempting treat in his hand.

"Absolutely. Right now, I love you more than any other person on the planet." Her words hit her. "That is, I mean, thanks. I'm so grateful. I didn't mean...I hardly know you." She floundered to a stop, her face burning in mortification.

"Relax, Hazel. I get it." He smiled broadly and flipped open the sauce and squeezed it over her bowl. "I know an exaggeration when I hear one. Enough?"

"Yeah. Perfect. Thanks."

"Besides, I have a sister and know how chicks are with ice cream."

"You did not just say that," she mumbled around a mouthful of ice cream. She groaned: part pleasure for the delicious treat, part exasperation. She laughed to herself at how she'd just proved his point.

He returned the sauce to the fridge and popped the brown package into the microwave. The ice cream went into the fridge's freezer rather than wherever it came from.

"I did say that. You know you can't deny it. Chicks, stress, and ice cream. They go together like cookies and milk."

She heard the laugh in his voice.

"You're yanking my chain, you jerk. I'm dying and you're messing around?" She feigned indignation. Only a few bites and the frozen treat was perking her up.

"Just lightening the mood. You're looking better. How are you feeling?"

"I'm getting there. I'm probably good to go home now." At least, she thought she might be.

"Suck it, girl. It's late. We're both tired and you need sleep. I've got a spare bed. Or I'll drive you home and pick you up in the morning."

She rolled her eyes. She did not need to deal with an overbearing male right now. She had to let her family know about her sudden power drain, although there wasn't anything they could do about it in the middle of the night. But they probably sensed something was wrong.

The microwave dinged and Dennis opened it to check the meat. "I'll just pop this on the grill. Sit tight."

Sit tight, her ass. If she had the energy, she'd grab her stuff and disappear. She was beyond exhausted. Maybe he had a point. Sleep would do her a world of good. She pulled her phone from her pocket and shot her grandmother a quick text, letting her know she wouldn't be home and where she was. Pearl wouldn't sleep deeply until she knew all her granddaughters were safe at home.

Reporting her plans never felt like an intrusion, or a violation of privacy. Since she and her sisters were old enough to go out without adult supervision, they'd been reporting their plans to a family adult. Being a magical in a world of mundanes made you cautious.

She finished her ice cream, stood and stretched. Her muscles burned like she'd spent hours in the gym. Not good. Yoga was definitely on tap for morning. She bent from the waist to touch her toes.

"What are you doing now?" Dennis asked, sounding incredulous.

She tipped her head to grin at him. "Working out some kinks. Don't worry, I feel much better. That ice cream was just the thing. Thanks." Straightening up, she grabbed her bowl and went to the sink to rinse it.

Dennis crossed his arms over his chest. "I could have taken care of that."

"Yup. But dishes are women's work, and I wouldn't want those fragile man paws to get dishpan hands. Do you want me to take over the cooking too?"

"Funny." He leaned against the counter and studied her.

His stare was unnerving.

"You are funny," he said at last. "But you're hiding something."

"Nope. Not me." She turned away to slip the bowl into the dishwasher and conceal the heat in her face. She sucked at lying, she always had.

"I told you. My ex is a witch. She works magic for everything, and I never once saw her sucked dry like you were. What went wrong?"

He was way too perceptive. Spending the evening with him had been a mistake. His concern was touching but if someone was stealing her power, he could be in danger, just from being around her. She returned to her chair and rested her elbows on the table. "I'm just super drained."

"And I'm the queen of England. You do know you wince when you lie? Your face is all screwed up and pinched together. I'm not magic, but I'm not stupid either."

"I am super drained. The universe is punishing me for using magic for personal gain." It was a partial truth. She should have stuck to their original agreement and not used magic on his property.

"You said you don't keep bugs away for yourself, you have a pendant. You did it for me, so not personal gain. Try again."

She didn't want to pull him into this. Sometimes, ignorance was bliss. This time, it could mean his safety. No way was she putting him in danger. A good night's sleep and she'd be right as rain. And they could go back to a boss-employee relationship. As if that could happen with the attraction she felt for him.

"I must have been more tired than I thought. It was late. I had wine. I was hungry. I've never done it for two people before. I guess it all added up." She tried to keep her facial muscles relaxed and un-bunched.

"Do all witches lie like you? How about your sisters? Is it just you? I know we got off to a rocky start, but aren't we friends?" His voice was level, but not quite calm. There was an undercurrent of tension and frustration. "I need to check the steak." He stormed from the kitchen.

Remorse pulled at her conscience, like the sun drawing water inexorably toward the clouds. Relentless and draining. She didn't have the strength for emotional gymnastics, and he had a point. If she wanted to see where her attraction for Dennis went, she had to be honest.

He came back but didn't say anything. He started setting the table.

She searched for something to say, but he left before she found the words. He returned and set a platter with two large T-bone steaks and a baked potato on the table.

"Eat up." He said and slid the smaller steak onto his plate. "The potato is for you. It's a premade, frozen stuffed one, but they're not bad."

"Thanks," she replied, subdued. She loaded the potato with butter and sour cream. They ate in awkward silence until she'd eaten half her steak.

She dropped her silverware onto her plate with a clatter that reflected her guilt and exasperation. "Fine." She swallowed the lump in her throat. "Something went wrong. I was completely fine. Just feeling a normal drain. I should have been fine for another half hour at least, maybe more. Then it got really difficult to hold the shield, just after I started massaging your shoulders. I thought it was me doing too much and was too tired. But now, I don't think that was it." She snatched up her fork and shoved a bite of the tender meat into her mouth. She was going to choke to death eating this fast, trying to keep her secrets to herself.

Dennis set his silverware gently on the edge of his plate and folded his arms loosely. "I don't know what you mean. If it wasn't exhaustion, what was it?" Concern creased his brow.

"I can't prove it, but I think someone was pulling my magic away. Stealing my power, or at least the energy I was using." She pleaded with her eyes for understanding. "It's like this. Everyone knows energy cannot be destroyed. It can change. High school physics. I pulled power, energy, from the earth and transformed it into a bug screen. Slowly, the residual energy dissipates, returns to the earth or is sort of used up by bugs battering against it. I have to keep feeding more energy into the shield to keep it up. When I drop it, the power returns to the earth. But somehow, it was disappearing too fast. Someone was sucking away either the energy in the shield, or my power." People with the ability to siphon a witch's power were incredibly rare.

He blinked rapidly. "Who?"

Succinct and to the point, but impossible to answer. "I have no idea. I've never felt anything like it before." Well, except for Keres. "I've pulled power from my family and sent them power. Normally, it takes consent on both ends. But this was different. Subtle. I didn't even notice until I was practically dry. Then it felt like the tide pulling water from the shore or a vacuum, sucking in everything I had."

To her relief he didn't say she was crazy, or demand she leave. He looked thoughtful. "What do you think it was?"

Again, a reasonable question. If only she knew. Her mind kept going to Keres, but he was still locked up. She hoped.

"I don't know for sure. If someone is tapping into my power, he's strong and experienced. I didn't feel him, and he didn't leave a trace I can find. It could be a she, I don't know. I didn't get a sense of gender, or anything else." The much-needed meal she'd eaten threatened to come back up. She rubbed her stomach.

"And that scares you." Dennis said with certainty.

"It terrifies me." She was beyond frightened. She wanted to bolt to the safety of her magically reinforced home. She was too vulnerable here. But if someone was after her, he could still be out there.

Waiting.

If he was, she was too tired for a magic battle. She'd lose for sure. She didn't dare leave now. She had to consider Dennis's safety too. Her burgeoning feelings for him could make him a target too, a way to get to her. They were safer in the house than in a moving vehicle.

"Okay. Say you're right," Dennis said, scraping his hand over his jaw. "How can we protect you? Should I drive you home?"

As strong as the pull of home and its protection was, her gut told her to stay put. "I need to talk to my family about it. But not tonight. Tired minds solve nothing. If it's okay, I'll crash here."

"Of course, it's fine. I'll find you something to sleep in. Do you need to do a spell, or something? I don't know magic protection."

He had a point. Protection could help, but she didn't have the strength. Maybe tonight was just a warning.

"I think I'm okay. I'm too tired to magic anyway. Besides, if what happened to my sister, Amber, is any indication, this is a warning."

"What happened to your sister?" His eyes widened and he jingled the change in his pocket.

"A couple months ago, a stranger approached her in our shop, just after we opened. He was—weird. Creepy. Eerie. He kept hassling her. Almost stalking her until he finally kidnapped her."

"What? Is she okay?"

"She was pretty messed up, but Kody, her fiancé, found her. She's okay now."

Several conflicting expressions crossed over his face. Relief. Worry. Fear. Anger. Confusion. He opened his mouth without saying anything. Twice. "It feels like you aren't telling me something. What else is there?" He pinned her with a stare, and she squirmed in her chair.

She could see the moment the light went on and he mentally connected the dots.

"He was magic." Dennis stated, no doubt in his voice. "When the guy was hurt on your land, that was him wasn't it?"

"Yes."

"Oh my God. He didn't burn himself. You guys did it." The concern he'd showed for her sister visibly morphed into wariness bordering on fear.

"It wasn't like that. We were all in danger. I nearly died at his hands. Amber did what she had to. It was the only way to stay alive." How could she explain when grievously injuring someone to survive was the only way to live? It wasn't a choice. It had been their only option. Either strike back or die.

"I know words don't convey what happened. I swear on my own life, on my family's lives, if there had been a way to avoid the confrontation and walk away from Keres, we would have." She choked up; her throat started to tighten with fear at the memory. Swarms of wasps surrounding her, stinging her, flying into her mouth and ears. She'd gone into anaphylactic shock after the attack Keres had magically unleashed on her. Her brain and body recalled every single sting, every sharp jab. Hundreds of them, deadly to anyone, even more to someone cursed with an allergy to wasps.

Her skin twitched as if they still crawled over her. She'd had nightmares for weeks. Her body trembled; she swallowed back her terror, reminding herself it was just a memory. Of the worst day of her life.

She sat, unable to move, torn between past terrors and the fear Dennis would recoil from her and send her packing.

"You swear? Swear you had no choice except what you did?" He asked harshly.

She nodded weakly. "I swear. Until that day, I would have sworn I couldn't hurt a fly. I still can't. We had no choice. None. It still sickens me when I think of it. The guilt is crippling, but I'd do it again if I had to. We all would. But only to save our lives."

"And this guy, Keres, was he stealing magic, like you felt tonight? Could there be someone out there, right now, who could be dangerous? Could it be him?"

"Probably not him. He's incarcerated. Magically."

"But there could be someone?" Dennis persisted, not even blinking at the idea of a magical jail.

"Yes." Her mouth was dry, her tongue thick and awkward.

Chapter Twelve

"Son of a bitch." Dennis's guts felt like lead as tears welled in Hazel's eyes. Her body trembled; she was scared. What the hell had actually happened the night they were attacked? And, equally important, what *exactly* had happened to her tonight to bring back that fear? She looked so broken. From the memories as much as what happened outside earlier.

"Come here," he said, his voice croaked. He opened his arms.

She hesitated half a second; indecision clear on her face, before she stepped into his embrace. Her skin was icy against his arms as he wrapped them around her.

"Relax, Haze. Try and breathe. I'll keep you safe." Right, like he could combat magic. He was getting in too deep. He never should have hired her, but he couldn't resist her spunk. She was gutsy and tough. Although now he sensed a much softer side beneath all her bluster.

"Someday, you're going to have to tell me the full story. But not tonight." Definitely not tonight. He'd had enough shocks to assimilate. What was the world coming to when a man and his guests weren't safe on his own land? Dammit. Was someone wandering, uninvited on his property?

He rubbed his hands up and down her back, hoping to soothe her, to calm her nerves, and still her shaking. Her arms snaked around his waist, drawing him tighter against her. It was a wonder she wasn't totally freaked out and calling the police. Of course, how could she convince the RCMP she wasn't nuts? Who would believe in magic?

He knew magic firsthand, had for his entire five-year engagement and he'd had no idea how dangerous unchecked magic was. Almost too late, he'd learned people could control your mind.

He'd read about this shit in fantasy novels, saw it on television, but this was real life, not fiction. He'd been wrong to dismiss the true power of magic.

He needed a lesson on what to watch for, and how to protect himself. The woman in his arms was just the person to help him. After he helped her through the night and delivered her, safe and sound, to her family and she felt better, he'd be asking for lessons. He suspected she needed family support, emotionally and in dealing with her assailant. After they slept.

"Come on, I'll show you your room," He grasped her cold hand and led her down the hall to the guest bedroom. "You can sleep in here. I'll be right next door if you need anything. All you have to do is call."

She nodded and stood staring into the spacious room.

Did she like it? His sister had decorated it in vibrant red and black, with gold accents. She'd told him it was bold but not garish. It was the room she used when she visited, and he let her decorate it to suit herself. Until this moment, Dennis hadn't cared what it looked like. Maybe he should have insisted on something less jarring. Too late now.

"Hold tight, I'll get you a T-shirt to sleep in." He hurried to his own room and was back in under a minute. "Here you go. One T-shirt, suitable for nightwear." He'd grabbed his softest shirt, hoping it would be more comfortable to sleep in.

She took the shirt but didn't move into the room. "Thanks," she said woodenly.

He hadn't known her long, but he'd never seen her so indecisive. She was really rattled. Maybe he should phone her family.

"Are you going to be okay? Should I call someone?" He hated this feeling of helplessness.

She pivoted to look at him with sad, worried eyes. "No," she said, her voice soft. "Tomorrow is good. I'll just catch some sleep." She stepped into the room.

Deep inside, he wondered if she was making a mistake staying with him. Part of him wanted to object, to drive her home. But she was an adult, capable of making her own decisions.

"If you're sure?" He lifted one shoulder in a questioning shrug. "There are new toothbrushes in the drawer of your ensuite. Help yourself and call me if you need me. Good night, Haze. Sleep well." He backed out of the doorway and eased the door shut.

Her barely whispered response came through the door to where he stood, indecisively, not sure he should leave her alone. He couldn't wrap his mind around what happened. He had a vague idea based on his own experiences with Natalia trying to push thoughts into his head. But to steal her power and strip her strength? It sounded similar to a flu or virus. A magical virus. Maybe even mental abuse. He shuddered.

Behind the door, she moved quietly, her footsteps nearly soundless on the carpet. Water ran. The light he'd turned on earlier clicked off. A few more footsteps and silence.

He banked the urge to go into the room. It felt wrong to leave her alone. Not just because of the potential threat, more so because she was so emotionally wiped and distressed. He tried to rationalize it by telling himself she'd ask for help if she needed it. The ache in his guts and tension in his neck told him he was wrong to leave her and equally wrong to go to her.

He trudged back to the kitchen and quietly cleaned up the dishes before setting the house alarm and going to bed to toss and turn as sleep evaded him. Strange, uncomfortable worries plagued his over-active imagination.

He'd barely drifted off to sleep when a whisper of sound had him jerking to his feet and snapping on the bedside lamp.

Hazel stood at the end of his bed, blinking at the sudden light.

He rushed to her side. "What's wrong? Are you okay?" He ignored the way his shirt brushed her thighs, drawing his gaze to her shapely legs. Now was not the time.

"I can't sleep. Not alone." Her cheeks turned pink, and her hands twisted together. "I know it's a lot to ask…"

He waited thirty seconds for her to finish speaking. "Go ahead, ask," he suggested, dreading and hoping she wanted to share his bed.

"Can I sleep with you?" she mumbled.

"What?" He didn't know whether to panic or do a happy dance.

"It's okay. Never mind." She turned to go.

"No. Wait! It's okay, you just surprised me." He waved toward the bed. "Pick your side. I'll take the other." His cock leaped to life at the vision of her in his bed. He willed it to behave. She was pretty, sexy, strong and vulnerable. All his protective instincts kicked in. He was definitely not going where his libido tried to lead him.

Nope. Not happening.

She slid into the left side of his bed and pulled the covers to her chin. "Thank you. Sorry to be such a wimp."

He joined her, careful to keep his hands and body to himself. "It's okay. You've had a brutal night. Sorry about that."

"Not your fault." She rolled to face him; her leg brushing his.

He managed to stay still, not jerking away or pulling her closer. This night had already been an eternity, it was about to get longer.

She didn't appear to blame him for what happened, but he blamed himself. If he'd put on bug spray instead of having her magic away the insects, this never would have happened. They never should have eaten together. Not inside and definitely not outside. They should have closed the store and gone their separate ways, avoiding this unforeseen disaster entirely.

No time together would have meant, no meal, no shield, no magic thief.

Wait. Exactly how close did someone have to be to steal magic? Miles? Feet? Meters? Was someone on his land right now?

"I'll be right back." He slid out of bed and quickly checked all the doors and windows. All locked. Probably futile against magic, but it eased his mind a little. He'd done what he could to keep her safe. Back in bed, he checked the security app on his phone. The greenhouse was shut tight, and all the motion sensors armed.

"What are you doing?"

"I was distracted when we closed up. Just making sure I locked everything up." And desperately sucking up any comfort he could find. He was partially responsible for this. Keeping her safe for the night was the least he could do.

"I don't think he'll be back tonight. I hope." She curled her hands under her head and looked at him.

"Then why are you in my bed?" Dennis grinned to show he was teasing. Anything to ease the tension. Sexual and otherwise.

"Because you're irresistible?" she teased back.

"Don't start something you have no intention of finishing," he warned and tucked the covers under her chin. "It's late, almost morning. Get some sleep." He stroked one finger down her soft cheek and turned off the light. Maybe if he couldn't see her, he wouldn't be tempted.

Fat chance.

In only minutes, her breathing slowed and deepened in sleep. He should be so lucky. Nothing moved in the stillness of the night.

Her breath whispered in and out, bathing him in fresh mint. Her soft earthy, lemony scent stole the air from his lungs. Though he was nearly a foot away on the king-sized bed, he swore he could feel her heat. He ached to pull her into his arms to keep her safe.

She shifted in her sleep; her hand came to rest on his chest. He clasped it in his and lay in the dark, praying for sleep. But what man could sleep with a beautiful, vibrant, woman in his bed? Certainly not him.

Chapter Thirteen

A small beam of sunlight on her face woke Hazel. She lay there, letting her body and mind come to life.

The bed was unusually hot and smelled like spice and leather. A warm weight was over her waist and something hot was pressed against her back. Realization came slowly. She was in Dennis's bed.

Shit. Heat flooded her face. She'd been such a wimp last night, terrified to be alone. She'd found comfort in his bed, even though the man cuddled up to her would have been powerless to protect her.

Remorse flooded her. She'd used him. She wasn't a user. That wasn't who she was, but she'd taken advantage of him in an act of cowardice.

Still, she couldn't bring herself to pull away from the warmth and strength of his comfort. She justified it by reminding herself the alarm on her phone hadn't gone off, yet. It was still early, before six, and he was asleep. They'd gone to bed after two. No sense waking him.

She ran over the events of last night in her head. The fun and companionship of working alongside him. The peace and joy of their moonlit picnic. The soul crushing terror of feeling her power sucked away.

Her body tensed. Her fight or flight instinct kicked in. She was tempted to bolt for home, where she should have gone last night. Only knowing how late she'd kept him up held her in place.

"You think really loudly."

Dennis's soft words brushed across her neck.

"Morning, Haze."

"Sorry. I didn't mean to wake you. Why do you call me that?"

"You mean Haze? I don't know. Hazel seems too formal, too up-tight for friends. Is it okay?"

She'd never really had a nickname. Being the youngest of four, she'd often been tagged as brat, but rarely an abbreviation of her name. She liked it. "It's fine. But probably not great in front of the rest of your staff. It might seem overly personal."

"Good point."

"We should get up," she suggested without moving. She was too content right where she was. Safe and protected, in his arms.

He brushed her hair off her shoulders, his fingers barely grazing her skin. He leaned close and kissed her shoulder. "I like waking up with you. Did you sleep okay?"

Surprisingly, she'd fallen asleep immediately once she was beside him, and she felt fairly well rested considering she'd had, at best, three hours of sleep. "Better than I thought I would. You?" Maybe if she kept this conversation going, she could hide in his arms all day. The arm around her waist tightened and pulled her closer.

"I slept well. Not long enough, but well. Thanks. Maybe we should try and sleep a bit longer?"

Right. Like she could sleep with his hard body against hers and his erection pressing against her backside.

"Or," she said and rolled toward him. "We could do this." She slid her arms around him and brushed her lips across his. She felt his smile against her mouth.

"This is a bad idea." He leaned up on one elbow and devoured her mouth with his. "Such a bad idea." He kissed her again.

He was so wrong. This was the best idea she'd had in months. She wiggled closer, tangling her legs with his. Her hand explored the muscular plane of his back. He felt so incredible against her. There was a security in his arms she hadn't known before last night. Similar to, but different from the safety of home.

What was she doing? She didn't sleep around. She could barely remember the last time she'd had sex. Making love to someone she cared deeply for had been even longer. But Dennis? By the Goddess, she wanted to climb into his skin and become part of him.

She'd known he was a decent guy, except for his magic fears. She'd been tempted to seduce him under the moon last night, before things went south. Then, he'd been so kind, so caring and concerned. Despite his own fear, he'd cared for her. He'd even let her into his bed, which was the only place she wanted to be right now. She slid her land lower, into the back of his boxers.

"Whoa, slow down, honey. There's no hurry." He grabbed her hands, rolled her onto her back and pinned her down with his body. "I'm going to enjoy every second of this, of you." He trapped her arms over her head and nuzzled her neck.

"Let me go," she protested lightly, wiggling underneath him.

He released her arms immediately and lifted up to look at her. "Sorry, I got carried away."

"You should be." She jerked out from under him, pushed him onto his back and straddled him. "I want to be on top." She bit his lip and wiggled her hips.

"You'll pay for this," he laughed and reversed their positions, once again taking control.

"No, you don't." She jerked away and leaped off the bed and bolted out of the room laughing.

"Vixen," he shouted and chased her.

She let him catch her in the living room. He flopped onto the sofa and pulled her onto his lap.

"Come here, beautiful," he whispered huskily. "I want to kiss you."

"I can live with that. I hope you're up to the challenge." She bit his lip again.

"Are you questioning my sexual prowess?" His hands slid to her waist, below her T-shirt.

"Yes, Mr. Belanger. I am. I have specific needs and I need to be certain you're up to the task." She ground against him, wished he was already inside her. This was fun, but she wanted more.

"I assure you," he kissed her deeply, stealing her breath, and making her heart pound, "you won't be disappointed." He stripped the shirt over her head and tossed it aside, knocking over a lamp. "Whoops." He leaned back to look at her, his hands resting just below her breasts. "My god, you are beautiful. Breathtaking."

She stared at him. He looked awestruck. If he was a character in a movie, she'd say he looked smitten, there was such caring and passion in his eyes. She could drown in those sea blue eyes. How could she possibly resist his expression or the caring he'd shown her?

She cupped her breasts and leaned forward, bringing one rock hard nipple to his mouth. "Make love to me, Dennis. Please."

"Your wish is my command." He flicked his tongue over her nipple. She jerked at the electric jolt which followed. *Holy shit.*

Somewhere a phone started chiming. "Sorry," he whispered against her breast. He lifted her from his lap and set her on the sofa. "I have to get that. It's the alarm."

She padded after him to the bedroom, enjoying the flex of his backside under his boxer-briefs. The man was delectable.

He snatched his phone off the nightstand and keyed in some numbers. She leaned in to look.

"What in the world is he doing here this early?" Hazel demanded, staring at the picture of Matt Brown on the screen. "It's not even six." The chills racing down her back had nothing to do with being nearly naked.

Dennis frowned at the phone. "Good work ethic?" he said unconvincingly.

Hazel bit back a smart remark. The man was up to no good. All traces of arousal evaporated as she stared at the phone. "Mind if I take a shower?"

Dennis looked disappointed. "Sure, go ahead. I'll go talk to him. Don't leave before breakfast."

Water sluiced over her body as she soaped up. Aside from anger and concern about Brown's early arrival, she felt better than she'd expected to after last night. She'd slept like the dead, quickly dropping off and not waking until morning. At least she had, after crawling into Dennis's bed. Before that, her mind had spun in crazy circles, driving her insane and keeping her awake.

She paused in the middle of washing her hair. Brown's early morning arrival set off alarm bells in every cell of her body. Usually, her intuition wasn't great, but it was screaming at her right now. Mathew Brown was going to be a problem. After last night's energy sucking, it was too big of a coincidence he'd show up so early. He made her uneasy. More now than ever.

Did Brown have something to do with last night? She didn't get a sense of magic from him, but he could be masking it. She needed to head home for a confab with her family. They'd have some insight. She hoped.

What a way to ruin a beautiful morning. Heat flooded her face and flowed down her body along with the suds. She couldn't believe her behavior. She'd actually set out to seduce Dennis and had nearly succeeded. They'd been minutes away from the main event. Yikes.

Fate, in the form of Brown, had saved her from making a big mistake. It wasn't that she didn't want to make love to Dennis. She did. But their relationship was still in its infancy. Barely just friends, and maybe moving on toward something deeper. It was too soon to make the jump to lovers, no matter how tempting he was. No matter how right it felt.

She was full-on ready to see how compatible they were, despite his biases. People could change. Sleeping together would be a mistake before they explored their compatibility. Even if Dennis was fit, toned and muscular from moving plants and bags of soil around all day.

He was drool-worthy for sure. She'd known he'd be buff long before she saw him half dressed. He'd amped up his physical appeal with his concern for her welfare. Him helping her refuel and standing solid when she was exhausted and scared counted for a lot. She didn't need a man to take care of her but liked knowing he was willing.

She finished her shower, dressed in yesterday's clothing and headed for the kitchen.

Chapter Fourteen

"Morning, Matt," Dennis called out as he opened the front door of the greenhouse. "What brings you here this early?" He looked pointedly at the watch he'd slipped onto his wrist on the walk over.

Matt stepped inside.

"Just thought I'd get a head start on moving those bark chips." His eyes shifted away and he shuffled his feet.

"How'd you plan to get in? Only managers have keys." Something about the ridiculously early arrival bothered Dennis. Even the most dedicated employee didn't show up three hours early. The yard was gated, and unless he'd planned to climb over the fence, he had no access.

"Yeah. I forgot I didn't have keys. After years of working on-site, I'm used to starting when I can't sleep."

Dennis sensed the truth in Matt's words but heard a deflection as well. He had no intention of letting his newest employee have unsupervised access to his livelihood. "I guess I understand that, and I appreciate your work ethic, but you'll need to find something else to do until your shift starts. It's early and I haven't had my coffee yet." He let his words hang, hoping Matt would agree and leave without pressing the issue.

"You sure? I could start now and not clock in until nine?" His smile grated on Dennis's nerves.

"I appreciate your generosity, but store policy is that only managers have unsupervised access to the premises." This conversation was getting old, fast.

"Aren't you the owner?"

God, this guy was used car salesman pushy. "I am, but I have a partner. We set the rules together and I don't have the power to change them without consultation." Technically true. He'd given his sister ten percent and paid her a monthly dividend. He hadn't needed a partner, but his sister could use a bit of extra income. Her share was a way to help her out financially without giving her money for nothing. She needed the money to finish medical school. They had discussed business, but she trusted him to run everything and rarely had an opinion on any of it. She'd be thrilled with the petting zoo.

"You're sure then?" Matt persisted.

Frustration spiked. He was sorely tempted to fire Matt on the spot. "One hundred percent." Dennis pushed the door open and held it for Matt to leave. "See you at nine," he said pointedly.

"Later then." Matt frowned and stepped outside. "But I see Hazel's car is here already." He made the statement heavy with insinuation.

Dennis glanced at the parking lot. Shit. "So it is. I guess she got a ride home from someone yesterday." The man had colossal nerve. The insinuation infuriated Dennis. Even if it was sort of true. "See you later." Dennis snapped the lock shut and stood there until Matt climbed into his car, which was backed into the handicapped spot, close to the door, rather than in the designated staff stalls.

"Unable to sleep, my ass." When Matt drove way, Dennis double checked the locks, all of them, and went back to the house.

The enticing scent of coffee welcomed him when he stepped inside, and relief washed through him. The tension in his shoulders floated away. He'd been half afraid Hazel would vanish while he was gone, even if her car was still there.

"You're still here," he greeted her with a kiss. She turned her face, so his lips brushed her cheek. Guess he should have expected a cool down.

"Coffee?" She selected two mugs from the mismatched collection hanging under the cupboard.

"I'd love some, it smells greats." Not as delicious as she'd smelled in his bed. He accepted the mug she held out to him and sat down. He'd half suspected the morning fun had been situational and spur of the moment but he was still disappointed.

She took the chair across from him and stared into the mug cradled between her hands. "What did he want?"

"He said he couldn't sleep and decided he'd come to work early."

"I hear your doubt." Her gaze flicked up to his and retreated to the mug.

"He lied. I don't know why, or what he was actually up to. He doesn't have a key, so he'd have to break in, and he was backed into a handicapped spot."

"Weird." She opened her mouth and snapped it shut again.

He knew what she was going to say. She'd told him not to hire Matt. Maybe she was right, but he had seemed a good fit, even if this morning's behavior was suspicious.

"It makes me wonder why he really was here. Robbery? Or something else. There's nothing worth stealing. I'm certain he wasn't here to work." Dennis admitted. He wasn't one for instincts, but this made him uneasy, especially on the heels of last night's attack. He mentioned his concern to Hazel.

"Yeah, that crossed my mind. Where is he now? Are you going to fire him?" She sounded hopeful.

"He's gone. I can't fire him; he hasn't done anything. Even though he's on probation for three months, he could complain to the labor board. I don't need the hassle. I'll give him the benefit of the doubt, for now. But I'll keep my eye on him."

She nodded, but a scowl creased her brow.

Honestly, keeping Matt on left him uneasy as well.

"Is it okay if I take the morning off? I'm out of sorts and I'd like to talk to my family. I'll make up the time over the next week."

Their gazes tangled and he realized she was still upset about last night and their strange morning visitor. Was she running from their physical attraction as well?

"Take all the time you need. Don't worry about time. You put in extra hours before our picnic last night." He had no concerns about her taking a couple hours off. "Do you want breakfast?"

The question seemed to shock her. "Oh. No. Thanks. Gramma Pearl will want to feed me. Food is her go-to method of offering comfort," Hazel chuckled, "and of leading off an interrogation. And you know she'll have questions about me being out all night. She'll freak when she hears what happened. Although I'll be shocked if she hasn't sensed something wrong already."

He was glad Hazel had a strong support system at home, but it made him wonder about her safety at his place. His worry morphed into concern for all his employees.

"What?" she asked.

"Sorry? I was lost in thought." The lie tumbled off his tongue.

"That was an enormous sigh. What's on your mind?" She tapped her thumb against her leg and stared at him until he spoke.

"Mostly your safety. Will you be safe here? Is there something I, we, should do to protect you?" He kept his broader worries to himself. No need to burden her further.

"Not really, no. Thanks for asking."

"You're telling me there is no magical way to guard you? I don't believe you." He knew about wards and magic sigils, even if he had no idea how to use them.

"Magical yes, but I agreed no magic on your property. I broke our agreement last night and look what happened." She chugged her coffee before knotting her fingers together.

"Screw that. Do what you need to do. Magic or otherwise. You could have been badly hurt. I won't let that happen again." Anger at whoever tried to hurt her rocked him. He forced his hands to relax before he crushed the ceramic mug between them.

"If I don't perform magic, he'll have no reason to attack me. Don't worry. It won't happen again."

"Bullshit!" His expletive startled her, she jerked back. "Whatever was going on wasn't a one-time thing. He's on to you now. He'll come again." He thought she'd leap at the chance to put up some protection. Why wasn't she? It dawned on him. "You feel guilty, don't you?"

She nodded.

"This isn't your fault. Not in any fashion. Full blame lies on the asshole who attacked you." No, the attack wasn't physical, but it had had devastating physical consequences for her. Her attacker had stolen from her. She must feel violated. His college apartment had been broken into and had left him feeling nervous and uncertain. She had to feel worse.

"Haze, listen to me." He paused until she lifted her head to look at him. "This wasn't your fault. There is no way you could know anyone was out there waiting to drain you." That brought up the question of who it was, and why they were on his land. He tabled the questions for later. Hazel was his first concern.

"You told me about your sister. I don't want you hurt like she was. Put up the wards, do a protective spell. Hell, do a dozen spells to keep yourself safe. Do what you need to do. I retract my stipulation. All I ask is don't let the rest of the staff see you."

He rounded the table, grasped her hands and pulled her gently to her feet and into his embrace. "I don't ever want to see you like that again. Please, for the love of God, put up some protection."

She leaned into him, her arms slid around his waist and her cheek pressed against his chest. "That's a sudden change of opinion, but I will, since you insist." Relief and pleasure were heavy in her voice.

"I insist," he said and stroked her back. "The sooner the better. Now, how about breakfast?"

She laughed outright. "Not today, but I'll take a raincheck. I really should get home."

He smiled when she pressed closer rather than moving away. "I'll drive you."

"What? Why? I can drive." She looked up at him.

For a moment, he was lost in the depths of her beautiful brown eyes. "You're still tired. It's been a long night. Besides, until you get your protection set up, I'm your bodyguard."

His urgent need to protect her unnerved him. He'd never felt so protective over another person, except his sister, and his brother's kids. He'd put the words out without thought, and he'd abide by them. He traced a dark circle under her eye with the tip of his finger. "Try and get some rest. Take the day off and sleep."

"I'll be back later," she whispered. "But I'll need to catch a ride if I leave my car here. It's easier if I just drive home."

"I'll take you home and bring you back when you're ready. Just text me." He tipped her chin up and stared down at her. "Damn," he muttered and slowly lowered his head. He paused a fraction of an inch from her lips, giving her time to object.

"Okay, you can drive me home." She sighed and pressed her soft lips against his.

Renewed desire sliced through him. He let her set the pace, banking his yearning to ravish her mouth and her body.

Her kiss was soft and gentle, slowly flowing into firmer and more insistent. He grasped her waist in an urgent battle to keep his hands from straying. Her hand slid lower to cup his ass.

He leaned back. "Hey. Slow down. We can't. We shouldn't. You're still shaken after last night. We need to wait until this isn't fueled by reaction to what happened. I need you to be certain this is, that I am, what you want."

"I'm sure." She nibbled his lips.

He groaned. "Maybe so, but you need to talk to your family first."

"I am not going to discuss my sex life with my family," she said indignantly.

He chuckled and brushed his thumb down her cheek. "Not what I meant, and you know it. Don't think I don't want you. Because I do. I'm rock hard with need for you. Later. Okay?"

"Fine." She brushed her hand over his erection and turned away. "But you'll pay for this."

"I already am." She had no idea how much he ached. The physical was nothing compared to the agony of knowing he'd been responsible for the attack on her. If he hadn't asked for a bug shield, she wouldn't have been attacked. Nothing was going to release him from his guilt.

They'd had a lovely dinner last night. They'd talked easily. She was great company, and a joy to be with. He was pissed off at himself. He'd potentially ruined a good relationship because he didn't like insects or bug repellent. Now, he wanted to protect her, and she needed her family. He felt guilty and useless.

"Let me guess," he said as the two enormous wrought iron gates opened at their approach, "magic gates?"

She blushed. "Yes. Most people assume they have a remote."

"Just how magical is your family?" He imagined it would take considerable strength and power to put long term enchantments on inanimate objects.

"Pretty magical."

"Nice evasion." Her family must be stronger than he thought.

"Okay, we're direct descendants of Margaret Hawkes, one of the accused witches of Salem. We're the product of more than sixteen generations of witches. We've lived on this land for decades. Somehow, our magic has seeped into the land itself. The closer to the house, the stronger the magic."

"Shit." He whistled. Impressive. And scary. "Maybe I should bring your work to you. You'd be safer here." There was no way he could offer the protection her home could.

"I'm not going to sit in hiding. If Keres taught us anything, hiding or avoiding confrontation doesn't make trouble go away. I'm going to go about my life and deal with shit as it comes."

Feisty. Arguing would be a waste of breath and effort. "Okay. But you'll be careful, right?" He hated the doubt in his tone. He was more worried than their new friendship would account for, and more than his troubled past with a magical ex justified. He was falling in deep, like he was swimming out of his depth. In her life, and in his emotions.

When the house came into view, he saw four women sitting in chairs on the porch. Waiting.

Her home was a blend of Victorian and Colonial styling, two stories tall, with dormer windows in the attic. An octagonal turret graced either end. Flawless white woodwork was balanced with brick trim. It screamed comfort and welcome; except for the women on the porch.

"A greeting committee? Firing squad?" He was only half joking.

"I texted them I was on the way home. I didn't mention you though." She groaned. "I should have just shown up. I'm sorry."

"No worries. I'll just drop you off and go."

"You wish."

He slowed to a stop alongside the walkway to the front steps. "I'll be back, call me when you're ready."

The truck stalled.

"They didn't," Hazel complained. "You might as well get out. They won't let it start until you've undergone the fifth degree."

"They can control machinery?" He'd never heard of that skill and he'd done a lot of research since Hazel had come for her interview.

"No, but Lazuli, the one on the left, controls air. She probably just sucked the air out of your air intake. Evil witch."

Her comment made him laugh. He turned the key off. "Let's get this over with. No sense fighting the inevitable." He squeezed her hand reassuringly. "I'll live through this. Did you tell them about last night?"

"No. Just that I'd be out all night."

"So why the porch brigade?"

She winced. "We have, sort of, a mental connection. We can feel each other's really strong emotions. I tried to block them. I should have known I didn't have the strength. I did text to say where I was. You being here isn't a surprise to them."

"I'm in trouble then?" This group of women didn't scare him. Much.

"No. They'll grill you, but they know I stayed willingly. You'll get bonus points because I trusted you." She grasped his arm. "I apologize in advance. Don't let them scare you away. Okay?"

Fat chance of that. "Relax, Haze. I'll survive Let's get you inside and safe."

"Just know Gramma Pearl has a bias against mundanes getting too close to the family." She shrugged. "Don't take it personally, please."

"I'll try not to." He climbed out of the truck and hurried around to open her door. Maybe some old-world manners and chivalry would win them over.

"You didn't need to do that," she chided with a smile. "But thank you."

He took her elbow and led her toward the waiting firing squad.

"I do know how to walk," she teased.

"True, but you've had a tough night. I want to be certain you're okay. If I thought you'd let me, I'd pick you up and carry you." He winked at her.

Her laughter tickled over him, chasing away most of his trepidation over meeting her family for the second time and under such questionable circumstances.

They paused at the base of the stairs. Three cats lined the steps, their gazes as judgmental as her family's.

"These guys," she stopped to pet the solid black cats, "are Meeka, Calista and Apollo. You've met my sisters and my Gramma Pearl."

He greeted each family member in turn, ending with her grandmother. "Nice to meet you again Pearl. Sorry to be the cause of your night of worries. Had I known your family had a psychic connection, I'd have rushed her right home."

"Psychic connection?" Pearl asked, her expression bland and dead panned. "I don't know what you're talking about."

Dennis laughed aloud at the blatant lie. "Yes, ma'am. Hazel isn't the first magical I've known, but she is the kindest." Hazel's blush emboldened him. "I know your family has a metaphysical shop. Magicals purchase their supplies in your store, and mundanes think it's a hoax or a way to ply on tourists. I know you all have specials skills, gifts if you will, though I don't know specifically what they are."

Pearl frowned at him and then at Hazel.

"Don't blame your granddaughter. She's extremely closed mouthed about your family, but there are rumors around town. I made a few deductions. Rest assured, your secrets are safe with me and I mean your family no harm."

"And yet she was attacked when she was with you," Pearl accused, dropping all pretense.

Hazel's sisters looked uncomfortable at their grandmother's accusation.

"It wasn't his fault," Hazel snapped. "We were outside, on his land, private property. I put up a bug shield and someone sucked away my strength. They fed on my power and it wasn't Dennis." She crossed her arms over her chest and glared at the family matriarch. "And stay out of his head."

"I would never enter another person's head without permission."

All four sisters snorted in derision.

"Right," Hazel drawled, sarcasm heavy in her voice.

"Anyway," Dennis injected into what appeared to be the start of a fight. "After the attack, I took Hazel inside, fed her and did my best to help her recover. I'd have driven her home if she'd let me. I feel terrible this happened while she was with me." He paused and met each sister's gaze. He ended by looking right at Pearl. Save the worst for last. "I'd like your help to ensure she's safe at work. What can I do to protect her?" His question seemed to win over her sisters. Pearl, not so much.

"How do we know you didn't do this?" the old girl demanded. "Maybe you're a magic sucking vampire."

The idea was totally offensive, but he had to admire her spunk in throwing the concept onto the table. Wait, did she mean actual vampire? Or just someone who sucked magic like a vampire sucked blood? Did he even want to know? He shoved his questions aside. She wasn't going to distract him.

"You don't know if I'm responsible, but maybe you could trust Hazel knows it wasn't me, she was there." He waited for Pearl to process his challenge, hands loose and relaxed at his sides.

Her response was a simple nod of acknowledgement. She rose re-gally to her feet. "Come inside, the tea's ready."

Everyone filed inside. He and Hazel brought up the rear. As he stepped through the front doorway, he felt a moment of resistance, as if passing through an invisible membrane. No doubt a protective barrier. He wondered how it worked, and how it knew who to admit.

"Weird," he whispered to himself.

"What you felt is conditional acceptance. We invited you in, the house let you in. if you arrived and we weren't home, it would keep you out."

"You make it sound as if the house is sentient. How can an inani-mate object physically prevent entry? Aside from a locked door?"

She shrugged. "She just does. It's magic. I've seen it with my own eyes. I've seen the hose turn itself on and put out a fire caused by a lightning strike. I know, it's totally far-fetched. Hang around long enough and you'll believe it too. We never do maintenance beyond cleaning. The house never needs it, she heals herself."

Animated, self-protecting houses? He'd heard of everything now. What next? Flying cars? Flying witches? "Can you fly? Do you ride a broom?" he blurted, immediately wishing he hadn't.

Her laugh was spontaneous and joyous and not at all mocking. "I wish. Our brooms, or Besoms, are strictly for ritual purposes. Magic can do things you can't even imagine, but it can't make us fly; although I sure wish it could."

He followed her through the hallway and living area, taking in the abundance of family pictures, dozens of candles and massive bookcases. It was cluttered, but clean and tidy. He couldn't put a name on the scent lingering in the air, but it smelled like home.

As they entered the kitchen, the aroma morphed to ginger and spice. One of the sisters, he couldn't recall which one, maybe Lazuli, pulled a tray of muffins from the oven.

The kitchen was enormous with several large work surfaces and an island. The countertops were virtually clear of clutter. He counted two pantries and at least eighteen upper cupboards. These people must take food very seriously.

"Take a seat. Time for muffins, cookies and brainstorming." Hazel gestured toward the enormous, round, kitchen table set in the alcove formed by a bay window. It looked like solid oak and seated eight. A shimmering crystal bowl overflowing with fresh fruit sat on an old school lace doily in the middle of the table.

"And a family meeting," said Pearl from her place near the window. Somehow, he understood the spot was considered the head of the table.

He wasn't family, but they'd invited him in, which must mean he was included. Besides, he had no intention of leaving until he found out the best way to protect Hazel while she was at work.

"Did you sense anything from your attacker?" the muffin sister asked as she joined everyone else at the table.

"No, Laz, I didn't. I didn't even feel it at first. Then, just before I shut down the bug shield, it hit me like a brick. He was subtle enough I had no sense he was doing it."

Hazel turned toward Dennis. "Laz is the most intuitive and psychic of us all."

"Don't give away our secrets."

"Relax, Amber. Dennis wants to help, not publicize our secrets. He's not new to magic, his ex was a practitioner."

Oh great, now his past was up for public consumption. He hadn't counted on that.

"Why'd you break up?" Hyacinth asked. Since Hazel had put names to the other two sisters, this one had to be Hyacinth.

"Plenty of reasons, but primarily because she wasn't who I thought she was. We were growing apart and I ended it when I realized she was trying to control my mind and influence my thoughts."

Everyone gasped.

"I swore I would never let myself get tangled up with another witch."

"So, why did you?" Pearl asked.

"Honestly? I like Hazel. She's kind. She's helpful, she's got a strong work ethic."

"She's sitting right here," Hazel snapped.

"Sorry," Dennis apologized. He'd been flinging out reasons and trying to keep from blurting out how wonderfully sexually appealing she was. Just because she appealed to every single masculine instinct he had, didn't mean he had to confess his baser emotions.

He grabbed Hazel's hand in his and looked her in the eye. "I like you and I'd like to get to know you better. As for your magical side, you haven't done me wrong, and I'm prepared to give you the benefit of the doubt." He suppressed a wince at how condescending he sounded.

"Gee, thanks." Sarcasm dripped from Hazel's words as she dropped his hand to pour tea for everyone.

"I didn't mean it the way is sounded. Sorry. I do want you to be safe at work, even if we decide not to pursue a relationship."

When she smiled, he felt like he'd come through a challenge un-scathed. Weary and elated; both physically and mentally. Being around her family was going to be difficult to say the least.

"I can live with that," Hazel said, squeezing his fingers lightly, her hand warm from the tea pot.

"Cut the PDA," Amber teased. "Save it for private."

"Right." Hazel laughed. "Like you and Kody never kiss or touch in front of us. Talk about a double standard."

Dennis lifted Hazel's hand and brushed his lips across her knuckles. "Okay then. How do I keep her safe? I felt the barrier when I came in. How do I get similar protection at my place?"

"You can't," Pearl said. "It's the result of generations of magic seep-ing into our home and our land." She sipped her tea. "But we can help you put up wards, which we'll do before she returns to work, just to be safe."

They discussed strategy; a lot of unfamiliar terms and concepts were thrown around. Frankly, it sounded like a foreign language and a lot of mumbo-jumbo. But after seeing how badly Hazel was affected last night, he was prepared to go along. Anything to keep her safe.

Two hours later, the entire group stood inside his kitchen. Hyacinth was prepping with a small jar of protective oil containing bergamot and cinnamon, as well as a bottle of clear nail polish. She would paint protective runes on all the windows and doors with the polish and protective sigils on the wood frames with the oil.

Pearl and Lazuli were prepping to lay a protective circle comprised of witch's black salt, crushed eggshells and red brick dust, around the outside of the house.

Amber and Hazel filled a small glass jar with herbs, pins, tacks and nails and bits of broken mirror. They filled it with white wine and sealed it shut with wax.

"What's the bottle for?" he asked as curiosity battled unease.

"It's a witch's bottle, for protection. We'll bury it in the yard to keep evil and unwanted visitors at bay." Hazel explained.

"And it actually works?" It seemed unlikely that a random collection of scrap items would work. He didn't know how to fully express his disbelief without seeming dismissive or downright rude. He'd asked for help and they were providing it. And he was grateful.

"We have no proof it works, but we use witch's jars or balls anyway. Besides, hundreds of years of witches can't be wrong, right?" Hazel grinned and snuffed the candle they'd used to seal the bottle.

He shrugged. "Who am I to argue with tradition? What's next?"

"We'll do a protective spell. Double duty. Part to keep me safe and part to guard your house."

"Okay…" How did that work? He wished he'd been able to research all this before they started. At least then he'd know what he was getting into. Well, in for a penny, in for a pound. He guessed. He was nervous, but he was more concerned with Hazel's safety.

"You can participate, or not, as you feel is best," Pearl advised. "Since it's your house I'd suggest you take part, to make the spell stronger."

"But I'm a mundane, to use your terminology." He knew almost nothing about rituals. He could really screw this up, for all of them.

"Irrelevant," Pearl said. "A huge part of magic lies in the intent behind it. Your focus on what you wish to achieve, Hazel's safety, will help the spell to manifest. The more complete your focus, the stronger the magic."

God, what if he screwed this up? Was magic sensitive to negative thoughts? He expressed his doubts aloud.

"Relax." Hazel slipped her arm around his waist. "You won't mess this up. Just visualize your house and me being safe and we'll do the rest."

They reconvened in his living room. Laz and Cynth lifted his coffee table onto the couch. Hazel swept the room with his kitchen broom while singing nonsense words in time to Pearl's chiming of a small bell. They said the musical chiming and singing cleared the room of negative energy which might impede the effectiveness of the spell.

Sweeping complete, Hazel pulled a large glass jar of white crystals from the box they'd brought with them. "Salt for protection." She drizzled a rough ring of salt around the room, encircling them all.

Lazuli set four candles inside the circle. Cynth followed her around, calling Athena and Heka to join them for the ritual. He'd heard of Athena but needed to research Heka. The hair on the back of his neck stood up.

This was real and way beyond anything he'd ever seen Natalia perform. It was like something out of a movie. Completely far-fetched, yet totally serious and gut wrenchingly real. He'd never hear stories of the old gods the same way again. He'd almost swear he could feel their presence.

Pearl lit a bundle of herbs on fire and set it to rest on a large abalone shell. It smoldered there, smelling of burning grass. He recognized sage. He had a native friend who used sage for cleansing.

Hazel took Dennis's left hand; Pearl grasped his right. One by one, they joined hands until they formed a circle of people, inside a circle of candles, inside the ring of salt.

"Focus on keeping Hazel safe," Pearl advised him. He did his best to keep his mind on the task, on keeping Hazel from harm. It was hard to concentrate, but he kept forcing his attention away from what was happening in the room, and back to protecting her.

With her sisters and grandmother humming softly, Hazel began to speak.

"Mother Earth, Father Sky,

Join us here, the time is nigh.

Darkness creeps upon us now.

To you we promise with our vow.

Protect the lands and our homes.

Keeping safe where we roam.

Someone comes within our midst.

He has a bent and evil twist."

The seemingly ad-libbing and awkward rhyming went on for several minutes until Hazel raised her face to the sky and declared,

"By the powers of earth, air, sky and water,

Mother Earth, protect your daughter."

Together they added, "As we will it, and with harm to none, so mote it be."

Hazel expressed a brief thank you to the Goddess, the God, and all the deities they'd invoked earlier, and everyone released hands.

One by one, they snuffed the candles and Hazel swept up the salt.

"What do you do with that now?" he asked. It was the easiest question. He wanted to know if spells always rhymed, why they called the deities they chose, and how long the spell would last.

"Seal it in a jar and save it until the danger has passed. Then, wash it away with running water. It is simple sea salt; if we lived near the ocean, we'd pour it there. Since we don't, it goes down the drain rather than risking the salt destroying our local ecosystem."

Logical. He tabled his other questions for later. He looked around the room at the women gathered there, they were all pale and exhausted. They'd put a lot of themselves into their spell. He had felt the energy flow through the room as he concentrated on his desire. Come to think of it, he felt a little drained himself. Brunch was definitely in order; it was well past lunch and those muffins only kept you fueled for so long.

"Thank you," he said to them all. "Come to the kitchen. I'll make coffee and something to eat." Thank goodness he always kept his fridge, freezer and pantry full.

Working side by side with Hazel, they whipped up a feast of sausages, bacon, eggs, biscuits and fresh fruit.

After everyone departed and Hazel went into the office, he stood in his living room, looking around. It felt...different. Cleaner, more vibrant; the room had an energy of its own. It felt...alive.

No damn wonder their house could protect itself if a simple ritual like the one he'd just taken part in could alter a room so drastically. Decades of magic would have an enormous residual effect. Stonehenge sprang to mind. Millions of people believed the stones had magic powers during the solstices. Perhaps they were right.

Chapter Fifteen

"Look," Hazel said to her grandmother, a week after they'd cast a protective spell over Dennis's home and office. "Dennis will be here in half an hour to help us search for clues."

A frown marred Pearl's face, aging her at least ten years. Pearl, who usually looked decades younger than her sixty-five years, was starting to show her age. The stress was wearing on her. The change, though only evident when Pearl frowned, reinforced Hazel's decision to invite Dennis to help them search their enormous library of family grimoires, or books of spells.

The more eyes searching, the better, as far as she was concerned. First Amber was attacked and abducted by Keres, now someone had stolen Hazel's magic strength. She couldn't shake the conviction that the two incidents were related. They might even tie into the witch killer her mom and stepfather were chasing. It was time to end all of this trouble.

"I can bring books downstairs and not let him into the library if it makes you feel better, but he's coming and he's helping. I'll keep him from the oldest books. End. Of. Discussion." She hid a tremble of unease at her boldness. Nobody in the family stood up to Pearl on anything serious. She was the family matriarch and they listened to her, even when they disagreed with her dictates.

Hazel frowned. It wasn't like her thoughts made it sound. Pearl was rarely unreasonable and was decidedly more experienced than the rest of them. But this time, Hazel knew, beyond all doubt, they needed Dennis's help with this. Call it a hunch, call it intuition. They had already called on their magical friends to search their own records for anything that might tip them off to Keres' intent. Pearl had even invited a few of her oldest friends over to help search; but there were hundreds of books to go through, many of which had virtually indecipherable handwriting. Hazel understood Pearl's reticence to invite Dennis in, she really did.

Pearl smoothed her silk blouse and frowned. "This is a bad idea. Mark my words. When your parents hear about this, they'll kick your ass."

Pearl rarely cussed.

"Really? I'm twenty-three and you're sicking my parents on me? Go ahead. Call them. I think they'd want to hear about what's going on." Initially, she'd agreed to keep the troubles at home secret from her parents. Now, she wasn't certain it was a good idea. They probably already felt the stress through the family emotional connection.

"She's right," Cynth joined them in the kitchen. "Mom would want to know about this." Her long blonde hair was pulled into a neat bun at the nape of her neck. Comfortable jeans and a serviceable blue T-shirt completed her outfit, a sure sign she was on her way to a call. "Are there any of those energy balls left?"

"Only half a dozen," Pearl replied. "In the blue star tin in the freezer. "Take them all. I'll make more today. And we're not disturbing your parents. Yet."

Hazel glanced at Cynth who nodded slightly. Okay. They'd keep quiet, for now. Sooner or later, they'd have to pull their parents into the loop, because something wasn't right; something terribly wrong, was going on. The attack on Hazel was only one symptom. The air had a heavy feel, like the entire world was holding its breath in fear. Or as if something was feeding on positivity leaving darkness behind.

Hazel transferred the energy balls into a small container while Cynth prepared herself a travel mug of herbal tea.

Pearl slipped a floral skull patterned apron over her head and tied it at the waist. "Have you got time for something to eat before you go?" she asked.

"I'm good, but thanks. I ate earlier and now; I have a baby to deliver. I can help search the library when I get home, assuming no complications. I'm not expecting any, this is her fourth child." She crossed her fingers.

"What about you?" Pearl looked at Hazel.

"Dennis is bringing dinner for all of us. You don't need to cook." Pearl was a nurturer. She cooked and fed them in every crisis. It was simply part of who she was as a kitchen witch. Magic was all about intent. Everything she cooked was prepared with love and a bit of her own special magic. Nothing overt and definitely not harmful to anyone, just blessings for good health and happiness.

The energy balls were another story. Magically crafted, using only the purest ingredients, they gave you a magical boost to restore flagging energy. That power had helped them defeat Keres.

"I guess I'll make more energy balls then. Do I have time before Dennis arrives?"

Hazel nodded her agreement. "I'll help." She began pulling ingredients from the cupboards. Cynth waved and called goodbye from the doorway. Hazel worked silently beside her grandmother until Pearl spoke.

"Do you really, I mean really, trust this man? He's new to town. Nobody knows anything about him." She didn't need to remind Hazel that Keres had been new to town as well.

"Tell me you haven't been asking people about him." Hazel groaned.

Her grandmother had the grace to flush. "Only other witches and magicals. They have a vested interest in keeping Three Moon Falls safe as well."

"Can you just quit?" Hazel snapped, her frustration mounting. She got it; she understood the stakes. Just as she knew Dennis could and would help them.

"What's she done now?" Lazuli asked, coming in the garden door from outside, bending to untie her steel-toed boots.

"She's snooping into Dennis's life. Asking people what they know about him." Exasperation made her voice harsh. She banked her irritation rather than cause a fight.

"Gramma? Is that true? You need to leave us some privacy. Room to make our own mistakes. Give us breathing space. Please." She glanced down at her shirt. "Shoot, I thought I had all the sawdust off." She stepped back outside, boot laces trailing and brushed herself clean before coming back in and placing her boots neatly to the side. "I'm going to shower. What's for dinner? I'm starving."

"I don't know," Hazel replied. "Dennis is on his way with supper. Shower fast."

"I will, but first, we may have a problem. Frank Perrum's daughter, Rosie, showed up in my workshop today. She skipped school and walked from town. I don't know what to do, this is the third time, and it scares the crap out of me when I turn around and see her standing there watching me. She could get hurt if she turned on one of the saws. I can't even think about the dangers of walking all the way from town."

Lazuli was a carpenter and specialized in custom woodwork. She had a large workshop on the family property. Filled with saws of all types, lathes, planers, plus hundreds of sharp hand tools, it wasn't a safe place for an unsupervised child.

"Oh, no! What did you do?" Hazel's hand flew to her chest to still the racing of her heart.

"Called her father. Let me tell you, he was pissed. She's run away and hidden before but I guess it's getting out of hand. He's got no idea how to stop it. I feel bad for both of them. What makes a six-year-old make such a long trek alone? On foot?"

"She came to the house a couple times last year, but it's not far from their house to ours. Still, it's not right that she's wandering around alone. The girl needs a woman's steadying hand." Pearl waved her spoon in the air.

Hazel and Laz ignored the antiquated idea that a single man couldn't raise a child alone rather than sidetrack the discussion with an argument.

"She has a nanny," Lazuli said.

"One in a long line. They never last long and she needs stability. I think that's why she comes here. There's almost always one of us around. I feel for her." Pearl shook her head sadly.

"She precious for sure. I made her promise not to come again without permission, and Frank agreed to bring her to visit once a week. With luck that'll keep her off the streets. By the Goddess, I'd die if anything happened to her."

How tragic it must be to be motherless. Rosie's mother had died shortly after she was born, and life with her father was all she'd known. Rosie's mother, Celine, had been a close family friend. She'd known their great-grandmother and named her daughter Rosie, with her husband's reluctant agreement. Hazel identified with Rosie's sense of something being missing. Hazel had met her own father only a few times. He had wanted nothing to do with her or the rest of the family. Growing up, she'd often wondered what it would be like to have an actual, loving, caring, father. Trevor Moon was a wonderful man, but he hadn't been around when she was young and impressionable. She felt like she'd missed out on having father-daughter time. She hoped to do better for her own children.

Missing a parent wasn't an easy thing. She had the full support of her sisters, her mother and grandmother. Later, her stepfather. She could see how being a young girl cared for by nannies who never lasted long would be difficult. How did you explain to a child that they would never meet their parent? Hazel had always known she could approach her father, even if he wasn't interested.

Chapter Sixteen

D ennis was struck by a feeling of belonging when he entered the
Hawk family home. The invisible barrier he'd felt the first time
didn't seem to impede his entry. Whether that was because he didn't
notice it or because it wasn't there, he had no idea. But the feeling
of welcome definitely was stronger than before. It felt like...coming
home...was the only way he could describe it.

He paused, recalling the last time he'd been inside and how the
house had smelled like home. Now it felt like walking into the house
he'd grown up in and finding his mom busy making her famous meat-
loaf. He paused, box of takeout in his arms, to enjoy the feeling.

"What? Are you okay?" Hazel asked, her hand on the doorknob,
ready to close it behind him.

He stepped farther inside and toed off his running shoes. "Nothing.
Just admiring the decor. Your house is eclectic. I like it." Good grief.

He sounded like an idiot but there was no way he'd admit how he felt right then.

She stared at him and blinked twice before closing the door.

"I know. Men don't usually notice that stuff. I'm looking to change some stuff in my place. A lot of the furniture came with the house. Except the bedrooms. I'd like to make it more personal, more my style." He dropped the subject, feeling awkward. "Where do you want this food?"

"Kitchen, please. We're all set up for dinner." She pointed the way, though he remembered from his prior visit. "What did you buy? It smells delicious."

"A mix. I ordered from Sensations. I got three types of pasta, garlic toast, salad, pizza, two vegan dishes and a mix of Chinese food." Sensations was an old-school, small town restaurant. One of those places that served a little of everything. Italian, Chinese, western. It often reminded him of one of those random truck stops that had the best food in three hundred miles.

Hazel's laugh made him smile.

"How many people are you feeding?"

"I figured I'd take the leftovers home and not have to cook for a few days. It's busy at work, and I'm inherently lazy." He smiled and shrugged. "And you can help me finish it for lunches." He wanted to invite her to eat with him every day, but he was carefully keeping his distance. He was still friendly and his need for her hadn't dropped one iota, but he didn't want to pressure her. Their relationship had settled onto more solid ground, but she seemed a bit skittish sometimes. Although the way she looked at him now, he could have sworn she wanted to kiss him.

There were more people in the kitchen than he expected. Hazel, her grandmother, two of her sisters and a man he didn't recognize. Hazel introduced him as Kody Wilkins, local diving instructor and Amber's fiancé. It was a damned good thing he'd ordered so much food. He set the box on the table and shook Kody's hand and started unpacking the food.

"Who's that?" he asked, pointing outside where a young, black haired girl stood in the yard, staring at them. Hazel had never mentioned children as part of the family and there were no other homes in sight.

Everyone turned to look.

"Dammit," Lazuli jerked to her feet. "I thought I had her convinced not to come over alone. I'll go bring her inside."

"I'll set two more places," Pearl said.

Two places?

"That's Rosie Perrum, our neighbor's daughter. She's got a bad habit of sneaking away from her father and her nanny. She usually ends up here. Her dad will only be seconds behind her."

"Wow. That must make him crazy, my brother would have a fit if one of his kids wandered off." A tall man with jet black hair loped across the lawn.

"Rose Celine Perrum, get back here this instant," he shouted.

Rosie froze for a fraction of a second and bolted toward Lazuli who stood on the steps outside the kitchen. Lazuli staggered backward, almost falling, when Rosie launched herself and flung her arms around Lazuli's waist.

Laz knelt down and hugged Rosie. Her softly chiding voice drifted through the open window. "Hey. Didn't we have a deal? You promised to stay home until Daddy could bring you."

Rosie looked down and scuffed her feet. "But I needed to see you," she whined. "I came to help."

Lazuli glanced back toward the house; one brow raised in question. "Help with what?" she asked, her voice soft and kind. Obviously, Lazuli was good with kids. She reminded Dennis of his brother's wife.

Rosie shrugged.

"Well, if it's okay with your dad, maybe we can talk a bit."

"I should take her home. Visits are treats for girls who don't run away." He frowned and slammed his hands into the pockets of his jeans.

"Maybe, just this once, we can make an exception?"

Dennis winced. Parents hated when people interfered with their routines and discipline. He'd made that mistake once and his sister-in-law had ripped him a new one.

Frank closed his eyes. Dennis imagined the man was counting to ten to regain control of his emotions the way his brother did when his kids were out of control.

"Fine. But just this once," he agreed.

"Come inside. We were just about to eat. There's plenty." Lazuli waved toward the house. "Hazel's friend, Dennis, is here and he brought dinner. Join us."

Another round of introductions followed. Learning Frank ran the local lumberyard was fabulous news. Increasing the size of his petting zoo would require lumber. He also had some repairs to do to a couple of his displays. Until now, Dennis hadn't realized there was a place to purchase all his wood needs just outside of town. He'd planned on hitting a big box store in the city. This was better because he preferred to shop local when he could.

Dinner was a lively event. Between getting to know one another and Rosie's gregarious comments, Dennis was highly entertained. It was nice to connect to other people and expand his circle of friends. He just wished the impromptu party would break up so they could get after the task at hand. Hazel had invited him over to search some old books for ways to prevent someone from harvesting her energy again. He wanted to get started. Finally, Hazel rose from the table.

"Well, this is fun, and I hate to leave, but I have to start my research." She started clearing their plates.

Dennis jumped to his feet to assist. Everyone followed suit and the mess was cleared away in minutes.

"Thanks for dinner," Frank said. "And sorry for interrupting your evening. I promise I'll find a way to stop the unscheduled visits."

Hazel knelt before Rosie, looked her right in the eyes and took her hands. "Listen, sweetie. We know you like to visit, and you are welcome to come anytime," she paused, "but you have to get Daddy to bring you. Okay?"

Dennis felt bad for the youngster who withered under Hazel's kind remonstrance. Then Rosie stiffened her shoulders and glared at Hazel.

"I had to come help look," she declared belligerently, crossing her arms. "You need help."

"Look for what?" Hazel asked, her tone soft and understanding. She was very good with the child. She'd make a great mother.

"I dunno," Rosie looked up, her eyes pleading for understanding. "In the books."

Hazel shared a glance with her family. How in the world did Rosie know they were searching books? It was uncanny or the biggest coincidence she'd ever seen.

"Your Daddy can read you books at home," Hazel suggested.

"I sure will, sweetheart," Frank agreed. "Let's go now. Say thank you for dinner."

"No!" Rosie stomped her foot. "Your books."

"You want to borrow a book?" Hazel asked, confused. "We have some books you could read." They had a shelf of children's books from their childhood.

"The other books." Rosie put emphasis on the word other. "The ones upstairs."

Shock raced through Hazel, making her gasp. "What books upstairs?" When had Rosie been upstairs? Probably never. Their collection of family grimoires wasn't public knowledge. Even Rosie's deceased mother hadn't been taken to their private library and hadn't been told about the collection.

They weren't even planning on letting Dennis up there. She was going to bring books down. Now, she realized keeping the library a secret was harder than they realized. Apparently, word had really spread, especially if this child knew about it.

"In the library," Rosie said.

"I'm sorry. There is no library upstairs," Pearl said.

"Yes, there is.," Rosie stomped her foot. "I just wanted to help. I'm big enough and I'm a good reader. Right, Dad?" She looked to her father for validation.

"You are a fabulous reader. You read better than some grade four kids," he agreed. "But you don't need to borrow the Hawks' books."

"Fine." She turned toward the door, clearly angry at being excluded. "I just wanted to read the purple ones."

"Sorry," Frank apologized to her and to the family.

"Don't worry about it," Hazel said. "Kids get funny ideas sometimes. She's welcome to visit any time you say so."

"I can't believe this family. They're blind. It yanks my skirt." Rosie crossed her arms over her chest with a frown.

Hazel did a double take at Rosie's strange comment. It yanks my skirt had been her great-grandmother Rose's favorite expression.

"Don't be rude, Rosie. Thanks again," Frank said. "Say thank you for dinner, Rosie Posy."

Her response was grudging, bordering on insolent. Hazel let it slide. There was a time for discipline and technically, she'd done as asked. "You're welcome. Have a lovely evening."

Nobody said anything as the duo walked across the yard.

"What was that all about?" Kody asked, raking his fingers through his hair. "I saw the look you guys shared. What aren't you telling us?" He gestured at Dennis and himself.

Dang. Hazel had hoped they'd miss the visual exchange. Intelligent, perceptive men...a blessing and a curse. "It's nothing." Not an outright lie, more an evasion.

"Bullshit," Kody said. "I haven't been around long, but I recognize that look." They'd only met Kody a couple months ago. After a rocky start, Kody and Amber had become a thing. Nothing like near death experiences to draw people together.

"Just tell him," Amber declared. "You know he won't shut up until you do." She kissed her fiancé on the cheek in a 'no harm meant' gesture.

"I'd like to know as well," Dennis said. "I've read about psychic links between members of strong families and Hazel mentioned yours." He pulled a chair out, pivoted it around and straddled it, his arms resting on the back.

There was no way Hazel was going to avoid this discussion. Both men had stubborn expressions on their faces. She moved about the kitchen, filling the kettle and putting it on the stove to boil. All hard discussions went better with tea. Especially those which involved difficult to prove statements.

"It's possible that Rosie is our great-grandmother reincarnated."

Dennis blinked rapidly and rubbed the back of his neck. "You believe in that stuff?" Disbelief filled his words.

Kody's expression mirrored Dennis's. She'd known this wouldn't be easy. She looked to her family for help. This was precisely why she wanted to avoid a discussion. "Yes, we believe in reincarnation. Though it hasn't been scientifically proven, there is a lot of anecdotal evidence."

"So, everyone comes back?" Dennis said doubtfully. "Then what about ghosts? People swear ghosts are real."

"It's not hard science, but no, not everyone comes back. We've got two ghosts at the shop and we can, in dire circumstances, call our ancestors for help. It's difficult, powerful magic not to be engaged in lightly."

"I'm skeptical, but for the moment, let's pretend I believe. Why do you think that little girl could be your great-grandmother?" Dennis asked.

Kody remained quiet. He had firsthand experience with the ghosts at the shop as well as the shop's talking cat. He was more likely to believe in reincarnation than someone who was new to all this.

"That yanks my skirt, was our great-grandmother's favorite expression. Plus, nobody, outside the family and Kody, who is family now, knows about our upstairs library. Friends know about our collection down here, but only family knows about our grimoires. Besides," Hazel paused for a breath. "We've never been able to call great-gramma Rose, nor have we ever seen her ghost. It just all adds up."

"Call? What does that mean?" Dennis shook his head in confusion.

"Call, like a séance. Talking to the dead. Many people, particularly magical ones, can be called back to talk to," Pearl explained impatiently.

"You're saying you can call the dead, like on some crazy television show?"

"Yes." Hazel looked uncomfortable. "I know it's hard to believe. Since we can't call her, and Rosie is quoting her, we believe there's a chance she is our great-grandmother reincarnated."

"Bizarre," Dennis said. "Coming back as someone else would really mess with your mind."

"No. Except in rare circumstances, they have no memory of a past life. Maybe a vague sense of dèjá vu. But nothing concrete. Rosie would never know she was great-gramma's spirit come back. She might just know things she might not otherwise know." She poured the hot water on some tea leaves. Mint and lavender filled the room.

"Is that where old souls come from?" Kody asked. "My grandmother talks about people being old souls. Wise beyond their years and stuff like that."

Pearl spoke up. "Exactly. I believe if you've been around enough times, your soul has to be wiser."

"I don't know," Dennis said doubtfully. "I'm not sure I can believe in ghosts, or souls being recycled."

"Most people can't," Hazel agreed, wishing this was easier to explain. Sometimes the beliefs you held your entire life didn't seem so easy when questioned by others. "But don't stress if you don't believe, not many people do believe. I actually have trouble believing in reincarnation sometimes and I grew up with the idea."

"But if she doesn't remember, how did she know about the library? Doesn't that contradict itself?" Dennis asked.

This whole evening was turning into a massive disaster and they weren't getting anything done. Hazel pushed back her frustration. If she was going to pursue a relationship with Dennis, and she did want to, she needed to help him understand her world and her beliefs. He didn't have to share them, but he did need to respect them.

"Haven't you ever just known something you shouldn't and assumed you must have just forgotten hearing it before? It's similar. Like a kid that sits down at the piano and starts to play without ever taking a lesson."

"I guess so." He definitely didn't sound convinced.

"Anyway," she said and poured the tea into china mugs. "Let's get started. Gramma Pearl and I will bring down some books and we'll skim through them. Maybe we can find a reference to this power stealing and a way to stop it. Plus, we can keep looking for clues to whatever Keres was after."

"You think they could be related?" Kody asked, stirring a ton of sugar into his tea.

"I don't know for sure, but my gut says it is. We just have to figure out how, and that starts with finding some information in the library," Hazel said. "Hang tight while we get those books."

"These are old," Dennis said ten minutes later as he opened a grimoire. "This one is dated 1842. Shouldn't we be wearing gloves, or something? Isn't the oil on our skin bad for books? I had to wear special gloves to read an old herbal reference at the university."

"Normally, it would be prudent to protect old books, but ours are spelled to prevent damage." Hazel slid into a seat across from him and pulled a book toward herself.

"How far back do these go?" Dennis asked.

Everyone else was upstairs in the library. If Dennis was upset not to be asked upstairs, he showed no sign of it. "They go a long ways back. I'm not exactly sure how far."

He gave her a mocking look. Obviously, he suspected she was fibbing but didn't call her on it.

"Just look for anything which mentions stealing power, a talisman, a waterfall or raising the dead."

"What?" His voice lifted in alarm. "Are you serious?" He gulped half of his tea.

"Yup. Frankly, I don't think it's possible, but Keres seemed to think so."

"That's terrifying. Wouldn't that be dark magic? You said you didn't do dark magic?"

He looked ready to bolt, so she reached across the table to stroke his hand. "I don't, my family doesn't do dark magic. Which isn't to say some of our ancestors didn't do it or record something they heard about elsewhere. Research is an important part of magic. My own book has a number of spells and recipes I've recorded for interest's sake. Like a chef might save a potential recipe. That's what we're looking for."

"This whole thing really makes me uncomfortable. I'm so sorry my aversion to mosquitoes lead to this."

Hazel laughed. "Don't be. This isn't your fault, or mine. Whoever did this would have done it anyway. People who abuse power always find a way. It's sad, really. Aside from what happened to Amber and I, Mom and Dad are tracking a witch killer. One would think, in this day and age persecution would be ended. But no." She kept the idea the witch killer was stealing power for his own use to herself. No sense freaking Dennis out any further.

"This could be about power, not persecution." Dennis turned the page in his book. "Either way, I'm worried about your safety."

"Your concern means a lot. Thank you." She gave him a grateful smile. She might have been shielding him from bugs when the attack happened, but it was weirdly nice that she hadn't been alone during the attack. He'd helped her through the aftermath. His conclusion that this was about power surprised her. He was smart, but she didn't think he'd make the connection so quickly.

They studied long into the night. It was nearly four when Dennis declared himself done for the night. "Sorry, Hazel. I can't read any more. I keep falling asleep."

"Yeah, me too. But I don't want to give up."

"Me either. But at this rate, we're likely to miss something. I'm going to head home. You should sleep in tomorrow. Come in when you wake up, and if you text me when you're leaving, I'll make you breakfast." He lifted her hand and pressed a kiss to her palm.

His lips were soft and warm against her hand. She smiled at him. "I suppose you're right. Sleep might help clear my brain. I'll be in, eventually. I appreciate the offer of breakfast. Something simple, I don't eat much in the morning."

She pulled the leftovers from the fridge and walked him to the door. "Thanks for coming, and for dinner. Thanks for helping with the research."

"I'm just sorry we didn't find anything. I'll help you look anytime you want."

"You have a business to run, but if you find yourself at loose ends..."

He took the box of food from her and brushed a kiss on her forehead. "As soon as I can spare a couple hours, I'll be back. Are you okay to drive to work? I can pick you up."

"I'll be fine. But thanks." She stood on the porch; arms crossed around her middle until he was out of sight. By the Goddess, she didn't want to be interested in him, especially now while her entire world was upset by whoever had stripped her energy, but she couldn't help herself. He was kind, generous, helpful, and a good boss. All his employees liked him. He'd even brought food tonight and was going to feed her again tomorrow. The old adage about the way to a man's heart being through his stomach might not be true, but she was a foodie and feeding her was a sure way to win her over.

She laughed at the silly idea. It took much more than a hot meal, but Dennis had that, and a whole lot more going for him.

Chapter Seventeen

"**G**ood morning, Hazel." Dennis stuck his head through the office doorway to smile at her. God, she was breathtaking. Her hair was piled on top of head in a messy bun, she wore some kind of lacy T-shirt and matching cloth headband. She looked like an angel sitting there with the morning sun highlighting her hair, turning it shades of gold and red.

It was barely nine and she was already hard at work entering receipts and getting his finances in order. One thing she had, in spades, was dedication to her job. She hadn't missed a single day in the ten days since they'd warded his house. She'd produced reams of reports. She had to be nearly caught up.

"Oh." She looked up and blinked as if it was taking her a few seconds to adjust to his presence. "Morning, Dennis. How are you?"

"Lonely." He winked. "Want to join me for breakfast?"

"I already ate, but thanks." Her smile stole his breath.

He leaned against the doorjamb. "I hate eating alone. Join me for coffee while I eat?" He really just wanted to spend time with her. He'd like to take her to dinner soon. Something nice and relaxing, in public. Somewhere she'd be safe from attack. At least he hoped she would be safe in public.

"You do realize you're paying me to work, not to socialize?" Her voice was light with laughter. She clicked a few keys, stood and picked up her mug. "I could use another cup of go juice. Besides, you're the boss and whatever the boss says goes."

"Somehow I doubt you're serious, but I'll take it." He gestured for her to go ahead of him and instantly regretted it. She wore a short skirt that floated and shifted as she walked. He couldn't draw his gaze away from the enticing motion where the fabric brushed against her tanned, shapely thighs. Every time he looked at her, his attraction grew. But it was more than physical, there was something earthy and ethereal about her. It was almost as if her magic shone from her.

He shook his head. He was getting fanciful. Maybe he needed to start dating in his spare time. Ha. What spare time? He was head down, ass up, all day every day. He'd be happy with a quiet dinner. With Hazel.

Hazel went straight to the coffee maker and started a fresh pot while he pulled food from the fridge. "Are you sure you don't want something? I'm cooking anyway."

She laughed. "I'm good. Are you trying to fatten me up?"

"What?" He laughed, realizing she was teasing. "No. Definitely not. You're perfect the way you are. I guess it's part of how I was raised. If you're eating, feed everyone. If company comes, offer them a beverage. Since you're handling the drinks, I offered food. Again."

"Tell you what," she said, pivoting to grin at him. "I'll let you buy me dinner tonight." Her face turned red. "That is, if you want to. Or

I can pay, or we can go Dutch. Or nothing." She pivoted to focus on the coffee pot.

He set the eggs, bacon and some peppers on the counter. "I'd love any of those options; except the nothing one. And, of course, I'll buy. Pick a time and I'm in."

"Excellent. It won't interfere with work will it?" She turned back toward him, her face slowly returning to a normal color.

She was adorable with the heightened pink in her cheeks. He'd realized she didn't seem to wear makeup, yet she never looked pale. "That's where I was this morning. I hired four new part-time staff and promoted three people to managers. Between my tree farm, the greenhouses, petting zoo, and retail area, I have thirty people working for me. I never imagined this business would grow so quickly. I'm optimistic this will reduce my workload. I have my fingers crossed."

"Oh, fabulous. Who'd you promote?"

They discussed the changes while he fried bacon. He'd tried cooking it in the oven or microwave, but he always got the timing wrong and overcooked it. Hazel started chopping peppers and an onion she pulled from the fridge.

She snuck the first slice of bacon he set on a plate to cool. "I thought you weren't hungry?"

"Dude, it's bacon. Who can resist bacon, even when they're not hungry? You didn't mention bacon when you offered food. I figured you for a cold cereal guy."

He clutched his chest. "You wound me. I'm a fairly decent cook when I want to be. Breakfast is my specialty." He laughed when he realized she was teasing again. "You've eaten here, more than once." He shook his finger at her.

"You should try my summer berry oatmeal. It'll make you purr." A vision of her purring for other, more risqué, reasons entered his head. His mouth went dry, and his heartbeat accelerated. Wow. He had to get his errant thoughts under control. He stole another look at her delicious legs and felt his body harden in response. Oh yeah, he was definitely out of control. He cleared his throat.

She glanced at him. "Are you okay?"

"Um. Yeah. I'm good. Just a frog in my throat." He was grateful when she turned her attention back to slicing vegetables. He'd been worried about hiring her, and that worry had passed; but this was a whole new dimension on dangerous. She was dangerous to his libido and his sanity, and damned if he didn't like it. He could get used to having her around. She brightened his kitchen and when he was with her, he felt his tension slide from his shoulders.

He hadn't been expecting to find running a business without a partner so stressful. Growing plants from seeds and shoots was one thing. Retail operations and a petting zoo also added to the workload. He shrugged the worries aside. He'd made the decision to work with the public on a larger scale and he loved his greenhouses. He'd adapt to this, especially now that Hazel was here to help with the bookkeeping.

He mentioned his worry to her.

"I can see that," she said. "Working with the public can be stressful and there'd be much more public with a greenhouse than in landscaping. Give yourself time to get used to it. The people in Three Moon Falls are a good lot. Yeah, there's a few bad seeds, if you'll pardon the bad gardening reference." She grinned at him and poured the coffee and added flavored cream to hers. "You've got more staff, which will help too. Before long, you won't know what to do with yourself."

"I'm going to start by taking you out to dinner. Where would you like to go? Heaven is nice, but hard to get into sometimes." And could be quite intimate. He wanted to get to know her better but wasn't sure their relationship was ready for a full-on romantic dinner.

"True. What about Romero's? Frankie Romero is the best Italian cook in the province. He's won dozens of awards for his cooking. He even has a Michelin star."

"That sounds great. I haven't had Italian in ages. What's a Michelin star chef doing in small town Alberta? Couldn't he have a place in the city?"

"You'd think so. He left the restaurant he ran in Chicago when his grandmother got sick. He came home to look after her and ended up staying when her cancer treatments were finished. She's been cancer free for two years. He's got no plans to leave, or at least he didn't last time I talked to him."

"I'm glad his grandmother is doing well. But I'm even gladder you and I will be sharing delicious Italian food together."

Hazel looked at him with her brows bunched together.

"What? I'm a foodie. I love good food. I work hard. Physical labor all day. I'm afraid if I don't get enough to eat, I'll waste away to nothing." He patted his flat stomach and flexed his biceps, making her laugh.

"You are incorrigible." She set his mug on the table and sat down with hers cradled between her hands, in front of her chin.

"You do that a lot," he observed.

"Do what?" She sipped her coffee.

"Hold your mug between your hands, just below your mouth." Her pose struck him as both calm and contemplative. Like she was surveying the world around her and was content with what she saw.

"There's something about the smell of coffee. It's almost as good as the smell of bacon. While drinking it gives me energy, and sometimes makes me hyper and twitchy, the smell is both invigorating and peaceful."

"Funny, peaceful is exactly what came to mind when I saw you sitting with your mug under your nose." She smiled warmly over her

cup, sending his heartrate skyrocketing. How could one simple smile
affect him like that?

Dennis's hand was warm against Hazel's back as he gently steered
her toward the front door of Romero's. She had debated meeting him at the restaurant, but in the end, agreed to let him pick her
up at Four Seasons Metaphysical. It had been her policy to meet her
dates, what precious few of them there were, at the restaurant or club.
No sense getting into a car with someone she didn't know well. But
she'd worked with Dennis for weeks, and she trusted him. Besides,
her family knew where they were going. It was nice being back in her
hometown. Dating in the city while she was at school meant telling her
friends where she was, and with whom. Just in case. She liked having
the backup of her family close at hand and in the loop.

It wasn't that she didn't trust people, she was just innately cautious.
Being with a man she knew and liked; in the safety of the place where
she grew up, was freeing.

"That's a beautiful smile," Dennis said as they waited for the host-
ess. "What are you thinking about?"

"Honestly?

"Honesty is always best."

"About how nice it is to go out. With you."

His smile sent a fresh wave of happiness through her. "Smell that."
She breathed deeply, inhaling the mouth-watering aroma of melted
cheese, garlic and basil. "Oh, I think I need garlic bread. Maybe bruschetta. Seafood linguini. Or maybe lasagna."

"Wow. You must be starved. Didn't you eat lunch?" he teased. "I
thought skipping lunch was my go-to move, not yours."

She chuckled. "I'm always like this when I come here. I can never make up my mind. Oh, they make the best calamari. Maybe I'll have calamari."

"An appetizer, main course and dessert sounds good. I have seen you eat that much." He winked to show he was teasing.

She fought back a smile. He was right after all. She'd nearly eaten him out of house and home the other night. But those were exceptional circumstances and tonight was going to be fun. Pure and simple entertainment. She had zero intention of using magic and attracting unwanted attention.

"Maybe two appetizers, and an Irish coffee after dessert."

He looked at her, as if he was assessing her mood, or her thoughts. He smiled softly. "You're pulling my leg."

"I am," she agreed. "Although I do wish this place had a sampler platter. A little of everything. I hate to miss out on some of my favorites."

"I know the feeling well. My partner and I used to hit wing night at a local pub. Ideally, I'd have ordered one wing of each flavor. All fifty-seven of them. Instead, I picked two and he picked two and we made do. We actually managed to work down the entire list. I had my favorites, but I'd like to go back and have a mixed platter."

"You really are a foodie, aren't you?" she asked, enjoying their easy banter.

"Don't say it like that. I suspect you're just as bad."

"Hazel. Nice to see you," the restaurant host greeted them.

"Amir, good to see you too. This is my friend Dennis. He owns the garden center." She returned the greeting to the twentyish man who returned to the entry after seating another couple in the dining area.

"Nice to meet you, sir. Follow me." He led them to a quiet table in the back. It was set with a burgundy tablecloth and glasses for water and wine. After filling their water glasses, he returned to his station.

"Quiet in here tonight," Dennis commented. It was early enough the restaurant wasn't busy. There wasn't anyone seated nearby and only four other tables of diners.

"It usually is quiet until after eight when families have put their kids to bed. Though Friday and Saturday evenings are always packed. You need reservations on weekends. They've got a Sunday brunch which is to die for."

"There's your sample platter. Come to brunch."

She laughed. "It's more a traditional brunch with a bit of Italian thrown in. Good thing too, or I'd be here every weekend, eating my weight in pasta."

Their small talk was surprisingly comfortable. She should have expected it, they'd spent hours together since they met and were past the awkward stage. She'd half-expected first date jitters. They ordered their meals and shared plates of calamari and bruschetta.

When the server brought their main courses, Hazel looked up to thank her. A motion near the doorway caught her eye. Mathew Brown stood in the entrance.

"Shit."

"What?" The server asked. "Is there something wrong with your food? Did I make a mistake?"

"Oh, no. Sorry." Hazel smiled at the woman. "It looks and smells delicious." She'd barely glanced at her food. "My mind was elsewhere," she lied.

"Oh. Okay then." She grated fresh parmesan onto their meals and left.

"What was that all about?" Dennis asked.

"Nothing. I thought I saw someone." He'd been there, but when she looked back, Mathew had disappeared. She looked surreptitiously around the room but didn't see him. What were the odds he'd show up at this place, at this time? Nil. Dennis's back was to the door, so he wouldn't have noticed the unwanted man.

"Someone who makes you swear. That can't be good. Mind if I ask who?"

As much as she'd like to drop the subject and get back to enjoying her dinner, the brief glimpse of Mathew continued to distract her. "Fine. I swear I saw Mathew Brown in the doorway. Then he disappeared."

"Disappeared? Like magic?"

She chuckled. "No, like a person. I turned away and he vanished. Why is he here?"

"It is a public place," Dennis said reasonably. "Why wouldn't he be here?"

"Three Moon Falls has about two dozen restaurants. What are the odds of him picking the same one at the same time?"

"Okay, when you put it that way…" He paused. "But don't you run into people you know all the time? Coincidentally?"

"Yeah, I guess." He was right, but she couldn't shake the feeling Brown was following her. If she was in a business, he was there. She'd caught sight of him at the grocery store, drugstore, and post office yesterday. He walked by the family shop too often to be coincidence. He'd even been in once, though he hadn't purchased anything. She'd have to let Corporal Stone know that he seemed to pop up too often.

"I don't know how to explain it. He feels like a threat to me. He's never done anything wrong." She paused. "And I don't like him being at the garden center so early the morning after my powers were stripped. He frightens me."

"But there hasn't been an attack since."

"I know. I can't decide if that makes it better, or worse. I feel like I'm waiting for the next disaster. Crazy as it sounds, I wish he'd attack again. Give me someone to fight. I need to solve this. It's making me nuts. I'm barely sleeping at night and not at all if I don't take an herbal sleep remedy my grandmother creates. I can't live like this."

"That's not good."

"Look." She nodded to the doorway behind Dennis. "There he is. Coming this way."

"Hi, Dennis. Hazel," Brown greeted them. Hazel was said dismissively. "What brings you guys out tonight? Celebrating?"

Hazel nodded but didn't speak. She was afraid if she opened her mouth, she'd demand to know why he was here, why he was following her.

"Hi, Matt," Dennis returned the greeting but didn't answer his question.

"Want some company? I'm here alone, I'd love to join you."

His gall was unbelievable. It was all she could do not to say something incredibly rude.

"Not tonight, we'd prefer to be alone. Perhaps another time," Dennis responded civilly.

Hazel was torn between admiring Dennis' restraint, and wondering if he was making a mistake brushing Brown off.

"I had the impression you didn't see your staff casually," Brown accused.

"This," Dennis waved back and forth between himself and Hazel, "This is a business dinner with my bookkeeper. Have a nice evening, I'll talk to you at work."

With a glare, Brown walked away.

"Dinner with your bookkeeper?" she asked slyly.

'Dennis looked chagrinned. "I know you don't care for him, and I certainly didn't want him interrupting our date."

"Which is it? Dinner with your bookkeeper or a date?" She was joking, mostly. She'd have preferred if he told the truth, this was a date, or at least two friends sharing a meal. She didn't like the lie, even if it was to avoid a third wheel.

"This is a date," he stated categorically, grasping her hand in his. He squeezed lightly. "Have no doubt. This is about a man and a woman getting to know each other better. I choose to be with you. Alone."

A thrill ran through her, erasing her unease at Brown's proximity.

Dennis was a wonderful companion, thoughtful of her needs, complimentary, generous and kind. He was, in a nutshell, the kind of man she was looking for. The kind of man her family would approve of. If only he were magical. She paused as she reached for her water glass. She'd only known him a couple weeks and already she was thinking long term. She was getting ahead of herself. The question she had to unpuzzle for herself, was how much her family's opinions mattered to her. Were they critical? Could she just disregard them?

It wasn't like her family would disown her, but if she was going to place family opinion above her own, she needed to decide. Now. Before she got further involved. It wasn't fair to Dennis to lead him on if she was going to dump him later.

"Where do you see this relationship going?" she blurted, immediately wishing she'd kept her big mouth shut. Why did she always speak before thinking?

"Um." He blinked twice. "I hadn't really thought about it and I had not planned anything." He winced. "I mean..."

"It's okay. Never mind. Forget I asked." She gulped her water, nearly choking on her mortification.

"I see us dating. Seeing where it goes. Maybe pursuing something long term if we're compatible." He paused thoughtfully. "I'm not rushing anything, but frankly, eventually, I'll be looking for a permanent relationship and children. I'm not saying that's with you, and I'm not saying it isn't with you. Those are my goals. I'd like to see where this goes. Follow along and see if we are compatible. I find you attractive, entertaining and intelligent."

Wow! A man upfront about wanting a family. Men like this didn't come along every day. And being open about seeing where their friendship went was an enormous plus. Too bad he hadn't mentioned her family's magic. He'd been so adamantly against it initially, though he had softened his stance.

"And magic?" she asked at last, unable to hold the question in.

"Magic isn't an automatic hard no any longer. I'm researching different things you've mentioned, and I've seen the positive it can do—like when we warded my house to keep you safe."

"Does this mean you aren't wary anymore?" She felt compelled to press the issue. Like her family's opinions, his stance on magic could, potentially, be a relationship ender.

"Less wary would be more accurate, to be brutally honest. The things you can do are unnerving. But I'm more open minded than I was the day I hired you."

She considered his words. His honesty was refreshing. He wasn't mincing words to save her feelings. "I'm glad to hear that. I respect your honesty. I like you, Dennis Belanger. You're a good boss and friend. I'd like to carry this forward as well." She rubbed her hands together and picked up her fork. "Now, let's eat this incredible food before it gets any colder. I'm starved."

"And family? Are you wanting a family?" he asked after a few bites.

"Definitely. Having siblings is the best," she paused, "and the worst. I want at least two, maybe six kids." She winked to show she was teasing. "Seriously, yes. I want to get married, eventually, and I want children. Having a life partner who understands magic is part of my life, part of who I am is important. In fact, it is critical."

"I can understand that. I'm trying to get my head around what you do and what it means. Both to me, and to a relationship. Which is why I've been researching magic and its history."

"I can't ask for anything more."

Chapter Eighteen

"I was thinking we could go for a walk," Dennis suggested as they exited the restaurant. "Maybe stroll along the creek? You could share some witchy observations with me. You know, to introduce me to your way of thinking."

"You'll likely be disappointed in my thoughts," she demurred. "But I'd love to walk with you. Good thing I wore comfortable shoes." She looked down at her flat white sandals.

"You always wear sensible shoes. I like that. Heels might make a woman's legs look longer, but there's something about a woman who's secure enough to be who she is." He gestured for her to lead him around the corner toward the creek.

"Are you saying a woman in heels isn't secure in who she is?" She raised one eyebrow as she slipped past him. If so, he had a thing or two to learn about women.

"No! Not at all. I mean…You know what? I'll just shut up now. There's no way I'm digging myself out of that hole. All I'm going to say is I didn't mean it the way it sounded. I fully respect a woman's footwear choice, though I don't understand the appeal of heels. They look as uncomfortable as hell." He stepped up beside her and grasped her hand lightly in his. "Forgive me for being obtuse?"

"Hm." She tapped her lip with one finger. "I'm not sure I should." Squeezing his fingers in her hand, she tugged him closer until their shoulders touched. She pointed to his cowboy boots. "Me, I never could see how those things could be comfortable. They're so clunky."

He chuckled. "They took some getting used to, but they're durable for some of my messier chores. I guess I wear them because my grandfather gave me my first pair when I was twelve. I spend half my time in these and the rest in runners. Barring the occasional stint in good old rubber boots or my winter Sorels."

She chuckled. "No offense, but this is the weirdest date conversation I've ever had." She nudged him with her shoulder.

"I'm deeply offended." He winked at her. "I'm fascinated by everything about you. Are you saying you aren't enthralled by my footwear?"

"Not even remotely."

They laughed together and fell into a comfortable silence as they walked.

"Are you good to walk for a while? There's a beautiful meadow with a bench just over a mile down the creek. It's a great place to sit and watch the wildlife."

"Sure," he responded. "A mile isn't far."

Giddiness flowed through her. Walking was her thing. She could walk for hours, especially in the wilderness. Walking along the creek, in town, wasn't true wilderness, but they'd be separated from town by a thick shelter belt of trees teeming with wildlife. Squirrels, deer and rabbits thrived in the area and the red shale pathways were perfect for walking.

The path was busy with families. Fathers teaching their daughters to ride two-wheelers. Moms pushing strollers. One set of grandparents were busy trying to corral five young children determined to race wildly along the path.

"This is incredible. I love watching the families interact." Hazel nodded to a family she knew well. "It makes me want a family of my own."

"It makes me miss my brother's rats."

"You call your brother's children rats?"

"Rats, brats, heathens, depends on the day."

She smiled at him. The depth of his caring for the kids was evident in the affectionate tone in his voice. Clearly, he adored them. "Do you see them often?"

"Not as much as I'd like. They're coming in for a visit in two weeks. Which means I have to get the play structure I ordered built by then. I hope I find the time."

"You have to make time! They'll be so disappointed if you don't. Hire my sister to supervise. She's a carpenter. Get some of those young guys you hired to do the work. It'll be done in no time. Come on," she urged. "You only have days. It takes time for concrete to set, and you'll want it to be sturdy, right?"

"Do you really think she'd be game to help? It would save me time." He slowed their pace to a stop; a thoughtful look crossed his face.

"I can ask her. The worst that happens is she says she's too busy. She focuses on her own designs and does a lot of custom orders. I don't know how busy she is. Want me to call her?"

"Yes. Please. I really would like to have it ready for them."

Hazel made the call. After a moment she handed the phone to Dennis and listened to him explain the structure to her sister. It sounded massive. Two slides, a climbing wall, a rope jungle gym, six swings and four monkey bars. It even had a tree house loft.

When he finished the call, he handed her back the phone. "Thank you."

"Those kids are darn lucky to have an uncle like you," she exclaimed. He was going to be a great father if this was any indication. She stepped tight to his side. "Come on, Uncle Nice Guy, let's go check out the meadow. Maybe we'll see a few deer. There might even be fawns."

As they walked along, the crowds thinned out until it seemed they were alone on the paths. "I love this time of evening," she gushed. "It's peaceful. At home, I love to sit out in the gazebo and just listen to the sounds change as day fades to night. I love watching the bats swoop and catch bugs. As long as they stay far away." She shuddered. "Far, far away. I got one in my hair as a kid. It really freaked me out. I keep my distance now."

"Did it get hurt? Was the bat okay?" he asked.

"Was the bat okay?" she echoed. "I'm revealing a childhood trauma and you're worried about a bat? Harsh. Very harsh," she teased.

"Clearly, you're fine. A little mentally damaged, but fine. But a wee little bat, you might have hurt him."

She huffed out a fake sigh. "He was fine. Flew away like nothing happened once Amber got him untangled."

"All's well that ends well."

They walked past an enormous clump of evergreens into a large clearing. A small stream flowed from the creek into one end of a large oval pond and out the other end. A fish jumped in the pond. "That was a trout," he exclaimed.

"No fishing, this is a provincial park. Not even catch and release. Let's sit." She gestured to a decorative concrete bench adjacent to the water. "The bench is new. It used to be a wooden one, like the others."

The bench had a small plaque. She paused to read it. "In loving memory of those lives lost in the Raven Falls explosion." It listed the names of the people who died when Keres blew up a portion of the waterfall.

"I can't believe someone blew up a waterfall," Dennis said. "What a waste of nature."

"Keres was a jerk. He had a mission, a nasty plan, and he didn't care what he had to do to get what he wanted. I'm glad he's locked up." Just remembering the incident and the ones which followed sent her heart racing. Her near-death experience wasn't something she liked to think about. She probably should book herself an appointment with a healer, one who wasn't her sister, to help deal with the aftermath. *He was still locked up, wasn't he?*

"What did he want? Did you ever figure it out?" Dennis sounded sympathetic and interested.

"We can't figure it out. He claimed to have a spell to bring his wife back from the dead. Necromancy isn't something you mess around with. Frankly, I'm not even sure it is possible. We wonder if he needed another spell, or a sacred item, a talisman if you will. We're one hundred percent sure we won't stop searching until we figure it out. If we can't find what we need in our library, there are bigger, central, magical libraries we can turn to, but not everyone is granted access. And if they are, it's only for serious research. Life and death stuff. I'm hoping it never comes to that."

She wrapped her arms around her middle and drew her feet up to sit cross-legged on the bench. He sat beside her, turned slightly toward her.

"If there is something to his claims, we need to find a way to stop it. Get rid of the talisman, give it to the council, remove all mentions of the spell. Whatever it takes to end this."

"But if he's locked up, isn't it over?"

"You'd think so. We hope so. Think it through. Keres figures we had, or have, something he needed. We're not famous or notorious. How did he conclude we had what he needs? Who else might figure out the same thing? Can we take a risk?"

"Good point. Isn't there a paranormal police force who can deal with this?"

She chuckled at his wording. "There is a witch's council who deal with law breakers. They're handling Keres now. But it isn't like police patrolling the streets, looking for criminals. Most police forces have at least one member of the council high up in their ranks. Even in small towns."

"So, Three Moon Falls has a witch officer? Which one?"

She mimed zipping her lips. "That's for me to know and for you to...forget you ever heard about. You aren't supposed to know these things. Hell, you aren't supposed to know magic exists at all."

"That brings up a question, can a muggle, or mundane, as you call us, learn magic? Is it a training thing or is it genetic? Genetics I understand."

"There are stories of mundanes learning magic. It happens. But the question always arises about their backgrounds. Were they actual mundanes, or did they have magical ancestors? Take Kody for example. We were certain he was mundane. Turns out his grandmother was a witch, and his mother had his powers blocked because she didn't approve of the magical lifestyle. In the end, he was able to tap into his powers, with his grandmother's help to assist us in defeating Keres."

"Are you saying I could be magical and not know it?"

"Could be. I guess. I don't know. History of magic was my worst subject. Gramma Pearl would be the one to ask. She might even know how to figure out if you had magic genetics and how to tap into them if you did."

Dennis frowned. "You know, I think I'll give that a miss. I'm not sure I'd want to be magical. Seems like it might be riddled with problems."

"No more, or less than regular people. Not unless you didn't know about your magic and you suddenly started casting accidental spells. Which would be a problem." She scanned the area as they talked, alert for wildlife and anyone who might overhear their somewhat forbidden conversation. She loved sitting here, talking to him, building their friendship. "Oh, look." She pointed to a break in the trees a hundred yards away. "A doe and two fawns."

"They're whitetails and they're playing," Dennis exclaimed. "I've never seen deer play before. Although, I suppose, like bears and cats, play is part of the learning curve."

"I think it is for most animals. It's the first time I've seen it." The fawns raced around one after the other, nipping and nudging as they went. The doe grazed placidly, keeping her head turned in the fawns' direction, ears twitching. Hazel leaned into Dennis, resting her head on his shoulder. They sat in silence until the animals wandered back into the woods.

"Ouch," Dennis exclaimed, slapping his arm. "Mosquitos are out. We better head back."

"I can put up a shield," she offered without any real enthusiasm.

"Hell no. I don't want a repeat of the last time. But thank you." He stood and held out his hand to help her up. "Thanks for bringing me here. I didn't realize we had something like this right in town."

"The path system is about five miles, end to end and runs on both sides of the creek. There are six, maybe seven bridges to cross back and forth. Lots of hiking trails in the bush too. And more of the shale paths and a few paved ones as well. It was all done with money left by a witch. He left the money, and a plan, when he passed away."

"Male witches are witches? Not wizards or warlocks?"

"They're whatever they want to be called. Our family calls them witches. It's really just terminology. Our family knew the donor, he used the term witch. The rest of town just called him the crazy old guy on Barker's Hill."

"I read something about him in a Three Moon Falls history book. Kept to himself, but always donated money to local causes. The book didn't mention the pathways. Or the fact that he was a witch."

"Perhaps you're reading the wrong history books," she said dryly.

He groaned. "Let me guess, there are magical history books, not just those grimoires of yours?"

"Got it in one." The walked along chatting about how regular people were oblivious to the magic all around them.

"I'm certainly guilty of that," Dennis said as they rounded a corner close to the restaurant. A couple walked toward them. "Do they look familiar?" he asked.

Chapter Nineteen

"I was just thinking the same thing." Hazel squinted at the on-coming duo. "He seems familiar." They walked forward and the couple became clear. "I don't freaking believe it," she said as it dawned on her that it was Brown coming toward them. With a woman on his arm. An unfamiliar woman and Hazel knew most of Three Moon Falls' residents.

"You've got to be kidding me. What the hell is she doing here?" Dennis grumbled.

"She? She who?" Hazel asked. "Do you know her?"

"That woman is my ex-girlfriend. There's no way she should be in Three Moon Falls."

"What is Brown doing here? I told you he was following me."

"The better question might be what is she doing with him and why are they both here?" Dennis made a frustrated sound. "I apologize in advance for the bullshit she says."

She looked at Dennis. His brows were pinched together in a frown and his hand, the one not holding hers, was clenched into a fist. He was more tense than she'd ever seen him. He wasn't just puzzled, he was angry, like he was going to blow his top and she'd never seen him lose his temper. This was not good.

"Hi, Dennis. Hazel," Brown greeted them. "I'd like you to meet my friend, Natalia."

"We've met," Dennis growled. "Natalia. What are you doing here?"

"Why, I came to visit you. To talk some sense into you. I bumped into Matt while I was having dinner. I knew him years ago. We chatted. When I told him, I was looking for you, he mentioned you were out walking with her." The pronoun rolled off her tongue like acid.

"Her name is Hazel, and I'm standing right here," Hazel snapped, displeased with being judged and dismissed on sight.

"I can see that," the lanky blonde woman drawled, tilting her head and cocking her hip. "What, precisely, are you doing with my fiancé?"

"We're not engaged," Dennis bit off the correction. "We were done a long time ago."

His teeth ground together audibly. Hazel winced. "As it happens," she mimicked the icy blonde's stance, "I'm on a date."

"You said it was a business meeting." Brown squinted at them.

"Semantics." Hazel waved his comment away with a flap of her hand. Brown didn't show any outward signs of magic, but the woman beside him almost glimmered with the dark nothingness of black magic. "Besides, what we do with our time is hardly the business of either of you." She made her tone as unconcerned as possible and slipped her arm around Dennis's waist.

She discretely massaged his tense back and gave the couple in front of them a dismissive look. "Now, if you'll excuse us, we'd like to finish our walk. Come on, Dennis. I feel like ice cream. Goodnight, Matt, Natalia." She put pressure on Dennis's back, urging him past the duo.

When she risked peeking back at them, they stood on the path, two feet apart, staring after her and Dennis.

"What's wrong with her? She's practically bleeding negative energy," Hazel said after they rounded a corner out of sight. "You actually dated her?"

"I dated her," he said defeatedly, his shoulders slumped. "Sometimes I wonder what I was thinking. I don't know why she's here. She's never set foot outside Drayton and her witchy little empire there; except to go shopping in Calgary."

"She'd be pretty if it wasn't for the total blackness of her energy. You can see the black magic. She's messing with some dark stuff. Really dark. It's not my business, but I'd steer clear of her if I was you."

"Trust me on this. There isn't a chance in hell of me hooking up with her. Not to date, not for coffee, not even to say hello. She was nice when I met her, quite charming. She changed over the years. Plus, I rode that train wreck once, never again."

"You rode that?" She wrinkled her nose. "Ew. I did not need that image burned into my mind. Pass the brain bleach. Maybe Gramma Pearl can do a memory erase on me," she joked.

"I didn't mean it like that. We dated. We were engaged. I ended it when I realized she was trying to influence my thoughts."

"I understand, now, why you were so adamant about me not doing magic at work. It still doesn't explain what she's doing here and what she's doing with him."

"I don't get it. She's never so much as called me. Sure, in the first couple months after I dumped her. Then I got a new phone number. She called me once, and I warned her I'd have a restraining order put on her. She never called again. I didn't know she was aware I'd moved out of Drayton."

"And bumping into Brown? That's an enormous coincidence." She stopped walking, closed her eyes and tilted her head up to the darkening sky, trying to regain her calm. "What on earth is going on? This feels, I don't know, wrong somehow. Seeing the two of them together sets my nerves on edge." She paused and looked at him. "Have you ever had the feeling something is going to go wrong? Like shit's going to hit the fan?"

"Not really. That sounds like a premonition. But I hear what you're saying. If you take everything; Matt showing up super early for work, and right after you were attacked, him showing up at the restaurant while we were there, my ex showing up with him; honestly, it makes me as nervous as hell. Too many coincidences."

"She really did a number on you, didn't she?" How horrible to realize someone was manipulating you. Especially someone you cared for. No wonder he was wary.

"I didn't even realize it was possible. I guess, by the time I realized what she was up to, I was ready to end it anyway. She didn't show me her magical side initially. Then, it was just the odd thing here and there. After a while, I began to question some of the things she was doing. But the mind manipulation was the last straw. How do you abuse someone's trust like that?"

"I can't even fathom that. I grew up knowing about mind reading and influencing. It isn't something we do, but every now and then, Gramma Pearl would stick her nose into my head. Not to influence me, but to see what I was up to. Even that is invasive and unacceptable. But not knowing…" she trailed off with a shudder, unable to express her revulsion, knowing he understood her feelings.

"Do we worry about it?"

"I think we have to keep our eyes open for sure. I swear he's magic, though I can't sense it. I don't feel blocked, but he isn't open either. It's really hard to explain. It's as if I can almost sense something; kind of like a word you can't remember but it's right on the tip of your tongue."

"You've read him? Is that what you call it? Doesn't that cross a line, or something?" Dennis's voice wobbled almost imperceptibly.

"Not read, like poked into his mind, but magicals have a distinctive look. We talked about dark magic leaving behind darkness. I can't fully explain, but when I look at him, something isn't right. Something is missing. A skilled practitioner can hide what he is, to a certain extent. I did not try to probe his mind," she stated, hoping the declaration would set Dennis's mind at ease. His shoulders relaxed and he half smiled. "It's more of a witches can sense each other thing."

"I'm glad to hear that, actually." He shrugged. "I don't like her suddenly showing up here. Not one bit. It reeks of, I don't know, manipulation. Or something. I guess there isn't much to do, besides keep our guard up."

"Are you going to fire him?" she asked hopefully.

"I admit, I am tempted. He's still in his probationary period, and technically, I don't need a reason to let him go. But, frankly, I'd like to keep him close so I can keep my eyes on him. Who knows, maybe he'll tell me how he met Natalia, and what they are doing together."

"I don't like it. I'd let him go. Maybe he'll move away and forget this place and take her with him." Unease crawled down her back and settled in her stomach like a dozen tiny bouncy balls.

"Or maybe he'll get angry and stir up trouble. I'd rather have them both where I can see them. I can't decide if they planned on being together here. Just meeting is a huge coincidence." He shook his head. "Maybe I'm overreacting to a coincidence. I don't know."

"I doubt it. My instincts are screaming. But Mom always said, "Don't borrow trouble." I say we take her advice and try and enjoy the rest of the evening. Whatever's going to happen, if anything, will happen even if we don't worry about it."

For a moment, he looked skeptical; then he smiled weakly. "I guess you're right. Care for an after-dinner drink? Maybe ice cream or a coffee. Sorry, tea. You drink tea in the evening, don't you?"

"I do, and I'd love a cup. Why don't we go to the shop? I can introduce you to some of our family blends. You'll love them."

She laughed at his wince.

"Um, no thanks. I'm more a coffee guy. How about we hit Brewsters? They've got coffee and tea. We can both be happy," he suggested. "I'd kill for a half-caf."

As they walked toward the café, she kept her eyes and senses open for signs of Brown and Natalia. After a while, she almost managed to relax.

"That was delicious," she exclaimed as they left the café nearly an hour later. "I never would have thought they'd have something so delicious, and I'm a tea snob. I feel bad I've never gone there before; they haven't been open long. I assumed they'd serve the usual corporate teas, not their own blends. I'm definitely coming back. I'm going to have to get to know the owner and talk tea."

"The éclair was good."

She gripped his arm excitedly. "Good? It was divine. Heavenly. Delightful. How can you just call it good? Have you no appreciation for fine desserts?"

She smiled widely, her brown eyes sparkling. He loved the laugh in her voice.

"Fine," he feigned exasperation. "They were delicious. I could have eaten another one."

"Want to go back? I could eat another one. I'll go for a super long run tomorrow to make up for it." She bounced on her toes.

"I think, we'll save that for another day. I hate to break up a nice evening, but I need to get some sleep. I'm running on empty." He'd love to continue their date, but he was exhausted and now, with his belly full of food, he was having trouble staying awake, despite the pleasant company.

"I thought it was going better at work. Didn't you delegate?"

Her concern was touching. "I did and it is better, but I think months of overwork and fatigue have finally caught up with me. I'd rather continue this..." He waved vaguely to indicate their being together.

He'd like to end the night in a different way entirely. But not only was he too bushed, he didn't want to rush Hazel into a physical relationship and risk ruining what seemed to be blossoming between them. He stifled a yawn hoping she didn't notice.

"Are you okay to drive home? I can give you a ride."

"I'm sure I'm fine." He yawned again.

"You are not fine. The sugar in your éclair was your undoing. You're crashing on top of being exhausted. Let's go back to the truck. It's only a couple blocks. I'll drive you home and bring the truck to work in the morning. I'm not letting you hit the highway in this condition."

She tugged him forward and he followed along rather than risk stumbling. Maybe she had a point. Suddenly he could barely keep his eyes open. "Yeah, let's do that." The words came out as a mumble. By the time they reached his truck, he was leaning on Hazel for support. This was messed up. Something was wrong with him. Maybe he had the flu.

"Up you get," she declared, shoving him into the passenger seat of his truck.

The next thing he knew, she was urging him to get out of the truck. He opened his eyes and realized he was home. One of her sisters, he couldn't recall her name, was there, helping lead him into the house.

Chapter Twenty

"I'm telling you; this isn't right." Hazel stared down at Dennis who lay asleep, on his bed, arms and legs splayed where she and Cynthia had dropped him. He hadn't moved an inch in the past five minutes. Her stomach clenched. "What do you think it is? I mean, he said he was tired, but this is ridiculous. He slept twenty minutes before I called you. I didn't want to risk dropping him on the way into the house. I'm worried."

"It could be exhaustion. I guess. I'm not a doctor, just a midwife. But I don't really think he's just tired. It's something else." Cynth checked his pulse and lifted one eyelid to check his pupil.

"By the Goddess. Could he have been drugged? Poisoned?" Brown and Natalia were behind this, she'd bet her best broomstick on it. "Is he going to be okay? What do we do? I can't stand to see him like this."

"You really like him, don't you?" Cynth's tone was understanding and compassionate.

"I didn't want to. He was a jackass when we met. But he's grown on me and now he's less of a jerk about magic, I like him. A lot. More than I should. But forget that, let's figure out what's wrong with him. Should we call Gramma Pearl? A doctor?"

"Honestly, I don't know what's wrong with him. He seems to be asleep, but since we can't rouse him, I'm fearful it could be something else. I think we should call Dr. Carter. She'll know where to start."

"You call her, I'll stay with him." Hazel sat beside Dennis and stroked his head. Dr. Carter was their best bet. The mundane offspring of magical parents, she was a trusted source of medical information. If she didn't have any ideas, they'd call in some of the more experienced members of the magical community. Surely someone would figure out what was wrong with him.

Fifteen minutes later, Doctor Carter arrived. Half an hour after that, Gramma Pearl, Leticia Stone and another close family friend, Danica Maes, arrived.

"Did he eat or drink anything unusual?" Pearl asked after her initial examination.

"I don't think so. We went for dinner and a walk. Then had tea and dessert at Brewsters. Nothing weird." Hazel wrapped her arms around her waist. She wanted to push the doctor away and climb up beside Dennis, as if being closer would help him.

"Oh, he's been magicked for sure," Leticia said after examining Dennis. "Someone very skillful did this." She rose and flipped her dreadlocks over her shoulder. "I can't tell what the spell is, but I'm certain there is one. What do you get Pearl?"

"Nothing. I get a big fat nothing. A vague hint of darkness. I'd say a sleeping spell. What exactly, I can't tell. Nor do I know why. I don't like this."

"Did you see anyone unusual? Go anyplace weird?" Danica asked. "He's out so cold, his brain is beyond sleep. I can't pick up anything."

She held up a hand. "His brain seems fine, but he's not dreaming, and I can't detect much subconscious or unconscious thought. Whatever caused this, it's either going to last a long time, or end abruptly."

"What the hell?" Hazel cursed. This was so wrong. She felt like this was all her fault. She'd been attacked on his property and now he'd been attacked while he was with her. Someone was seriously trying to screw up her life. "It's that f'ing Brown and Natalia."

"I know who Brown is, but who's Natalia?" Leticia asked, sliding smoothly into cop mode.

"His ex," Danica said. "I got that much from him. I didn't mention her because I didn't know if you knew about her, Hazel."

Hazel appreciated Danica's discretion. Occasionally, the petite woman with her brightly colored, pixie cut hair, could be indiscrete. She called it a side effect of working in a beauty shop where gossip ran rampant. Her disclosures weren't deliberate, just a result of her innate enthusiasm and tendency to babble. It was a miracle she kept her mouth shut about magic.

"Yes. Natalia is his ex. She showed up tonight with Brown. Neither Dennis nor I could figure out why they were together. It felt weird. I didn't like Brown from the minute I met him. He works at Get Growing." She explained how she was later attacked and Brown showing up super early for work the next day.

"I'll have a deep search done on him, and on this Natalia. Maybe they've got something in their pasts we need to know about. I'll also put the Witch's Council on notice there is something going on." Leticia started typing on her phone.

"We should move him somewhere safe until he wakes," Danica suggested. "If this is magic, he needs protection until we figure out who is behind it."

"We'll take him home with us," Hazel declared. "Safest place in town is our house. Nobody gets in there without an invitation." Keres had made it onto their property, but not into the house. Instead, he'd egged them on until they went to him, which had turned out to be a colossal mistake. "Help me get him to the truck."

"Don't be hasty. Let me call for help," Leticia said. "I can have a couple of big, burly officers here in no time. They can do the heavy lifting."

"I don't know. He might be embarrassed when he comes to," Hazel objected. Dennis was probably going to be chagrinned enough as it was. Nobody likes to be helpless in front of others, let alone a bunch of cops. She wouldn't want strangers seeing her like this.

"It's safer to have trained people carry him than a bunch of light-weight women. I'd suggest firemen, but I can't call them out without you paying ambulance fees. Plus, how did you get an ambulance to take someone to a location that isn't a medical facility without stirring up a bunch of questions?"

"Call your officers." Hazel frowned. She sure couldn't afford an ambulance ride, and it didn't seem right to make Dennis pay when he had no choice. Dennis was going to be mad enough when he woke up in a strange place. Maybe he should be in the hospital, someplace where qualified people could watch over him. Yeah, Hyacinth had medical training. Tons of it, but she wasn't a doctor and she certainly didn't have sophisticated monitoring equipment.

Ugh. She shouldn't dismiss her sister's skills. She was a gifted healer and midwife and definitely had the knowledge to keep a proper eye on Dennis. Still, sometimes modern medicine seemed the better alternative. Maybe this was one of those times.

No! If her suspicions and everyone else's opinions were correct, this was a magical malady which demanded magical treatments. Conventional medicine wouldn't know anything about magical ailments. Home was the perfect place for him. Her home, not his.

"Should you have someone keep an eye on his house and the green-house?" Pearl asked before Hazel had a chance to. "If this is magical, as we all know it is, someone wanted him out of the way for a reason."

"Access to his business would be a good reason," Leticia agreed. "I'll have the night shift do regular drive-bys of the property and your driveway.

"What about what happened to Hazel? Someone tried to suck her magic strength dry. Maybe they wanted Dennis out of the way to get closer to her," Hyacinth asked.

Hazel felt the blood drain from her face. It hadn't occurred to her they could both be in danger. She was going to have to be extra cautious and alert. She rubbed her palms up and down her arms. Her mind flashed to the three most terrifying incidents in her life. Nearly drowning when she was ten; nearly dying when Keres attacked; and having someone suck her strength away when she was practicing magic. By the Goddess, there was no way on earth, or in the galaxy for that matter, she was going to leave herself, or Dennis, open and vulnerable.

This all seemed linked to Keres' attack somehow. Whatever he was after must have become public knowledge. Otherwise, how did Brown and Natalia know about it? Did they know about it? Was this all a huge coincidence? How did she and her family figure out what they were after? How did they keep this from escalating out of hand as it had with Keres?

Before Hazel had time to get her wits together, Dennis was asleep in the spare bedroom on the main floor of Hawk's Manor. She sat in the bedside chair, watching him. They had concluded he was in a magically induced sleep. It didn't seem to be dangerous. To the untrained eye, it was just an extra deep sleep. She just didn't know how long it would last.

There wasn't much they could do except watch him. The magic caster could remove the spell, or time could weaken it. There was also a chance it was cast with a limited duration. Once again, the local magic community was hitting the books on behalf of the Hawk family, in search of a spell to reverse the one making Dennis sleep.

Hazel wanted to find Brown and his new friend and question them. Find out what they knew, what they had done. There was no doubt in her mind they were responsible for Dennis's condition. Of course, they wouldn't easily give up their secrets, she'd have to find a way to trick them into talking. She'd give the police a couple days to investigate, then she was starting her own investigation.

Chapter Twenty-One

H ours passed with no sign of a change in Dennis's condition. Hazel spent a sleepless night in the chair beside his bed, waiting and hoping he'd awaken. With every passing moment, her worry deepened, gnawing at her stomach like a dog chews a bone. He was her boss, her friend, and more. She was falling for him and didn't know what she'd do if he didn't recover.

"Come on, sister mine. It's time for you to get some sleep." Amber leaned on the door frame; Kody close behind her with his hand on her shoulder. "We'll watch him. You need some sleep. It's important you go to work in the morning. Keep up appearances and all that. We can't let whoever did this know we're affected. Get some rest. Nobody can harm him here. We've got your back."

Knowing she wouldn't sleep a wink, she agreed to try and trudged upstairs to her room. It was a blessing to have someone share the burden of watching Dennis. But he damn well better be awake in the morning.

She changed and climbed into bed hoping for the best.

The river was icy as she splashed across to the other side. Her toes curled up, threatening to cramp from the chill. Clouds scudded across the moon, obscuring its glow as she stumbled up the steep bank. Brambles scratched her shins as she pushed through a wild rose thicket toward a small grove of trees. An owl screamed in the night, swooping low over her head, its eyes glowing like coals.

Hazel jerked awake, panting in terror. She shivered in the breeze blowing through her open window. Open window? She'd shut it before going to bed, hadn't she?

The first glimmer of false dawn lightened the sky. Too early to get up, but she doubted she'd ever get back to sleep with the adrenaline coursing through her system, and fears gouging at her mind.

Years of habit had her making her bed before she dressed and brushed her teeth. Pearl's voice rang in her mind, "A tidy bed is the sign of an organized mind." Hazel crept down the stairs, avoiding the third step which creaked when you stepped on it. No sense alerting Gramma Pearl that she was up and about. She peeked in on Dennis; Amber and Kody sat, holding hands, whispering back and forth, half their attention on their sleeping guest. She waggled her fingers at them and made a drinking motion with her left hand.

The microwave's numbers shone red in the near darkness of the kitchen, reminding her of the glowing eyes in her dream. Nasty. Apprehension scraped down her spine. She froze there, staring at the red glow unable to move.

"Hazel, what are you doing up?" Her grandmother's voice jolted Hazel back to reality.

"I had a bad dream, couldn't sleep so I got up. I'm making tea."

"You were standing, staring into space. You look half terrorized." Pearl drew her into a comforting hug. "Last night was tough but we'll find a way to bring Dennis back. We'll get through this."

"The dream, it was so weird. So real. Crazy real."

"Was it a premonition?" Lazuli asked, joining them in the kitchen.

Amber strolled in, followed by Hyacinth. What was with her family? They should all be in bed.

"I don't know. I don't have premonitions, or visions. I've got virtually no psychic abilities. Aside from talking to ghosts."

"Tell us about it," Pearl said, bustling around to make tea.

Hazel nodded and her sisters gathered around her for a group hug. Wrapped in their embraces, feeling their love, she could almost believe things would work out okay.

"Kody's going to call us if anything changes with Dennis," Amber advised. "Luckily, he's got no early dives today. He can nap later."

"I appreciate that, and all the support. You guys are the best." They settled at the table and she related her dream. "That's when I woke up."

"Why were you standing, staring when I came to the kitchen?" Pearl asked.

"In the dark, the microwave lights were like the eyes. They caught me, like I was trapped."

"Premonition," Amber declared. "We need to research glowing eye spells and how to break their bond. I vaguely remember seeing something while we were searching for talisman stuff. I'll try and find it again. Thankfully, I recorded what books I've searched to prevent duplication."

"Being magic sucks," Hazel pouted.

Pearl reached across the table and patted Hazel's hand. "Come on, sweetheart. You know better. Everyone's lives have troubles. We're just going through a rough spot. Magic is who we are. Like everything, it has its ups and downs, but magic is epically awesome."

Hazel couldn't stop a chuckle at her grandmother's use of epically. A sigh followed the laugh. How in the world was she going to get through this?

"One day at a time," Lazuli said, answering the unspoken question.

"Reading my mind?" Hazel groused.

"Nope, you're casting off emotions loudly enough they might as well be verbal. "Ask anyone."

Her family nodded their agreement.

"Sorry, guys. I'm not doing it on purpose."

"I suspect, this is what, or at least part of what, the spell caster wanted," Hyacinth said. "To throw you, and maybe all of us so far off our game we can't function."

"But why me? Why Dennis?"

"Why did Keres go after me?" Amber countered.

"Why doesn't matter," Pearl advised. "Who is the question we need to be asking."

Hazel wrapped her arms around herself. She couldn't seem to erase the chill she'd gotten last night, and the uncertainty was making it worse. "What will I do if he doesn't wake up? I need him." She swallowed hard and whispered, "I love him."

To her surprise, Pearl didn't grumble about Hazel falling for a mundane. "We'll work this out. We have to. We would even if you hadn't met your only chance at love."

Hazel had been avoiding thinking about her family's inability to find a second love after meeting their soulmate. From the earliest records of their family, the Hawk women only found true love once in their lives. Look at her mother, she'd fallen for Trevor Moon as a teenager and had never loved deeply again, until they found each other again. Sure, she'd had boyfriends and lovers, in serious, long-term relationships, but not another deep, lasting love.

If Dennis didn't recover, Hazel would spend the rest of her life alone. Grief pulled heavily on her heart. "No way, no freaking way am I going to let Brown win. Not a chance. I'm going to find a way to beat this, to get past it and bring Dennis back. I'll get him back if I have to kill Brown with my bare hands."

"Violence is not the solution," Lazuli declared. As the empath, she was the most sensitive to the feelings of others. "But we will get through this. Even if I have to kick some ass."

The joke lessened the tension in the group. It was still there, hanging over them like a thundercloud. "I'm headed to the garden center later," Laz said. "I'm working on the play structure. I told Dennis I would start today. I'll give you a ride, Hazel. You can tell me who to pull from the staff as my construction crew."

Chapter Twenty-Two

The day was interminable for Hazel. Rather than work on book-keeping, Hazel chose to spend the day in the greenhouse itself. She started by delegating four strong youths to help her sister erect the play structure.

Having spent a few hours working with plants and customers last week, her presence wasn't unusual. Her goal was to be close to Brown, watch him. Study him. Catch him doing something wrong. If he stepped one foot out of line, she'd fire his ass.

Technically, she didn't have the right to do that, especially after Dennis said he wanted the man close. But Dennis was incapacitated, Brown didn't know she lacked the power to fire him, and she was freaking pissed.

By ten o'clock, he hadn't shown up. She checked the schedule to ensure he was on shift. Yup. Scheduled for nine. She asked around the center, nobody had seen him since the previous day. His absence was suspicious. She shot a quick text to her family, the mayor, and Leticia Stone, telling them and asking them to keep an eye open.

She worked hard, trying to keep her mind off Dennis lying pale and unmoving in the spare bedroom. In his absence, staff turned to her for help when they would normally turn to Dennis. It was a heady, but uncomfortable feeling. She wasn't the boss; she was just the bookkeeper. But she'd act like the boss until he got back.

Several employees questioned his absence. She told them the half-truth that he was sick in bed and would be back as soon as he recovered. Close enough to the truth she didn't feel guilty. Except for her role in getting him magicked.

She left the greenhouse after eight that evening. With only an hour left before closing, she was certain the shift manager could handle things. Good thing too, because nothing was going to keep her from racing home to check on Dennis. Surely there would be some improvement by now. It had been nearly twenty-four hours.

At home, nothing had changed. Dennis was still out. The doctor had been by, and Pearl was watching him closely. None of their friends had uncovered any useful spells or information. Hazel's heart sank. The last of her hope died. What if this was forever? Another day and they'd have to take him to the hospital. He couldn't survive without food. They were already dribbling water into his mouth to keep him hydrated.

After last night's pathetic sleep and an exhausting day, Hazel hoped to sleep well. Her hope was in vain. After tossing and turning for hours, she woke in worse shape than when she went to bed.

After breakfast, and a couple of her grandmother's energy balls, she hauled herself to work. Again, Brown didn't show. The morning dragged on. By noon, she was virtually nonfunctional.

"Sarah, I'm heading home to sleep," she told Dennis's employee as they did the daily check on the petting zoo. "I can't stay awake another minute. Call me if you need anything."

"Should you call a cab? Maybe one of the boys can drive you. You look like death warmed over."

"The boys need to keep working on the play structure. It needs to be finished before Dennis's family comes to visit." If he was awake by then.

She struggled to keep her eyes open on the short drive.

And failed.

She woke up to someone banging on the window of her car.

She blinked and looked around. Matt Brown was banging on her window, a rough grin on his face.

"Hazel, wake up." He pounded the glass.

It took a moment to reorientate herself. Her car had stalled, half on the road, half in the ditch. She must have dozed off. Thank the Goddess she drove a standard. It must have stalled when she fell asleep and took the pressure off the accelerator. Good thing she didn't drive an automatic, she might have ended up in the trees. In a bad way.

Brown tried the handle of her door.

Hell no!

No way was she letting him into her car. And how the hell had he known she was here. Again, the odds were staggering that he'd be the first to arrive.

"I'm fine. Go away," she shouted.

He tried the handle again.

Nope. Not happening.

Her old car had quirks, the driver's door would open from the inside, even though it was locked. She'd meant to have it looked at but had forgotten. Good thing too.

"Let me help you," Brown said, an oily smile on his face.

As sensitive as she was to the feelings of others, she could feel his eager glee.

No. F'ing way.

He released the handle for a second.

She grabbed the inner handle, gave it a yank and slammed the door into him with all her strength. It made a mighty crack against his head and he dropped to the ground.

Careful not to hit him, or his vehicle, she restarted hers and backed out of the ditch. Luckily, she wasn't stuck. She slammed into first and stomped on the accelerator.

A hundred yards down the road, she glanced in the rearview mirror. Brown was still on the ground unmoving. Good. As happy as she was to escape, part of her was upset she might have hurt him. Maybe he'd been trying to help.

Nope. He'd been committed to harm; malicious intention had rolled off him in waves. She was still sickened at experiencing his ugliness. She pulled over, opened her door and puked onto the road.

Their yard gates opened before she got there and Hazel careened through them, fishtailing on the corner, narrowly missing the left gate. Heart pounding, she barreled up the driveway, slid to a crooked stop, jumped out and raced for the house. The cats scattered at her approach, meowing their distress and abandoning their guard posts on the porch.

The front door opened itself and after she thundered through, slammed shut.

"Gramma Pearl?" she hollered from her knees, gasping to regain her breath.

"What?" Pearl raced into the room from the kitchen. "What happened? I heard your distress long before you got here."

Breathlessly, Hazel spewed out her story. Her grandmother helped her stand and with an arm around Hazel's shoulders led her to the kitchen table before she bustled around putting on the kettle.

"Text the mayor, and Leticia. Let them know what happened. This isn't right. Something has to be done about that man," her grandmother demanded as she worked.

Calmed now that she was in the safety of her home's protective magic, Hazel's heartrate started to settle. She shot off some texts and Lazuli exploded through the kitchen door. "What's wrong?" she blurted.

Sometimes, having an empathic, nearly psychic sister was a blessing.

The phone rang.

"That's Amber," Laz said.

Within minutes, the mayor, Leticia and the entire family were gathered around the kitchen table, trying to figure out what to do.

"Sorry I'm late," Leticia said. "I had to wait for the ambulance. Brown was still unconscious when I arrived." She shrugged. "I have to do my job, no matter what I believe. Although I can tell you this, I'll be making a report to the witch's council and demanding a full investigation. Unfortunately, he didn't commit a conventional crime and I have no proof he committed a magical one." She held up a hand to silence the group's objections.

"I know. He's as guilty as the Salem witch hunters. We all know it. But without evidence, the witch council won't do anything. I've reported my suspicions and Hazel needs to file a complaint. Magical law enforcement isn't much different than regular law enforcement."

Hazel banked the scream clawing at her throat. Being pissed off wouldn't help. Still, she felt twitchy, like she needed to do something, or hit someone.

Pearl slid a tray of her famous pineapple cookies onto the table. Hazel snatched one up and bit into it. Instantly, she felt calmer. These little tidbits of sugary delight only came out when things were super stressful. These cookies, like Pearl's energy balls contained more than good wishes. Pearl put a lot of extra magic into them, and they helped bring calm to whoever ate them.

Some of the panicked pressure eased from Hazel's chest. "Thanks, Gramma. I needed these." She grabbed another one.

Everyone sipped their tea and nibbled on the calming cookies. Pearl slid a large plate of normal cookies onto the table. Everyone munched as they debated the next course of action and how to protect Hazel and her family.

A deep groan came from the doorway. Hazel jerked around to see what it was.

Dennis stood there, wobbling on his feet. "What happened?" He groaned again. "What's going on? How did I get here?" The questions dribbled out, his exhaustion evident.

Hazel leaped to her feet and threw her arms around him. "Thank the Goddess, you're okay." She plastered little kisses all over his face. "You are okay, aren't you?"

"Yeah. I think. I need to sit down." He teetered, nearly knocking them both over.

"Come on. Sit. We'll get you some food." With Hyacinth's help, she managed to get Dennis to the table and safely seated.

Pearl gave him tea, a large glass of water and made him a sandwich. Like casting magic, being the victim of black magic left you hungry. The body consumed enormous amounts of energy fighting the unnatural state.

Hazel sat beside Dennis, one arm around his shoulders, her other hand stretched across her body to clutch his hand. She was almost sick with relief. Her body trembled and she got lightheaded thinking about the possibility of Dennis not recovering and thinking about her own near miss accident and Brown's untimely arrival.

Slowly, her voice shaking, Hazel related everything that had happened since they'd had their dinner date. Dennis devoured his sandwich while she talked. Surely his hunger was a sign he was fully out from under the spell.

"What the hell?" Dennis exploded, spewing sandwich crumbs all over the table. "How does shit like this happen? How can people not know what was going on?"

Hazel's heart sank. This was it. He'd dump her now for sure. Her heart stuttered, and her breath stuck in her throat as an invisible band of fear tightened around her chest.

Chapter Twenty-Three

"What do we do now? How do we stop this son of a bitch?" He slammed his fist on the table. He'd meant to make the room jump, to demonstrate his anger, but his hand landed like a toddler's. *Damn, he was weak.*

How long had he been out? It felt like days. Sometimes, he'd been aware of the people around him, sitting by his bed. He'd tried, more than once, to reach out to them but couldn't struggle past the black fog clouding his mind.

"How long was I out?"

"A day and a half. It's one thirty, Tuesday." Hazel told him.

"Shit. The store." Great, not only was he the victim of a magic attack, but his business was also in danger too.

"It's okay." Hazel rubber her fingers along his arm. "I borrowed your keys and opened up. I pretended you were sick and took over as boss." She grinned at him. "Everything is okay. They know to call me if they need anything."

"And they went along with that?"

"I sort of lied and said I found you sick when I went into the house for work, and you told me what to do." Her blush was adorable.

"That's fine. Thanks." Damn he was feeble. "I'm as weak as a baby kitten. I've got a headache like a five-alarm hangover." Another need surfaced. "Where's the washroom?" He struggled to get to his feet. "Crap." He dropped back into his chair.

Hazel and her sister helped him stand and led him to the bathroom just off the kitchen. He tried to ignore them waiting just outside the door. When he managed to stagger, with their help, back to the table, there was a plate of cookies and little balls on the table in front of his chair.

"Eat those," Pearl demanded. "I'll make some real food."

He glanced at them and then at Hazel. "Energy balls and calming cookies."

"Magic food?" he asked warily. He'd had enough of magic. Was there anything in this family's life that wasn't magicked to hell and back?

"Relax," Lazuli, advised. "They won't hurt you. The balls will pep you up, help you get back on your feet and the cookies will take the edge off your stress.

He eyed them warily but didn't pick one up.

"It's okay," Hazel said. "I swear on my life, they won't hurt you."

Something in her eyes, her eager but calming expression, told him he could trust her. Battling reluctance, he picked up a ball and bit into it. It was delicious. He gobbled it down. After only seconds, he felt stronger.

"That's weird," he mumbled around the last bite. "I feel better." He looked around the table at the tolerant grins. "Do you guys put magic in all your food?" Too late, he realized how judgmental the question sounded. "Sorry. I worded that wrong."

"We'll let this one go, for now," the mayor said with a chuckle. "You've had some shocks. It'll take a while for you to regain your balance." She paused. "And your manners."

"Thanks." He gobbled the rest of the treats, no longer caring that they were magic.

"To answer your question," said Hazel, "No, we don't put magic in everything. Those are, or rather were, for special circumstances only. We try not to rely on magic unless we have to."

His ex had used magic for everything she could. If there was a magic way to do things, she used it. These people were so different. He hadn't stayed with Natalia after he realized how weird her magic had gotten. Hazel and her family didn't seem like Natalia had been at all. She didn't seem to feel the effects of her magic like the Hawks did. But then, she'd eaten like a horse all the time. Maybe she was constantly fueling up.

"Is Natalia still around?" he asked.

"I haven't seen her," Hazel said. "I didn't see her with Brown earlier, but I didn't exactly stop to look for her either."

Hazel looked thoughtful.

"If I had to venture a guess, I'd say she was still around. She was way too cozy with Brown for it to be a coincidental meeting. They're up to something."

Everyone agreed. Especially Dennis. His ex was no good. She had an evil side a mile wide.

The longer he sat at the table, the more he ate, and the longer he was awake, the better Dennis felt. He was regaining his strength and his head was clearing. "I feel almost human."

"If it's okay," Hyacinth said, "we'd like to examine you, and have the doctor examine you to see if you're clear of magic now, and to see if we can figure out what spell was used. Half the battle in magic is in knowing the right counter spell."

"Doctor?" *What doctor?*

"Doctor Carter. She's a friend of the magic community. We had her examine you when you first fell asleep. There wasn't anything she could do." Hyacinth's voice was calming, like she was calming a skittish child. "I think it's important we give you the best once-over we can."

Hell yes. After having an ex who prodded his brain and being under a stupid sleeping spell, he wanted to be sure he was free of magic.

The doctor came to the house and examined him from head to toe in one of the bedrooms. Finally, she announced him fit. Leticia and Hyacinth inspected him as well before leaving the room for a few minutes. When they came back, Hazel was with them.

She dragged a chair up to the bed he sat on and took his hands.

"Listen, you're healthy. But there is lingering darkness. It looks like traces of dark magic, and, honestly, we don't know what long term effects they could have on you. There is speculation among the magical medical community that dark magic remains might be one of the causes of cancer."

She held up a warning hand, stilling the objection he was about to make.

"It's just speculation at this point. From what the doctor says, they've started studying it, but it's not exactly easy to find participants in a study like that." She squeezed his fingers and looked up at him.

Her eyes were dark and solemn, lacking their usual spark.

"Hyacinth is a healer. She believes, and I trust her completely, she can remove the remaining mess so it can't affect you anymore."

"What does that mean?" He sure as hell didn't want to wander around with dark magic having free reign in his body. But how, exactly did they get rid of it?

"Remember when we did the spell to ward your house? It's similar. But instead of casting protective magic, Cynth will use her magic to bind and remove the negativity left behind from the spell. It won't hurt. You won't feel anything, except maybe some relief when it's gone."

"How does she do it?" This sounded like a bad idea all the way around, but he didn't feel like he had much of a choice. He certainly didn't want cancer if he could avoid it.

Hyacinth stepped into the room to stand behind Hazel. "I'll touch you, with my mind and my hands. I can't really explain how it works. I don't understand it myself. I just do it. With my mind." She shrugged. "Think of it as sweeping a room. I'll sweep your body, gather up the dirt and get rid of it."

That was the craziest thing he'd ever heard. Total insanity.

He was equally intrigued and terrified.

"Where does it go? The negativity, the bad magic?" Was it like conservation of energy? It couldn't be created or destroyed? Where did it go? A thousand questions plagued him.

"I don't know," Hazel said. "But once, when I was a kid. I was sick. I got the chicken pox and three weeks later, I was still down and out. Cynth didn't have her skills yet, but my mom called my aunt. A healer. She came and did her thing and I got better almost overnight."

"Wow." He'd heard of miracle healers but chalked them up to a scam.

"You're right," Cynth said. "There is a balance we can't or rather shouldn't tinker with. A balance between good and evil. Dark and light. Everything needs balance. My way of dealing with the dark of illness, which is balanced by health, is to envision myself sweeping all the icky stuff together. Exactly like sweeping a floor. Only instead of sweeping it into a dustpan and throwing it away, I sweep it closer together. I imagine it getting smaller and smaller, until it disappears altogether. I'm not willing it to be anything other than it is, I'm just willing it gone. You've heard of cancer patients who will their sickness away? It's like that." She had a resigned look on her face as if knowing he'd refuse, or he'd laugh at her.

"Crap on a cracker. Half of me thinks you guys are bat crap crazy. The other half almost believes you." What did he have to lose? They seemed sincere.

He closed his eyes and breathed slowly for a few minutes. Focusing on everything he'd learned or suffered through with his ex, he also reviewed what he'd read on magic since meeting Hazel. Witches magically cleaned a room's energy in a similar fashion. Hell, they'd done it at his house without ill effect. He considered her family, their behavior and how they'd taken care of him.

Three Moon Falls was wary of them, but overall, they had a solid reputation.

Then there was Hazel. He couldn't help himself. He wanted to keep his distance, but they kept getting closer together. He was half in love with her already. And, unless he missed his guess, she was falling for him too.

He opened his eyes and stared into Hazel's pleading eyes and for a second, he thought he could see his heart, his destiny.

He banked a mental eyeroll. Romantic claptrap. That's all it was. Physical chemistry.

Hazel squeezed his hand again and he capitulated.

"All right. Let's do this. I sure as hell don't want cancer."

Hazel leaped at him, wrapping him in her arms and knocking him backward on the bed, her body on top of his. "You won't regret this."

Her lips brushed his. Suddenly, he was kissing her back, lost in the sweet, sugary taste of her mouth. He pulled her closer, deepening the kiss. If anything went wrong, he wanted to take this memory and her taste with him.

Someone clearing their throat and giggling brought him back to reality.

The ritual started the same as the one at his home only this time, they called different deities. Hygieia, Airmed, Lugh, Asclepius. Dennis hadn't heard of any of them, but that wasn't surprising. Hazel told him, before they started, they would call healing gods this time.

Circle cast, stones laid, candles lit, Dennis lay down in the center of a nearly circular room upstairs in the Hawk home. The family, and their friends, gathered around him holding hands and chanting.

The air thickened, then thinned. A soft breeze blew through the room, ringing a small windchime hanging from the ceiling. Hyacinth knelt beside him. "Close your eyes and try to relax."

Relax. Right.

She held his hand and talked to him. Explaining where she would touch. Her words were comforting. Like his mother's had been when he was sick as a child. Slowly, his apprehension fled. When he was relaxed, on the verge of sleeping she started.

Her hands ran slowly up and down his arms, across his shoulders and chest. Back and forth. Up and down. She touched him with light, massage like strokes. As she moved, he felt tension dissipate from his limbs. By the time she was finished touching his entire body, he felt lighter. Freer. It was like a massage, but more.

Finally, Hyacinth declared herself finished. They broke up the circle and headed to the kitchen to refuel.

He was surprised to learn the healing ritual had taken over half an hour. The family and friends had stood there, by his side, chanting lowly and singing for the entire time. He was touched they'd stick by him. He was a virtual stranger in their world.

Still, after his experiences with Natalia, he couldn't shake a lingering unease. Sure, the magic was cool. Beyond anything he'd ever experienced but it frightened him as well.

Was this what life with witches was going to be like? Magic, good and bad, happening all the time? If so, he wasn't sure he wanted any part of it. Even if Hazel was awesome.

He rubbed his chest, trying to sooth away sudden heartburn and the anxiety lodged there, chasing away his earlier calm.

How could he care so much for Hazel, knowing she was a witch and possessed these sorts of skills and probably some he'd never imagined?

Images, memories, flashed through his head. Hazel interviewing Sarah, putting her at ease, asking her about her children. Hazel's kindness with staff and customers. The way she muddled through things she found difficult. Her dedication to work. The way she shared her food with him. Her cautiously walking with him in the creek, despite her fear of the water. The way his heart pounded when she was close. How delicious her kisses were and how deeply they'd reached into his soul.

Natalia's duplicity. Brown's evilness.

So many memories, most of them good.

Hazel might be a witch, but she was a good person. That had to count, right?

Chapter Twenty-Four

"I don't know what to do," Dennis said to Bert as they leaned on Jellybean's paddock.

"What do you mean? She's doing great. You just said she rarely faints at all now. The kids love her." He gave Dennis a quizzical look.

"Not with the drama llama. With Hazel."

"What about her? She's hot, right?"

"Yes."

"I'm sensing a great big but in there somewhere."

"Her butt is not big," Dennis joked, but the joke fell flat.

"Dude," Bert complained.

"Beer?"

Bert studied him. "I should get home. I've got chores. But yeah, I can spare time for one."

They walked in silence to the house, through the kitchen where they grabbed some brews and headed out onto the deck. There, with their feet up on the railing, Dennis found the courage to speak.

"It's like this," he started, hoping his friend wouldn't think he'd lost his mind. "I hired Hazel. She's great. I like her. A lot." When Bert nodded, he went on, telling the entire story of his life since Hazel entered it. He hesitated briefly before spewing out the magic parts, but Bert was one of the most open-minded people he'd ever met.

"My little sister has started reading about magic. She studies magic, not sleight of hand. She claims it's real. Maybe she's right."

"No maybes about it," Dennis declared. "It's the realest, scariest shit I've ever seen. Shit that would make your hair curl."

"What's the problem, aside from being freaked out?"

Leave it to Bert to hit the nail on the head.

"What do I do?" It was the simplest question he could muster. What did he do about Hazel, about knowing magic was real, about the bastard he'd hired and how to get rid of him? Brown needed to be locked up in the Hawk's damn magical jail.

"Walk away from it all." Again, curt and to the point.

"What if I can't?" Another minimalist question with far too many meanings.

"Then don't." Bert scrubbed a hand over his face. "Honestly, dude. I can't believe most of what you're saying. It's like some damned episode of *Charmed*. Fantasy. A B-grade movie. I don't know." He glugged the rest of his beer. "I'm gonna need another beer to swallow all this crap."

Dennis finished his drink and grabbed a couple more. He threw some burgers in the microwave to thaw. He wasn't about so send a friend home on an empty stomach after two beer. Likely, Bert would crash here and get his neighbor to check in on his place.

Back on the deck, Dennis struggled to organize his thoughts.

"She's not like Natalia." Not even close. "She's nice."

"I told you to stay away from her. She's a witch." Bert shook his head in disgust.

"I know. I tried. Something about her just pulls me in. She's a good person. Kind. She makes me happy. But the whole witch thing. I swore I'd never get involved with another one."

"That lasted a long time, didn't it?" Bert had never cut him any slack when his dating life went awry.

"Yup. Days. Not even. But there is just something...I don't know. She's irresistible."

"Magic?"

Dennis considered the idea and discarded it. "I'd say no. Definitely not. It's more chemistry." He sounded like an idiot. Why were they even having this conversation?

"Bang her and get it done with. Burn off that chemistry. Do her and move along."

He leaped to his feet. "What the hell? I will not bang her and move along. She's not like that. She's a long term, maybe forever, type of woman. The kind you make your wife." He dropped to his seat stunned by his explosion.

"Dude! You are gone. Give it up. Date her. Keep an open mind. What can go wrong? I mean besides getting your mind probed and being put under a sleeping spell. Suck it up and try, sleeping beauty."

"You did not just call me sleeping beauty," Dennis laughed.

"Well, if the nap fits."

They laughed together.

"This is supposed to be a serious discussion," Dennis complained.

"We discussed it. I heard your story. You like her. I told you last time I was here. Take a chance on her. Despite my ex and yours being bitches, good women are out there and if you like Hazel, take a chance. See how it goes. And if you end up under another sleeping spell, maybe

Prince Charming will kiss you awake." His outrageous comment had them both laughing.

"I swear to god, I have no idea why I'm still friends with you," Dennis declared as his mirth faded.

Bert was right. He was in up to his neck. Hazel's kisses and touches made him feel alive. Why not follow and see where it went? He was half gone on her already.

Chapter Twenty-Five

Hazel skipped through the garden center after work on Saturday. She had a dinner date with her boss. She'd worried he might distance himself after their ritual, but he hadn't. They'd even shared a few kisses in the office. She was trying hard to separate business and pleasure, but she really liked Dennis. More than liked him.

She might even, her mind whispered the word, love him. The idea made her giddy.

Too bad she didn't dare tell him or let herself get much closer until they dealt with Brown. It had been nearly two weeks since Brown had attacked. Released from the hospital and recovered from the head wound she'd given him, he'd disappeared. Too bad he hadn't taken Dennis's ex, Natalia, with him. The woman was getting on Hazel's last nerve.

She rounded a corner, past a display of miniature lemon and orange trees.

"Hey, good looking." Dennis snagged her around the waist and nibbled her neck.

"No public displays of affection," she reminded him before turning in his arms to devour his mouth. After a single kiss, she pulled reluctantly out of his arms. "I was just heading home to change. Where do you want to go for dinner?"

"How about we save time and have dinner at my place? I can whip up something quickly and there's salad in the fridge." He clasped her hand and led her toward the back exit. "I'd like to eat and then show you my private greenhouse."

"Why Mr. Belanger, are you inviting me up to see your etchings?" She batted her eyes like a classical movie heroine.

"Why yes, Miss Hawk, I believe I am." He winked and pushed open the door. "And don't worry about changing your clothes, you won't be in them for long."

"Is that a fact?" She burst into laughter at his audacity. "Pretty confident, aren't you?" Especially since beyond a bit of necking and heavy petting, they'd never...

"Call it cautiously optimistic." He slung his arm around her shoulder. "Or maybe hopeful."

"Life is nothing without hope. And dreams. Dream on, Dennis, dream on." She laughed and he joined in, the deep rumble rolling across her skin, raising goosebumps. The man had the greatest laugh.

He was probably right. It wasn't going to be long before they ended up together. She wasn't one to sleep around but her heart was fully into this relationship. She worried a bit over the inevitable, because taking the final step to intimacy would bring them closer, and until Brown was dealt with, she wasn't sure it was a good idea. Her heart was screaming for her to take the next step, but her mind knew better. Men like Keres and Brown would stop at nothing to get what they wanted. Keres was out of the picture; Brown was another problem altogether.

"I think," she stopped walking and pivoted to look at him, "I'd like dinner in town. Nothing fancy. Just a nice meal and then I'd love to come back and see your greenhouse." She tried not to sound pleading. If they went straight to his place and ate, she wasn't sure she could resist him. She'd end up in his bed having way more fun than she should.

His disappointed look bothered her.

She placed a hand on his forearm. "It's not because I'm not interested in your etchings. I am. Very much so. I'm worried we're taking this too fast. There's a lot of crap going on and I can't fight the idea Brown is due to show up any day. I can't believe he hasn't already. People like him don't give up that easily."

"Not sleeping with you isn't going to stop me from caring about you." He scratched his forehead. "Honestly, I'm just as worried as you are. I don't trust Brown or Natalia and I still want to know why they were together. But..." he waggled a finger under Hazel's nose, "I'm not going to let them stop me from living my life."

He slung his arm around her waist and puller her to his side. She nestled into his warmth and leaned on him. Damn he smelled delicious. He smelled...kissable.

"Come on then," he said. "Let's go to dinner. Where would you like to eat?"

"Just like that, you're giving in?"

"I'm not a sex crazed idiot. If you want a restaurant, that's what you'll get."

A rush of pleasure ran through her. How could she not like a man who considered her wants and needs ahead of his own? Dennis Belanger was a keeper for sure. Suddenly, she wanted to stay home with him.

"Let's grab a pizza and eat here instead," she capitulated.

Half an hour later, she was sitting on his sofa, feet on the coffee table, delicious, ooey gooey pizza in her hand.

"It was so busy today, I didn't have a second to ask, how's the book search going? Find anything new?" He bit into his pizza.

"Oh my gosh! Yes! Last night we found a reference to Chickadee Falls, that's the smallest one. It was quite vague; you wouldn't even pick up on it without knowing the landscape. It's a poem, written by one of the first Hawks to settle here. But not when she first arrived, in her last grimoire. I checked our family tree, she died later the same year."

"Oh, that's terrible."

Hazel shrugged. She didn't want to seem insensitive. Every life was valuable, but her ancestor had been dead since 1890, only four years after she settled here. "She left a lot of good information behind for us. I feel like I know her after reading so many of her entries. The clue is not enough to figure out what she hid, but obviously it was something and it's near the falls." Hazel recited the poetic entry from the grimoire.

"That's pretty vague."

"Not so much if you know the falls on our land as well as we do."

"You mentioned you can call your ancestors; can you ask her?"

"It's not that easy. The longer ago a person passed, the harder they are to reach and the greater the need has to be. Nobody is in imminent danger. Yet. There's also a risk in calling the long dead back. Plus, we never know if she was reincarnated. There are a billion factors to consider. For now, it's not worth the risk or effort." She chewed her pizza thoughtfully. "We're going to have to keep reading, though it's doubtful there'll be another entry."

"Don't give up. Maybe you can fully decipher the clues better. Or perhaps someone else has read her journal and dug up whatever she hid."

He had a point. She'd spent hours reading old grimoires, even before this crisis. She loved reading her great-great-grandmother's entries.

She'd been a ghost talker, just like Hazel and had had some hilarious encounters.

"**N**ow we've eaten, are you going to show me your green-house?" Hazel asked, shocking Dennis. He'd been certain she'd forget. Accidentally or on purpose. His passion wasn't hers; even if she'd let him blather on endlessly about his attempts to breed a pink striped daisy.

"I'll probably just bore you." He couldn't wait to show her what he was doing but didn't want to seem selfish. Despite the issues hound-ing Hazel, and potentially himself, he was interested in developing a relationship with her. Thinking about it astounded him. Only weeks ago, he didn't even want her on his property. Now he wanted her in his life.

"I love plants. Don't think I haven't noticed how healthy the plants you sell are. Initially, I thought you might have some plant magic." She laughed lightly. "But I've concluded it's just your love for growing things coming through. Most of your staff seem to have the same passion." She carried her plate to the kitchen, forcing him to follow her with his and the leftovers. "Show me your plants, please."

For a second, his brain blipped, and he heard show me your pants, and his mind nose-dived into the gutter. He was going to have to get a grip on his wayward libido if he wanted to respect her need to go slow.

"Sure." He tried to sound calm, but inside, he felt like he'd just hit a home run. He resisted the urge to thrust his fists in the air and shout. Instead, he said, "Grab a jacket, the wind's come up. I don't want you to get a chill. If you didn't bring one, use one of mine."

Two minutes later, he took a deep breath and led her through the outer door to his private greenhouse. We can leave our jackets here." He hung their jackets on a couple nails.

"Two doors?" She looked up at him, questions in her eyes.

"Yup. Keeping as much outside contamination down as I can. Typically, this type of work would be done in a lab. Sterile conditions and all that. I'm not a breeder, so I'm not stressed if something funky happens. Just be cautious. There are bees inside. They help with the pollination in each area." He opened the second door and urged her through.

"We won't be in here long. Just a few minutes."

"Why?" she asked. "Don't you want to show me?"

Wow. She'd hit the nail right on the head with that one. He wanted her to see his work. But what if she was like Natalia, dismissing it as unmanly or a waste of time.

"Wow. Dennis, these are incredible." She stood, hands clutched to her chest, staring at the rows of pink daisies. They're so healthy." She reached out with a hand and froze. "Can I touch them? I won't spoil anything will I?"

Exhilaration rocked him and nudged away his worries. This woman didn't think his hobby wasn't worth pursuing. She looked enthralled and her beauty put the flowers to shame. "Go ahead, touch them. Just avoid the centers. I've got other varieties in separate sections." He waved at several, smaller, plastic cordoned off areas.

"Right. Cross contamination."

God, he adored her enthusiasm and understanding.

"Isn't this usually done by gene blending, or something?"

"Usually. But I'm no geneticist, and I don't have a laboratory. I like the hands-on approach. Working with the plants and the soil it..."

She looked at him with understanding. "It feeds your soul. It's calming and exhilarating all at once." She raised an eyebrow.

"True." She really did understand his passion.

She ran a finger down the petal of the largest blossom. "So pretty."

Yes, she was. Her pleasure, her vitality floored him. He stepped closer. "Any questions?"

"Only one." She turned to face him, stepping closer until their bodies almost touched.

He could smell her light lemony scent, it snuck into his heart nearly stealing his breath. Her gaze caught his. "What's that?" he responded at last, remembering she had a question.

"Are you ever going to kiss me?"

Oh, hell yeah!

He placed his hands on her arms, just above her elbows and slid his hands up to her shoulders. Her skin was like silk beneath his palms. His hands were rough from all the outdoor work; he hoped he didn't scratch her delicate skin. Cupping her face between his palms, he leaned closer. Not quite touching her lips with his. He waited for a sign, any sign, she wasn't interested. Yes, she'd asked for this, but he wasn't going to push it, just in case she changed her mind.

Before he realized what was happening, her lips brushed his, stealing his breath and his sanity. He yanked her to him, ravishing her mouth with his. He explored her arms, her back, her hips, with his hands. He wanted her. With every fiber of his being. But not here. In his home. In his bed. She deserved better than a romp in a dirty greenhouse.

Her hands yanked at his shirt sending buttons flying. Her hands burned a trail across the skin of his abdomen, around to his back before delving lower. When they touched his backside, he was lost. Nothing had ever felt this perfect, not even his passion for flowers.

She reached inside him and touched his heart, crumbling the walls he'd built to protect himself.

Chapter Twenty-Six

"Holy. Wow." Hazel almost stuttered the words. Her heart pounded and her lungs struggled to suck in air. That was incredible. Dennis was an amazing lover.

"Yeah, wow."

Wow didn't even cut it. Making love to Dennis had blown her mind. She didn't even care that she was on her back, atop his shirt, naked on the floor of the greenhouse. She was a nature girl at heart but...

"Are you okay?" He lifted himself off her, kneeling between her thighs. "I shouldn't have..."

To her surprise, he blushed.

"Hey," she reached up to caress his cheek. "I started it." She winked. "Although I hadn't intended this." She waved generally, to include them both and the greenhouse. "But I have to say it again. Wow. Good thing you were prepared."

"No kidding." He helped her to her feet and gently brushed the dirt off her back.

His arms stole around her, his hands locking against her belly. He was scalding hot against her back.

"We should get dressed," he whispered against her neck.

His breath was hot, his mouth hotter. Damn. She could go again. When had she ever felt like that? Never. There was something special about Dennis which touched her inside.

"Yeah, we should. I feel a bit exposed."

The sun was sinking, but there was still plenty of daylight and anybody walking past could see them. Not that there should be anyone on his property. Her mind skittered to Brown and Natalia.

"What is it?" He turned her to face him. "You went rigid."

"Nothing. I just...what if..." She sighed. She was ruining the mood.

"I know where your mind went." He bent and picked up her shirt and helped her put it on. Once she was dressed, he slipped into his own clothing. "Let's get back inside."

"I want to see the rest of your work."

"Another time. We're hot, we're sweaty and I'm not finished yet. Let's get inside and cleaned up."

"Oh no. Look." She pointed to a couple of plants they must have knocked from the table. "They're bruised." She picked up one and set it back in its place, tamping the dirt down in its pot. Dennis picked up another. It only took minutes to restore order.

She looked at them. They weren't badly injured but could use some healing magic to help them mend. She wasn't much of an herbalist, but she knew what to do.

All around them, the energy, the power of their lovemaking, lingered. She closed her eyes and gathered it together and channeled it into a healing spell directed at the plants. It wasn't an instantaneous spell; the magic would take time. It wouldn't heal entirely; it just gave a boost to help the plants along.

"What was that?" Dennis looked around. "I felt something."

Hazel couldn't stop the heat from stealing into her face. She hadn't expected him to notice the change in the air's energy. She closed her eyes. Might as well confess. "I took the energy in the air and turned it into a healing spell."

"What energy?" he sounded as puzzled as he looked.

"When people have sex—"

"Make love," he interrupted quietly.

"When people make love, the energy they create lingers in the area until it is used. I channeled it into a spell. A healing spell and sent it to the plants we damaged." She looked down at the floor. She understood his restrictions against magic. She should have asked.

"It's that easy?"

His question surprised her. She'd expected objections, if not outright anger. Maybe there was hope for him after all.

"Not easy, exactly. But it's something I can do. Part of my heritage. I'm sorry for magicking without asking first. I broke my promise." She looked up at him, hoping he'd understand. "I couldn't stand to see them hurting from our enthusiasm." She smiled weakly.

He looked at the plants, then back at her. "I don't see a difference."

"It's not healing, exactly, more just giving them the energy so they could heal." She shrugged; magic wasn't always easy to explain. "It's kind of like how your love of plants, your passion, helps you grow better plants than someone who doesn't care or is apathetic."

"Cool. Thanks." He smiled. "Is this energy there after every..."

"Always, sometimes more than others. The more energy and emotion expended, the more there is just floating around." He nodded as if he understood. "I don't always channel it, you shouldn't. There's a balance. But in rare cases, you can turn the energy toward something special."

"Sounds complicated. How do you keep all these magic rules straight?"

She chuckled. "Sorry, I'm not laughing at you. You're right. There are a billion rules. Spoken and unspoken. When you live with magic, from the day you were born, you absorb them like breathing. Like learning table manners by watching your parents. Manners from hearing them. Specific things are taught, but there's a lot of just picking things up by example."

He looked thoughtful. He slung his arm over her shoulder. "Enough magic lessons for now. Thanks for caring for my plants. Let's get back inside."

His gratitude embraced her like a warm embrace. Standing between the entry doors, he helped her into her jacket, like a gentleman. It was nice to be pampered. She could get used to his little kindnesses. And his lovemaking. She'd felt so cherished, so adored.

"You shower first," he said once they reached the house. "I'll make you a snack. You probably expended some of your own energy with your spell. I can't have you getting too tired on me."

She headed down the hallway toward the bathroom.

"Let's take tomorrow off and go to the lake. There are some wildflowers on the island, and I want to collect some seeds."

She froze. The island? Across the lake? Over that massive body of water? Being in a boat fed her biggest fear.

"You have life jackets?" she voiced her anxiety.

"No. But the boat rental place does."

Reluctantly, she agreed, hoping she wouldn't regret it.

Chapter Twenty-Seven

Hazel climbed out of the boat and dropped to her knees on the island's sandy shore. Every inch of her body ached from sitting tense and unmoving on the ten-minute boat trip. Why in the world had she ever agreed to come here? Her hands ached from clutching the seat and it had been all she could do not to barf. Only panic induced terror had kept her from leaping from the boat.

"Are you okay?" Dennis asked after he'd tied the boat to a nearby tree. "You're as white as a sheet." He held out his hand to assist her up.

She accepted the help and rose, unsteadily to her feet. "I'm good. I just wasn't expecting the trip to be so rough." By normal standards, it hadn't been bad, just a little choppy in the earlier breeze. Dennis looked like he didn't believe her. "Honestly, I'm fine. Let's find those plants and eat the picnic you brought."

Food in her stomach might not be the smartest idea she'd ever had. But she'd skipped breakfast, unsure how her body would treat a lake crossing and her biggest fear. Water. How could she be scared of water? She was a water witch, for Pete's sake. She sighed. Nearly drowning as a kid hadn't done her any favors mentally.

"Come on then, if you're sure you're okay. Let's pick some seeds so we can picnic in the sun. The wind blew away the clouds. It's beautiful out here."

It was lovely. Sunny. Not too hot. And the further away from the water she got, the better she felt. "What are the seeds for? Can you legally collect them here?"

"This isn't a provincial park, it's private land. I have permission to gather here if I do so responsibly."

"I thought this was crown land. Kids party here all the time."

"The owner's pretty forgiving. He has the party mess cleaned up occasionally. He inherited the property from a relative. I found him through a land database. He has a cabin on the far side of the island but rarely uses it. I gather he's a bit of a hermit. Anyway. We have permission and shouldn't be bothered." He paused to look at her. "So, if you wanted to wander around topless," he waggled his eyebrows.

She laughed. "Good luck with that, plant guy. Dream on."

The idea was tempting but she wasn't going to let him know. She loved the feel of the sun on her skin and had a bikini top under her shirt, just in case.

"What are the seeds for?" she repeated.

"I'm planning a line of wildflower seeds packets. I've started an online business. Lots of city people want a more natural garden. Native grasses and flowers. I'm hoping to fill that niche and grow my business. Step one is collecting seeds. I'll have to come out several times. Not everything goes to seed at once."

They picked seeds for a couple hours. Each one going into an appropriately labelled envelope. The seeds came from a variety of plants, they were careful never to strip more than a small percentage from each growing cluster. Nature had to be respected.

Hazel leaned against the base of an enormous poplar as Dennis picked seeds from a wild clematis, the seed head looking like something Dr. Seuss would have drawn. Creamy and fluffy, like a dense dandelion. Suddenly chilled, she left the shade of the trees to stand in a patch of sunlight. Despite the sun's warmth, the chill didn't go away.

Pivoting slowly, she searched the undergrowth. If she didn't know better, she'd say someone was watching them.

"You said the guy who owns this island isn't around?"

"Yeah, I guess he has more than one home. He said to feel free to come out anytime."

Knowing the owner was absent deepened her chill. She was certain someone was out there, and her mind eagerly provided two unsavory options. Try as she might, she couldn't spot anyone. In the distance, she heard birds; up close, nothing. Something was disturbing their song.

Wandering in slow circles, she followed some nearby game trails, keeping Dennis in sight, and after a few minutes the birdsong returned and the eerie feeling dissipated. Instead of being relieved, her worry increased. They hadn't been alone. Someone was watching.

"Gosh, it's hot," she complained as they trudged back toward the boat two hours later.

"I've got a perfect picnic spot. Just wait."

Fifteen minutes later, bottles of water in hand, they settled onto a blanket in a clearing, just off the beach. Trees provided just enough shade to cool them off, but not enough to make them cold. A creek ran past their spot, a deep swimming hole in the center. She eyed the water warily. As long as she didn't have to go in it, she'd be fine.

"This is perfect." She sighed, leaning back to study the sky. A red-tailed hawk swooped across the top of the trees and disappeared. Not far away, a crow called. And chickadees tweeted their song all around them.

"I love that, sound," she enthused. "I love the chickadee call. When I was a kid, I called them cheeseburger birds because their swee-dee-dee call sounds like they're saying cheeseburger. Of course, cheeseburgers were my favorite food at the time." She chuckled.

"No cheeseburgers today." Dennis started pulling containers out of the jumbo backpack he'd been carrying all day. "We've got French bread, cheese, ham." He set a container down with each word. "Veggies. Fruit. Cupcakes and chocolate covered strawberries." He made a flourishing motion with his hands, making her laugh. "And the pièce de résistance, champagne!"

She jerked upright. "Holy cow. That's a lot of food and you've been carrying it for hours. I'm impressed."

He leaned back on his hands and grinned. "My work here is done. I've successfully impressed Miss Hazel Hawk, witch extraordinaire."

She snorted. "Hardly, but it does sound like a great lunch."

"You aren't impressed by my forethought and planning?" He clutched his chest. "You wound me." He peeled away the foil and untwisted the champagne wire.

"Oh, I am impressed. Mostly that you toted our lunch all day without complaint. But I'm hardly a witch extraordinaire. More like ordinaire. But I thank you for the compliment."

He popped the top without spilling and filled a plastic flute for each of them. He handed one over. "To you. Hazel Hawk, witch more than ordinaire."

She raised her glass with a chuckle. "And to you Dennis Belanger, daisy breeder extraordinaire." Oh gracious, why had she brought up breeding and daisies? Her mind went right to the previous evening and her body heated. *Oh yeah. She'd definitely like to go there again. Soon.*

Lunch was delicious and the champagne divine. When they finished eating, Dennis cleaned up their containers and stowed them in the backpack. With a little work, he fashioned it into an acceptable, if lumpy pillow for them to share.

Side by side, they lay on their backs. Hand in hand, they chatted as the clouds floated by. "That one looks like a soaring eagle," she exclaimed.

"It's a dragon," Dennis responded sleepily.

She elbowed him lightly. "Is not."

The next thing she knew, he was whispering in her ear. 'Hey, beautiful. Wake up. We should get going. It's nearly five." His breath was warm on her ear. His arm draped over her waist.

"Or maybe you should kiss me." She rolled to face him; still half caught in the steamy dream she'd been having.

"Maybe I should."

Nothing else was said for a long time as they were lost in each other's arms.

"Come on, beautiful." Dennis stood and held out his hand. "Into the water. We can clean off some of our exertion before we head back." He rummaged in the backpack and extracted a towel.

"You came prepared to clean up?" She gawked at him.

"Yes, and no. I always carry a towel. *Hitchhiker's Guide to the Galaxy* ring any bells? Douglas Adams. Seriously. Seed collecting can be messy work. I like to be ready for cleanup if I end up face down in the mud. Prepared for what just happened between us? Just a coincidence. I swear. I wasn't planning on seducing you. Scout's honor." He saluted.

She raised an eyebrow and squinted at him.

"Honest." Well, mostly honest. He hadn't planned a sexual encounter, but he had planned to seduce her heart with food, wine and nature. She was an outdoor girl after all.

"Come on. Let's get washed up."

"I'm good. That water is probably freezing."

"Pretty sure it'll be refreshing after our exertion," he countered. When she finally grasped his hand, he pulled her to her feet.

Naked, they wandered through the grass, across the sand and small rocks to the water. Dennis strode right in, nearly yanking her with him when she stopped abruptly.

"I'll just wash here," she said, planting her feet and shaking her hand free of his.

"The swimming's great in the pool. Join me."

"I'm not much for swimming. You go ahead. I'll wash up and wait on shore." She inched backward, reminding him of her hesitancy to enter the water in the creek behind his house. He'd been right. She was afraid of water. A water witch, afraid of water. How did that even happen?

"The water feels great. It's actually not overly cold. It's refreshing. Come on, Haze. Join me." He wasn't going to force her in, but he'd really enjoy it if she were close beside him. If he was right, maybe he could help her overcome her fears. He loved the water. Swimming. Hot tubs. Long baths. The ocean. All of it. He wanted Hazel to share his joy.

She stood there for several long minutes, her gaze at her toes which were barely in the water. She didn't look up at him, nor did she move. Just when he was certain she'd rush back to land and abandon him, she took a hesitant step forward.

Her skin rose in goosebumps and she shivered.

The water wasn't that cold. He was standing, mid-thigh, in the creek. She looked absolutely, completely, one hundred percent, terrified. He was just about to scoop her up and carry her to shore when she took another timid step forward.

"You're doing great," he whispered, hoping his words didn't spook her.

Her head jerked up revealing a nervous smile. Her eyes flashed with unspoken emotion. Another hesitant step. Before long, she was standing beside him, the water lapping at the base of her belly.

"Whoa, it's really cold there," she exclaimed.

"If you go in deeper, all the way, it feels much warmer." Midnight swimming in the lake was the best. Chilly air, few mosquitos and water still holding the sun's heat. Bliss.

"I don't know. I'm not much of a swimmer."

Her voice trembled. She might not be much of a swimmer, probably due to her fear rather than a lack of skill.

"I'll hold your hand. You can touch the bottom, even in the deepest parts. I swim here whenever I can. Much preferable to a chemically laden pool."

"Pools have lifeguards." Another small step and she slipped her arms around his waist.

She stood there, shivering against him.

"Great job. Come with me. I'll be your lifeguard. Deeper. I'll keep you safe. I won't let you drown."

She jerked back and glared at him. "I'm not afraid."

He kissed her nose. "Liar," he whispered. "It's okay to be scared. We all have our demons, things we have to overcome. Like me. I was terrified of succumbing to magic, and you've taught me that not all magic wielders are bad. You for example," he kissed her again, "are kind and generous and wouldn't hurt a fly."

He ignored the little voice reminding him she'd admitted her guilt in the injury of Keres after he attacked her family. Desperate circumstances, he reminded himself. She wasn't the type of person to hurt people. He knew that, deep in his heart.

And, right now, her vulnerability was wrenching his heart.

"Another step, just a small one," he urged and inched backward.

She went with him, her arms locked around his waist.

Deeper and deeper until he was up to his waist and Hazel was nearly to her breasts. Her nails dug into his back, but he didn't care. Maybe he could get her beyond her fear, if only for a few seconds.

"I'm doing it!" Her voice trembled with fear and exhilaration.

A sharp boom-crack thundered through the air and they jerked apart.

Hazel scrambled toward shore in a blind panic.

Suddenly, she was out of his reach, and under water.

What the hell?

Chapter Twenty-Eight

S he was doing it!

"I'm doing it," she crowed.

She was actually in the water, past her waist and nearly to her neck. She was freaked. But she was doing it with Dennis's help. Maybe, in time, she could overcome her fear completely. One on one help might work. Goddess knows swimming lessons had only exacerbated the problem. They say that facing your fears was the way to defeat them, in her case it had only made them worse when faced with the ridicule of the other kids in her school swimming classes.

Okay, one more step. You can do this, Hazel. You've got this. He's got you.

BOOM!

A shot rang out.

She bolted out of Dennis's arms and scrambled toward shore. Someone was out there; she hadn't been mistaken earlier. Someone was out there, and they had a gun. A high-powered rifle! Shit.

They had to get out of the open!

Her feet skidded dangerously on the slippery rock bottom. Her left foot lurched sideways and jammed under the edge of the adjacent rock. She pitched forward, headfirst into the water.

Everything went dark.

Pressure clutched her chest, squeezing out the air until she sucked in a breath. Water surged in. She gasped again.

More water.

Darkness threatened to steal her.

Submerge her.

Down she went. Frantically searching for the bottom. It wasn't that deep! If she found the bottom, she could push up and out. Regain her feet.

She struggled forward, scrambling against the bottom. Jerking her leg, trying to free her foot. It was wedged painfully.

She forced her eyes open. Nothing except bubbles and muddy water.

She slammed them shut again as darkness began to overcome her. Another gasp.

Why had she listened to him? She was going to die here, in the middle of a stupid creek.

Strong hands grasped her, pulled at her.

She batted them away blindly, panic stealing her logic. She fought with everything left in her. She wouldn't die here!

They grabbed again and suddenly; her head was above water.

"Breathe, Hazel. Dammit. Take a deep breath!"

Dennis shook her. Jarring her from her panic.

She gasped. Sucked in a breath.

Spasms of coughing threatened to knock her back into the water. She struggled against Dennis, frantic to get to shore before she drowned, or the shooter found them.

She scratched and clawed. Fighting with every ounce of her strength.

Suddenly, she was airborne. Lurching crazily, Dennis stumbled toward shore with Hazel in his arms. She nearly wept when her feet touched the ground.

She scrambled away and scurried toward the blanket and her clothing. She had to get out of here. She needed to be home. With her family. Away from this place.

A towel came around her shoulders from behind.

"Hazel, relax. It's going to be okay. Let me dry you off."

Her teeth chattered. She wanted to crawl into a hole and hide until the panic ebbed and she was safe. Coming here was a mistake. Going into the water was pure stupidity. She was trembling too badly to grasp the towel, so she stood helplessly, letting Dennis dry her off.

He helped her into her clothing for the second time in two days. This time, she wasn't enjoying it. His tender motions and caring words bounced off her. Regret at falling for him and listening to his pleas to enter the water angered her. She just wanted out of there. Now.

Chapter Twenty-Nine

"You're going to be okay," Dennis said as he struggled to pull his jeans up his damp legs. He was dressing as fast as he could.

Hazel stood at the edge of the path leading to the boat, her back to him, her arms wrapped around her waist. Her head pivoted around, staring in every direction like a frightened animal. Even from nearly thirty feet away, he could see her trembling. This was all his fault, and he was going to find a way to fix it. Finally dressed, he slammed into his running shoes without untying them.

He grabbed the backpack and blanket and rushed to her side.

"I know it didn't end well, but you should be proud of yourself. You overcame your fear enough to enter water up to your neck." He wrapped the blanket around her shoulders and his arm around her waist.

She tried to shrug him off, but he refused. She was acting out of fear. Her shaking proved she needed comfort and his warmth. After one failed attempt to dislodge him, she stood rigidly inside his arm.

"Didn't end well?" she screeched. "I got my foot stuck, I nearly drowned, again. Somebody was watching us and shooting a damn gun! How is that even close to ending well?" She stopped to jab him in the chest with her index finger. "We could have been shot!"

She had a point.

"Wait! What? What do you mean nearly drowned, again? Again?" Why hadn't she told him that was why she was afraid of water? Never mind. She'd never even admitted she was afraid of water. "Tell me about it. What happened?"

She stormed away and he had to race to catch up. He grasped her by the shoulder and pulled her to a stop.

She whirled around, batting his hands away. "Let go of me!"

He let his arms fall to his sides. "Why didn't you tell me you were afraid of water and you'd nearly drowned?" He tried to catch her eye, but she kept looking away. "I suspected you were afraid, but I never, not even for a second, thought you'd nearly drowned."

"I was ten," she whispered. "We were playing in the water at the base of Chickadee Falls. There's a pool there. I slipped on a rock. I went under and cracked my head on a rock. Mom had to rush in and pull me out. I've never been in deep water since then. Nothing over my knees. I can't. I freeze up."

"You waded with me in the creek by my house."

"Only for a second. I could see and reach the bottom. And you."

He recalled how quickly she'd bolted out of the water. Maybe her running hadn't been only due to his kiss.

"You did well today. Fabulous, until the end. But we're okay. The day ended fine."

"Fine? You call this fine? Soaking wet. Shivering. Terrified to get back in that boat. Not to mention shot at?" Her voice rose with every word.

"Okay, I phrased that wrong. Look at what you achieved. Forget the bad ending."

"I'll never forget. I'll never take a risk like that again. I'm staying out of the water. I don't even want to get in a hot tub again."

So much for his dreams of hot tub sex. He shook off the errant fantasy. He had bigger issues to deal with. He had to get her calmed down before he tried to get her into the boat. It wasn't like he could afford a helicopter to come get them.

She stormed away again, leaving him to follow behind as he searched for the right words.

Jesus. She could have died, and it would have been his fault. And what the hell did she mean someone was watching them? When? How? As far as he knew, they'd been on the island alone. That is until he heard the shot. He wasn't a hunter, but it damn well wasn't hunting season, for anything.

Who was out in the woods, on an island, taking random shots? Or rather a shot. There had only been one. That in itself was suspicious. Not hunting. The other option was sighting in a rifle which took more shots than a single one.

This had to be a warning of some sort.

His mind went to the inevitable conclusion. This was Brown. Or whoever was trying to steal Hazel's power. What if she had drowned? What happened to her power then? Did it just die with her? He had a million questions, none of which were going to be answered until he had her calmed down, across the lake, and home.

If he hadn't dragged her out her to collect seeds, and then into the water, this never would have happened. She wouldn't have had another near drowning incident.

"What made you think someone was watching us?" *And why didn't you tell me and why did we make love with an audience?*

"Early in the day, long before lunch. I sensed something in the woods. At first, I thought it might be an animal, maybe a deer. Or a bear. It wasn't anything concrete. Just that feeling you get that someone's eyes are on you. There weren't any bird sounds near us. Birds go quiet when something unusual is in their area. The sounds came back, the feeling went away."

"You should have told me."

"And let you think I'm crazy. I'm not crazy! Something was out there."

"But we…"

"Yeah. We did." Her voice trembled.

"If you had told me, I wouldn't have…" It should have been safe. A private island. Two lovers. Nature. It should have been perfect. It had been perfect. He felt things with Hazel he'd never felt before. He didn't want to admit it, even to himself, but there was a chance what he felt, this tension and warmth in his heart, it might be love. He was almost afraid to even think it.

"I got caught up in the moment and it felt safe."

"Hazel, I swear, I never would have started something if I even thought there was a chance of someone watching us." Not that it had stopped him in the greenhouse yesterday. Damn. He needed to get a grip on his hormones. His attraction was turning him stupid.

"I could have refused. You'd have stopped. But I was sure we were alone. I wanted it too." She turned to rest her head on his chest.

The small action stole his breath. He'd make all of this right somehow. He hugged her close. "I'm so sorry this happened. I won't force you into the water again. I'll respect your boundaries."

"I have to get back into the boat, don't I?" she asked sadly, burrowing closer.

"Unfortunately, yes. Unless..."

"Unless what?" She looked up at him hopefully.

"Well, you are a witch. Can't you just fly home?" He grinned to show he was joking, trying to lighten the mood.

Her elbow gouged a hole in his ribs. He grunted in pain. "Sorry."

She laughed weakly. "It was funny, sort of." She raised up on her toes and kissed his cheek. "Thanks for trying to make me feel better."

She stepped away from him and scraped her hands through her sodden, messy hair. Even in total disarray, she was beautiful. He wanted to touch her lovely locks. If he had a brush, he'd smooth them for her.

She squared her shoulders as if preparing for battle. "Let's get this over with. No sense delaying the things you don't want to do."

He admired her bravery in the face of her biggest fear. He couldn't help but think that if she was a water witch, she controlled water, didn't that, or rather shouldn't that, make her safe in and around water? He must be missing something.

"Come on, honey." He wrapped his arm around her shoulder. "Let's hit the boat and get home. You'll feel better once you warm up and have a shower."

"I hope you're right." Her arm snuck around his waist and she slid closer.

Chapter Thirty

Hazel and Dennis sat in Corporal Stone's office with the door shut tight against prying ears. No sense letting mundanes in on what was going on. Few were equipped to handle what they'd learn if they did notice the magic around them.

They'd gotten home yesterday and taken a hot shower, but Hazel couldn't seem to warm up. The chill chasing her was more than the result of being doused and nearly drowning. It came from a deep fear that things were going to get worse before they got better. Way worse. Her intuition usually sucked, but she was afraid it was spot on this time.

"I can't prove it was Brown," Hazel said, twisting her hands together. She hated making accusations without proof, but she was certain Brown had fired the shot. "But I'm certain it was him. There have been too many coincidences for me to believe otherwise."

"Wait. That whole sex magic thing, if we released energy, was it magical, could he use it?" Dennis asked.

Hazel leaned into Dennis for the thousandth time in the last two days, seeking comfort in his arms and hoping her nearness would soothe him as well.

"Maybe," she admitted. "It doesn't hang around long. It dissipates quickly. The energy isn't magic, but it can be harnessed to do magic. He'd have to be really close." She shuddered at the idea of anyone watching them make love. Knowing it was Brown creeped her out. She needed another shower to wash away the negative vibes.

Another shower before coming in today hadn't warmed her. "I didn't feel him around after the shot, but honestly, I wasn't at my best. I don't think he was close enough to harness the loose energy. The shot wasn't close, just too close for comfort."

"Good." Dennis hugged her close, tipping his head so his cheek rested on Hazel's forehead. His warmth seeped in, heating her body, but her soul remained chilled.

"Unfortunately, there's nothing I can do without proof. It's your word against his and you don't know for sure. But I'll make a note in the file I'm compiling on him." Stone sucked in a deep breath.

"What?" Hazel asked. Her friend was shooting off negative energy like crazy. She had something on her mind and wasn't comfortable about it. "You're shooting bad vibes." Leticia Stone was usually the epitome of calm rationality. She had a firm grip on her powers and her emotions. She didn't leak strong feelings. She couldn't, not in her position as head of the RCMP detachment.

"I discovered something in a deep search of the mundane and magic databases."

Her tone, and still posture warned Hazel bad news was coming.

"Mathew Brown is probably Keres's son."

Hazel leaped to her feet, her elbow smashing Dennis in the process. She ignored his groan of pain. This was bad. Beyond bad. It was horrific. Was Brown after them for his own purposes, or for revenge, or something else? She hadn't expected Officer Stone to arrest the man without evidence, but she sure as hell wasn't expecting that tidbit of information.

"What?" Hazel stared at the woman across from her.

"Apparently, Keres was married." Stone frowned.

"Yeah, we knew that. Whatever he was after had something to do with his wife. We saw her picture when Amber and I snuck into his house. There was the weird spell too. The one to raise the dead." She shuddered. What kind of fool wanted to reanimate the deceased? Idiocy. And dangerous as hell. She didn't really believe it could be done. The idea terrified her.

"It seems they had a son who had moved away from home long before the wife died. I found an old neighbor who says the son was estranged from Keres. I started following up on the son. He legally changed his name, shortly after he left. Even so, I don't think it's a coincidence that he showed up here so soon after his father's incarceration."

You think? Hardly a coincidence at all.

"It sure as hell isn't," Dennis blurted, echoing Hazel's thoughts.

"No way! What do we do now?" Hazel sank back into her seat and dropped her face into her hands. This was so messed up. If she told her family, they'd lock her in the basement for the rest of her life to keep her safe. Occasionally they still treated her like a child instead of a twenty-three-year-old woman.

But how could she not tell them? They were in as much danger as she was. Holy crap! Amber was trying to get pregnant. No way in hell was Hazel going to let Brown put a baby at risk. She was going to have to solve this. Now.

For a moment, she froze in place. How the hell was she going to defeat someone with enough power to totally hide his magic, his evil intentions, and his emotions? That took skill. More skill than her family possessed, even Gramma Pearl. Leticia had skills too, but even she leaked now and then. How the hell had Brown managed to accumulate enough power to hide everything he was?

By the Goddess, the terror creeping over her was worse than the total panic she'd felt nearly drowning for the second time. What the hell was she going to do? She'd need a plan. A foolproof plan and a way to keep her family out of it. She was going to take Brown down and protect her family while doing so.

She was drowning in fear. Sucked under in a whirlpool of panic. She wouldn't give in to the terror clawing at her calm. She had to get a grip.

"It's okay," Dennis whispered in her ear. "We've got this."

She looked up at the man she was falling for, despite their fight at the lake. She had to protect him too. If it was Brown at the lake, he knew how much Dennis meant to her and he wouldn't hesitate to use Dennis as a pawn in their war; and it would be a war. They needed to end this before it even started. They couldn't risk another fight like the one with Keres where she'd have lost her life if not for her sisters, Kody and their grandmothers.

She was not going there again if she could help it.

"What else do we need to know?" Hazel finally managed to still her panic and find the words to ask a coherent question. She looked back and forth between Dennis and Stone, hoping an answer, a solution, would magically appear out of thin air.

"That's all I've got. Estranged family. Up until Keres's wife's death, they were fairly normal for a magical family. Grey magic, nothing to upset the local magicals. No sign of dark magic until after her death. Keres went crazy for a while before he disappeared. According to his neighbors, he turned their house into a shrine for his wife. Then, he started doing magic in the open. Later, he turned to dark magic. Their house is still the way he left it. A trust pays the bills, and a maintenance company takes care of the house. The crazy thing is, their house is on an old farm, only sixty miles from here. I can't believe they never interacted with anyone in Three Moon Falls."

"Why the hell was Keres renting a place here when he lived so close?" Hazel demanded. Not that Leticia would know the answer. It was the first coherent question to emerge from the chaos battering her brain.

"I bet he was avoiding home," Dennis said. He rubbed a hand up and down Hazel's back.

She wiggled away from his touch. It wasn't soothing, it aggravated her irritation. Her nerves were strung too tight to accept his attempt at reassurance.

"If he was totally bent on resurrecting his wife, he'd be grieving too much to be where they lived together. Too many memories."

"Maybe," Hazel agreed. "If they weren't into dark magic when she was alive, he might know that she wouldn't have approved. Being there might remind him of her potential disapproval." She shrugged. Who the hell knew how another person's mind worked? Especially a grieving person. She was no shrink, that was for sure.

"Makes sense to me," Leticia agreed. "Anyway, that's all I have for now. I'll keep you posted. Sorry about your mishap yesterday. Watch your backs, both of you."

Hazel rose, Dennis stood beside her, taking her hand and squeezing it lightly.

"We'll be careful. Thanks for warning us about what we're up against." After they shook hands with Leticia, Dennis opened the door for Hazel, and they headed outside.

"Do you want to go get dinner?" Dennis asked before he started the truck.

"No. I mean yes I'd like to, but I have to go home and talk to my family about this. They're already upset about what happened earlier. This news isn't going to improve their concerns. Might as well get it over with."

"Okay." He started the truck and pulled out of their parking stall.

She heard the understanding and disappointment in his voice. He had a stake in this too. He hadn't wanted to hire her and if she wasn't magical, he wouldn't be involved in this crap. This was her fault. She sucked in a deep breath. Not exactly her fault, but he wouldn't be in danger if not for Brown coming after her family.

"You should stay. You're involved in this." Guilt wracked her, making her stomach ache and shoulders burn with tension. "I feel terrible for dragging you into this when you were kind enough to trust me against your initial judgment."

"That judgment was wrong. I was acting in anger at my ex. You've taught me to trust, and to try not to jump to conclusions." He grasped her hand and pulled it onto his lap. "I should have listened when you told me not to hire Brown. You were right about him."

"It doesn't matter. But thanks for saying so. Unfortunately, you hiring me is what dragged you into our mess. I apologize for that." If she had walked away when Dennis displayed his witchaphobia, he'd be safe, as would the rest of his employees. She couldn't change the past, and an enormous part of her was glad she'd stayed and gotten to know Dennis. He was a good man and she really liked him. Maybe more than liked him. What she didn't like was knowing she'd put him at risk.

What if something bad happened while his brother's kids were visiting. The danger was skyrocketing out of control. She was going to have to confront Brown. Sooner rather than later.

Her cell phone chimed, and she checked her messages.

"Head to the shop. Everyone is there waiting for me. Family discussion time."

"Am I family now?" Dennis teased, obviously trying to lighten the mood.

"Not yet. But you are a close friend." *Maybe more.* "And you're in this up to your neck whether you like it or not. Please stay and find out what's going on. Maybe you'll have some ideas we don't think of." She rolled her hand from his and squeezed his thigh.

Everyone was at the shop. Gramma Pearl, Hyacinth, Lazuli, Amber and Kody. Mayor Quinton in her colorful clothing and hipster sandals. Corporal Stone had beaten them there somehow. She looked stern and uncompromising in her uniform. Her family had called in several other local magicals. Danica Maes and her favorite couple, Mel and Jerry who stood holding hands. Nobody but family had been in on the fight with Keres. It was a testament to her family's fears that they called in reinforcements.

Mel rushed to Hazel's side as soon as she entered and threw his arms around her. "Oh Hazel, why didn't you tell us how bad this was? I know you've been looking for information on Keres and what he might have wanted from your family, but you never told us your family was in danger." He hugged her close, squeezing tightly.

Jerry joined the embrace. "I've seen Brown around town. Weird that he could be a dark magician and not give off dark vibes. Usually, I can get a sense if someone is magic. Unfortunately, not seeing it in him is a sign of his strength and power. Be careful." He turned toward Dennis. "Thanks for standing by our girl when she's going through this crap. I'm Jerry this is my partner, Mel." He nodded toward the other man.

"Um. You're welcome?" Dennis looked vaguely uncomfortable.

"Oh, Dennis, sorry. Let me introduce you to some of the members of the Three Moon Falls magical community." She made introductions. "Don't worry guys," she addressed the others. "Dennis is a good guy. He knew about magic before he arrived in town. His ex was, er is, magical." She slapped a hand over her mouth. "Oops. Not my story to tell," she mumbled through her fingers, casting Dennis an apologetic look.

He shrugged. "No problem. This feels like an all-hands-on deck minute. I don't know what I can contribute, but I'll try. I don't want someone with bad intentions hanging around town. Just so you know, my ex, Natalia, showed up in town the other night. With Brown."

The room erupted in chatter about the coincidence until Amber snapped the store's deadbolt shut. She hung a Back in an Hour sign on the door. They gathered in the back room. Pearl made tea and handed out cookies. Hazel smiled at her grandmother. There was no stopping a kitchen witch. When trouble was at hand, kitchen witches broke out the food and drinks.

Two hours later, nothing had been solved. They were at an impasse until Brown did something he could be arrested for. Until then, they were all going to keep their eyes and ears open for signs of Brown.

"I'll drive you home," Dennis said.

"Sure."

"Can I ask you something? Something weird?" He asked as they climbed into the truck once again. They buckled up, but he didn't start the engine.

She wrapped her arms around herself against the early evening's chill. It might be July, but the evening was cold and overcast.

"Sure. Anything. But I can't guarantee I'll answer." She grinned to show she was teasing.

"This is going to sound nuts." He grimaced. "But I swear you were having a separate conversation from the rest of us. What was with all the whispering?"

Dang. She'd hoped he wouldn't notice. She debated for several minutes before deciding to answer. She was involved with Dennis. Deeply. He had to know everything.

"Okay. I know you won't believe this. The shop is haunted. We have two resident ghosts," she blurted the words out without giving him a chance to respond. "We don't know why they haven't moved on and if they know, they aren't telling. They're tied to the shop. Most ghosts are restricted to a specific area or item. They can't run willy-nilly anywhere they want. Or rather, most can't. They want us to let them loose to search for Brown."

"What?" He stared at her like she'd lost her marbles. "Seriously?"

"Seriously." She crossed her arms over her chest. Was this the breaking point in their relationship?

"I mean I believe in ghosts. Sort of. More or less. I read the book on Three Moon Falls ghosts. I chalked it up to rumors or a tourist thing to drum up business. But if they're real, why would you release them? I mean, if most ghosts are tied down, so to speak, wouldn't it be a risk to let them go?" He paused. "I'm assuming they aren't malevolent."

She chuckled. "Not malevolent no, but Kansas, she's a teenager, is belligerent sometimes. And Evelyn who ran the drug store that used to be in our space can be grumpy. But overall, they're okay. They've been asking to be let loose since Keres showed up. I'm not sure it would be a good thing. They won't explain why the sudden interest in being free, although they swear, they aren't up to anything nefarious."

"I'm going to be honest; this all has me rather freaked out. Ghosts, magic, witches. I suppose the mayor is magic too?"

She recognized the tiny tremor in his voice, though if you didn't know him well, you'd probably miss it. He was more concerned than he let on.

"Hey, I've lived with this stuff all my life and lately, I'm freaked out." She couldn't ask him to stick around, but she wished he would. Just thinking about being separated from him for more than a few hours made her heart hurt. She offered anyway. "Look, if this is too much, you don't have to hang around. No harm, no foul. I understand."

"Did I say that? Did I imply that I wanted out?" Now he was full on glaring. "Brown is messing with me now, and I'm not about to put up with it. I'm all in. I'll protect you."

Hazel smiled. He was so cute, offering to protect her against dark magic when he couldn't even protect himself. She didn't ridicule him by laughing. His offer was sincere. "Thank you. Honestly, I'm glad you're hanging around. I feel braver when you're at my side." The words popped out without thinking, but it was the stone-cold truth. He made her stronger. She leaned over and kissed him on the cheek.

"Why don't we go back to your house?" she suggested. "My family will be headed home any minute and I'd like some time to think." She just wanted to be with him, to touch him, and know the comfort of his embrace while she figured out how she was going to deal with Brown.

When she woke in the morning, she was alone in Dennis's bed.

Hazel glanced at the bedside clock. Ten a.m. She'd slept for hours and slept so deeply she hadn't even heard Dennis getting up to go to work. She'd expected to be awake most of the night, but after they'd made love she'd gone right to sleep. Damn. Dennis Belanger was the best lover she'd ever had. She couldn't get enough of him.

She suspected it wasn't just technique. When she was with him, she felt adored and cared for. Like she was valuable and wanted, which wasn't a feeling she'd had from her few previous lovers. This relationship was turning into something serious, and she was okay with that.

But, before it went any further, she had to deal with Brown.

She climbed out of bed and headed for the shower. Taped to the bathroom mirror was a note.

Haze,

Sorry to abandon you. Got a text that I was needed in the store. I slept so well by your side, I overslept. I'll be back for coffee mid-morning. Hang around and wait? I'll make breakfast.

D.

She was tempted, too tempted to stay, but she had things to do. Plans to make. She needed to take Brown down. Before he did any real damage. She popped into the shower, determined to be done and gone before Dennis got back. She'd leave him a note.

She stepped out of the shower to the scent of bacon and the sound of off-key singing.

Damn.

She'd missed her opportunity to slip away. No sense fighting the inevitable. She might as well enjoy more time with Dennis before heading off to battle Brown. Food might be just the thing she needed to jumpstart her mind. Before she did anything else, she had to find Brown.

Chapter Thirty-One

B reakfast was delicious. What followed was even more so. Dennis was definitely relaxing and letting his staff do more of the work. She smiled to herself thinking about their intimate moments. So much for keeping her distance. Dennis had gone back to work, leaving her to shower, again, before heading home. She was taking the day off.

She locked up the house and headed around the greenhouses, toward the petting zoo. It was a chance to enjoy the sun and visit Jellybean. She hadn't been by to visit the friendly llama in days.

Things had changed in the small zoo. Dennis had been busy adding proper paddocks and the number of animals had doubled. Chickens, geese, a cow and calf, a horse, ducks, puppies and kittens. The last ones were on loan from a local shelter and were adoptable. There was one enormous cage housing three beautiful peacocks. Their plumage was incredible, but their call grated on her ears.

She ambled through the zoo. It was quiet, not many guests and most of those were focused on the puppies. She stopped in front of Jellybean's paddock and the llama immediately trotted over, sticking her head out for attention.

"Morning, girl. How's zoo life treating you? Is it good?"

Jellybean nodded.

"You actually understand me, don't you, girl?"

Another nod.

Hazel couldn't help but laugh. Despite the trepidation clouding her mind, there was joy in the moment, and she was going to take it.

"What are you smiling about?" Brown's voice startled her.

She whirled around to face her nemesis. "What are you doing here?"

"I work here." He smirked.

"Not anymore. Pretty sure you got fired." She kept her temper and banked her fear. She wasn't about to give him the upper hand by revealing her emotions. Her chest tightened and she did her best to ignore it.

"Does it matter? Nobody out here knows I don't work here." He was wearing a Get Growing T-shirt. "I've been chatting them up. Making friends." His smile turned oily and malevolent.

She needed to get out of here. She couldn't fight him in public, even if she had figured out how to do it.

Her chest tightened again. She coughed, trying to loosen it. She wasn't allergic to animals, just wasps, but it felt like an allergy attack coming on. She pushed against the feeling, trying to shake it off.

Her throat tightened. Beside her, Jellybean hummed loudly and raced around her pen.

Damn.

He was trying to squeeze the breath from her chest. She hadn't expected a daylight attack in public. The man had balls. She struggled to put up a shield to push him away.

It wasn't working. Breathless, her mind was fuzzy and her powers weak. He ambled toward her until they were nearly toe to toe. "Bitch. Your family killed my father. I'm going to make you all pay."

His eyes glowed red. Like the eyes from her nightmare after Brown had cast his sleeping spell on Dennis.

Shit. Her dream had been a premonition.

She had to figure out a way out of this. Get rid of him. Stop him.

Darkness encroached on her vision. She was going to pass out. She couldn't let him win this easily. She struggled against the invisible pressure. Her mind was flooded with a vision of Brown, holding a rifle, standing near their picnic spot on the island. Then darkness folded in. Her mind went dark. She felt herself falling.

Chapter Thirty-Two

Dennis was straightening a display of miniature rose bushes in decorative pots.

A seventy-something customer rushed in. "You've got to help. The llama got out!" The woman grabbed his hand and yanked him toward the door. "There's a woman on the ground I don't know what happened to her. I can't get close to her. The llama keeps chasing everyone away."

"What?" Panic froze him for half a second. What happened? Oh no, what if a customer got hurt by his friend's stupid llama? He'd be sued. He'd be ruined. He shook the thoughts off. So selfish. Someone might he hurt. He had to help them.

"Come on," she urged, dragging him forward.

The petting zoo was a good idea. It had brought in a lot of new customers. What if he'd been wrong? Accidents were never a good thing. He raced through the greenhouse and the yard, the aging customer hot on his heels. In the petting zoo, a crowd had gathered around, keeping a safe distance from the very vocal and agitated Jellybean.

The llama paced back and forth making a weird humming noise. The sound meant she was warning her pack of danger.

Dennis pushed through the crowd. First things first, he had to calm the upset animal so they could get close to whoever was hurt.

"Jellybean. Calm down girl." How the hell did you calm an upset llama?

Her head whipped toward him and the humming dropped in volume. Okay, that had to be good, right? He really had to make the time to learn more about the animals in his care. He'd studied up on the basics but obviously not enough.

Focus, Dennis. He had to get a grip. Panic was bouncing his thoughts around from the immediacy of the moment to random stupidity.

"Let me through," he demanded when the last few people refused to step aside. "Back away. Give her some room. She's upset."

Slowly people began to move. He wanted to pick them up and hurl them out of the way. Finally, a path was clear.

Jellybean stomped in agitated circles around a prone figure.

Shit! That was Hazel!

She was totally motionless on the ground. He leaped forward and dropped to the ground at her side. He touched her gently on the shoulder. "Haze? Are you okay? Wake up, honey."

She groaned and her eyelids fluttered.

He sucked in a relieved breath. At least she was alive. He'd be lost if she was gone from his life. "Hey, honey. Wake up. What happened?"

She groaned and looked up at him. "Brown," she whispered, her voice sounding raw and painful.

Crap on toast! He never should have left her alone in the house. Brown was out there waiting to strike, and he'd failed to protect his girl. Self-recriminations and anger nearly overcame his common sense.

"The petting zoo is closed. She's fine. Clear off. Let's get this place calmed down so we can get Jellybean back into her pen."

Sarah rushed forward and started shooing people away. He was grateful for her calm insistence.

Once the crowd cleared, Jellybean stopped pacing and settled down to sit beside Hazel, almost as if she were standing guard. He'd read that llamas could be great guard dogs.

Hazel struggled to rise and dropped back onto the gravel path.

Her hair was messed, there was dirt on her cheek as if she'd landed on her face. Her neck was darkening with bruises, the dark color bleeding down under the neck of her shirt. She was a wreck, but those brown eyes looking up at him were the most beautiful things he'd ever seen.

"Take it easy. The crowd's gone. Don't rush. Do you want me to call your sisters?" They'd know what to do. He was panicky and irrational, and he knew it. Seeing her lying there had ripped his heart out. "Lazuli is at the house; she's finishing up the play structure. Do you need her?"

Hazel nodded weakly.

He tossed his phone to Sarah. "There's no screen lock. Call Lazuli. Get her over here."

Kneeling beside Hazel, he talked quietly, encouraging her to stay put and wait for her sister.

"Lazuli's on her way. Do we need to call an ambulance?" Sarah asked.

"No," Hazel whispered hoarsely, clutching her throat.

"Don't talk. Wait for your sister."

Two minutes later, Lazuli nudged Jellybean aside and dropped to her knees beside Hazel. "Hey, sis. What's up?"

Surprisingly, the llama moved back into her pen and stood there, placidly watching over them. Crazy animal. He'd be giving her an extra ration of feed tonight for protecting Hazel from the crowd.

"Brown," Hazel croaked, her voice sounding stronger.

"Don't speak, just nod. Are you hurt anywhere besides your throat? It's bruising like crazy." She run her hands lightly over Hazel's limbs as if looking for injury.

Hazel shook her head weakly.

"Let's get her inside, off the ground." She looked up, scanning the area. "You called me?" she asked Sarah.

"Yes. What can I do?"

"Get that crazy llama penned up. Then you can help us get my sister to the house." She turned toward Jellybean. "Okay you. Good work. But we've got to move her now. Don't get upset."

Dennis nearly keeled over when Jellybean nodded as if she understood what was being asked of her. "Good girl." He felt ridiculous praising the animal, but it felt right. Weird.

"Lift up just a bit," he told Hazel. "I'll get my arm behind you and we'll ease you up, a few inches at a time. Take it slow. Don't rush."

Inch by inch, they got Hazel to a sitting position. She drooped forward, rubbing her neck.

By God, he was going to kill Brown the next time he saw him. Nobody hurt women like this and got away with it. Not on his watch. Hazel being hurt tripled his ire. He was almost vibrating with anger.

"Back off, stud," Lazuli warned him. "Anger isn't helping."

Damn, meddling, psychic witches!

Lazuli had the audacity to laugh. "I heard that."

Luckily, Sarah was busy trying to repair the damage Jellybean had inflicted on her pen in her attempts to get free. "Back in a second," she said and raced off. Two minutes later, she was back. "I'm good to help move Hazel. One of the students is coming with supplies to repair the enclosure."

"Thank you." Dennis looked at Jellybean. "You stay put now. I'll be back to reward you later." He wasn't surprised when she nodded, but he couldn't stop rolling his eyes. His life was spiraling into pure lunacy.

Lazuli on one side, Dennis on the other, they managed to get Hazel to her feet. She groaned and teetered. He slipped his arm around her waist. Sarah pulled Hazel's arm so it draped over his shoulder. Slowly, carefully, they crossed the short distance to his home. He handed Sarah his keys and she let them in. Minutes later, they were settling Hazel on the living room sofa.

"Thank you, Sarah. We couldn't have done it without you. I don't know what happened, but we'll let you know when we find out. Can you double check on Jellybean and give her a treat?"

"Got it boss. She loves apples. I've got one in my lunch. I'll feed it to her. I'll let the staff know you're busy and can't be disturbed."

"Thanks." The single word didn't express the depth of his gratitude, but he hoped his tone did.

Sarah disappeared and left the three of them alone.

"I'm calling Hyacinth. Hazel needs medical care. Cynth'll be able to help with the pain."

It was a tribute to Hazel's shock and discomfort that she didn't voice an objection. Dennis settled beside her on the couch, careful not to jostle her. "Should we get her water or something?"

"Not yet," Lazuli advised. "Judging by the bruising on her neck, she might need traditional medical attention. We don't want to fill her stomach in case they need to do any testing. She'll be fine for a few minutes."

Lazuli cocked her head to the side for a second and then grinned at Dennis. "She's sending me the idea she's fine and doesn't need a drink. Yet. I think we're good for now. Where will I find a cloth to clean her up with?"

"Bathroom. End of the hall. There's a first aid kit in the hallway linen closet. Second shelf from the top, left hand side." He didn't know what they'd need, if anything, but he had a full kit.

"I'll do it," he said when Lazuli came back with a damp washcloth. Gently, careful not to hurt her, he wiped Hazel's face. Every stroke of the rag stabbed his heart. This was his fault for leaving her alone. He didn't start this fight, but by God, he was going to finish it.

Lazuli chided him again for his strong emotions.

"Sorry, I can't help myself."

"Hazel's not psychic, but she can read you right now. Tamp it down or you'll have to leave. Got it?" The glare on her face was tempered by the understanding in her eyes.

She was going to kick him out of his own house. She was crazy. No, she was right. He was out of control. It wasn't easy to see the woman you loved in pain.

Whoa! The woman he loved?

Lazuli chuckled. Obviously, he'd cast that thought out too.

No sense denying it. He reigned in his emotions as best he could, though he had no idea how to stop broadcasting. Could he even do that? He'd ask later, when shit was done hitting the fan.

He'd fallen for this pretty little magic wielder and he'd do anything to keep her safe. He'd take on Brown single handedly if he had to. But first things first. They had to help Hazel. Physically and emotionally. She had to be ruined by the attack.

His anger spiked again, and Lazuli groaned.

"Fine. I'm doing my best here. Nobody ever taught me how to shut off the broadcast."

"Why don't you go for a walk, watch for my sisters and my grandmother. They'll be here soon. They're on the way. Maybe make some coffee or something and put on the kettle. Cynth will have a healing tea if she decides it's okay to give it to Hazel."

Resigned, he tossed the cloth aside and kissed Hazel lightly on the forehead. It was making him crazy that she just sat there, looking back and forth between him and her sister. Not saying anything. She was a fighter. What had happened to take away her fight?

"Call me if she needs me," he said and left the sisters. He put on some coffee, threw some premade cookie dough in the oven, and plugged in the kettle before going outside to wait. He paced back and forth on the front walkway. Over to the driveway, back to the front door. Over and back. Over and back.

With every turn, he scanned the area for Brown. Where had he gone? Was Natalia with him again? He couldn't get beyond the coincidence of them being together. Meeting in Three Moon Falls wasn't a coincidence. Not a chance. Maybe she'd been involved in the attack.

His musings were ramping up his disquiet and anger. He was relieved when Hazel's family pulled up. He rushed them inside, took the cookies out, and stood back while her family did their thing.

There wasn't any magic he could see. No wand waving, or spell casting. Just a lot of whispers back and forth before Hyacinth placed her hands on Hazel's bruises. From where he stood, he could see Hyacinth close her eyes. She did nothing, she just sat there, eyes closed, hands unmoving. An eternity passed. When she leaned back and wobbled, her sisters grabbed her and helped her to a chair.

Torn between his concern for the two women he chose Hazel. He rushed to her side and clasped her hands in his. He looked at her.

Holy hell.

The bruising on her throat and neck was significantly lighter. What the hell?

Hyacinth was a midwife and they said she was a healer, but what in the world? Had she taken those bruises? Lifted them? Healed the damage? The bruises were still dark and ugly, so ugly, but they looked days old rather than fresh. Amazing!

He stared at the marks until Hazel reached out and touched his cheek.

"Hey," she whispered, her voice sounding better. "Don't cry. I'm okay."

What? He wasn't crying.

She stroked his cheek with one finger, and he felt the wetness there. Shit. "I'm just so glad she could help you. It looks better." He faked a laugh. "It still looks awful, but not as bad as it had."

"It feels better. Can I get a drink now?"

"Right here," Pearl responded from behind Dennis. "Healing tea. Then the cookies Dennis baked and an energy ball or two." She nudged Dennis aside. "Out of the way, boy. I need in there."

Dennis moved to the couch and wrapped his arm around Hazel's shoulder. Maybe she could pull energy from him. He was nearly vibrating with pent up emotion and unspent energy.

Across the room, Lazuli and Amber hovered over Hyacinth. Helping her drink tea and eat something. He'd seen firsthand how much using magic could sap your strength. She must be exhausted from healing Hazel. Food. They needed to eat.

"I'll get food." He leaped to his feet and headed for the kitchen.

Rather than cook, he called Romero's and ordered enough food and desserts for a dozen people. He paid extra for a rush order and long distance delivery without hesitation. He threw some mugs of coffee on a tray, added cream and sugar and a plate of cookies and lugged it into the living room.

"Okay, ladies. Time for a snack while we wait for real food to arrive. I've order Italian, including dessert and several vegetarian dishes. It'll be here soon." He walked around the room offering the drinks and cookies.

Chapter Thirty-Three

"I can't believe I'm getting into a boat again," Hazel grumbled as she fastened her life jacket.

"I can't believe I let you talk me into this," Dennis retorted.

They stood on the dock outside the boat rental. It was the darkest night of the month, the New Moon. The night when there was no visible sign of the moon. The stars shone like beacons in the sky, and it seemed the darkness had become a physical thing encroaching on her.

"Yeah, me either. I thought for sure you'd tell me to drop it and let the police handle it." If the truth were known, she'd have preferred to go alone. But if she were going to face down Brown, she had to go back to the island. She couldn't get there without Dennis.

There was no way she'd ask her family to help with this suicide mission. She was taking on the enemy with Dennis's help. If she didn't need him to drive the boat, she be here alone. She couldn't take the risk of freezing up halfway across the lake and leaving herself vulnerable to Brown.

She didn't want to be here, but she had no option. It was time to end this, before she lost someone she loved. Brown had gotten to her, in a public place. Only Jellybean kicking up a fuss and knocking down her pen had saved Hazel's life. She had no doubt he would have killed her, just to make a point. He'd choked her, without using his hands. He hadn't tried to read her mind unless he'd done it after she blacked out. He'd bled her power off after he choked her. Weirdly, he didn't break her or take her power. It was more like he'd fed off her. Like a vampire.

A psychotic, psychic, magic sucking, vampire.

She'd done six Tarot card readings in the last three days and every one of them spoke of travel, water, danger, endings and new beginnings. The Rune stones had told her now was the time to face her danger.

She was as ready for this as she'd ever be. After hours of shoring up her strength and building mental blockades, she'd fueled her body and sought out Dennis. Here they were, at the side of the lake, at nearly midnight, preparing to climb into a boat.

She blew into her hands, trying to erase the chill taking over her body. Refusing to focus on the fear climbing up her spine, she ran over her supplies. She'd brought food, water, energy balls, a thermos of tea, and her wand, though she couldn't remember the last time she'd used it. She had a lighter, paper, cellphone, a backpack with dry clothing and a blanket.

It was hard to prepare for magic battles. This wasn't like getting ready for a boxing match or an MMA fight. It was impossible to train for, except raising your mental blocks to keep your enemy out. She prepared herself for the possibility that Brown might have Natalia with him. She could be another adversary, or Brown could use her and throw her away like his father had done with his minion. He'd taken the man's power and killed him to gain strength.

Never once growing up had she thought about power vampires. Doubt plagued Hazel. This was an idiotic move. There was no way she could do this alone. But she was going to try. Brown hadn't yet gone after her family. This was personal. It was her battle to fight, and she wished she hadn't needed to get Dennis to bring her to the island.

"You sure he'll be here?" Dennis asked, untying the boat they were "borrowing" from the dock. Hazel had sneaked into the boat rental shop and stolen a set of keys that afternoon.

A snip of bolt cutters snapped the chain securing the boat and they were prepped and ready to go. Well, as ready as you ever were when heading out to face your nemesis, over water, on an island, virtually alone.

"I'm sure."

"I don't doubt you, but how do you know?" He stopped to stare at her, questions in his eyes. "Are you sure you don't want to bring your sisters?"

"No sisters. This is personal. This is about me and Brown. If I knew how to get there without a boat, you'd be out too. Sorry. I don't mean that the way it sounds. I just want everyone to be safe. Ending this quickly when Brown thinks I'm down and out is the only way. Surprise attack."

Doubts marched across his face. He opened his mouth and snapped it shut. "I should have protected you."

She smiled and leaned forward to brush a kiss across Dennis's cheek. "Thank you. That's the sweetest thing I've ever heard. You can be my backup." She took in a deep breath and prepared to ask the unaskable.

"I didn't mention one thing," she confessed.

"What's that?" Dennis took her hand and helped her into the small motorboat.

"I might need you for actual backup. If I get weak, I'll need to touch you, to hold your hand, so I can draw on your strength. You don't have magic, but you've got physical strength I can use to fuel my own. In desperation. Only if you agree."

"What?"

"It's hard to explain. I can't put it into words. Remember how Brown sucked my power when we were picnicking? It's similar. If we're touching, I can feed," she winced at the harsh word, "Feed on your physical strength. I'm saying this poorly."

"And that's the only way I can help?"

"Unless you can knock him senseless, it might be the only way. Honestly, I have no idea what's coming. It'll be dangerous. There's a time to cut and run and a time to fight. The time to fight is now, while we have the advantage of surprise. Plus, it's the New Moon. There's power in the full moon, just like in the movies. But there's also power in the New Moon if you're starting something new or ending something. I'm doing both. Ending Brown's reign of fear, and starting a new, fear free period."

Dennis's look of confusion had her struggling to explain.

"It's like this. Your house has two types of power. 110 is regular for the lights and outlets. 220 is for the stove and dryer. Think of the moon phases like that. Brown is probably strongest at the full moon. I've always been drawn to the New Moon. My power lies in the dark moon."

"Honestly, I don't get any of this. I've been reading up on magic, but I don't think anything can prepare you for a fight like this. I'm here for you. Do what you need to. Take what you need. Let's end this. Today. I've got your back. Get comfortable."

They zoomed across the lake, much too fast for Hazel's peace of mind. Two hundred yards from shore, Dennis cut the motor.

"What are you doing? We can't stop here," she hissed, her hands white knuckling the sides of the boat.

"Sound travels further at night. I'm going to row us in. Approach with stealth. If I had to guess, I'd say he's squatting in the cabin on the far side of the island. I'll row us around the bend. There's a beach close to the cabin. We can sneak in from there."

"Oh. Good. Smart thinking. I was freaking out a bit."

"A bit?" Dennis said as he dipped his oars into the water.

"Okay," she whispered back. "Maybe a lot. Just row. Please." Her voice quivered on the last word. She'd been counting on a speedy trip, but Dennis had taken it slow and easy. Now, they barely crawled along.

Thankfully, as he got in a rhythm, the boat sped up.

Chapter Thirty-Four

Relieved to be out of the boat, Hazel resisted the urge to lay down and rest. Dennis tied off the boat and they crept up the shore toward a cabin set back in the trees. There were no lights visible, but she wasn't foolish enough to think everyone inside was asleep. Blackout curtains could hide light. Especially if whoever was inside didn't want to be noticed. For all she knew, Brown could be hiding outside after sensing their arrival. She didn't dare let down her guard even for a second.

Watching her step wasn't easy. The moon cast no light on this darkest of nights. She inched forward, carefully placing her feet after checking for obstacles. At this rate, they'd never get there. She just wanted this over and done.

Trees loomed ahead of them, past the sand and the boulders littering the shoreline. She'd feel better when they reached the forest's protection. Each step seemed an eternity. Seconds felt like hours. And the distance didn't seem to be decreasing. It wasn't far, maybe twenty yards. But crouched low, creeping in the dark without making a misstep was painful. Her thighs and calves cramped.

Inside the tree line, she relaxed. Not fully, just enough to take a slow deep breath. Fresh moist earth and pine filled her senses. The cold night air blew past, erasing the nervous sweat from her brow. Dennis sidled up beside her and grasped her hand. His thumb stroked hers, his fingers calloused and rough, yet comforting. She squeezed back.

They crept forward again until they were directly across from the cabin. They stood side by side, watching for signs of life. It remained still and dark, as if nobody had been there in ages. If not for the recently cut grass, it appeared abandoned and forgotten. The owner's groundskeeper must have stopped by.

"No sense delaying this. I guess." Despite her declaration to start a massive fight with Brown, she didn't move. Doubt swirled around her as she second guessed her decision to come here without backup. Part of her, tired of being the baby of the family, wanted to bust out all the stops and hit Brown hard. Take him down. Knock him out and end this. Her family had barely survived one magical battle this year, they didn't need another. No way could Brown be as strong as Keres had been. Her magic was strong, and she had the advantage of surprise. She'd be able to take him.

At least she hoped she could.

"It's not too late to get back in the boat," Dennis whispered.

Damn, was he reading her thoughts? She turned to look at him. Did he doubt her abilities or was he trying to be supportive? She was terrified and without magic, he must be in worse shape. Was terrifieder a word?

Focus! She mentally shouted at herself. They'd get their asses kicked if she didn't pay attention.

A crash came from the cabin. She whipped around. The front door stood wide open, Brown backlit by the light streaming through the cabin door.

"Come out and face me, you cowards. I can almost smell your fear."

His mocking voice scraped her nerves, doubling her dread.

"Jesus," Dennis whispered, his voice quivered. "So much for a surprise attack or strategic retreat."

Yeah, no shit. They were totally screwed. Now instead of saving the day, she'd have to listen to her sisters dis her for acting without thinking.

Screw it! She'd mulled this over, more than once. Dozens of times since she was first attacked. She could do this. They could do this!

Brown was going down and she was the one doing it.

"We've got this," she murmured, trying to sound confident. "Let's go."

She strode forward as quickly as she could without tripping and landing on her face.

"All right, Brown. I'm here." She stopped outside the tree line, hands on her hips. "I'm tired of your crap. I'm telling you to leave me, my family, and my friends alone. Get the hell out of Three Moon Falls, or you'll regret it."

"Oh, boo hoo. Poor little witchy girl. You've got no power over me. You're weak and powerless." He lifted his right hand and with a flick of his fingers, a ball of white light shot toward her, crashed into the ground at her feet and exploded bits of sod and dirt up at her, coating her face.

She shifted left, moving further onto the lawn, more in line with the cabin than beside it. Slightly closer to the water she feared but needed.

Suddenly, Dennis was at her side, his fingers tangled with hers. Strength of purpose flowed through her like a current

"She's not alone. You'll have to deal with both of us."

Brown's mocking laughter followed Dennis's statement. "You're less of a worry than she is. Mundane, you have no idea what, who you're dealing with."

Dennis's mouth snapped shut with a click of his teeth. He mumbled something under his breath. Anger poured off him in a tsunami of waves.

"I'm going to ask you, politely, to leave town and never come back," Hazel declared, doing her best to sound like she was granting him an enormous concession.

Another flash ball flew toward them. She just managed to avoid flinching, though Dennis wasn't so lucky. He jerked back several steps and cursed before returning to her side. From the corner of her eye, she saw his grimace.

"Is that all you've got?" she sneered. "I thought the great and powerful Mathew Brown would have some skills beyond a simple parlor trick." His energy balls were far more than a trick; she suspected if you were actually hit with them, you'd take serious damage.

"Where is it?" Brown demanded, his arm raised for another strike, another ball glowing on his fingertips, larger and bluer than the previous two.

"Where is what?" She cocked her hip to the right, feigning nonchalance.

"Don't play coy with me, witch. Give it to me!" he shouted. The ball glowed with red and orange highlights.

What the hell type of magic was this? She'd never seen anything like it. Simple energy balls, yes. Multicolored, morphing ones? No. They were in deep shit. Fear shook her knees and she struggled to remain straight until Dennis squeezed her fingers. She debated trying to shield Dennis in case Brown tossed the ball more accurately; and decided against it. Brown was probably set on destroying her, not Dennis.

"How about, you tell me what you want, and I'll tell you if I have it." She flicked her fingers dismissively. "I mean, if I have no idea what you want, how could I possibly know where the mystery object is. Oh," she snapped her fingers, "is this a game? Kind of like I Spy, or Twenty Questions? Is it bigger than a breadbox? Smaller than a house?"

"You're testing my patience." He tossed the glowing orb up and caught it in his other hand. It brightened the area, illuminating his face, turning it to a rocky façade of bones and shadows. He looked like death.

"So, this thing. What does it do? Seriously, man. I can't help unless I know more." She was pushing her luck. Trying to piss him off. One of the first rules of magic was to never cast with your emotions, because things could get out of hand. Brown was so fired up and emotional he could lose control. If he did, she might be able to take him down.

Her neck started to itch, right at the base of her skull. She scratched it idly, thinking it was a mosquito. The feeling didn't go away. It intensified. Deep in her mind, she heard her grandmother's voice asking where she was.

Busy! She mentally shouted back. The pressure eased but didn't dissipate.

She refocused on Brown who was blathering on with random threats. He was crazy. Bat-freaking-crap crazy and starting to crack.

"I'll say it again. Tell me what you want, you remind me of your father. He was always screeching about something. We never did find out what he begged for before he was hauled into custody. Can you get to the point?"

Dennis whispered, "Stop provoking him."

"Shh," she growled through gritted teeth. "I have a plan."

"Bloody good thing," he murmured. "I'm starting to worry."

"The talisman!" Brown screamed, launching the ball their way.

Hazel panicked a bit and snatched water from thin air to extinguish the ball. The sudden magical action cost her a chunk of strength. Damn, she needed to stay focused.

"You're exactly like your father. Exactly." She shook her head condescendingly and popped an energy ball into her mouth.

"I. Am. Nothing. Like. My. Father. Give me the damn talisman," he screamed, and rushed off the cabin step toward them.

Another, decidedly female figure appeared behind him.

Natalia.

"Natalia, what are you doing with this idiot?" Dennis called.

"He's a powerful magician, not a useless, chickenshit tool like you. Matt and I are going places." She strolled up to Brown, her hips swaying like a cheap prostitute on the prowl. She rested her hand on Brown's shoulder.

"Don't touch me," he snarled, dislodging her hand.

Her arms crossed over her chest and she glared at him.

Hazel laughed at the anger and disappointment on the other woman's face. Trouble in paradise.

"I thought we were a team," Natalia whined. Brown ignored her as another ball grew in his hand.

Was that his only trick, besides stealing energy? Hazel felt a moment of hope, until the ground beneath her feet trembled and started to crack. Shit. This was going wrong. Fast. She pulled Dennis with her and moved toward their foes. Backward wasn't an option, too many obstacles hidden in the dark.

An owl screeched nearby, and three crows flew overhead, cawing raucously. Unusual for them to be around at night. She heeded their warning that something big was coming. "Brace yourself," she ordered Dennis. "Feet apart. Be ready to move."

"Ready." His instant obedience was a sign he was scared, but ready to follow her lead.

The ground heaved again, knocking them sideways, tearing her hand from Dennis's grip. A crack in the ground appeared to her left, the earth inside it moist and full of water. Excellent. She could use the power in the water. Struggling to maintain her balance, she toed off her runners and scraped her feet on the grass to slide her socks off. The closer she was to the earth and water, the stronger the bond she could forge.

"I'm tired of waiting." The ground shook again. Hazel and Dennis managed to maintain their stance, Natalia was knocked sideways, landing on the ground with a painful thump. She groaned but didn't get up.

"I don't have a talisman. I don't know anything about a talisman." Okay, maybe they had uncovered some clues to a potential magical item, but no proof and they sure didn't know what or where it was. Not that they'd give it to Brown or anyone else. "What's this talisman of yours do anyway? Your father seemed very determined to find it."

"Its powers are legendary. Don't pretend you don't know anything about it. Your family stole it when they fled from Salem."

Damned ancestors.

The itch at the back of her neck intensified. An image rolled into her mind, her grandmother and sisters gathered together at the shop, frightened, worried and wanting to know where she was. She tried to ignore them. She didn't need the distraction. Finally, she shot back a mental image of the island and a demand to back off and stop distracting her.

The last thing to come through was a wave of fear and disapproval. Good. Now she could focus on Brown.

"There's no talisman in our house. I'd know. I've lived there my entire life. Whatever rumor you're chasing, it's false. You won't find what you need here."

A ball of light exploded in front of them, knocking Dennis to his knees and shaking the ground again. Her foot slipped to the right into a pool of water. After the first second of shock, calm returned along with a sure connection to her powers. Focusing her intent, she pushed against the water with her mind until it shot up at Brown's feet, dousing him and the ball forming in his hand.

"That won't stop me," he screamed, his face red and mottled in the light of a new ball. It was working, he was losing control. She had to find a crack in his armor to break him, to throw him over the edge. If she could knock him down, knock him out, she could temporarily bind him using the spell she'd researched last night. It was similar to the one Kody's mother had used to bind his magic when he was a child. It was breakable, but it would hold until help arrived.

If she could manage it.

Doubt rocked her, making her stomach hurt. She never should have come here alone. Dennis as backup was inadequate and she'd known it all along. She was just too stubborn wanting to prove herself to her family. Her family was right, she was still a baby and needed a keeper.

Screw it.

She moved further into the wet earth at her feet. The ground flowed with moisture. Being on an island provided countless miniature currents of water in the earth. She pulled their power toward her. Storing up power and water to use when she needed it.

Belatedly, she realized this fight might have been easier closer to the water. In the water, if she could overcome her total terror of water.

Too late now.

She wanted to approach him, to anger him. Shake his balance and throw him off. She couldn't move from her spot, from the connection she'd formed with the water, or she'd lose its power. Dammit she should have planned better.

Natalia groaned. Brown tossed her a casual glance and kicked her in the side. She rolled away from him, coming to her feet behind him, clutching her ribs.

Good! He was losing it. His distraction allowed Hazel to help Dennis to his feet and reestablish their connection. His hand trembled in hers, but he squeezed reassuringly, the small action bringing comfort.

S hit. Dennis glared at the man across from them. He'd known this wasn't going to be any fun. But fireballs and earthquakes? Seriously. This was freaking insane. Terrifying. They were doomed. Hazel's hand was cold within his. He squeezed it again trying to show his support. They might not live through this, but he'd stand strong every second of this battle. Whatever Hazel needed; he'd give it to her.

Energy ball! The thought hit him like lightening. He fumbled in his jacket pocket for the zipper bag of the chocolate balls Hazel had given him earlier. One handed, he dug one out, leaned toward her and when she opened her mouth, he popped it inside. She nodded her thanks and a warm feeling flooded through him. Maybe he wasn't magic, but at least he wasn't useless. He took one himself and felt the instant surge of strength.

Natalia stood behind Brown, her unhappy glare pivoting between Hazel and Brown. She was upset and likely to do something stupid. "Natalia," he called out, "You aren't like this. You're not a bad person. There's good inside you. Somewhere, deep down, is the woman I fell in love with. Do the right thing here."

Natalia rocked back on her heels, a sneer on her face. The next time he glanced at her, she seemed confused, like she couldn't make her mind up about something. If they could turn her against Brown, it might be to their advantage. Nothing ventured, nothing gained. Unless he pissed her off of course.

Beside him, Hazel taunted their foe, yet again. With each of her jeering comments, he grew angrier, and the ground shook worse. What was she thinking? The ground trembled again, not as badly as the last few times, and he slid off the lip of earth he was standing in and into the crack in front of him; his shoes were immediately soaked through with frigid water.

That was it! She was a water witch. She got her power from water and could control it. The deeper the water got, the better she could use it.

Chapter Thirty-Five

"I'm telling you," Kansas said. "Let us out." We can find her.

Lazuli looked at the two ghosts hovering in front of her. This was nuts. Her sister was missing, well, not exactly missing, she was in danger and refusing or unable to relate where she was telepathically. Some island based on the images, but there were several islands in nearby lakes.

Kansas and Ev's idea to be freed was total insanity.

Laz was psychic, it was her biggest magical gift, but she couldn't read non-corporeal entities. Ghosts were tied to a place, or an item, for a reason. Releasing them from their binding was an enormous risk. How could she trust them to come back? But how could they not let them go to find Hazel?

"I don't think it's a good idea," she said. "You're here for a reason."

"We'll come back," Ev stated. "I promise. Just a bit of freedom, I've been trapped here for years. A break would be nice. I don't know why

I'm still here either. I don't feel any unfinished business. But I swear, we'll come back and if she doesn't want to, I'll drag her back kicking and screaming." She nodded at the surly teenaged ghost beside her.

"I'll come back," Kansas declared. "She needs us, I can feel it."

"We're not letting you out," Gramma Pearl injected. "Our primary rule is do no harm. Once released, there is no way to control you which could constitute harm. Give it up. We'll have to find Hazel another way."

Hyacinth spoke up as she slid her cell phone into the back pocket of her jeans. "Dennis isn't answering his phone. It's possible he's with Hazel."

"That's not good. He'll be in danger too." Pearl shook her head.

"It could be good," Lazuli said. "I think Hazel loves him, and if he loves her, he could give her strength, back her up." She crossed her arms over her chest. "What in the world was she thinking? I can't wait to give her a piece of my mind."

"Let us loose. We'll find her and come back. Cross my heart and hope to..." Kansas frowned. "Too late for that, but you know what I mean."

"Let us go, we'll find Hazel so you can get to her," Ev said. "I don't know how, but I know she needs you. Seriously needs you. In person." Ev might be a ghost but before she passed, she'd been a witch, like the entire Hawk family.

"Did some of your skills pass over with you?" Lazuli asked.

"Truthfully, this is the first time I've noticed it. I think it might be because Hazel can talk to all ghosts, and she sees us when others don't. You guys know how she's helped other ghosts pass through the veil to the other side."

"Not. Letting. You. Loose." Lazuli decreed. "There's no way to guarantee you'll come back. Your word is not enough."

"There might be a way," Hyacinth said. "I was reading the grimoires..."

Chapter Thirty-Six

"I've had enough," Brown shouted, the power of his voice shaking the ground and sending birds screaming into the inky black night sky. "Tell me where it is. Now."

"We don't have it." Hazel stood her ground. She wasn't going to back down from this bully. He needed to be put in his place, in custody, beside his father. "What makes you think we have this, whatever it is?" She wasn't mean by nature, and she was having trouble making herself taunt him.

"I followed the notes my father gathered, and the notes he made during his own research. You have it. Somebody in your family knows where it is." The ground rumbled again.

"We don't even know what it is, let alone where it is," she countered, sending a splurge of water up at his feet.

"The chalice. I want the chalice."

"You mean like a wine glass? Come to the house, take all the wine glasses. We rarely use them." His face darkened and he hurled another ball their way, narrowly missing them. Shoot. Maybe she'd gone too far with that one. She wanted him off balance, not totally out of control. Behind him, Natalia laughed.

"Enough insolence. Tell me where it is, or he dies."

Suddenly, Dennis was flying through the air. He landed a hundred feet away with a thump and didn't get up.

Son of a...

Abandoning her fortifying pool of water, Hazel raced to Dennis's side, her heart in her throat. He'd pay for this.

She knelt beside Dennis and placed a hand on his chest. It rose and fell beneath her touch. She wasn't a healer by any stretch, but she mustered her strength and pushed a small burst of energy into him. Nothing happened.

He had to be seriously injured after being flung and landing so hard. Quickly, with only half an eye on Brown, she felt Dennis's limbs for breaks. Finding nothing, she pushed more energy into him, leaving herself reeling with the effort.

Dennis's eyes fluttered, but he didn't wake.

Dark boots appeared beside her.

"Give me the chalice," Brown screamed in her face, his breath rancid, his aura reeking of evil and evil emptiness.

He was way gone to the darkness. Probably beyond saving.

Weak and trembling from unsuccessfully sending so much energy into Dennis, she fumbled in his pocket and found the energy balls. She devoured three of them, leaving only one in reserve. Why hadn't she brought more? Stupid.

"I don't have your damned chalice. I've never heard of it." She pulled herself upright and faced him, head on. She'd had enough of his crap. She was scared to the marrow of her bones, but this had to end. She had to finish it. Before it was too late.

Brown's arms came up, glowing balls in both hands. "Stupid witch, you'll pay for not giving it to me."

Before she could muster a counter spell in her weakened state, the balls slammed into her chest, knocking her backward toward the rocky shore. She landed with a thump; her breath rushing out in a heavy grunt. Winded, she struggled to breathe, too stunned to prevent the next attack.

She'd barely hit the ground when she found herself flying through the air to land on her back on the edge of the lake, one hand flung over her head in the water.

Water!

Finally, she'd provoked him into a mistake. Water was her strength. She lay there, gasping for air and at the same time, pulling strength from the water, drawing it in, building her power.

Gasping, she rolled over, coming to her hands and knees. Mentally chanting a spell, she called in clouds, bringing a rainstorm to the clear night. Messing with the weather wasn't easy, and if it happened too often, it could permanently shift an area's weather patterns. She had to go carefully. Gather what she needed, and nothing more. Later, she'd have to restore what she'd shifted. If she lived through the fight. Restoration would come later, after she fixed this and regained her str ength.

With one eye on Brown for more sudden moves, she focused her intent on rapidly evaporating the water around her and turning it into thunderclouds over his head, wishing she had the power to call electricity from the air like some of her ancestors. Hitting him with a blast of lightning would be extremely satisfying. She'd have to make do with a serious dousing from the storm. The rain would distract him further but sending it would weaken her. Nature had a frustrating way of demanding balance.

Rising to her knees, she pushed more and more water into the cloud, ignoring Brown's ranting and raving. His voice rose in volume. From the corner of her eye, she saw him raise his hands. Balls started to glow and the ground trembled. A slight twitch of his hands warned the shot was imminent. She pushed the water harder until it spilled from the sky, dousing him in a torrent of water, extinguishing the orbs.

He recovered quickly. Much too quickly. Where had he learned such skills? Nobody expended such powerful magic without extracting a physical cost. This was dragging her down, she barely had the strength to move, let alone fight, and he was as strong as ever.

Damn.

He might beat her, even though she was pulling strength from the water she was surrounded by.

"Enough." His voice boomed, thundering through the air like a physical blow, knocking her backward. "Give me the chalice, or he dies."

Brown backed up until he was beside Dennis and bent down. He grasped Dennis by the throat and lifted him from the ground one handed. His other hand glowed fiery red with a growing orb. He lifted both hands, Dennis dangled, his feet barely touching the ground, his face turning red, then blue, in the orb's light.

No! Her mind screamed at her to do something. Her heart echoed the cry, threatening to break in half. She might not live through this battle, but by the Goddess, he would not kill Dennis. She wouldn't allow it.

She had to do this! She had to end it. To live without Dennis would be to die, piece by piece. Better to perish now, than suffer forever.

A glimmer of motion stirred beside her. First on the left, then on the right. With a flick of her gaze, she glanced at the motion. Ev? Kansas?

How in the world had they gotten here? Who had let them loose? Brown?

Their voices urged her to fight. Her spirits lifted and her strength grew. Knowing they were behind her, not on his side helped.

She dumped more water on Brown, but the ball didn't go out. She had to act now. Before it was too late. The wind rose to a roar, and the ground shook. Brown's face screwed up in concentration. He was calling something big. Too big for her to handle alone. She should have brought her family.

"Get in the water. All the way," Kansas screamed.

"It's the only way to save him," Ev shouted.

"I can't," she cried, tears streaming down her face. She could die if she went in the water. She'd spent more than a decade, over half her life, terrified of water. She couldn't handle anything deeper than a bathtub. Just days ago, she'd tried to overcome her fear, right here on this island, and had nearly died. She couldn't go through that again. Not even for Dennis.

She dropped her face in her hands and wept. Tears of failure crushing her soul, tearing out her heart. Her guards dropped down as she gave in to despair.

She had failed. Herself. Her family. Her magical friends. But most of all, she had failed the man she loved.

Chapter Thirty-Seven

"U seless witch," Brown screamed. "I'll kill him."

The threat cut through her heart, and she wept harder. She never should have dragged Dennis here. She never should have come.

This was all her fault.

Hawk women only loved once in a lifetime. Only once. When Dennis died at Brown's hands, she'd be alone for the rest of her life. Her heart cracked further.

If she was going to have to live without her one true love, she might as well be dead.

Screw this. A plan formed in her mind. Gathering her resolve, she struggled to her feet. Her legs trembled; her knees knocked together. Upright and shaking, she backed slowly into the water. Deeper and deeper.

When the water reached her waist, she froze, unable to go further. She couldn't do this. Water had nearly killed her once. Flashes of her near drowning flooded her mind, stealing her breath as if it were real.

No!

She had to do this.

She'd save Dennis or she'd die trying. Time was running out; her lover was limp in Brown's hand. He'd die without her.

"Give me the chalice," Brown screamed again.

Water splashed up around her, coating her body filling her mouth. Spitting the water out, she stepped backward. "I'm coming Dennis," she screamed, praying he would hear and hang on just a few seconds longer.

Decision made, she committed herself, and her life to saving Dennis. She dove under the water, forcing herself to stay submerged, despite her fears and exhaustion. She fought back choking panic. Dennis would not die here, at the hands of this asshole.

With courage she didn't know she had, she funneled the water's power to her own magic and prepared to blast Brown. She pressed the power, tighter and tighter, like a compressed spring, until she couldn't contain it any longer.

She shoved the magically charged water outwards, toward Brown. Into his mouth, down his throat and into his lungs. She felt, rather than saw Dennis slump to the ground free from Brown's death grip.

Voices whispered at her, Ev and Kansas. "He's down. He's out. Bind him. Quickly."

Fighting for breath and power, she recited the binding spell she'd read, her mouth moving under the water. She couldn't risk leaving the water and having her power ebb and fail before he was bound. Exhaustion dragged at her. She was spent, but not beat.

"He's down! He's bound!" the voices crowed in her ears; the sound distorted by the water.

She eased her pressure and let off entirely. Giving in to fatigue after spending every molecule of her magic, she sank beneath the water and succumbed to its power. Dennis was safe!

Peace washed over her. Dennis was safe, Brown was contained. Her lungs were exploding. Drowning was a horrible, painful, way to die.

Chapter Thirty-Eight

Dennis gasped for breath, his throat raw and burning with every agonizing pain. Beside him, Brown lay on the ground, curled up in a fetal ball. He glowed lightly with a weird energy. Magic! Hazel must have managed to bind him.

Hazel!

Where was she? He searched around frantically and didn't see her anywhere. He screamed her name. He had to find her. Where was she? Where had she gone? Had Brown killed her? He was alone on the beach.

He dropped to one knee, broken. He'd die without her.

"She's not dead," a voice whispered in his ear.

"You can save her," another added.

He jerked to his feet. He was alone.

He was hearing voices. He must have brain damage.

Something shoved him from behind and he stumbled forward. He spun in a circle, he was alone, except for Natalia who sat crumpled on the ground near the cabin, head in her hands. Another shove.

"What the hell?" he mumbled, staggering toward the shore.

"She's in the water," the voices urged in unison. "She needs you."

He raced ahead, afraid of the voices, but desperate to see if they were right. Something large floated in the water twenty feet offshore. The water would be deep that far out. Hazel hadn't...she couldn't.

He ran toward the shape, staggering as his feet met the water. Two shimmery shapes raced past him, the voices egging him on, fueling his feet. Ghosts? The idea hit him like a brick wall. Where had they come from?

He dove into the water, swimming toward Hazel. He was certain now. It *was* her. The ghosts cheered. He sputtered to the surface with barely any strength left and hunted around him.

There!

Just out of reach to his left, he stumbled her way, feet barely reaching the bottom. She was face down in the water, limp and unmoving.

He was too late.

No!

He could save her. He had to save her.

He grasped her shirt and pulled her toward him. Shaking with weakness, he dragged her onto his shoulder and swam toward shore and trudged brokenly out of the water and eased her gently onto a patch of sand and pressed his ear to her chest.

Nothing.

Tears rolled down his face as he started a pathetic attempt at CPR. Why in hell hadn't he taken a recue breathing class? He was an idiot. If she died, it would be his fault.

Natalia! She had magic. She could help him save the woman he loved!

"Natalia," he screamed. "If you ever felt anything for me, anything at all, you'll help me." Beneath his too weak chest compressions, Hazel groaned and fell still.

She wasn't dead. Thank God.

"Natalia," he screamed. "Get over here."

Suddenly, she was beside him.

She stilled his hands. "Stay back," she whispered brokenly. She rubbed her palms together briskly, until he could see a small buildup of crackling energy between them. She closed her eyes, took a deep breath and pressed her hands to Hazel's chest.

Hazel bucked against the pressure, groaned and rolled over.

Natalia flopped to her back on the sand and lay still, her chest rising and falling in deep sucking breaths.

"Hazel, are you okay?" He grasped her shoulders and pulled her up to sit. Water dribbled from her mouth and she started coughing. Choking, wet, gagging coughs. Slowly, her struggles eased, and she took a deeper breath.

"What happened?" The words were a whisper, he heard the pain in her voice.

"I don't know," he confessed. "Are you okay? I woke up and you were gone. Voices in my head told me to save you. I mean real voices."

She laughed weakly.

"It was us," the voices chimed.

"Ghosts," Hazel murmured with a chuckle. "From the shop."

"I thought...Never mind. It doesn't matter. We have to get you home."

"No, I can't leave him unsupervised. Help me up. I need to check the binding." Together, weakly leaning on each other, they staggered toward Brown. He lay on the rocky ground, unmoving except for the uneven rise and fall of his chest. She looked almost giddy with relief. "The spell worked and held. I was worried I was too weakened and could have messed it up, or failed entirely. I'm glad he's still bound. I need to call someone to come get him." She looked around. "Where's my backpack, my phone?"

"You must have lost it in the water." Dennis fumbled for his phone. Dead. The water had destroyed it. "My phone is ruined. I expect yours is too."

"Use mine," Natalia shoved her phone at him.

He looked up at her, stunned at the sorrow in her eyes.

"Thanks." He handed it over to Hazel who called Corporal Stone and then her family.

"Come inside," Natalia said. "It's warm."

"I can't leave him. I'll stay here."

"Suit yourself." Natalia walked off; her shoulders slumped forward.

Dennis sat ten feet from Brown, Hazel nestled into his embrace. They shivered in the glowing light of early morning. Thankfully, the sun would be up soon. They could use the warmth while they waited for help.

A pile of sticks dropped nearby. "I'll make a fire," Natalia said and walked away. Minutes later, she had a cozy fire blazing and brought them blankets to wrap around their shoulders.

"Why?" Dennis asked, unable to put a more precise point on the question.

"Because, for all your faults, I did care for you. A lot." She swallowed hard. "I can see now, not all magic is good. There's a balance to maintain. Earlier, before you arrived, he tried to kill me, to steal my power. I'd heard it was possible but didn't believe it. He was going to kill me to get it. I'm sorry I took part in this disaster. He'd have sucked me dry and left me to die if you hadn't arrived." She shuddered and her eyes welled with tears.

"You helped me save Hazel. Thank you."

"I did it for you, not her."

"You should go," Hazel said. "Before the police get here."

"No. Not after nearly dying at his hands, then watching him try and kill you both. I don't deserve freedom. I'll stay and take my punishment. After that, if there is an after, I'll find a new home and a way to make retribution for what I let happen. For what I helped cause."

Hazel climbed unsteadily to her feet and hugged Natalia. "Thank you, from the bottom of my heart, for not helping Brown defeat us, for saving me. And honestly, for scaring Dennis away. Your loss was my gain and there aren't words enough to express my gratitude for the gift you've given me. I've fallen for him. Hard. He's my soulmate and I love him. I never would have found him without you. I owe you my world, and my life."

Natalia's laugh was weak and a bit forced. "You're welcome. I think. I made a big mistake losing him. But if you're right and he's your soulmate, he couldn't be mine."

"Can I get in on this hug?" Dennis asked, wrapping his arms around them. "You guys are making me jealous." *And more than a little uncomfortable*, but he kept the last part to himself.

Crazy witches. They were stirring up his life and setting it on end, and he couldn't be happier.

Flashing lights in the distance alerted him that the police boat was close.

Thank the Goddess, as Hazel would say. He could take her home, warm her up and cuddle her until they'd both recovered from this ordeal.

Chapter Thirty-Nine

H azel cuddled into Dennis's embrace.

It had taken hours for them to give their statements. This time there were no questions or doubt about Brown's guilt. Brown and Natalia were locked up.

Dennis had wanted to go home, to his place, but she'd insisted on going home, to her family. They'd showered quickly and now sat cuddling each other, drinking mugs of hot chocolate, rather than the usual tea. With a warm blanket around their shoulders, another on their laps, she was finally starting to warm up.

She didn't know if she'd ever have the energy to cast spells again. The long night had taken its toll on her. Her sisters and grandmother strolled into the living room, a tray of cookies, sandwiches and energy balls in hand. Here it comes. The inquisition.

"I'm proud of you both," Gramma Pearl said, startling Hazel.

"What?"

"I'm proud of you. But don't go thinking you're out of trouble. You'll never be so big I can't paddle your backside for doing something stupid. And this was stupid."

Hazel chuckled. Her grandmother had never laid a hand on them. Her stern words and cross looks were usually enough to deter any mischievous behavior. Add in the occasional grounding, and the Hawk girls kept tight to the line. That behavior of respect had become habit as they aged into adulthood.

"This is no laughing matter, I'm dead serious. What the hell were you thinking?"

Oh, this was bad. Her grandmother never cussed. Hazel shrugged.

"Going off on your own, putting your life, and Dennis's on the line. This should have been left for the Witch's Counsel, or the police. Not a baby witch and a mundane." Pearl turned to glare at Dennis. Then her expression softened. "Thank you for saving my granddaughter."

"My pleasure."

Hazel felt the chuckle he was keeping inside. Chastised for being a mundane and praised as a savior all in one breath.

"It's in the hands of the authorities now," Hazel said. She leaned further into Dennis, drawing strength from his warmth. "I can't believe I did that," she whispered. "I went in the water and took Brown out."

"You saved me." Dennis pressed a kiss to the top of her head.

She turned her face toward him and kissed him back.

"Gross," Lazuli teased. "Stop it already."

"Suck it," Hazel murmured against Dennis's mouth.

"What happens now?" Dennis asked when they finally ended their kiss.

"Brown will be incarcerated at a different facility from his father. They're searching his apartment for more information. Unfortunately," Pearl said. "I don't think this is going to end here. Until we find, and destroy the chalice, we're all in danger."

Hazel's heart fluttered and fear pressed down on her. "No sense buying trouble. We'll just take it as it comes and be ready for it."

Her sisters chimed their agreement. Her grandmother pressed her lips together disapprovingly.

Outside, a masculine voice called, "Rosie, you get back here, right this instant."

A knock sounded on the front door.

"Rosie, I presume," Dennis quipped, earning him another sharp look from Pearl.

"I've got this." Lazuli invited her Rosie and her father inside.

"I'm sorry," Frank exclaimed. "I turned around and she was gone. Again." He sighed heavily. "I don't know what to do with her."

Rosie climbed up on Hazel's lap and patted her cheek. "Are you okay, love?"

Hazel's heart wept. Her great-grandmother Rose had called her love.

"I'm fine, Rosie. A bit of trouble, but it's over now." She folded the blanket back to hug the black-haired girl. "You need to listen to your father."

"I can't," she proclaimed. "You were in trouble."

The family shared a look. Every time they saw Rosie, they became more convinced she was the reincarnation of their great-grandmother, despite never experiencing reincarnation firsthand.

"You're still in trouble," the child proclaimed wisely. "This isn't over yet. And don't forget to send those ghosts home." She pointed to the corner where Ev and Kansas were sitting quietly.

Frank's gaze darted to the corner and he shook his head. "Sorry, she gets these weird ideas."

"It's okay," Lazuli grasped his forearm. "We don't mind. This whole family is a bit weird. Come into the kitchen, I'll make you some coffee. You prefer coffee to tea, don't you?" Frank looked befuddled but followed Lazuli to the kitchen.

Once they were out of earshot, Kansas spoke. "We don't have to go back, do we?"

"Wait," Dennis jumped up, nearly dislodging Rosie from Hazel's lap. He jabbed a finger toward the corner. "I heard that. They were there. At the lake."

"Yes, we were."

He shook his head like a dog trying to shake of water. "No freaking way."

"Way," Hazel said, setting Rosie aside and standing to slide her arms around his waist. "I told you we had ghosts. Because they've chosen to reveal themselves to you, you'll see them more often."

"Crazy."

"Crazy about you," Hazel said, wrapping her arms around his waist.

"You're pretty okay too." He laughed.

"I guess this disaster is finished," Hazel said.

The ghosts vanished with an audible pop.

"What the heck?" Dennis asked, blinking in surprise.

"I found a spell," Hyacinth said. "It released them and then retied them to the shop when the crisis was over. Your statement rebound them."

"Good," Rosie said, hands on her hips in a ridiculously adult pose. "You can't disturb the natural order."

Everyone chuckled at her wise words.

"No, you can't." Hazel agreed, lifting the girl into her arms.

"Now, you have to marry him," she said, returning to little girl mode. "If you kiss, you get married. I learned that on TV."

"I'd like that," Dennis said, taking Hazel's hand. "Hazel, what is your middle name?"

"Hazel Pearl," Rosie piped in as if he were stupid.

"Hazel Pearl Hawk, will you do the honor of marrying me?"

"Oh my," Hazel couldn't stop her enormous smile from bursting forth. "Yes. Yes, I will marry you. The sooner the better."

"Halloween weddings are nice. I can wear a beautiful princess dress," Rosie said. "Got any cookies?"

"We do indeed," Pearl said, taking her hand. Everyone except Hazel and Dennis trooped into the kitchen.

"This isn't over, is it?" Dennis asked warily, concern heavy in his voice.

"No. It's not. Not until we do something about that talisman. But like they say, no sense buying trouble. We'll prepare and deal with trouble when it comes knocking."

"But not alone next time, right?" He shook a warning finger at her, and she nibbled it.

"Definitely not alone." She leaned against him, her heart full. Her body tired, yet strangely elated. "Do you think we can sneak out, to your place? I need to be alone with you." They crept toward the door, eager to escape to privacy. Any remaining reprimanding would have to wait.

"Nefarious plans for my body?" He grinned.

"Yeah, definitely. But after I nap."

"I'll agree to that. And to the Halloween wedding. I don't want to wait any longer than I have to."

"Me either." Her heart swelled. The past few months had been insane. Between the fight with Brown and falling for Dennis, life had changed. For the better. And who knows, she might even be brave enough to swim again. Maybe.

L ove the novel you just read?

Be sure to check out the rest of the series!

Your opinion matters.

I'd love it if you would review this book on your favorite book site, review site, blog, or your own social media properties, and share your opinion with other readers.

Thanks in advance. Katie.

A Bit About Salem

The truth about the Salem witch trials is too many innocent people died. Were they witches? Perhaps. Most, for certain, were ordinary people. Several theories have evolved in the decades since the executions. Mass hysteria. Poisoning from rye flour gone moldy. A vicious land grab. Jealousy over healthy crops. I'm sure there are many more theories. As time passes, we get further and further from a truth we'll never be able to attain.

There were, however, some truths recorded at the time. Interestingly, none of the accused in Salem were burned, though one man was pressed to death. Witch burnings did, however, take place in many other locales, particularly in Europe. Nineteen people were hanged. Four died in jail. Of the twenty executed, five were men. Sources indicate over two hundred people were accused in Salem.

According to the Salem Award Foundation website, there are roughly 25 million people around the world who are descended from the Salem Witch Trials victims and the other participants in the trials. (Source: https://historyofmassachusetts.org/salem-witch-trials-victims/)

Various sources indicate that Wilkins is alternately spelled Wilkens. Hawkes is also referred to as Hawks. I've selected the most common versions for this story.

As a witch, Pagan and Wiccan myself, the entire history of witch trials and massacres worldwide, breaks my heart. I mourn for those who died by hanging, by pressing, by fire, and in prison. Persecution and prosecution without cause is always a tragedy. I'm optimistic that as we grow to learn more about others, and to accept others, tragedies like this will become a distant memory.

Disclaimer:

There is no Three Moon Falls, nor is there a Three Moon Falls Lake. I've taken considerable liberty with the geography of Alberta in the creation of this narrative. The scenery depicted is an amalgamation of random mountain waterfalls, the Athabasca River, which I've canoed down on more than one occasion, and a number of small towns; not the least of which is Fox Creek, Alberta; the town where I spent my high school years.

About Katie O'Connor

Best-selling author Katie O'Connor lives in Calgary, Alberta, Canada. She married her high school sweetheart and is living her happily ever after. She is the mother of two grown daughters and is extremely proud of her five grandchildren.

Katie is the founder of The Write Chicks, a private romance writers' group set up with the sole purpose of supporting each other's writing careers. She was a 2025 Story Coach for the Alexandra Writer's Centre Society in Calgary.

Katie's career path has been long and twisted, with most of her life devoted to her family. Her jobs have included being a waitress, chambermaid, cashier, store manager, as well as a lab and X-ray technician. She's been a small business owner and is an avid quilter and crafter.

She's dabbled in writing since high school because something drives her to create stories, and swears it's impossible for her NOT to write. Unsatisfied with one genre, Katie writes contemporary romance, erotic romance, fantasy/paranormal romance, romantic suspense, and erotica.

She believes in all things magical, including dragons, fairies, UFOs, ghosts, and house pixies. But most of all, she believes in love, romance, and hope. If you need her, she'll be over by the coffeepot, eyeing up the cookies.

Where to Find Katie

Website: https://katieohwrites.com
Email: katie@katieohwrites.com
Newsletter Signup: http://eepurl.com/Q2nRr
Facebook: http://www.facebook.com/katieohwrites
Bookbub: https://www.bookbub.com/profile/katie-o-connor
Instagram: https://www.instagram.com/katieohwrites/
Goodreads: https://www.goodreads.com/author/show/5362469.K
atie_O_Connor

Other Books by Katie

Their Christmas Heart
Their Christmas Love
Their Perfect Christmas
A Silver Fox Christmas Box Set

Heart's Haven:
Running Home
Building Trust
Saving Grace
Loving Winter
Heart's Haven Box Set

Three Moon Falls:
Fire Magic
Water Magic
Earth Magic
Midnight Magic
Air Magic

Stand Alone Books:
Carly's Heart
Matchmaker Christmas
Cupid's Charm
Gingerbread Dreams
Christmas in Silver Creek
Fake Dating at Half Moon Bay
Playing for Keeps in Half Moon Bay
Sleigh Bells Inn
Hearts in the Spotlight
To a Tea
Bulletproof Heart
Protecting Josie
Rekindled Fire
Winning her Love